GW01191293

SIDE HUSTLE

THE DAWSON FAMILY SERIES

EMILY GOODWIN

To my dad. Thanks for teaching me to never give up. (Ps…skip the sexy parts when you read this.)

COPYRIGHT

Side Hustle
A Dawson Family

Copyright 2018
Emily Goodwin
Editing by Ellie McLove
Editing by Lindsay, Contagious Edits
Proof reading by Jessica Meigs
Cover Photography by By Braayden Photography

∽

1

SCARLET

For as long as I can remember, there's been an emptiness inside of me. The more I try to ignore it, the deeper it sets into my bones, seeping down, deep down, until it becomes part of me. It's easy to blame the emptiness on my shitty upbringing. Having to give up my dreams of a future to take care of my brother and sister. Growing up with an addict for a mother and being the one who found her cold, stiff body after an overdose.

But I felt it before then, and sometimes I wonder if the emptiness isn't empty at all. Maybe it's darkness, and it's always been a part of me. And when you have darkness inside of you, you have two choices: hate yourself for it or embrace it.

I chose the latter.

The bathroom door closes with a heavy thud, and I step up to the mirror, pulling out cherry red lipstick from my purse. I carefully apply it, fluff my hair, and stare at my reflection, avoiding the tiny bit of judgment my moral compass is giving me. That thing's been broken for years anyway.

I close my eyes and think of homeless puppies, conjuring up images from those heartbreaking commercials I usually fast-forward through. It doesn't take much to make myself cry fake tears. If my cards had been dealt a different way, I'd be one hell of an actress.

Fake crying? No problem.

Real crying? I haven't done in years. Crying means feeling, and feeling isn't a luxury I can afford. My life is such a mess that if I stopped and looked at it—really looked at it—I'd be a blubbering mess.

Tears well in my eyes, and I let a few fall, smearing my mascara, before heading back out to the bar. It's a little after noon on a Tuesday, and the bar just opened up. It's inside a swanky hotel, and I can afford exactly half a watered-down whiskey here.

Spotting my target, I take a seat at the bar and order a vodka tonic with top-shelf liquor. I'm getting cocky, perhaps, but I didn't wear this uncomfortable-as-fuck pushup bra for nothing today.

I slowly sip my drink, crossing my legs and leaning back on the bar stool. I squeeze my eyes shut, and more tears roll down my cheeks. Setting the glass down, I angrily wipe them away, looking down at my phone and shaking my head.

"Excuse me, miss," the man in the blue Armani suit says, striding over. He extends a designer monogrammed handkerchief, flashing his Rolex at the same time. "But I have to ask who made a pretty thing like yourself cry?"

I'm not a thing, asshole. I'm a human-fucking-being. "Thank you," I sniffle, taking the handkerchief. I blot up my tears and turn to him, doe-eyed. "My boyfriend is here on business and I thought I'd surprise him. But when I got to the room…he wasn't alone." I turn away, waterworks in full force. I wish I could give myself an Emmy.

"He's a damn fool," Blue Suit says, taking a seat next to me. I can feel him eye-fucking me. "You're exquisite."

I shake my head. "Tell him that." I pick up my drink and down it. "I just want to forget him."

Blue Suit signals the bartender and orders us two martinis. "Here's to forgetting," he says, sliding the drink in front of me. I angle my body toward his and reach out, putting my hand on his bicep.

"Thank you," I say slowly, giving his arm a little squeeze. Blue Suit narrows his eyes and grins.

"Drink," he orders, eyes dropping to my cleavage. I know his type, and I can't fucking stand them. Relatively young for making so much money, they usually hail from trust-fund families to begin with. I bet Blue Suit posts selfies with his Lamborghini at least twice a week on Instagram and has to constantly remind people of how much pussy he gets.

Overly full of himself, he thinks wearing that fitted suit makes him the living embodiment of Christian Grey. Sorry, buddy. I'm not going *Fifty Shades* on your cock today.

"I hardly ever drink," I say, making my voice a little breathy after I take a big swig. "I'm such a lightweight."

His thin lips pull into a grin again, and I wish I could take the toothpick from my drink and stab it into his dick. I'll be doing all women a service from this snake in a suit.

"Well, sweet thing," he starts, leaning in and brushing my blonde hair over my shoulder. "That'll work in both our favors."

I giggle, doing an impressive job of hiding my cringing on the inside. I sip at my drink again, purposely spilling it. A little stream of alcohol runs down my chest, and I make a show of wiping at my breasts.

Like a hungry dog, Blue Suit has sunk his teeth into me, but it's only a matter of time before I walk out of here as *Best of Show*.

"I'm such a mess right now."

"You're too sexy to be a mess."

I mentally roll my eyes. *You're a beautiful mess* was a much better line, dude. "I'm so embarrassed. It's been one hell of a day, and I get a little flustered around attractive men. Oh—" I bring my hand to my face, and right on cue, my cheeks flush.

He chuckles and moves in. I rub my hands up and down my arms, shivering. Blue Suit takes off his jacket and drapes it around my shoulders, smoothing it out just so he has a reason to touch me.

"You're such a gentleman," I coo, pulling the jacket around my slender body. I can feel his wallet press into my side, and it only takes another few minutes of small talk for me to reach inside and pull out his cash. It's not the first time I've done this, but I always get a little rush. I'm right there literally in front of him, picking his pocket under his nose. I've yet to be caught, but there's a first time for everything, I suppose.

I fold the bills up in my hand and reach for my phone with my other. Sandwiching the money between my palm and my phone, I tell him I need to use the bathroom. I leave his suit jacket hanging on the back of the bar stool and slip right out of the bar, through the lobby of the Four Seasons and fall into step with the fast-paced Chicago foot traffic.

~

"THIS'LL COVER what insurance doesn't." I hand over crisp one hundred dollar bills, silently cursing the woman behind the counter. She holds each bill up to the light, making sure they're real, and proceeds to ring me up.

"You need to confirm the address for delivery." She slides the paperwork to me, and I can feel her judgment digging into me like a knife hot out of the fire. I'm still in my strappy Valentino dress, still showing more cleavage than your average street-corner hooker, and still have mascara smeared across my cheeks. I wiped it up the best I could, but I really don't give a damn right now. I changed out of my heels for two reasons: I'm down to one pair of designer shoes, and they're not the most comfortable to be trekking along the south side of Chicago in.

I'm now wearing a pair of worn-out Nikes and have twisted my hair into a messy bun on the top of my head. I had to hurry to get to the medical supply store in time to put in the order and have it delivered with tomorrow's shipment.

I've had this wheelchair on hold for weeks now, and after arguing with insurance for days on end, I knew it was either make my father suffer in his current ill-fitting chair that pinches his thighs and causes sores on his lower back or do whatever I can to get the money to get him this new one before the sores open up and turned into pressure ulcers. Again. We've been down this road before and it almost ended his life. The sores get infected and he's too old and too weak to fight off another infection. It would take me weeks if not months to earn enough from my waitressing job to cover this expensive as fuck wheelchair.

I confirm everything, making double sure the wheelchair will get delivered to the nursing home and then the right patient tomorrow afternoon. The cashier throws out a catty, "Well, you could be there if you're so worried," that I respond to with a glare and a roll of my eyes. I don't have time for her shit.

The wind picks up, carrying a cool fall breeze with it. It's the end of September, and it's been unseasonably warm all week. Not that I'm complaining, though. The lake-effect snow will be here before we know it, and I'll be trudging through it to work and back.

But today, though it's nice enough out to walk, I have enough leftover cash from Blue Suit to take public transportation and buy myself something for lunch. I put on my headphones and sit at the back of the bus, ignoring the world around me.

I get off a block away from the nursing home, intent on grabbing a taco from a hole-in-the-wall Mexican place. My stomach grumbles, and the last remaining twenty is burning a hole in my pocket. I round the corner a little too fast and almost step on a homeless woman sitting close to the side of a building. Her eyes are red and glossed over, but not because she's high. It's because she's been crying.

A sleeping toddler is tucked under her arm, wearing dirty clothes. They're both in desperate need of a bath, and suddenly tacos seem irrelevant. I come to a stop, digging the twenty out of my purse.

"There's a church three blocks over that'll take you in for the night," I tell her. I know this because I stayed there before years ago, back when it was me, Heather, and Jason against the world. "They'll have clothes for her too."

The woman takes the twenty from me, bottom lip quivering. "Thank you. My boyfriend…he got arrested, and we've had nowhere to go." She starts to get to her feet, struggling to keep her child nestled against her body and pick up her shit at the same time.

"Want some help?"

The woman eyes me suspiciously, and if you're going off my looks, I can't blame her. Two-bit whores aren't known for their generosity.

"I've been in your shoes," I offer.

"You have kids?" The woman gets to her feet and grabs a duffle bag full of baby clothes. She only has a backpack full of stuff for herself.

"Not my own, but I looked after my siblings for a few years." I take the duffle from her and lead the way down the street. We walk in silence, and when we get in front of the church, the woman tells me a tearful and heartfelt thank you.

I hike back to the nursing home, sweating by the time I get there. Dammit. This dress is dry clean only. The smells of body odor, urine, and bleach hang heavy in the air, mixed together like some sort of stomach-churning perfume. I turn down the hall and head in the direction of my father's room. I slow, seeing the curtain pulled around his bed.

The nursing assistant behind the curtain hums "Don't Go Breaking My Heart," and I hear him plunge a washcloth into a basin of water.

"Hey, Corbin," I say, knowing who he is without having to look.

His shoes squeak on the tile as he steps over to peer at me. "You pulling tricks again, hooka?"

"Magic tricks," I say, snapping my fingers. "And for my next act, watch that new wheelchair appear tomorrow."

"You didn't."

I raise my eyebrows. "I did."

He waggles a finger at me. "Girl, you are something else."

"How's he doing today?"

"We've had some good moments today, haven't we, Mr. Cooper?"

I perch on the edge of the other bed in the room, not wanting to go behind the curtain. My father's been in this shithole of a nursing home for the last several years, thanks to heavy drinking in his youth, a brain injury acquired during a bar fight, and most of all, early-onset Alzheimer's.

"Good."

"I'm going to take him down to Bingo after I get him cleaned up. He got a little messy during lunch."

"How'd that happen?"

"New CNA. Let him alone with a bowl of soup."

I let out a sigh. You can't leave food out around Dad. He'll try to feed himself and will end up spilling it everywhere. I pull my phone out of my purse, checking the time. I'm going to have to cut my visit with Dad short today if I want to make it over in time to see Heather, which I need to do. It's been a few days, and I have to make sure she's staying out of trouble.

Once Dad is up and dressed, I wheel him down into the cafeteria and sit him at a table along with a few other residents. I stay through one round of Bingo and then give him a kiss on the forehead and rush out, getting to the prison with only minutes left of visiting hours.

I've gone through the process of signing in and going through security so many times I could do it in my sleep.

"Hey, Scarlet," C.O. Benson says as I pass through the metal detector. "Looking good."

I flash him a smile and bat my eyelashes, just enough to keep him hanging on. "You too. Have you been working out?"

"I have," he replies with a wide smile. "Starting some new supplements."

"Keep it up. I can tell." I grab my purse, holding the smile on my face until I turn away. He's not a total loser but isn't my type. And by that, I mean, I'm not into guys who live in their parents' basement and find taxidermy a fun way to pass the time. But I know how helpful it can be to have that flirty relationship with someone in his position, and I never know when I'll have to ask for a favor.

For my sister, that is.

I get seated in the visitor area and lean back while I wait. My mind starts to wander, and I quickly reel that fucker in. *Don't think. Don't feel.*

"Scar!"

I look up and see my sister quickly walking over.

"Jesus Christ, Heather." My eyes widen, and I shake my head. "What the fuck did you do to your hair?"

She flops into the chair with a huff. "I knew you'd hate it."

Reaching over, I run my fingers through the rough cut. A natural blonde like me, Heather has butchered her long locks into a terrible above-the-shoulders bob with streaks of black and red throughout.

"It looks like a prison haircut."

"Well, it is a prison haircut. I'm in fucking prison, Scar," she spits out, nostrils flaring. We glare at each other for a few seconds and then burst out laughing. She reaches over the table and gives me a quick hug, ignoring the C.O. telling us not to touch.

"How are things?" she asks.

"As good as they can be," I say with a shrug. "I got Dad the new chair, and Jason was able to call home a few days ago."

Heather's face lights up. "God, I miss that little shit."

"Me too." Two years ago, our younger brother shipped off to the Middle East with the Army. I hate that he's away, but I'm proud of him for making something of himself. He's the only Cooper to do so…so far. We're a dysfunctional family, but we care about each other something fierce.

"Hey," she says, lowering her voice and leaning over. "I was talking to one of the girls in here."

I raise my eyebrows, knowing what comes next. It's usually a harebrained idea like all of her ideas are and never ends well for her. Hence why I'm visiting my baby sister in prison.

"And?"

Her lips curve into a smile. "I have a job opportunity for you."

"*D*ad, catch!"

I make a wild dive, over-exaggerating everything to humor my son. He throws the football, which only makes it a few feet before hitting the ground. I slide on the grass, making Jackson laugh.

"I won! I won!" Jackson chants, jumping up and down.

"Ouch!" Owen shouts from the patio. "Did you break something, old man?"

With a dramatic roll on the grass that makes Jackson laugh even more, I grab the football, pop up, and throw it at my younger brother. He's holding a beer in one hand and lazily reaches out with the other to catch it and misses. Luckily our sister, Quinn, is standing next to him and catches it before it crashes into the house.

"Seriously, guys?" She laughs and tosses the ball to Jackson. Shaking her head, she goes back to her fiancé, who's holding their sleeping baby. Emma looks so small in Archer's arms, reminding me of when Jackson was that little.

They really grow up so fast.

"Try to catch me!" Jackson shouts and takes off through the yard. I don't know where this kid gets his energy from.

"How about Uncle Dean come and chase you around?" I ask

loudly so both Jackson and Dean hear. Jackson loves the idea and
runs over to Dean, grabbing his hand and pulling him off the
bench. Logan steps out of the house, carrying two more beers. He
hands one to me and cracks the top back on the other, and we
both find a place to sit on the patio with the rest of our siblings.

It's a rare afternoon when we're all off together, and while my
parents don't usually have us over for a big dinner on a Tuesday,
we couldn't pass this up. It's nice out for late September and
might be one of the last times we can grill and eat outside before
the cold sets in.

"How's wedding planning?" I ask Quinn, watching my sister-
in-law, Kara, out of the corner of my eye. She's still harboring
resentment toward Quinn for going into labor on her wedding
day and has said more than once she doesn't see the point of
Quinn and Archer having a big wedding when they already have
a kid.

It's made for some awkward get-togethers, but hey…at least
I'm not the only one with a wife not everyone in the family is
crazy about. Though other than the stupid wedding drama, no
one has an issue with Kara. She's been good for Dean in a sense
as well.

"Good. Disney makes things easy." Quinn smiles and rests her
hand on top of Archer's. "I ran into Mr. Pickens today," she starts.
"And he thinks you should up your game. We all know you'll win
if we give this one-hundred percent."

I shrug off her words and take a sip of beer, turning and
watching Jackson run around the yard with Dean. All four of my
mom's dogs are following, barking and yipping and thinking
Jackson is running around solely for them.

"I couldn't even if I wanted to," I say.

"So you do want to?" Logan asks.

"I guess." I haven't wanted to admit it to myself that yes, I'd
fucking love to be Sheriff of our little county. I've been an
Eastwood cop for years, and I always planned on moving up in
the ranks. I officially threw my hat in the ring and am currently
running for sheriff, but as we get closer and closer to the election,
I'm feeling more and more inclined to drop out. It's weird to get

close to a long-time goal like this and want nothing more than to pull out. To stop trying before you fail, or worse, you win, and the results aren't what you expected.

And I did expect this. Well, maybe not being sheriff, but being more than a run-of-the-mill cop in this small town. But then Daisy up and left when Jackson was just a baby, putting a screeching halt on all our plans. Jackson is—and always will be—my first priority. He comes before anyone else, even if that means passing up on what I used to call my dreams.

My dreams have changed, and all I want in life is to see him grow up, happy and healthy.

"Having a brother as a cop around here has gotten me out of a few jams," Owen starts. "Having a brother who's the Sheriff... now that could come in very handy."

Quinn laughs. "Maybe you should just stay out of trouble."

"Where's the fun in that?" Owen counters and finishes his beer. Out of the five of us, Owen has the biggest sense of adventure. Which is a nice way of saying he has a lot of growing up left to do.

"You'd be great at it," Quinn goes on, being the voice of reason. "I know the crime rates around here aren't staggering or anything, but being in a position of political power—no matter how small—can have a big impact on the community."

Watching Jackson throw the football as hard as he can, I think back to when he was a newborn and I sat in the hospital room, talking to him as Daisy slept. I promised him the world, and so far, I've done a damn good job giving him everything he needs. But I'd love to be able to give him more.

"He'd be proud of you," Quinn says softly, knowing exactly what to say to get under my skin, not that she does it to upset me. Like our mother, Quinn is freakishly perceptive when it comes to her family.

"I know," I agree. "But...think about it...if I were the Sheriff, I'd be responsible for the whole county, not just Eastwood. It's hard enough now trying to figure out who can watch Jackson when I'm at work."

"You know I'm happy to help," Mom says, listening to our

conversation from inside the house. "Jackson is a great little helper when I'm at the office."

"Thanks, Mom. But what if I'm called out in the middle of the night or can't make it to pick him up from school and you're out on location for a job?" I look at Archer. "You get what it's like being on call."

Archer, who's a surgeon at a nearby hospital, nods. "I couldn't just leave, either. But Quinn is there to watch Emma," he adds almost guiltily.

"You need a hot nanny," Logan and Owen say at the same time. They're identical twins and do that quite often.

"It's not a bad idea," Archer says, earning a quizzical look from Quinn. "She doesn't have to be hot, but I mean, that won't hurt."

Quinn rolls her eyes. "I used to work with several people who had live-in nannies. That way they're always there, which would solve the issue of being called out to a crime or whatever."

"A live-in nanny?" I ask dubiously.

"We talked about this," Quinn reminds me. And we did, several months ago. The only way for me to be the Sheriff around here requires having someone at home to watch Jackson, and while I agreed to it back then, I'm having second thoughts. "It sounds more pretentious than it is." She tips her head toward Archer. "You know we're willing and ready to contribute to our town by enabling you to be our Sheriff. Just say the word and we can move forward."

I take a long drink of my beer, not answering, but not saying no either.

~

"I WANT ABSOLUTELY nothing to do with this." I put my arm around Jackson, who rests his head on my chest. I rake my fingers through his hair, dark and slightly wavy like mine, and hope I remember to take him to get a haircut this weekend. He needs it.

Then again, so do I. I've grown used to having longer locks, and it's one less thing to worry about. Maintaining a short cut requires too much work.

"I'll handle it," Quinn promises, nursing Emma with one hand while she opens her computer with the other. "Bethany from my old job swore by this site, and so did the CEO of our company."

"Sounds expensive," I grumble. Having invented and sold an app to Apple and then taking a high-paying position at a prestigious software company, Quinn has plenty of money. She cut back her hours of work now that she has Emma, but she's engaged to a surgeon for fuck's sake.

Quinn waves her hand in the air, dismissing me. "Think of this as us investing in our beloved community. Lots of people give big donations to the city, you know."

"If I don't like this, you're dealing with it," I go on. "Which means firing the nanny."

Quinn does a good job of ignoring me. In her defense, when we talked about this the first time, I was much more open to the idea. But that was because it was so far in the future I was able to not actually think about it. "Jackson is in school Tuesday and Thursday, right?"

"Right."

"Okay." She types away with impressive speed for someone one-handed, and a few minutes pass before she looks up, smiling. "I put up your profile and, in a day or two, we'll get applications from nannies who are fitting."

"And then what?"

"I'll screen the applications—Owen made me promise I'll let him help, which we both know means he's going to pick the prettiest one." She looks up from her computer with a hopeful smile. "Which really isn't a bad thing. Who knows what could happen?"

"You too?" I ask dryly.

"What?" She shrugs, acting like she has no idea what I'm talking about.

If Jackson weren't here cuddled up with me, I'd remind Quinn —again—that I'm technically still married. I haven't seen Daisy in years, which means she hasn't signed any divorce papers. I know I could push the issue, file something with the courts, and could be a single man in a few months. But what's the point?

Daisy was my high school sweetheart. Yeah, we broke up and got back together several times over the years, and I know my deployment was hard on her, but if over a decade of dating wasn't enough to see we weren't right for each other, then nothing is. I'm done dating. Done with women.

I've gone back and forth on my feelings for Daisy since she left that morning. She put us all through the wringer, worrying about her physical and mental well-being. I scoured the county for her, leaving our newborn with my parents while I drove around in a panic looking for her.

Her sister hadn't heard from her.

Her parents hadn't seen her.

Something terrible had happened. I was sure of it.

And then I found out she was partying in Chicago with a group of friends she met online in some sort of chat room.

She told me she didn't want to be tied down. Being a mom wasn't her thing. She spent years living on a military base, away from friends and her family, and felt like she deserved time to herself. She even thought I should give her credit for not cheating on me while I was overseas.

I spent the first year of Jackson's life hating her. Cursing her name. Wishing I could forget everything related to her—except Jackson, of course. She showed up on his first birthday, played the part of perfect mother for a few days, and we haven't seen or heard from her since.

"All I'm saying is having a good-looking woman around might not be a bad thing." Quinn readjusts Emma, who's done nursing now and is pulling on Quinn's hair, and closes her computer.

"I second that," Logan says, coming into the living room. His eyes meet mine and he gives me a tiny nod, knowing how much I can't fucking stand it when Mom and Quinn get on me about dating again. He sits next to Quinn and takes Emma from her

arms, holding her up and making a silly face. "And wh
feeling generous, Quinn, how about hiring a maid for me?"

"I think most of them prefer to be called house-cleaners n
and no. Owen's capable of cleaning."

Hearing his name, Owen rounds the corner. "Are you
insinuating that I'm the messy one?"

"We all know you are, Uncle Owen," Jackson quips and makes
us all laugh. He pushes himself up and wiggles his way in
between Logan and Quinn, cooing and talking like a baby
to Emma.

"Ready to head home, buddy?" I ask Jackson, knowing he's
going to protest. We have about half an hour before we have to
get home, and I'm buying my time to avoid a meltdown. We've
gone back and forth a lot this week, and while my parents and
Jackson enjoy the time they get to spend together, it would be nice
to keep him home during the week, especially now that he's in
preschool.

Admitting I need help has never come easy for me, but I know
deep down that this might be exactly what we need.

3

SCARLET

I pinch the bridge of my nose, gripping my phone so tight in my other hand I think it might break. I sink down on a creaky kitchen chair, looking at the bills laid out on the table. I'm behind on everything, like usual, and I don't have enough to cover the bare minimum this time.

Trying to get Heather the best outcome possible, I skipped the public defender and hired a lawyer, who was able to cut her sentence in half. But the lawyer fees weren't cheap, and I've been without TV or internet all month, making me go over on my data plan, but hey—that bill's not due until next month. The next to go will be my electric and water, though not by choice.

And now I'm dealing with insurance, who randomly decided to stop covering several of Dad's medications that he's been taking for the last three years. I've been on the phone for over an hour, mostly on hold, of course. I rest my head in my hands, zoning out as I continue to listen to crappy elevator music through the speakers on my phone.

Finally, I get through to a new person, whose accent is so thick I can hardly understand a word they're saying. I argue some more, but in the end, there is nothing I can do. The insurance company no longer deems the blood pressure medication necessary and will no longer cover it.

I hang up and let my phone clatter to the table. The fall is cushioned by the million bills covering the surface. Seething, I close my eyes and clench my jaw. I want to beat someone up, preferably Steve at the insurance company who has as much empathy as a pile of dirt.

"I am so fucking sick of this," I mutter. I'm sick of taking one step forward and two back. I'm tired of never having enough. I'm tired of everyone else's shit always falling on my shoulders.

I want out.

Out of the ghetto. Out of poverty. Of working my ass off for measly tips and dealing with rude customers who see me as that trashy girl from the south side. I want to make a life for myself. I want to do better.

Picking pockets will only get me so far. I need to do something big, something like I used to do before, and get enough money to finally start the life I know I deserve. Picking my phone back up, I log onto a caregiver site. I have a profile on here, though it's been a while since I used it.

Two years ago, I was a live-in nanny for a rich couple, looking after their entitled asshole children. Mostly I saw them off to school, spent the day hanging around the pool, and picked them up after school. I made sure they did their homework, but they each had separate tutors for their different subjects.

My biggest job while working there was constantly turning down advances from the children's father. He was a decent-looking guy, ten years older than me and working the salt-and-pepper hair hard. He was funny, cultured, and totally infatuated with me. He started sending me gifts, which is how I acquired a few designer items.

Then the gifts turned into dinner dates, and after a night where he flew me to New York City on his private jet, I drank too many mini bottles of vodka and took things a little too far with him. I threw up before we actually had sex, but that night opened up a whole new window of opportunity for me, not that I'm exactly proud of it.

Afraid I'd tell his wife of what almost happened, he started giving me cash in exchange for my silence. I had photographic evidence of him shoving his tongue down my throat, after all. I quit working for his bratty-ass children and was able to live off hush-money for a good six months. Then he got caught cheating on his wife with someone else and she left him, so my silence wasn't worth paying for anymore.

Not letting myself think about how deplorable I am, I make my account active again and update my resume a bit. I don't think Mrs. Milton ever knew about me, and to be honest, I don't care if she did. She was an awful woman who didn't deny marrying for money and openly admitted the only reason she had children was because she saw it as a way around the prenup.

Still, her name looks good as a reference. I'll leave it. I spend a few more minutes tweaking my resume, not exactly lying but making myself sound way better than I really am. I submit it to the site for review and answer a few questions to see if I can still pass a background check. Luckily for me, background checks don't go into my family history.

～

"You make sure Jason does his homework, you hear?"

I press my lips into a thin line. "Dad, Jason isn't in high school anymore. He's in the Army now."

Dad gives me a blank stare and tries to get out of his wheelchair. The new one is much more comfortable than the old one, but I guess I was overly optimistic that he'd keep his ass in this new chair better than the last. He's too unsteady to be up walking on his own.

"And you tell your skank-ass whore of a mother to stop drinking my beer."

"Mr. Cooper," Corbin scolds as he comes around the corner. "Now I know your pretty little daughter didn't take that nasty old bus and then walk two blocks in the rain to get her ass badgered by you." Corbin stops in front of my dad's wheelchair and pops his hip, holding out one hand.

Dad grumbles something I can't discern but hefts back in his chair with a sigh. I mirror his actions, letting out a breath of frustration.

"He doesn't mean it. You know that, right?" Corbin tells me, leaning against the wall.

"I know."

"It can be hard to see family like this, but it's the nature of the disease. Don't take it personally."

"I don't," I tell him, blowing a loose strand of hair out of my face. "He wasn't very involved when I was a kid. It's not like I have all these good memories of him to tarnish."

"Maybe that's a good thing."

"I should have been there," Dad says in a rare moment of clarity. "I should have been there for you and Heather and Jason. I should have made your mother get help. I'm...I'm sorry."

I close my eyes, shoving all my feelings aside. "You're here now, Dad."

Corbin pushes off the wall. "Anyway, Mr. Cooper. It's time for dinner. You coming, Scarlet? I can get an extra plate for you."

"What are they having today?"

"Sweet potatoes and fish."

I try not to cringe. "I'll take some sweet potatoes, but I'll pass on the fish."

"Smart choice," he mouths and unlocks Dad's wheelchair. I follow behind as we head to the cafeteria, pulling out my phone to see who just emailed me. It's a response to the nanny position I applied for a few days ago, which specific one is beyond me. I applied for any and all that I could.

I quickly skim the email, looking to see who sent it. The email was sent from a work account, and the name *Quinn Dawson* is at the bottom as an e-signature. Once I get to the table next to Dad, I enter her name in a Google search.

"Holy shit," I say out loud, earning a nasty look from the uptight nurse passing by. Quinn's made quite the name for herself, and she's younger than me. I find her on Instagram and creep through her photos. She has a baby, and it looks like she's either married or engaged to a doctor. I already hate her.

I don't care what the job description is. This is exactly the type of gig I need.

Corbin comes over with two plates of nasty-looking salmon that reeks like it's been left out on the counter all afternoon. Yep, I'm only eating the sweet potatoes. Swallowing the little bit of morality I have left, I turn to Dad and look into his eyes.

"I'm going to get you out of this shithole, I promise."

～

I FEEL like I'm drowning. Like I'm madly treading water just to stay afloat. I'm gasping for breath, but every time my lungs fill with air, it feels wrong. Like I shouldn't be breathing.

Like I should drown.

But like a cockroach, I keep coming back. Pulling on the cross necklace that's hanging from my neck, I push my shoulders back and step into the coffee shop.

We're meeting in The Loop, near Quinn's place of work. She already ran my background check and said she called my references, and it's a miracle she hasn't been scared off yet. I spot her sitting at a table in the back, typing on a laptop. There's an iced coffee next to her, and I can tell from back here her purse, clothes, and shoes are designer.

Her brunette hair is pulled into a braid that's perfectly messy, and she's not wearing much makeup. She's pretty and has a kind face. You can tell she's a nice fucking person just by looking at her, and I can't let myself fall into a trap.

I need money. Specifically hers.

My phone rings right as Quinn looks up, and our eyes meet for a fleeting moment before I glance down at my cell in my hand. It's the nursing home, and I hesitate before answering. They called this morning to tell me Dad was out of the medication insurance stopped covering and asked if I would be able to provide it until something was worked out.

I'm trying.

I silence the call and look back at Quinn, plastering a fake smile on my face.

"Hi," she says, standing up to shake my hand. "I'm Quinn."

"Scarlet. Nice to meet you."

"Do you want anything to drink? This new caramel frap is to die for."

"Uh, sure. Thanks."

Leaving her computer on the table with me, Quinn gets up and gets in line, returning a few minutes later after putting in an order for me.

"So," she starts, fidgeting a bit as she talks, "I've never interviewed anyone like this before. Sorry in advance if I'm a little awkward. And don't feel like you need to put up a front or anything. I'm not looking for Mary Poppins. Just someone who can help with basic household chores and make sure a four year old makes it to see another day."

Dammit, I kind of like her. "I think I can do that." My phone buzzes, and I glance down, seeing a text from Corbin. *Shit.*

Wait. Did she say a four year old? From my internet creeping, I only saw her with a baby who couldn't be older than six or seven months old. Doesn't matter. I'd rather take care of a four year old than a baby anyway. Changing diapers isn't my thing.

Quinn goes on to describe the job, and I hear her say the house is in a small town in Indiana, about an hour and a half away. I smile and nod as she explains the rest, not really paying attention because I'm trying to surreptitiously read Corbin's text. And when I see the words *your dad fell again*, nothing Quinn says stays with me.

The faster I can get to Quinn's husband, the better. I need to find a way to blackmail him into giving me money so I can move my dad to a place that's better equipped to handle someone with memory issues.

We go over pay, where I'll stay, and how my time off will work. She's pretty fucking generous and even offers to arrange a car to come get me since I don't own one myself. I can start tomorrow, and I have no doubt things will work out just fine. Being able to accommodate anyone is just one of my superpowers. Though, really, I don't see why it's all that hard. Find out what people want and embody it. Compliment them. Make them feel important.

And then you've weaseled your way into their lives enough to reach in and take whatever you want. Hey…I never claimed to be a saint.

∾

"Miss Cooper?"

My eyes flutter open, and I blink in the bright sunlight. "Yeah?"

"We're here."

"Oh, uh, thanks." I unbuckle my seatbelt, feeling a little disoriented. I had just slipped into deep sleep and am having a hard time pulling myself out of it. I smooth out my hair and pop the top button on this ridiculous pink sweater. It's not at all my style but gives me the image I want to portray. Squeezing my eyes shut to try and focus my vision, I open the car door before the driver has a chance to come out and open it for me. I'm capable of opening my own doors. It's just weird to sit here and wait for someone else to do it.

I blink once. Twice. Three times. "This is the house?" I ask, looking up and down the street. There's a good chance the driver took a wrong turn and accidentally drove us onto the set of a Hallmark Channel movie. We're parked along the curb of a postcard-worthy small town road, with well-maintained houses lining either side of the street. A handful even have white picket fences.

Forget Hallmark. There's an even better chance this is a horror movie and I've just been hand-delivered to a serial killer who spends her days knitting and offs her unsuspecting victims by poisoning their lemonade. Which she made. By hand.

"Yes," the driver tells me, coming around to get my bags. "This is the address Mr. Dawson provided."

"Oh, uh, okay." I hike my purse up over my shoulder and

grab the handle to one of my suitcases. This isn't what I signed up for. The house I saw on Quinn's Instagram is brand new and big, with curved double staircases greeting you from the oversized foyer. This house in front of me looks like a century-old farmhouse, safely nestled into the historic district of this small town.

The fuck?

I know I tuned out most of what Quinn was saying the other day at the coffee shop. I looked at her and saw nothing but dollar signs and was willing to watch two sets of hyperactive triplets if it meant getting a shot at some of her money.

But this...this has to be a mistake. On her part. Not mine. Because I didn't sign up for this.

"Uh...thanks," I tell the driver as he sets my last suitcase by the porch steps. I stand there like a deer in fucking headlights, taking in the perfectly groomed lawns on the surrounding houses and how nearly everyone is already decorated for fall. If I don't pull myself out of this living Pinterest board now, I fear I never will.

I'm about to turn around and leave, walking to the nearest bus station and pulling whatever trick I have to do to get enough money to get me back to Chicago. And then the front door opens. If anyone else stepped out of the house, things might have turned out differently. But the moment I lay eyes on *him* all I can think is, "Oh shit."

Tall and muscular, the man standing before me is just that: a *man*. His presence is intoxicating, intimidating, and impressive all at the same time. He has messy dark brown hair that's pulled away from his face, and the darkest navy-blue eyes I've ever seen.

His face is set, and I can tell just by looking at him that his guard is up, and for a damn good reason. Takes one to know one, I guess.

"Scarlet Cooper?" he asks, looking me over. His gaze slowly wanders over my body, but he's not checking me out. He's inspecting me, looking for flaws in the system and signs of obvious damage.

It's there, hiding in plain sight, but all he sees is a pretty blonde woman in a white skirt and a stupid fuzzy pink sweater.

"Yes. Nice to meet you, Mr. Dawson." I plaster a pleasant smile on my face, freaking out on the inside but otherwise appearing level-headed and cool as a cucumber. With practiced grace, I ascend the porch steps and shake Mr. Dawson's hand. His grip is strong and firm, and the skin on his palm is just rough enough to make me think he must work with his hands.

That thick skin would feel so good slowly making its way up my—stop. Get it together so you can get the fuck out of here, Scarlet.

His furrowed brows give way to a more friendly expression as he grips my hand for a moment before releasing it. He lets out a breath and his whole body relaxes. There are pounds of muscle under his black T-shirt, and it makes my body react purely on its own accord.

"Weston. But call me Wes," he says and steps aside. "Come in."

Suddenly, I can't move. This guy—Wes Dawson—isn't the surgeon I assumed I'd be working for. Is the con artist getting conned? Is the universe finally catching up to me, and this is its way of giving me the middle finger while laughing out a big *fuck you*? I have no idea what is going on or what I'm going to do, but I know one thing for sure. If I go into that house, there's no going back.

4

*S*carlet stands on the front porch, vivid blue eyes wide. Her blonde hair falls in waves around her face, and I can't help but notice how beautiful she is. Everything about her is soft and delicate, but there's a hardness to her I immediately recognize. Blinking, I sweep my hand up and over my hair, pushing it out of my face.

I don't know what I expected—Mrs. Doubtfire perhaps?—but I certainly didn't expect a blonde bombshell. Though really, Owen got the final say in who Quinn interviewed after she narrowed it down to her top five choices. Still…this woman before me belongs on the pages of a magazine, not living in someone else's house looking after strangers' children.

She freezes, looking around as if she has no idea what the fuck is going on, and then recovers fast. She blinks, puts on a smile, and comes up the porch steps. Scarlet is the definition of a hot nanny, even in that stupid fuzzy sweater. Perky round tits bounce underneath it as she walks, and it doesn't look like she's wearing a bra.

My dick jumps, and I turn away. She's been here all of a minute and I'm already reacting to her. Dammit. I don't even want her here, let alone want to find her attractive. She's here for Jackson, and he's all that matters.

He'll always be all that matters.

I don't move, and we stand there in a weird stare-off. My face is set, and my mind is made. Letting her into my house means I can't do it all, and that's not something I've admitted to myself. When Daisy left, I swore I didn't need her. That I didn't need anyone. Jackson was more than enough, and I have to be enough for him.

Knowing I can't stand here staring at Scarlet forever, I take a step forward. She smells amazing, like fresh flowers and clean laundry and sunshine. Impossible, right? I fucking wish it were. She sweeps her eyes over me, inhaling quickly. Her lips part, and we both reach for the same suitcase at the same time.

Her nails catch on my skin, and she jerks back.

"Sorry." She makes a move to grab my hand but stops, holding hers awkwardly out in front of her. "Did I hurt you?"

"No," I say gruffly, fully aware how easily a woman like her could hurt me. She shuffles back, and I grab her two big suitcases with one hand, pinching my fingers between the handles but wanting to get them inside so we can move off the porch. I'm suddenly sweating, and I'm blaming it on the hot sun.

Hah.

Once inside, she leans over to unzip her boots, and I get a clear view of her tits behind that sweater. She's definitely not wearing a bra. She's well-endowed, and I can't help but imagine what those gorgeous tits would feel like in my hands.

Obviously, I'm still attracted to women. Very attracted. But being married due to a technicality complicates the shit out of things, and even more pressing is not wanting to get Jackson's hopes up.

He's still too young to fully grasp what happened, but he knows his mother left him. I'm certain he doesn't actually remember her, but he understands the idea of a mother and asks every now and then if either his mom is coming back or if I'll get married again. I can usually sidestep those questions with an "I'm not sure" or "Mommy is busy," but what really gets me is when he asks why his mommy doesn't love him.

Because I don't fucking know why.

That kid is my moon and stars. He's my reason for getting out of bed every morning. He's everything to me, and the only reason this Scarlet woman is even here is to offer him a sense of stability that I can't on my own.

Everything I do, I do for him.

"So you talked to my sister yesterday," I start, stepping into the living room.

Scarlet's eyes zero in on me, and she takes a few seconds to study my face. She makes no attempt to hide it either, and her brazen move to check me out throws me.

"Quinn is your sister?" she asks, tipping her head to the side a bit. Why does she sound surprised?

"Yeah, she is."

Scarlet's long eyelashes come together as she blinks. "Oh. I thought she was your wife. You, uh, have the same last name."

I let out a strangled laugh. "No. She's my baby sister, and she won't be a Dawson for much longer anyway."

Scarlet's lips part, but no words leave her mouth. Then she smiles again and looks me over once more. "I can see the similarities."

I shrug. Dean and I look alike, Logan and Owen are obviously identical, and Quinn holds a resemblance to us all. Only prettier. "I guess. This whole thing is her idea," I add. I want to keep pretending I can do it all, play the role of perfect father and devoted police officer to our town, but dammit, I can't. Sticking to a schedule will do Jackson a world of good, especially now that he's in school.

"Oh." Scarlet brings her arms in, looking a little unsure of herself. The gesture throws me, and it takes me a few seconds to realize why. Her body language says she's shy and uncomfortable —expected in this situation, of course. But her face is set with determination, and she has a distant look in her eyes that reminds me of a huntress on the prowl.

I hate that I find it so fucking attractive.

"She was supposed to explain everything."

"Yeah," Scarlet says without missing a beat. "She did." She smiles and grabs the remaining bags, bringing them from the foyer and into the living room. I know they're heavy and she's struggling under the weight, but she doesn't let on or ask for help.

"But we can go over it again." She sets her purse down on the coffee table and looks around. The determination in her eyes gives way to a moment of panic, but she hides it well. I wouldn't be able to see it if it weren't something I've experienced myself.

"Jackson is watching cartoons in his room. He's excited to meet you." I give her another few seconds to look around. The house is historical and has been fully restored and professionally decorated. Buying and fixing up this place was a dream Daisy and I shared back when we first started dating, and we saved for years to have enough to do things right.

"Your house is beautiful," she says but almost sounds disappointed.

"It's haunted," Jackson quips, appearing at the top of the stairs. "The Tall Man comes into my room at night."

"Jackson," I scold, hoping Scarlet doesn't go running out the door. Though on second thought...nope. This is for Jackson. I can grin and bear anything for that boy. "We talked about this. Ghosts aren't real."

"The Tall Man isn't a ghost. He's a zombie!"

Scarlet smiles, going over to the base of the stairs. "Well, you're in luck. I just happen to know that zombies don't like cinnamon. All we have to do is put a little pinch of it by your door and he won't be able to come into your room anymore."

"Really?" Jackson's face lights up.

"Really."

Jackson comes down the stairs. "Are you my nanny?"

"I am. My name is Scarlet."

"I'm Jackson. I'm four years old. Did you know that babies grow inside their mommy's tummies before they pop out of their belly button?"

Scarlet smiles. "I didn't, but I do now."

I close my eyes in a long blink. It's Dean's fault Jackson won't stop talking about where babies come from.

"Want to see my room?" Jackson takes Scarlet's hand. "I got a new PAW Patrol blanket for my bed. I have a big boy bed!"

"Hang on, buddy," I tell him. "Let's show Scarlet around the rest of the house first and give her a chance to get settled."

Jackson makes a face but agrees—as long as he can hold Scarlet's hand during the tour. He's a friendly kid, loving pretty much anyone who'll give him the time of day. I try to remain pleasant for his sake, but this whole thing is pissing me off.

And for some reason, having Scarlet be as pretty as she is makes me even angrier. I don't want a nanny. And even more so, I don't want to *need* a nanny.

I give Scarlet a hurried tour of the house, ending with the small guest room upstairs. It has a tiny bathroom attached to it, and the entire room is rather plain in comparison to the rest of the house. The door to this room hasn't been opened in months prior to today.

"I'll bring up your bags," I say and turn to go down the stairs. Jackson starts to go in with Scarlet, but I call him down, telling him I need his muscles to help me carry Scarlet's stuff up.

She's sitting on the bed when we return and gets up to take the suitcases into her room. Her hand brushes across mine as she grabs the handle from me, and I'm taken aback by how soft her skin is. Has it been that long since I've felt the touch of a woman?

"Thank you."

"I'll, uh, give you some time to get settled. Jackson," I call, not wanting to leave him alone with this woman. Not yet. "Help me make dinner."

"I'll do it," Scarlet offers.

"It's fine. We got it tonight."

Jackson protests the whole time, wanting to stay and play with Scarlet.

"She's pretty, isn't she, Daddy?" he asks as I lift him onto the kitchen counter. On the evenings I'm home, we always make dinner together. It's never anything fancy, and tonight we're making spaghetti and meatballs. The meatballs are frozen and won't take long to heat up in the microwave. Like I said...we're far from five-star fancy around here.

"Sure," I say, not wanting to lie to my son but for some reason finding it impossible to verbalize out loud that this woman might be the prettiest person who's ever walked into this house.

"She looks like Elsa!"

I shrug. "I guess." I grab a box of spaghetti noodles from the cupboard and hand it to Jackson. He likes to pick at the cardboard until it opens. Grabbing a pot and filling it with water, I put it on the stove to boil and bring Jackson off the counter. He sets the table while I stick the meatballs and sauce in the microwave.

Hopefully Scarlet can cook.

My mind wanders back to her pert breasts under that sweater, and as if she can read my mind, the floor creaks under her feet.

"Hey," she says almost shyly, and this time her timidness seems genuine. She changed into black leggings and a gray T-shirt, and her long blonde hair is twisted into a bun at the nape of her neck. "Would you like any help?"

"No, thanks."

Jackson's in the living room, too distracted with his toys to notice that she came down into the kitchen. Scarlet sits at the kitchen table, body angled out toward mine.

"So, Wes," she starts. "Quinn told me about Jackson but didn't tell me about you."

"I'm not that interesting," I reply dryly.

"What do you do?"

I add the pasta to the water and turn to steal another glance at her pretty face. "I'm running for sheriff of our county, but who knows how that'll turn out. For now, at least, I'm a cop."

a cop.

I'm a con artist posing as a nanny for a fucking cop. What the hell did I get myself into? I can feel the blood leave my face at a dizzying rate. Stay calm. Freaking out won't do me any good now. I need to hold it the fuck together.

I squeeze my eyes shut. How did I get things so wrong? I wasn't paying attention, but how did I miss this? Surely that Quinn chick mentioned she was hiring me for *her brother*.

Her apparently-single brother who just happens to be irritatingly sexy with that whole dark and brooding thing going on. I can tell he doesn't want me here, that he's reluctant to accept help, and I'm trying really hard not to find that attractive.

"Have you always been a nanny?" he asks after a beat of awkward silence passes between us. Sweat rolls down between my breasts.

"No," I say with a shake of my head. "I was a waitress for a while." I swallow hard, carefully calculating my next move. It's not too late to back out and find a family that has money to blow. I could be gone in the morning and put this whole thing behind me. Move onto a bigger and better target.

Or I could stay and actually work as a nanny. You know. Do the job I was hired to do. But that's not my style.

"How long have you been a cop?" I ask, body going on autopilot.

"A while," he tells me, turning away from the stove just long enough to look at me. "I was in the Army before then and served two tours in Afghanistan before joining the police force."

"My brother is in the Army," I blurt, breaking one of my cardinal rules of *don't get personal*. "He's overseas right now. I haven't seen him in a few months."

Wes's brows push together, and his gaze drills into mine. "Next time you talk to him, tell him I thank him for his service."

Suddenly flustered, I bring my hand to my chest, tugging at the T-shirt. Why is it a million degrees in here? "I will."

"How long has he been in?"

"He joined a year and a half ago and has been somewhere in the Middle East for the last five months. I'm not exactly sure where he is."

"He probably can't tell you," Wes goes on, turning back around. His whole demeanor has changed, and I know his mind is taking him back to the days when he was overseas too. I've been soured by corrupt cops before, but I have the utmost respect for our military, especially soldiers since Jason is one.

God fucking dammit. Now's not the time to get a conscience, Scar.

"Jackson seems like a great kid," I say.

"He is." Wes grabs a wooden spoon from a drawer and stirs the spaghetti. My heart is beating with fury inside my chest, so loud I think it's going to give me away. I can't think, I can't feel. I just need to focus on the job at hand.

And that job is hustling every penny out of Mr. Weston Dawson that I can.

～

I SIT on the edge of the bed, running a comb through my damp hair. The window is cracked behind me, letting in a cool breeze. Everything is silent. Freakily silent. No one is yelling or drunkenly arguing with a street lamp outside my window. The walls aren't shaking from the Chicago L going by, and I haven't heard a single gunshot all night.

It's eerie as fuck.

Weston put Jackson to bed a few hours ago, and I basically just watched, getting familiar with their routine. It was pretty standard, I suppose, but wasn't something I've seen before.

My own parents didn't give me the time of day, and I suppose they couldn't even if they wanted to. Mom was drunk, high, or in jail throughout my youth, and Dad didn't enter the picture until I'd already dropped out of high school in order to take care of Heather and Jason. He stuck around long enough that time for me to go back and graduate the next year.

The family I nannied for in the past didn't have children out of love, and that love didn't foster and develop slowly over time as the children aged. I can't recall a single time either parent went out of their way to do anything for those kids, which only furthered my belief that loving and caring families only exist in movies.

But what happened tonight is shaking everything I've built my life on.

After dinner, Weston went over letters and numbers with Jackson and then gave him a bath. He read him a few books before tucking him in and stayed in the room with him until Jackson fell asleep.

Wes might seem a little cold and callous, but there is no denying he loves his son.

Pulling my hair into a braid, I wonder what happened to Jackson's mother. She's probably dead, because I can't see how anyone could leave that sweet little boy...or that beast of a man.

He's unlike anyone I usually work with—well, if you can call what I do work. It enables me to bring home money to pay bills, which is what work is, right? But Weston...he's closed off, and if he even has any weaknesses at all, he's not going to let me in on them.

I set my brush down and lay back in bed, grabbing a yellow stuffed unicorn. I've had the thing for years, and I'm well aware how weird some people think it is that I'm a grown-ass woman sleeping with a stuffed animal. But the thing brings me comfort, which is something I desperately need most nights. The mattress is comfy, and the quilt is thick and warm. I should be able to pass out, sleeping soundly, but I can't. I'm unnerved, but I'm not afraid. Wes won't hurt me, and unless the neighbors actually turn out to be Stepford wives, I'm as safe as I've ever been.

After an hour of tossing and turning, I'm risking a run-in with my conscience. Normally, I'd toss down a shot of whatever's cheapest at the corner liquor store, but I didn't bring any booze, and I can't exactly go downstairs and start raiding Weston's alcohol stash. Assuming he has one, that is.

Nevertheless, I get up to go downstairs for something to drink. I slowly open my bedroom door and look into the dark hall. Red light from Jackson's nightlight spills into the hall, but he's not in his bed. I panic for a brief second, thinking I lost the kid my first night on the job, and quickly tiptoe down the hall.

Weston's door is cracked open, and I can just barely make out his form laying in the bed. All rigid and muscular, he's a hard shape in the dark, and nestled up against his chest is Jackson.

I'm fairly certain the kid didn't have a nightmare. He was still in his bed after I got out of the shower, and the only reason he's in here, still fast asleep, is because Weston went in and got him, not trusting me enough to let Jackson sleep in his own room tonight.

Without meaning to, I find myself smiling. Wes is smart. Maybe too smart. The smile wipes off my face fast. I'm one wrong move away from being arrested and thrown into jail. Whatever I do next, I must proceed with caution.

The stairs are creaky, and long shadows are cast on the walls in front of me. Going slow so I don't trip, I hold my hands out in front of me and feel for the wall leading into the kitchen. I slide my hand up and down it, feeling for the switch.

I pour myself a glass of orange juice and slowly sip it, wishing for some vodka. Sitting at the farmhouse-style table, I look out into the dark backyard. It's illuminated just enough by the back porch lights to see the outline of a swing set, and the whole yard is enclosed with a white picket fence.

Freaky, indeed.

Finishing my orange juice, I put the glass in the sink and kill the light, taking another minute to stare into the dark and void my mind of all thoughts. Suddenly, the lights flick back on, and I jump.

"Jesus!"

"No, not Jesus. Just me." Weston stands in the threshold of the kitchen, eyes narrowed as they adjust to the light. He's only wearing navy blue boxers, and all the self-control in the world can't keep me from sweeping my gaze across his muscled torso, down to his defined abs, following the happy trail of hair that leads right to his—

"What are you doing?" he asks, diverting his eyes. Looks like I'm not the only one having trouble tonight. I'm wearing white underwear and a gray Columbia University shirt that barely covers the bottom of my ass.

"I came down to get a drink."

"In the dark?"

"I had the lights on, and then I turned them off."

Weston raises an eyebrow, bringing a hand up to push his hair back. I want nothing more than to run my fingers through it and see if his body feels as hard and chiseled as it looks. I want to slam him up against the wall, putting a crack in that shield he has around himself.

"What are you doing?" I shoot back.

"I heard something."

"Oh, I didn't mean to wake you."

"You didn't." He scrubs his chin with his hand.

I go back to the fridge and grab the orange juice again, pouring him a glass. I set it on the table and take a seat. Wes stares at the drink like I just poured poison in a glass and added a skull-and-crossbones warning for good measure.

"Can't sleep?" He finally takes a step and my god, men like him aren't supposed to be real. They're supposed to exist on the cover of romance novels or in magazines, digitally altered and giving us all a negative complex about the way we look.

"No," I reply.

"I suppose it's weird being here."

"A little. It's very quiet."

"I've never been a fan of big cities."

I shrug. "I've never lived anywhere else to compare it to."

His long fingers wrap around the glass of orange juice, but he doesn't pick it up. Maybe he *is* worried I poisoned him.

"Did you go to Columbia?" His eyes fall to the faded letters across my chest. I'm not wearing a bra, and it's chilly down here. I'm not ashamed to use my body as a weapon, but the flush that comes to my cheeks happens on its own accord. I lie to pretty much everyone I meet, and yet I find myself unable to lie to Wes. And more importantly, I don't want to.

"No, I didn't. Well, I've set foot on campus but not as a student." I fold my hands in my lap. "I didn't go to college." If he looked at my resume, he already knows that.

He picks up the glass and drinks all the juice and then gets up to put his glass in the sink. He has a scar on his back. It's faded considerably but hangs on to the red anger that was inflicted years ago. I can't tell what caused the scar...maybe a burn? My eyes drop to his tight and firm ass. The man does his squats and he does them well.

"You should go back to bed," he says, voice gruff again. "It'll be loud tomorrow once Jackson is up." And without so much as a look back, he crosses the room and disappears up the stairs.

He's brazen, a little rude, and it unnerves me. Wes Dawson is the last person I'd try to con, and not just because he's a cop. He's not looking for a hookup. He's not desperate and needing to prove something to himself.

Though deep down, everyone wants something, and finding out what drives Wes is key to getting what I want. I'll crack him eventually...as long as he doesn't crack me first.

6

I sit back at my desk and pull out my phone, logging onto the security company's app and checking the cameras inside the house again. For the fifth time. This hour. It's not that I don't trust Scarlet, it's just...I don't trust Scarlet.

She's well aware of all the security measures I have in place at our house, and I haven't given her the codes just yet. The only place she's going today is the backyard with Jackson, and there's no need to arm the house just to be outside.

The cameras aren't at all nanny-cams and show the front, back, and side door, as well as one looking down the steps with a view of the foyer. I can just barely see Scarlet and Jackson in the backyard. She's chasing him around with her arms outstretched, dragging one leg as she stumbles through the grass.

I can't help but smile, knowing exactly what she's doing. Jackson is currently obsessed with zombies and loves to be chased by them.

"Who are you sexting?" Officer John Wilson asks me as he passes by my desk on the way to his.

Another officer laughs. "The day Dawson sexts is the day we bust an underground crime ring in Eastwood."

"Fuck you," I shoot back. The guys never back down from a

chance to hassle me about my sex life, or technically lack thereof. "And don't fucking jinx us."

"Come on, don't tell me you don't wanna bust a crime ring?" Wilson goes on. He's a good cop, got his degree in law enforcement from a community college, but has never been in combat. Not the way I have.

"It'd give us something to do," I say with a chuckle. Movement flashes across the screen of my phone again, and I look down just in time to see Scarlet pull her sweatshirt over her head. She has a tank top on underneath, but I still feel like I just witnessed something I wasn't supposed to.

And fuck, I want to see it again.

A minute later, we're called out to a domestic dispute, which is probably the most excitement we'll see all day. I shouldn't complain, though. Eastwood is a safe, small town, and I couldn't think of a better place to raise my son. It's not to say nothing bad ever happens here. Our biggest problem is drugs, and given the rural setting of many of our residents' houses, we've shut down a surprising number of meth labs over the years.

Last year's big bust was arresting Marty McMillian, Eastwood's resident redneck, for threatening and harassing a gay couple. When we got to his house to take him in, hundreds of guns were laid out in his living room. Turns out he'd been stealing them for years and selling them on the black market.

We have a few burglaries and break-ins every year, but in my time on the force, I've yet to be called out to a murder. There was a body found two years ago, but it turned out to be a man from Newport who got drunk and stumbled his way into our township before passing out and succumbing to the elements.

It's obvious what's going on as soon as we pull up to the farmhouse. It's the second time we've been out here in a month.

"Here we go again," Wilson huffs and gets out of the squad car.

"Mr. Green," I start and shut the driver's side door. "I see you've been drinking again."

"Drinking!" his wife shouts. "He's been doing more than just *drinking*! Tell them, Earl, tell them what else you've been doing.

Or *who* you been doing!" She's holding a shotgun and has it pointed in his general direction. And I do mean general. Her hands are too shaky to take a clear shot.

The neighbors across the street are on their porch, and it looks like they've got popcorn. This is high-quality entertainment here.

"Put the gun down, Grace," Wilson says, holding up his hand. "We'll cart his ass back to the station."

I really don't want to put Mr. Green in the back of my car. He always ends up puking. But clearly, he's going to be spending at least the day sleeping this off.

"You take him, and you keep him!" Grace, Mr. Green's wife, pumps the shotgun.

"Come on now, Grace." I go around and take Mr. Green's wrist. If I can lead him away, Grace will start to diffuse. "You don't want to come down to the station with us."

"We'll put you in the same cell," Wilson goes on.

"Good!" Grace shrieks. "I'll beat him. I'll beat him to death this time!"

I wave my hand in the air, dismissing her. It's the same old song and dance, and it happens two or three times a month. The Greens have a daughter, but she can't be bothered with her parents anymore, not that I blame her. Mr. Green has been an unfaithful drunk for as long as I can remember.

I get Mr. Green around my car, and he doubles over and pukes on the grass. Score for me. I hate when we have to ride back to the station with a car full of vomit. I make sure he's done before putting him in the back, and Wilson deals with Grace and her shotgun.

Just a typical day on the job...which makes me want to run for sheriff even more.

~

OWEN: Getaway tonight. Drinks on the house.
    Me: You always say that, yet I always end up paying my tab.
    Dean: WHAT!? YOU'RE ACTUALLY GOING OUT?

Me: No.

Logan: Isn't the hot nanny there?

Dean: I'm sure she is, and that's why he's not going out.

Owen: If I come over and misbehave, will she spank me?

Me: Grow the fuck up.

Dean: I take that to mean she's as hot as her photo made her seem.

I roll my eyes, silencing my phone. Another slew of text messages come through that I ignore. My brothers and I have had an ongoing group text for years that we mostly use for hurling insults or sending crude GIFs to each other.

Putting my phone in the top drawer of my desk, I take care of the rest of the paperwork and grab a coffee from the breakroom. After leaving the Green residence, we had one minor car accident, teenagers trying to shoplift at one of the two gas stations in Eastwood, and ended the shift by helping Betty Perez round up her goats that broke out of their pasture.

I close the file and take it to Sergeant Lopez's office, dropping it off on her desk. Sipping my coffee, I get my phone out to check on the house once more and see I have fifteen missed texts from my brothers and one from Mom. Knowing the texts in the group message Owen named *Bros before hoes* are most likely bullshit anyway, I ignore them for now and see what Mom had to say.

Assuming she's asking about the nanny, her words almost take me by surprise. She wants to make sure I'm okay and not sad... and I have no idea why. Usually she'll text me and ask me that same thing—in the exact same wording every time—when the subject of Daisy is brought up. But we haven't talked about my almost ex-wife recently, nor is it our anniversary or any—oh shit.

Today is Daisy's birthday. It wouldn't have crossed my mind if Mom hadn't texted me. I respond back to her, telling her I hadn't even realized what day it is and yes, I'm fine. I put the phone down again, thinking that it's time to move on from this and file the paperwork after all.

ome on, get it together. I inhale and open the fridge, trying to find something to make for dinner. My first day as Jackson's nanny is almost over, and it did not go as planned at all.

Today wasn't miserable. Time didn't crawl, and I didn't want to claw my eyes out or drown myself in a bottle of wine. Instead—dare I say it—I had fun. I didn't expect to like Jackson. I hoped to mildly tolerate him while I formulated a plan on how to con his dad out of a large sum of money, but events unfolded differently.

Jackson isn't a spoiled and entitled brat. I can tell teaching Jackson manners is important to Wes, and even though he comes off as a mean old grump, I sense he's a gentleman at heart. After only a day, the kid is growing on me, and I need to press pause—if not rewind—on this whole situation and go back to not giving a shit.

But, dammit, I can't.

"Do you want help making dinner?" Jackson asks, little feet slapping against the hardwood floor behind me.

"Uh, sure. What do you want?"

"Chicken nuggets and mac and cheese and pickles and maybe a cupcake for dessert."

I laugh. "Well, we can do the mac and cheese for sure." I grab butter and milk, setting them out the counter. "Pickles too," I add when I see the jar. I preheat the oven, glad there's a bag of dinosaur-shaped nuggets in the freezer.

It's not exactly a home-cooked meal, but the kid's not going hungry tonight. That has to count for something, right?

As the food is cooking, Jackson asks me to sit down and color with him. I bring a coloring book and a big box of crayons to the table.

"I'm going to draw a picture for Daddy," he tells me. "And one for you."

"Thanks, buddy." I carefully tear out the pages he wants and take one for myself, absentmindedly coloring Mickey Mouse in different shades of pink.

"Are you from Chicago?" he asks.

"I am."

"Aunt Winnie lived there. I went there before. We took a train!"

"I used to take the train a lot. It's pretty cool." Cool if you like the smell of piss and dealing with the assholes that always seem to be on the same route I am.

"It wasn't like Thomas the Train."

"No, I guess it's not." I trade my light pink crayon for a darker one.

"Actually, I'm going to give this picture to Emma."

"Who's Emma? A friend?"

Jackson shakes his head, and hair falls into his eyes. He looks so much like his father.

"My cousin. She's a baby."

A baby cousin? Must be Quinn's. I just smile and nod, not wanting to know any more about the Dawson family. Don't know, don't care. Once I get enough money to take care of Dad, I'll be out of here and won't give them a second thought.

"Emma and Uncle Archer have the same birthday."

"Mh-hm." I need to tune this out.

"And Uncle Archer cuts people open. For his job!"

"Wow, that is cool. He's a surgeon, right?" Dammit. I already know too much.

"Right. And he really cuts people open!" Jackson says slowly, eyes wide. "He saved me from the pool once. I almost died."

I stop coloring and look at Jackson. "You almost died?"

He nods and puts on a terrified look. It's fake, but he knows he's supposed to be upset when he talks about this. Smart kid. "I fell in and water got inside my breathing. I had to go to the hos-able!"

It takes me a second to realize "hos-able" is hospital. "That's scary. I'm glad you're okay now or else I wouldn't get to play with you all day."

He nods and starts coloring again. "Daddy was scared. I think he cried. Don't tell him I said that. Daddy doesn't cry. Not even when Mommy left."

"Your mommy left?"

Abort. Abort. Stop asking questions. The less personal info you have about Wes, the better.

"Daddy doesn't know where she is."

"Oh, um…" I have no idea what to say to that. I'm no good at this.

"She didn't love me enough to stay here." A line of worry forms between Jackson's eyes, and I hurt for him. I put my arm around his shoulders.

"That's not true. She must have just, uh…uh…had something else to do." It's a good thing I'm not posing as a counselor. The gig would be up on that one within minutes. "I'm sure she loves you in her own way."

"I don't know what she looks like. Maybe she's pretty like you."

"If she's lucky." I give him a wink.

He goes back to coloring, telling me about something that happened on an episode of *PAW Patrol*. I wrestle with my mind, and my mind ends up winning. So Jackson's mother left him when he was little, too little to remember her. Why? And how?

It. Doesn't. Matter.

Water boils over from the pot on the stove, hissing as it reaches the burner beneath. I jump up and turn the heat off, hoping I didn't ruin something as simple as boxed macaroni and cheese.

Jackson keeps coloring as I drain the water, testing a noodle. It's a little overdone but isn't terrible.

I make the mac and cheese, cover it, and take the nuggets out of the oven. Weston should be back from work soon, and I suppose we can all eat together. My phone rings, and I know it's my sister right away.

"Hello?" I answer, waiting for the automated voice asking if I'll accept a call from an inmate.

"Hey, sis," Heather rushes out. "You didn't come visit me today. What gives?"

"I started a new job." Looking at Jackson, I step out of the kitchen. "I probably won't be able to come for a while, actually. I'm in rural Indiana."

"What the fuck are you—sorry, I won't swear anymore," she says to a guard. "What are you doing there?"

"I'm a nanny again."

A few seconds of silence pass, and I can only imagine Heather's stunned face. "Why?"

"I need money."

"But I had a job for you."

"I'm not doing that," I spit out, blood pressure rising. "No fucking way."

"But you've been all flirty with that C.O. He has it bad for you. Asks about you all the time."

"That doesn't mean I'll bring—just no. I keep him favorable in case you need an extra snack or if I ask him to look the other way if—no, when—you do something stupid. Like this. But I can't flirt my way into or out of this."

"You underestimate the power of your pussy."

"Heather," I start, pinching the bridge of my nose. She sounds manic, and she just went through a cycle a few weeks ago. "Are you taking your meds?"

"Yes! Jesus, Scar, stop trying to be my mother and be my sister for once, why don'tcha?"

"Trust me, I'd love nothing more." Unfortunately, I've been a mother to her since the day she was born. "I just...I just want you to get through your time and get out of there. No more talking with shady people who promise you protection in exchange for business, okay?" I step out of the kitchen and out of earshot. "Just keep your head down and behave."

She grumbles something but doesn't push the issue, mostly because she can't. Not over the phone. But even still, I'm not bringing drugs into a prison. I'm no Mother Teresa, but even I have my limits.

"So is this nannying gig going to turn out like the last one?" she asks.

"If I'm lucky."

"You *are* lucky, Scarlet. You're beautiful, and the world loves beautiful people."

"It's more than that." I sink down on the first step, feeling the threads I keep tightly wrapped around myself start to loosen. I tighten the threads back up until I can hardly breathe.

Not today, Satan.

"I have to go," I tell her. "Call me the next time you can, okay? And please, Heather, just keep to yourself."

"That's not how it works in here, sis. You gotta find a crew or you'll get eaten alive."

"You're in minimum security, Heath. Is it really that bad?"

"You have no idea," she says in a voice so icy it sends a chill through me. "Love you, Scarbutt."

"Love you too, bitch."

I end the call and close my eyes. She's in minimum security now, but I have a sinking feeling it's only a matter of time before she's sent to max. Dad's dying. My sister is in prison. Jason is overseas.

I'm so alone, and I just want my family back...though deep down I know I never really had one in the first place.

"Daddy!"

Jackson comes running, throwing his arms around me. Coming home to my son is the best part of my day. I never realize how much I miss this kid until his skinny little arms are wrapped around my neck. Scooping him up with one hand, I stand, pretending to drop him.

Jackson lets out a dramatic yell and then laughs hysterically. I do it again and get the same reaction.

"We made dinner!" he tells me excitedly, taking my hand as soon as his feet hit the floor. "Come eat!"

"Give me one minute, and I'll join you."

"It's just nuggets and mac and cheese," Scarlet says almost apologetically. She's still wearing the denim shorts she had on earlier but has added a button-up flannel shirt over her tank top. Her blonde hair is in a messy braid, with loose strands hanging around her face. Even a blind man would notice how gorgeous she is.

"Some of our favorites," I say and take off my shoes. I'm still in uniform with my gun strapped to my utility belt around my waist. I go upstairs to lock it up and change into gray sweatpants and a white T-shirt.

Scarlet is bringing plates to the table and does a double take when she sees me. I can't get a good read on her, and I don't get why everyday things seem surprising to her. Maybe it's a sign this isn't going to work out and I should let her go after the weekend is over, saying we're just not a good match.

Though that would be one hell of a lie. There are plenty of things I'd like to do with Scarlet where I think we'd be a match made in heaven.

"How was your day, buddy?" I ask Jackson, tearing my eyes away from Scarlet as she sets the final plate down on the table. Her shorts are tight in all the right places, and it's a battle of willpower not to steal another glance at her fine ass.

"It was so fun!" He puts his chicken nugget back down on his plate and bounces with excitement. "First, we played dinosaurs. Then Scarlet chased me around like a zombie!"

"Sounds like you had a pretty fun day." I smile, heart warming at the sight of his happy face.

"It was more fun than when I spend the day with Grammy, but don't tell her that." Jackson hunches his shoulders in as he speaks, making both Scarlet and me laugh.

"Your secret is safe with me," Scarlet promises.

Jackson takes one small bite of his food before starting up again, going through every single detail of the day. It sounds like he really did have fun, and it's nice knowing he was up and active and not stuck in front of a screen all day. Not that Mom gives him her phone with YouTube videos all the time or anything, but sometimes she has work to do and that's the only way to get shit done.

"Are we going to Grammy and Papa's this weekend?" Jackson asks.

"Yep," I reply and then flick my eyes to Scarlet. "We go to my parents' house for dinner almost every Sunday."

"That's nice." She pushes her mac and cheese around on her plate before taking a bite.

"Can Scarlet come too?" Jackson asks, eyes full of hope.

"Uh," I start, not knowing what to say. Scarlet lives with us —for now—but she's not part of the family. She has no obligation to do anything other than take care of Jackson, and

Sunday is technically her day off. "If she wants to, she's welcome to come."

"Yay! Did you hear what my daddy said? You can come!"

"If she wants to," I stress.

"Please!" Jackson begs her. "Please oh please say yes!"

Scarlet laughs. "How can I say no to that face?"

Jackson gets so excited he jumps out of his chair and runs around the table to give Scarlet a hug.

"Eat," I gently remind him. "We have to go over letters and then get a bath in."

"We already did letters," he says, giving me a know-it-all look.

"Excuse me?" I raise my eyebrows.

With a dramatic sigh that he learned from Dean no doubt, he points to Scarlet. "We already did letters, Dad."

"He showed me his workbook and asked if we could do a page. He got lowercase 'b' and 'd' mixed up a few times, but other than that, he did a good job."

I'm not sure how to feel about this. Can this woman teach Jackson as well as I can? It's not like I'm an overqualified child educator, but he's my son.

"Thanks," I say.

"Can we go to the park then?" Jackson asks.

"Yeah, we'll have time before bed now."

"Yay!" Jackson drops his fork and starts clapping. I shift my gaze from him to Scarlet, taking in the slight smile pulling up her full lips. "Will you come too, Scarlet?" he asks.

"Of course!" She beams at him, and he jabbers away about his favorite things to do at the park the rest of dinner. I take Jackson upstairs to change into something a little warmer. The evening air takes on a chill once the sun goes down.

The park is two blocks away, and Jackson usually rides his bike while I walk behind. He still needs training wheels and struggles a bit when the sidewalk is uneven.

Scarlet changed into black leggings and a long-sleeve T-shirt and is walking in step next to me. I turn my head, unable to help but notice the way her breasts bounce with each step even though she's wearing a bra.

"You don't have to go to dinner with my family on Sunday," I start. "Don't feel pressured by Jackson. He'll get over it."

She gives me a pleasant smile. "I don't mind, really. I have nothing else to do. But if you don't want me there—"

"No, that's not it," I say quickly. Why do I care about offending her? I shouldn't.

I don't.

"They're a bit overbearing," I warn. "And there's a lot of them."

"Jackson was talking about an Uncle Archer."

I nod. "That's Quinn's fiancé. She's the youngest of my siblings and has a baby. Then there's Logan and Owen—they're identical twins—and then Dean and his wife, Kara."

"Four siblings and two more by marriage?" She laughs. "I can hardly handle the two I have."

"It's a lot, but I like it," I admit. "It's always loud and crazy, but that's the way it's always been."

"You must be close to Quinn."

"We're all pretty close." We stop at the edge of the street, and after making sure Jackson remembers the concept of looking both ways, we cross and make it down half the block before either of us speak.

"So," she starts, voice soft. She pushes a loose strand of hair from her face and turns to me, blue eyes sparkling in the fading sunlight. "Jackson mentioned his mother. He didn't go into detail, but I don't know how you want me handling the situation. He seemed a little upset."

Well, shit. I didn't think this fun piece of conversation would come up already. Out of the mouth of babes...

"We don't talk about her." I set my gaze forward, watching Jackson peddle his little heart out. Indiana is relatively flat all around, but there's a slight incline on the way to the park that he sometimes needs help with.

"Oh, okay. I'll just try to change the subject."

I let out a sigh, knowing that sooner or later, this is going to all come out, and I'd rather have Scarlet hear it from me than anyone else.

"Jackson's mother left a few weeks after he was born. She came back once, stayed a few days, and that's the last time I've seen or heard anything from her. When Jackson asks, I tell him Daisy had other things to do." I shrug. "It's not the best response, but nothing is a good response in that situation."

"I'm sorry," Scarlet says, and I brush off her words. I don't want pity. I get along just fine, and raising my son on my own for the last four years allowed us to bond in a way we couldn't if Daisy was still in the picture.

"Slow down," I call out to Jackson, who spotted one of his friends at the park. We have one more street to cross. Picking up the pace, I catch up to him before he zooms across the street. We wait for a pickup to go by, and then he rides as fast as he can to the playground, dumping his bike to the ground and pulling at his helmet strap as he runs to the swing set.

I wave to Mrs. Hills, the mother of Jackson's friend, and motion to a park bench. Scarlet follows, eyes wide as she takes it all in.

"What part of Chicago are you from?" I ask.

"The South Side." She gives me a lopsided smile. "Yes, the ghetto."

Nodding, I decide that's enough information to share for one night. She's my employee, after all. The wind picks up, blowing in the scent of rain. Scarlet shivers and pulls her arms in around herself. The faint outline of her nipples becomes visible through her shirt, and I take off my jacket to give to her.

"Thanks." She slips her arms inside the sleeves, thinking I'm being chivalrous. Really, I'm helping out my dick.

"Dad! Scarlet!" Jackson yells from the top of a slide. "Come watch me go down the slide. It's super fast!"

We both get up, going across the playground to watch Jackson go down a twisty slide. He grabs Scarlet's hand and leads her up the playground steps. My phone buzzes in my pocket, no doubt more texts from my brothers.

"Good evening, Officer Dawson," Mrs. Hills croons, sauntering over. She got divorced last year and makes sure everyone knows just how single she is every time she talks.

"Hello, Mrs. Hills."

"Please, call me Terry. Our boys go to school together. We're practically family at this point."

I force a smile, realizing that running for sheriff means having to put up with bullshit small talk and pleasantries. Maybe I don't want to do it after all.

"I can't help but notice your companion," she goes on. "Finally free?" She wiggles her eyebrows hopefully.

"She's Jackson's nanny," I reply, sidestepping her question. Sometimes I hate this small town as much as I love it. Everyone knows Daisy ran out on us and I haven't petitioned for a divorce yet.

"Well, she's very pretty."

"I suppose so."

"Are you coming to the kids' fall party at school next week?"

Motherfucker. It's next week? "I'm not sure. We'll see how much crime happens that morning."

Terry laughs like it's the funniest thing in the world, and Scarlet snaps her head around. Her eyes flit from me to Terry, taking a second to watch us before turning back to Jackson.

"Well, I'm in charge of snacks, and if you want, I can bring you something extra. Maybe something a little sweet?" She angles her body toward mine, inhaling so her breasts rise up in front of me. "Or do you prefer salty?"

Doing everything I can not to physically recoil from her, my phone ringing at that exact moment is welcome.

"It's my sister. Gotta take this," I say.

"Quinn? Tell her I said hello!" Quite a few people in this town were quick to judge Quinn when they found out she was pregnant and not married. Then they remembered she was rich and suddenly are her best friend again.

"Hey, sis," I say into the phone.

"Hey. So...how'd it go today?"

"The day isn't over yet."

"Uh-oh. Is that a bad thing?"

I watch Scarlet run in slow motion as Jackson and his friend chase her around, pretending to be the zombies this time. "No. Jackson seems to really like her."

"Good! She was really nice when we met at the coffee shop."

I don't feel like getting into it with my sister tonight, but we've all tried to explain to her that just because someone seems nice doesn't mean they should be trusted. But that's just Quinn for you, always finding the good in everyone.

"We'll see how it goes. I'm still not sold on this, you know."

"Make up your damn mind. If you want to pull out of the race, just do it already. If not, we need to amp up your campaigning."

"I thought you were certain I'd win," I tease.

"I am. But people need to know you're running against that sexist old Sheriff Turner so they can vote for you."

Chuckling, I agree. "Okay. Give me to the end of the week. If this works out, we'll go all the way with this."

"Yay! Oh, shit. Emma just puked all over Archer and he was on his way out the door to do an emergency appendectomy."

"I don't miss those days. See ya later, sis."

"Love you. Give Jackson a kiss for me!"

"Will do."

I pull the blankets tighter around my shoulders and bring my legs up under myself. It started raining not long after we got back from the park, and it dropped the temperature by twenty degrees. A damp chill took hold of the house, and while the heater is on and running, I haven't warmed up yet.

Which has nothing to do with my cold heart, I'm sure.

Wes put Jackson to bed, and knowing that he actually *wants* to spend time with his son is charming. Wait, no it's not. There's nothing charming about him. Nope. Not at all. And he certainly didn't look good in those gray sweatpants. And offering me his jacket wasn't a smooth move or anything. And putting my arms in the sleeves of said jacket and feeling the heat from his body was a turn-off. Big time.

He's closed off but not socially inept, and his charm isn't lost on the people of this town. Ms. Soccer Mom at the park was flirting with him, and we got stopped three times on the short walk home. Two more single women just "wanted to say hi" and find out who I was, of course. His next-door neighbors are an elderly couple, and they thanked him for helping mow their lawn a few days ago.

He's the golden boy of this town, and pulling any sort of trick on him will probably cause the townspeople to grab their torches and pitchforks and march after me while singing "Kill the Beast."

I roll over, debating if I should get up and get socks or if moving out of the covers will make me even more cold. I cuddle my unicorn close to my chest and make myself into a little ball, too lazy to get up.

Someone softly knocks at the door, and I shoot up, thinking it's Jackson.

"Scarlet?" Weston calls, voice low. "Are you awake?"

Suddenly, I'm nervous, and it's not because I don't want him to come in here and make an advance. It's because I do.

"Yeah, I am." I get up, pulling the top quilt from the bed and wrapping it around my shoulders. Ignoring the urge to smooth out my hair, I open the door. Weston is standing there, wearing a white T-shirt and plaid PJ pants. The look is casual, completely appropriate, and not at all sexy. So why do I feel heat rushing through me?

"I never opened the vents in here." He motions to something on the ceiling. "I just remembered."

"Oh, um, how do you open them? I'll do it."

"I got it." He doesn't look at me, and for some reason, it annoys me. "You probably won't be able to reach it." Stepping aside, I flick on the light and pull the blanket tighter around my shoulders. "It's cold in here. Sorry," he mumbles and walks through the room, reaching up and opening the vents. Warm air rushes down on me. He turns to leave and spots the unicorn on my pillow.

"You sleep with that?" he asks, lips pulling up with a bit of amusement.

"Every night. His name is Ray."

"Interesting name," Wes says.

The half smile turns into a real smile and, dammit, it's doing bad things to me. I sit on my bed and pick Ray up. "He's yellow, like a ray of sunshine."

"That makes sense, I guess."

I shrug. "I've had him forever. I know it's weird."

"There are weirder things to have in bed."

I raise my eyebrows. "Speaking from experience?"

"Unfortunately, no."

"I suppose that's good to know," I laugh.

Weston smiles, holding my gaze for a few seconds, and I see the man under the tough exterior. He's a bit damaged, like me, and the strangest feeling takes over, making me want to comfort him. Then he stiffens, inhaling deep and pushing his shoulders back. I watch his chest muscles rise and fall, feeling so little next to him.

"Goodnight," he says and walks right past me out the door. He doesn't shut it behind him, and I watch him disappear down the hall. Jackson is in his own room tonight, and Wes closes his door halfway, probably leaving it open to be able to hear if I get out of bed and decide to kidnap his son or something.

I close my door, twisting the knob before it clicks into place, silently shutting it. Then I get back in bed, still cold but feeling hot and flustered inside. Along with having little experience with good parents, I have little experience with good guys. My track record is unimpressive, and I haven't had anything serious since I broke up with Tommy three and a half years ago.

I can feel warm air filling the room, but I'm still chilled. I get up and grab a pair of socks from my suitcase—no, I haven't unpacked yet and probably won't until I've worn everything at least once and doing laundry is a necessity. Hunkering back down into bed, I curl up with Ray and fall asleep.

It shouldn't surprise me that I dream of Weston. Of his large, rough hands running up the back of my thighs. Of his lips against mine as he kisses his way down my neck, over my breasts, and down my stomach. He yanks off my panties and dives between my legs, and his warm tongue against me is the best thing I've ever felt.

I wake up with my hand between my legs, body begging to go back to sleep and finish the dream. Rain patters against the window, and I let out a breath, no longer cold. I close my eyes and try to get comfortable, but I'm too hot and bothered to peacefully fall back asleep.

What am I doing wrong here? Well, besides wanting to cheat

an honest man out of money—don't judge me on that. That's a topic for another day, one that will require confession, ten Hail Marys, and hours of community service.

Weston isn't a wealthy asshole with money to burn. I can't convince myself I'm a sexy Robin Hood with him, stealing from the rich to give to the poor—aka me. I can't take anything from him. I don't want to.

I hoped to get through to him, to knock down his walls and see what makes him tick. But I think he's going to get to me first... and he's not even trying.

∼

I PLUNGE my hands into the warm, soapy water. I didn't sleep well last night, and around five AM I gave up and came downstairs to start breakfast. Wes works today and said he leaves the house around seven.

So far, I've made blueberry muffins, cooked an entire package of bacon, and have eggs whipped up and ready to scramble once the boys come downstairs. They're best fresh out of the pan and don't take long to make. I've piled the bacon onto a plate and put it in the oven to stay warm. The muffins are neatly arranged in a bowl on the table. I even found a white cloth napkin to put in the bowl first, making it look all fancy and proper.

And now the dishes are almost done, and the table is already set. Show me an attractive single dad and suddenly I turn into Betty fucking Crocker.

What.

The.

Fuck.

Compartmentalizing and not dealing with my feelings is my thing. My claim to fame. The only reason I've been able to get by this well for so long. My deck has always been stacked a few cards short, and in a dog-eat-dog world, I've never had the chance to stop and think about a better life.

And I mean really think.

Like muffins and bacon kind of thinking.

Opening the oven, I grab a piece of bacon before making a pot of coffee. The smell of French roast fills the air, and something inside me relaxes.

"Morning," Wes says when he comes into the kitchen. He's dressed in his uniform, and he looks so good I don't think I'd be surprised if someone started playing "Hot in Here" and he started taking off all his clothes in a private strip show just for me.

I'd grab the bacon, sit back, and watch.

"Morning," I say back, going to the cabinet to get him a coffee cup. Assuming he'll have his coffee the same way he did yesterday, I fill the cup and add just a little bit of cream and sugar. "Do you want eggs? I was just about to make some."

Wes's brows move together, and he looks around the kitchen as if I finger-painted the furniture, not made him breakfast.

"Sure."

"Okay. Have a seat. It'll only take a few minutes." I already preheated the pan. With my back to him, I focus on the eggs, doing my best not to turn around and make small talk, because I know if I look into Weston's dark eyes, there's a good chance I'll turn into a pile of goo on the floor.

And then who's going to finish making breakfast?

"You didn't have to do all this," Weston says in a level tone. "We usually eat cereal or Pop Tarts in the morning."

"I was up, and that's the kind of thing I usually eat too. Something hot for breakfast sounded nice."

I turn down the burner and risk a look back at Weston. He's pulled his hair away from his face and is leaning back in the kitchen chair. He looks right at me, and something burns behind his stormy eyes.

"Yeah, a hot breakfast is nice every now and then."

He's literally agreeing with words I just spoke, yet I'm feeling flush like he's filling every syllable with a secret innuendo. And dammit—I want him to. And now there's no denying that Weston Dawson has done the impossible: gotten under my skin and is weaseling his way into that dark cavity in my chest that some call a heart.

*G*oddammit. Bacon and eggs and blueberry muffins have never tasted so good. Scarlet piles bacon and eggs on her plate, fills a mug halfway with coffee and then tops it off the rest of the way with creamer. She dumps a spoonful of sugar in it as well, bringing her food over to the table. Her hair is pulled up in a messy bun, and the loose strands that fall around her face are begging to be pushed back.

She's wearing black leggings and a tight black T-shirt, with a loose-fitting red-and-black flannel shirt over top. She's effortlessly beautiful, and I can't find a single thing about her to complain about.

"Blueberry muffins are cliché." She reaches for one, setting it on her plate. "But it was the only kind I could make. You guys must like blueberries."

I smile as I finish chewing a piece of bacon. "Jackson eats them like candy."

"That's good. Better than eating candy like candy." She laughs at herself, realizing what she said. "You know what I mean."

"Yeah, I do. And I agree. He's always been a good eater in that sense."

She picks up a piece of bacon. "I can relate to that."

A few minutes of silence go by as we both eat our breakfast.

It's still gray and cloudy outside, but Scarlet is brightening up the whole room. "When does Jackson usually get up?" she asks.

"Eight-thirty or nine if he's able. Usually when I work on a Saturday, I take him to my parents' and have to wake him up early. He'll be happy to sleep in today."

Scarlet nods, finishing her bacon and eggs. She goes for the muffin next. "Are your parents retired?"

I shake my head, picking up the coffee. "No. My dad's a contractor, and my mom works with him running the office aspect of the business."

"What do your brothers do? Are any of them cops as well?"

I laugh at the thought of Owen or Logan in uniform. "No. Dean works with our dad, and Logan and Owen own a bar called Getaway."

"In town?"

"Yeah. It's pretty much the only good bar around here, and I'm not just saying that because my brothers own it."

"I've only seen quite literally two blocks of this town, but I'm guessing there's not much to it?"

"Eastwood isn't huge, but we have more than you'd think...I think." If she's used to Chicago, then she's not going to be impressed by our little town. "We're not some podunk town in the middle of nowhere," I go on. "If the weather clears up, I can show you around."

She smiles. "I'd like that. Better get used to things here, right?"

I open my mouth but can't make the word come out. It's easy. One syllable. *Right*. But saying that one word feels like I'm saying a magic spell that seals our fate. She's here. To stay. Which means there' s a good chance of winning this race, which of course is the end goal. But that means being away from Jackson more, and it's suddenly hitting me like a punch to the face.

"Yeah," I finally force myself to say and get up for a refill of coffee. Scarlet's almost done with her muffin by the time I get back.

"You eat a lot for someone of your size," I blurt, needing to fill the silence with something.

She smiles, finishing the last bit of her muffin. "I do a lot of bad things, and I think the guilt inside of me burns a lot of calories." Her eyes meet mine for a second, and I laugh.

"I didn't realize that was the key to dieting."

She winks. "It's a secret. Don't tell anyone."

Still smiling, I clear my plate from the table. "Thanks for breakfast. Jackson will be thrilled to have bacon when he gets up."

"Should I wake him up at any particular time?"

"No, you can let him sleep in. He might wake up when I go say bye to him."

Scarlet gets that surprised look again. "That's sweet you tell him goodbye."

"I always do."

She drops her gaze to her hands, blinking rapidly. I fill a to-go mug with coffee, fully aware of my caffeine addiction, though I think a caffeine addiction is almost a requirement when you're a parent, let alone a single one.

Quietly, I go into Jackson's room and pull the blankets back over him. The kid sleeps like an octopus, and his pillows, blankets, and stuffed animals always end up on the floor.

"Love you," I whisper and kiss him on the top of the head. "See you tonight, buddy."

～

"I HAVE no idea where Jackson is," Scarlet tells me, raising her shoulders in a dramatic shrug. The pile of blankets behind her on the couch moves, and Jackson giggles from inside.

"Oh no," I say back. "Where could he be?" Jackson laughs again, and I take off my shoes and stride to the couch. "I'll go look for him after I sit down for a bit." Perching on the edge of the couch, I slowly lean back against Jackson. "This pillow is lumpy." I pretend to fluff it, and Jackson pops up from under the blankets.

"Boo!"

"What?" I lean back, eyes wide. "I didn't know you were there!"

"I tricked you, I tricked you!" Jackson chants. He jumps into my arms, and everything is right in the world.

"What did you do today?" I ask, though I already have an idea. Scarlet texted a few photos throughout the day. It rained all morning, and they built a pretty epic fort in the living room. She was laying down inside it next to Jackson in one of the photos she sent. Jackson's face was scrunched up, eyes closed with a toothy smile.

Then it seems they played with Jackson's farm set the rest of the day, which is his current favorite thing. The handmade, wooden barn was mine when I was a kid, and Jackson thinks it's extra special knowing I played with it when I was his age.

Jackson tells me about his day, and Scarlet goes back into the kitchen. I can't see what she's doing, but it sounds like she's chopping vegetables. We don't have vegetables. Well, not fresh ones anyway. I desperately need to go grocery shopping, but Jackson's been a pain in the ass to take with lately, and I'm ready to bang my head against the wall by the time our shopping trip is over.

"Can I play at Dillan's house after dinner?" Jackson asks. Dillan lives across the street. His sister is in Jackson's preschool class with him, but girls currently have cooties, and Jackson wants nothing to do with her. Which is fine by me.

"Maybe for a little bit."

"Until it gets dark?"

"You can see if he wants to play here," I offer, liking it better when Jackson brings friends here as opposed to him going to a friend's house. I can keep a better eye on them...which is probably what every parent on the face of the earth thinks.

"Yay! Thanks, Dad!" Jackson gives me a hug and jumps off the couch.

Scarlet peeks out of the kitchen, knife in hand. Yep. She was chopping something. "You still need to go pick up your farm toys, buddy," she tells him. "You promised you'd pick them up before dinner."

"Okay," Jackson says without so much as a glare or a stomp of his little foot. He hurries up the stairs, and I look back in Scarlet's direction, thinking I hired a witch instead of a nanny because there's no way Jackson agrees to cleaning this easily.

Once the shock wears off, I go into the kitchen to make sure Scarlet is cooking dinner and not chopping up frog legs or eye of newt and adding it into a cauldron.

"Hey," she says with a smile, looking up from the cutting board. She's chopping carrots and adding them to a Corningware dish.

"Where'd the veggies come from?" I ask, bypassing telling her how spellbinding she looks with her hair in messy waves hanging around her face, wearing a simple black tunic and gray leggings.

"Ms. Hills *accidentally* bought too much at the farmers' market today." Scarlet raises her eyebrows. "Imagine that."

I plow a hand through my hair, smiling. "Yeah, she's...uh..."

"Totally hot for you?"

"That's not how I'd phrase it, but...yeah...I suppose so."

Scarlet chops up a few more pieces of the carrot and adds them to the dish. "I can't blame her." She flicks her eyes up, a small smile playing on her lips. Inhaling deep, Scarlet's breasts rise and fall beneath her scoop-neck shirt.

"What are you making?" I ask, trying to steer myself back into PG territory. Because my cock is making this conversation want to go into the *adults-only* section.

"I'm not really sure," she admits with a laugh. "I found this recipe on Pinterest." She grabs her phone to show me what she's making.

"Looks good."

She grabs an onion and starts slicing. "How was work?"

"Slow today, which isn't a bad thing."

"No," she agrees. "Not at all." She turns her head, blinking fast. "Oh my god. It really does burn your eyes."

"The onion?"

"Yes." Laughing, she sets the knife down and squeezes her eyes closed. "My eyes are watering like crazy!" She opens her eyes again only to shut them a second later. She wipes at them with the back of her hand, still laughing at herself.

"It can't be that bad," I say and stride over to cut up the rest of the onion for her. But the second I get next to the cutting board, my own eyes start to burn.

"Okay, you're right. This has to be the strongest onion in the world."

Laughing, she turns away and takes a step forward and walks right into me. Her supple breasts crash against my chest, sending a wave of heat right to the tip of my cock. She bounces off me, and I reach out, hands landing on the gentle curves of both her hips to steady her.

With her eyes still closed, she reaches forward with one hand, flattening it against my chest. Slowly, she trails her hand down until it's resting just inches above my belt. Her lips part, and my heart speeds up. I wonder if she can feel my pulse racing, if she knows what her body close to mine is doing to me. If she brought her hand lower or moved just a tiny bit closer, she'd feel it. My fingertips dig into her flesh, soaking up all the warmth I can through her shirt.

She smells like lavender and strawberries, an intoxicating scent on its own, but so welcome over the smell of the onion. I want to move close and breathe it in, but getting close to Scarlet is a bad fucking idea.

Clearing my throat, I tear myself away before this semi turns into a full erection.

"How are you able to keep your eyes open?" she laughs, blinks hers open for just a few seconds.

"I have superpowers."

"Well, then use them and chop up the rest of the onion." That smile looks so good on her, even with the red, watery eyes. She goes to the sink, washes her hands, and rubs her eyes. "Okay… that's a little better. But, oh my God, I had no idea it got that bad!"

"Have you never chopped an onion before?"

She shakes her head. "It's been a while. And I'm not the best cook, so don't hold it against me if dinner tonight sucks."

"I'm not a good cook either, so I won't." Besides…there are other things I want to hold against her. Swallowing hard, I take one last look at her before tearing my eyes away and going upstairs to change.

"Dad, look!" Jackson calls when I walk past his room. "I cleaned up!"

"You did a great job, bud!" I go into his room, impressed by how thorough the kid was.

"Do you think Scarlet will be proud of me?"

"I know she will be. I am."

"Really?"

"Of course!"

He makes a face. "You're just saying that because you're my dad."

I laugh. "Well, I suppose I am a little biased. But you are a good kid. Most of the time."

"What am I the other times?"

"Rotten. And a stinker."

Jackson laughs. "No, I'm not!"

"Yeah, you are," I tease and poke at his sides, making him erupt in giggles. He climbs onto my lap and runs his finger over my badge.

"I love you, Daddy," he says softly.

"And I love you."

~

I DOZED off putting Jackson to bed and woke up not knowing what time it was. Or what day it was. Or my name. Napping always does that to me. All I know is it's late, and I'm way too old to sleep contorted in a twin bed around my wiggling four year old.

Light from the living room TV filters up the stairs. Scarlet is huddled on the couch, knees drawn up to her chest. She's wearing a baggy sweatshirt and tight black shorts. Her hair is piled on the top of her head, and her eyes are wide.

The bottom stair creaks under my weight, and Scarlet jumps, knocking a pillow off the couch.

"Jesus!"

"Again, just me," I say with a cheeky grin. "You're jumpy." I flick my eyes to the TV. "And now I see why."

"Have you watched this?" she asks, picking up the remote and pausing the horror show she's watching.

"Not all of it. I'm up to episode four."

"I'm not even through the third episode and I don't know if I can handle the rest."

"It is creepy. They did a good job with this show."

She picks up the pillow and stretches her long legs out on the coffee table. "Want to watch it with me? You can hold me accountable not to chicken out."

"Should I indulge you with junk food too?"

A smile plays across her face. "I'm starting to think you get me, Mr. Dawson."

"You know you can call me Wes, right?"

The smile gets bigger. "It makes me feel like I'm on the *Titanic*."

"What?" I ask, my own lips curving into a half-smile.

"Seriously?" She pushes up on the couch and leans forward, and God help me, I can see down her shirt. She's dressed for bed and not wearing a bra.

"I'm not following." I run my hand over my face, needing to physically block out the sight of her perfect breasts.

"Isn't that part of the reason you named your son Jackson, so you could call him Jack Dawson?"

I shake my head again. "He's named after my grandfather."

"Oh. Well then, never mind." She leans back only to round on me again. "So you're telling me you've never seen the movie *Titanic*?"

"Can't say I have."

"We can't be friends now," she says seriously.

"That puts a strain on this whole situation, doesn't it?"

"It does." She slowly moves her head back and forth and picks up the remote again. "If only there was a way to solve it."

"You want me to watch *Titanic*, don't you?"

Laughing, she nods. "Not tonight, though. Tonight, we need to find out why angry spirits are haunting this family."

"Go ahead and keep watching," I tell her and cross the room. "I've already seen this episode."

Several minutes later, I come back with popcorn, Oreos, and a bag of chips.

"You delivered on that junk food," Scarlet says, folding her legs up under herself, freeing space on the couch. She pats the seat next to her and I can't move. Usually, the floor is lava and Jackson and I are jumping off it onto the couch, but right now it feels like it's the other way around.

"Do you like horror movies?" I ask, forcing myself to take a step forward and place the food on the coffee table.

"I do. I have a slight fascination with paranormal stuff. What about you?"

"They're okay. Most are lame nowadays, though. I miss the old slasher flicks from my childhood."

She tips her face up to me, eyebrow raised. "You watched a lot of slashers when you were a kid?"

"Actually, no. I watched them at a friend's house when I'd spend the night and then would have to lie about why I was so scared when I came home. My parents were kinda strict."

"Mine weren't." She grabs the bowl of popcorn, and I'm still standing there, eyeing her down like she's Kryptonite and I'm Clark Kent. "My dad wasn't around much until later." As soon as the words leave her lips, she leans back, almost as if she's surprised with herself for the confession. Seeming a bit flustered, she shoves a handful of popcorn in her mouth and grabs a blanket off the arm of the couch.

I go around the coffee table and sit on the couch, moving a pillow in between us.

"The flashbacks threw me," I say, wanting to break the silence. "I'm not good at remembering names in shows."

"Yeah, it took me a minute to get it too."

I watch her face, knowing a rotten body is going to fall out on screen when the closet door opens. Scarlet's eyes widen, but she doesn't jump.

I did.

"This house is old." She turns to me, pulling the blankets tighter over her shoulders. "But it's not haunted, is it?"

"I've never seen anything. And even though Jackson says he does, I don't really believe him. I'd think he'd be scared if he saw a real ghost."

"So you believe in ghosts?"

"I haven't seen enough to sway me either way."

"Smart man." She takes another handful of popcorn, and by the way she shuts down, I have a feeling she has seen something to sway her. But not necessarily a spirit. Something more real. Something that can hurt you in a way a ghost can't.

We finish the rest of the episode in silence, and then the next one starts. I'll admit, this show is creepy. There's something about weird shit happening to everyday people to get you thinking and make you become paranoid...which is exactly what the writers of this show wanted. They succeeded.

Halfway through the new episode, I reach for the chips the same time Scarlet does. My hand brushes over hers.

"Your skin is freezing," I say, using it as an excuse to take her small hand in mine. I splay my fingers over hers, sandwiching her hand between both of mine. Her skin is cold but so smooth and soft. Blood rushes through me, and the tip of my cock tingles, imagining that small, soft hand wrapping around it.

"My feet are even colder." She shifts her weight and pushes her freezing cold feet underneath me, laughing. "They get cold at night. I used to want a dog just so I could have them lay in bed and keep my feet warm."

"That's a good reason to get a dog."

"I know, right?"

I let go of her hand and move mine to her feet, cupping them both against my palm.

"You're so warm," she says quietly and leans back. I start to rub her feet—to be helpful, of course. There's no need to make her be cold.

"I tend to run warm. I'm always hot."

"I'm the opposite. I get cold easily and my hands and feet feel like ice if the temp drops below eighty."

I laugh. "I can tell."

She lays back, throwing the blanket over her legs. I don't mean to keep rubbing her feet, but I do, making sure she's properly warmed up. She twists, laying on her side but keeping her feet on my lap. I swallow hard, tempted to run my hands down to her thigh and see if the skin on her calves is as smooth and soft as I think it'll be.

She inhales deeply, slowly moving her feet against my thigh, and I can't help but think she's doing it on purpose. Does she know the effect she's having on me? Certainly a woman like Scarlet is well fucking aware of what she can do to a man.

Episode four ends and five begins, and Scarlet's legs are still draped over me. This episode is even freakier than the last, and Scarlet does jump a time or two. When episode six starts, we're both too far down the rabbit hole to stop. Scarlet gets up to use the bathroom, hurrying down the hall during the opening credits.

"I was convinced someone was going to jump out of that closet and bring me into the spirit world," she says when she gets back, taking her spot on the couch. Instead of leaning against the arm on the opposite side, she moves the pillow between us and scoots closer. "Feel." She holds out her hands, and I freeze, mouth going dry as I raise my gaze to her face.

Her blue eyes are wide, and red-and-blue flashes from the TV illuminate her face. A slight flush colors her cheeks, and her full lips are parted. She's so damn pretty it hurts.

"I think you were taken into the spirit world." I wrap my hands around hers. "You're even colder than before."

"Time probably stopped for you out here, and I was in there for like an hour at least, getting my soul sucked out by demons."

"That is the most likely explanation." Before I can stop myself, I push a loose strand of her hair back out of her face. She shivers, closing her eyes in a long blink and then inches closer. "I'll turn up the heat. Jackson runs hot too."

"He gets it from you."

I nod, eyes falling from hers to her breasts. "My brothers are the same way. My mom and Quinn were always freezing, but they learned to deal," I add with a laugh. Goosebumps break out along

her arm, and I slide my hand up, feeling each tiny [...]
her flesh. My heart hammers loudly in my chest as I [...]
every fiber in my being.

I want to pull her close. I have the perfect opportu[...]
screaming at me. It's like the universe is throwing me a bone,
trying to make up for the shit I've trudged through before. There's
no denying the attraction between us, and maybe I'm out of
practice, or all together too damn hopeful, but I feel something
with Scarlet.

Something I haven't felt in a long, long time.

Something I never even felt with Daisy.

But I can't. She's Jackson's nanny. She's here for him, and he's
the only thing that matters.

11

SCARLET

I forgot about conning this man. I forgot about wanting to squeeze every penny I could and leave without so much as a look back. I forgot about my old life, about the shit I have to deal with on a daily basis.

For the last four episodes of this scary-as-shit show, all I've been able to think about is 1.) we are probably going to die at the hands of evil spirits tonight and 2.) Weston is so big and so warm and it's taking every ounce of self-control I have not to move over and lean against him.

I want to feel his hands on me. His lips against mine. I want to at the very least press my hand to his muscular chest and see if his heart is racing, because mine is. And it's not only from being scared of this show.

It's because I know I'm walking a fine line, one that puts me at risk. And I don't take risks, not like this at least. When my heart is involved, I'm out. It hasn't been an issue for me before, because I've come to believe my heart is shriveled and small like the Grinch's, but unlike a children's story, no amount of singing and kindness can make mine grow and start beating inside my chest.

It can't.

Because beating hearts get broken.

The floor creaks above us and I tense, turning to Wes with

wide eyes. "Please tell me you have a cat I don't know about."

Slowly, he turns his head to look at me, eyes vacant. "No cat. Just the Tall Man." He looks at me, unblinking. My heart speeds up. I swallow hard, waiting for him to crack.

He doesn't.

"The Tall Man's coming for you," Weston whispers, almost scaring me before he starts to laugh.

I throw a pillow at him. "Jerk!"

"I totally got you," he says, still laughing.

"Not funny!"

Wes picks up the pillow and tosses it back at me. I tuck it behind me and scoot a little closer to him.

"But really...what was that?"

"When the heater kicks off it causes the whole house to creak. There's a lot of sounds you'll get used to. The pipes rattle when someone is in the shower. Or the dishwasher is running. If you open the windows upstairs, a draft comes down the stairs and blows the front door shut, and sometimes when you turn on the back porch light, it makes the hallway light come on."

"And you say this house isn't haunted."

Wes laughs again, and dammit, I need to look away. Because this man is beautiful when he smiles. "It's faulty wiring and a drafty old house with poor insulation."

"Keep telling yourself that, mister."

He leans back and puts his feet up on the coffee table. "It's three AM. You're sleep-deprived and it's making you paranoid," he teases. "We should probably call it a night."

I grab his arm before he gets up, and the moment my fingers touch his warm skin, I regret it. Because now I know he's as warm as I imagined, and I'm drawn to him like a moth to a flame.

Though, unlike the moth, I know what will happen if I succumb and fly right into the bright light. I don't feel like burning to a crisp today, so I pull back.

"We have two episodes left. I won't be able to sleep until I know how this ends. Stay with me?" I meant to say *stay and watch it with me,* but somehow the other words got lost on the way out.

Wes is standing above me, with the light from the TV

illuminating his back. He's so big and so tall, and with his long, messy hair hanging around his handsome face, it's like I'm sitting before Thor himself. I swallow hard, lips parting, preparing myself for him to go up to bed.

Alone.

Which would be a good thing. The *right thing*.

For him.

For me.

And for Jackson.

But I've never been good at doing the right thing.

"Sure," Wes says, and I watch his beautiful lips curve into a smile. My body is reacting *hard* to him, and I have to reel in my libido. Trying to convince myself his physical attraction is the only thing that's pulling me to him, I put a pillow in my lap and tuck my legs firmly underneath myself.

Wes settles back onto the couch, and the TV show cuts to a scene of a bright and sunny day, contrasting with the dark and gloomy mood of the rest of the show. The light illuminates Wes's face, and I take a few seconds to study him.

It's the middle of the night. We're both tired, and if he's anything like me, he's questioning the existence of ghosts and demons right about now and feeling very vulnerable.

Very human.

He rests his head against the back of the couch, and this is the most relaxed, the most *real* I've seen him with the exception of the moments he's with Jackson. Right now, sitting here in the dark, the walls have been lowered, and he's not resisting the fact that I'm here. I get not wanting to admit you want help, but what I don't get is why Wes seems resentful of the fact that he needs a nanny.

Maybe it has to do with Jackson's mother, who walked out on them?

"I didn't see that coming," Wes says, pulling my attention back to the TV. I look away from his face, and it takes me a few seconds to catch up to the twist that was revealed.

"That's fucked up," I mutter, shaking my head.

"Yeah, it is. But it explains why the shadows always

followed her."

"Ohhh, it does."

Tiredness grips me, and if I were to lay down and close my eyes, I'd be asleep in minutes. I want to see how this show ends because I know once I get up and walk up to my room, I'll be awake enough to lay there terrified the shadows cast by inanimate objects will manifest into dark spirits.

And I like being here next to Weston.

It's weird. It doesn't make sense. We're not talking. Not touching. Yet his presence is calming, and the faint scent of his woodsy cologne clings to his muscular body, and I know if I were to inch close and snuggle up, resting my head on his chest so I could count his heartbeats, the smell would fill my nostrils and I'd be a goner. There's something about an attractive man who smells good that makes them irresistible.

I'm so comfortable right now and feel so safe around him. I close my eyes for just a minute.

"Scarlet," Weston whispers. "Scarlet."

My eyes flutter open, and I realize I've fallen to the side, drifting to sleep. Wes is looking down at me, his face dangerously close to mine.

"You're falling asleep," he says with a chuckle. "Go to bed."

"No way." I stretch out, moving closer to him. "We're too far in to give up now. I don't take you to be a quitter."

Wes laughs again. "I'm not, though I never looked at turning off the TV because it's now almost four AM as quitting."

"We've got, what, one episode left? It's quitting in my book."

"Well, I guess we have to watch until the end." The smile is still on his face as he leans back, but the second he relaxes, he gets up again, moving in between the couch and the coffee table, reaching over to get the blanket that fell onto the floor. He grabs it and spreads it over me.

My heart speeds up, and suddenly I feel like I'm in a rickety boat, being tossed about in stormy water. Not because Wes scares me, but because he does the exact opposite.

You're walking the line of dangerous territory, I remind myself. He's my boss. Sleeping with your boss is never a good idea.

"Thanks." I smooth out the blanket and sit up, fixing the pillows. "Is it just my imagination or is it colder in here now?"

"It's colder. I have the heat set to go down a few degrees between midnight and five AM. It goes back up at six-thirty, around the time Jackson gets up." His brows furrow. "Though I suppose I can change it to seven-thirty now since he doesn't have to get up so early anymore."

I nod, knowing what he's talking about. They used to leave the house around seven in order to drop Jackson off at Wes's parents' before Wes went in for work.

"Are you cold?" I ask him, swinging my legs over the side of the couch and offering to share the blanket.

"I'm okay," he says and kicks his feet back up on the coffee table.

"Really?" I ask dubiously and reach out—against my better judgment, of course—and press my hand against his bicep. "You are warm." I push up and eye him suspiciously. "Are you really a shifter?"

"Huh?"

I shake my head and laugh. "Shifter. Or werewolf. In paranormal romance books, any sort of were or shifter is always described as being warmer than normal humans."

Wes raises an eyebrow, looking amused. "I didn't know that."

"I'm a little weird. Maybe I should have warned you."

Slowly, he angles his body toward me and brings one arm up, resting it on the back of the couch behind me. "I like weird."

"Well, you're in luck."

Our eyes meet and my heart flutters. This is the most real I've seen Wes, and this is the most real he's seen me. Because right now, I'm not Scarlet, the con-artist, scourge of the South Side. I'm just Scarlet, the quirky blonde who reads smutty vampire and werewolf romance novels in her spare time and gets way too wrapped up in scary TV shows.

Wes's fingertips brush against my shoulder, and I shiver. I tip my head towards his, lips parting. He moves his head down toward mine.

He needs to stop.

I need to look away.

But I don't.

And he doesn't.

Our eyes meet again, and I know he's feeling the exact same thing as I am. My heart flutters in my chest, like it's taking flight before it starts flapping its wings as hard as it can, beating away like a drum inside my chest.

He sweeps his hand down, and his fingers trail along my arm. His touch is gentle, making me want to lean in and feel more. He's doing it on purpose, knowing exactly what kind of reaction he's going to get from me.

I don't know if I should be mad at him for it or not. Swallowing hard, I take my bottom lip between my teeth and slowly lean in. He brings his hand up again and pushes my hair back behind my ear.

He's going to kiss me.

The little bit of logic that hasn't left me is screaming to stop, because if he kisses me, things won't end there. I'll climb into his lap, press my core against him, and feel his cock harden beneath me. I'll wrap my arms around his neck and buck my hips back, rubbing his cock against me once, maybe twice, before going in for another kiss. His hands will settle on my waist, pushing under my T-shirt, feeling the soft skin on my back. He'll shift his weight, rubbing himself against me until the top of his boxers dampens from the glistening tip of his cock.

He'll press his lips to mine again, and I'll push my tongue into his mouth. We'll fall back on the couch, kissing with fervor as we peel off each other's clothes. He'll want to carry me upstairs, but I'll be too impatient to wait even half a minute to feel his big, rough hands sweeping over my body, moving down my thighs, parting my legs, and rubbing over my clit.

If I let him kiss me, I'm going to end up sleeping with him. And nothing good ever comes from sleeping with your boss.

My heart flutters again, and the little bit of logic dissolves into nothing.

He's going to kiss me.

And I'm going to let him.

12

*I*f there was ever a rational part of my brain, it's now dead and buried six feet under. My cock has taken over, and right now it's screaming at me to kiss Scarlet. To take her in my arms, feel her breasts crush against my chest, to put my lips to hers and see if she tastes as good as I think she will.

It plays out before me, and I imagine her in my lap, legs wrapped around my waist, pulling my shirt over my head. My cock jumps at the thought, and I inch in closer and closer.

Somewhere in the back of my mind, I know this is a bad idea. She's Jackson's nanny and hasn't even been here that long and I'm already trying to make a move on her. But it's not like she's uninterested, and I can tell by the way she's biting her bottom lip and is moving toward me that she wants this too.

We shouldn't. We really fucking shouldn't.

But dammit, I'm tired of holding back, of going to bed alone. I've spent the last four years convincing the world that I'm not lonely, but you can only lie to yourself for so long before the smoke and mirrors gives way for the bullshit it really is.

I'm going to kiss her.

I bring my hand to her face, cupping her cheek. Her skin is so soft, and her long hair tangles around my fingers. I want to take a fistful of it, pulling it gently as I kiss her hard.

Scarlet's tongue darts out, wetting her lips. I'm officially a goner now. No logic is left, and I move forward, bringing my other hand to her waist. My fingers rest on the curve of her hip, and she tenses for a second before melting against me, bringing a hand up and resting it on my chest. She tips her head up, lips parting.

I inhale, heart beating faster and faster. I take one last second to look at her pretty face, to admire the sapphire blue of her eyes, the light freckles on her cheeks that she covered up with makeup the first time I saw her. I brush her hair back, moving it out of the way.

My heart is beating so fast I can hear it echoing in my ears, and I wonder if Scarlet can hear it. She brings her free hand up, placing it over my hand that's cupping her cheeks. Her thumb rubs over my palm, and she leans into my touch.

My cock is hard, pulsing, begging for me to get this show on the fucking road. To kiss her, bring her close, and feel the heat of her pussy hovering over me. She pushes herself forward, and the softest whimper leaves her lips.

God, this woman. If I don't kiss her now, I'm going to implode. I tighten my grip on her waist and pull her close. Her breasts crush against my chest, and she slides her hand up and over my shoulder.

And then I kiss her.

The moment our lips touch, desperation sparks between us, and she holds me close, pressing her body against mine. I run my hand down her waist and down to her ass, lifting her up and bringing her onto my lap. She straddles me, slowly easing herself over my cock, gasping slightly when she takes in the length, feeling it through my pajama pants. She stops kissing me for a brief moment, looking down in my lap, and the lust in her eyes paired with the shock does me in.

With an animalistic growl, I flip her over, moving on top of her. She curls her legs around my waist, rocking her hips so she rubs against my cock. Fuck, it feels so good even with clothes on I could come right now, dry humping her like a horny teenager. I haven't been with a woman since Daisy left, and the desperation is getting to me.

Scarlet grabs the hem of my shirt, but right as she goes to pull it off, the bottom stair creaks.

"Daddy?"

Jackson's little voice comes from behind us, and I move off Scarlet so fast I fall off the couch, hitting my shoulder on the coffee table.

"Dammit," I mutter, rubbing the spot where the corner of the wooden table hit. Scarlet scrambles up, smoothing out her shirt.

"Hey, buddy." She rushes around the coffee table. "What are you doing down here?"

"The Tall Man is back."

Scarlet glances over her shoulder at me, flicking her eyes to my cock. She knows I can't exactly stand up right now.

Sitting on the bottom stair, she pulls Jackson onto her lap and brushes his hair back. "Is he still there?"

"No. He went into Daddy's room, and then Daddy wasn't there. I thought the Tall Man got him."

"We were watching a movie," Scarlet says, wiping away a tear. I push myself up onto the couch. "No Tall Man down here. Let's get you back to bed, okay?"

"Okay," he says and pulls out of Scarlet's arms to run to me. "Daddy, will you tuck me in?"

"Of course, buddy." I wrap my arm around him and kiss the top of his head. Scarlet turns on a light, and I pause the TV, knowing watching even a few seconds of this show will make him have nightmares. In the light, I look at Scarlet. She meets my eyes and then looks away.

What the fuck was I thinking?

She's here for Jackson. Not me. We're lucky Jackson had a nightmare and stopped us before we got in too deep. Because getting in deep was exactly what I wanted to do. This can't happen again. It *won't* happen again.

～

SCARLET'S BEDROOM door is closed when I get up Sunday morning. Technically, Sundays are to be her day off. Unless some big crime happens in Eastwood and I have to go in, I'm always off on Sundays. It was discussed with her before she even started, but seeing her door shut like that makes a bad feeling form in the pit of my stomach.

Not that I'm in a rush to see her either. Because…what the fuck will I say? Hey, last night *almost fucking you* was fun? That I want to do it again but know we shouldn't. That my will is paper-thin at best and avoiding each other is ideal, but that won't work because *you fucking live here.* God, what the fuck did I do?

She's. Jackson's. Nanny.

"What do you want for breakfast?" I ask Jackson, plugging in the coffee pot.

"Can you make bacon and eggs like Scarlet does?"

"Sure," I say, internalizing my grimace. I'm no master chef, but I do try to eat healthy, and I want Jackson to grow up with good eating habits like I did. And it makes working out worthless when I eat like shit anyway, so the Pop-Tarts and cereal mornings should be over.

Jackson watches cartoons while I cook, and I'm putting his plate on the table when Scarlet comes downstairs. Her hair is messy, and she has pillow creases on her face. My mind immediately jumps to her waking up in my bed, rolling over with that bed-head in my face. I'd slip my arm around her and bring her close, not ready to get up.

"Morning," she says with a small smile and crosses the kitchen, going right for the coffee.

"Morning." I pull the creamer out of the fridge. Her fingers brush over mine as she takes it from me, and the small touch is enough to send a jolt through me, going right to my cock. I need to get it the fuck together.

"How'd you sleep?" she asks Jackson, looking over her shoulder as she prepares her coffee.

"I stayed with Daddy. He kept me safe," Jackson replies between bites of bacon. "The Tall Man didn't come back, but I did see him standing outside your door."

Scarlet's face blanks. "Well, I'm going to be sleeping well tonight."

I laugh, wishing I could give her a similar offer. My bed is open to anyone scared of the dark tonight.

"Are you still coming with us to Grammy's tonight?" Jackson asks Scarlet.

She flicks her eyes to mine, and in that half-second, the room fills with tension so thick it's hard to breathe.

"Yeah," she tells him with a smile. "I wouldn't miss it." Taking a sip of her coffee, she keeps her eyes focused on the floor in front of her. I pile bacon, eggs, and toast onto my own plate and take another down from the cabinet for Scarlet.

"Hungry?" I ask.

"I'm always hungry in the morning." With a smile, she sets her coffee down and starts to walk over to the stove. Her perky tits bounce slightly under her T-shirt, and I need to turn around and stop looking for my own good.

"Want to play zombies after breakfast?" Jackson asks Scarlet.

"Today's Scarlet's day off," I remind him gently. "She's here but not really here."

Jackson tips his head. "Huh?"

Scarlet laughs. "It's okay. I don't really have any plans other than showering and reading a chapter or two from my book."

"Are there zombies in your book?" Jackson's eyes widen.

"Actually, yes." Scarlet fills her plate and joins us at the table. "It's a romance set in the zombie apocalypse. It's really good."

"Can you read it to me?"

"When you're older." She smiles and then digs into her food. We eat in silence, and I'm a little jealous of the innocent way Jackson is completely oblivious to how fucking awkward things are right now.

"After breakfast, let's go grocery shopping," I tell Jackson, who groans in response. I'm sure Scarlet would appreciate a little time to herself, and Lord knows I need some time away. Or a cold shower.

Probably both.

Once everyone is done eating, Jackson goes back to his

cartoons and Scarlet clears the table. She's at the sink washing dishes, and I'm a few feet away from her cleaning the grease off the stovetop that splattered when I made bacon.

I need to say something. I pull the burner apart and wipe it down. *I really need to say something.* I put the clean burner back on and move onto the one behind it. Once that's cleaned, I put the grates back on and start on the other side, even though it's clean. I'm being fucking ridiculous. Has it been that long since I've had any sort of a connection to a woman? I can't remember how these things go.

And I've also never almost slept with someone and then had to see them like this in the morning. It's like some sort of tight-rope version of the Walk of Shame. I need to suck it up and tell her I enjoyed last night, I like her, but we have to keep things professional for Jackson's sake.

"So, last night," I start and at the exact same time she asks,

"Should I bring something to—sorry, what?"

I shake my head. "Go ahead."

"Should I bring something to your parents' tonight?"

"Nah, you don't have to. I never do."

She smiles and scrubs at the pan, trying to get the baked-on eggs off. "I've never done a family dinner like this before. I don't know the etiquette."

I know our family isn't the norm. There's seven of us, plus a few spouses and children now, and the fact that we get together once a week goes above and beyond what a lot of people do. But hearing her say she's never done a family dinner takes me by surprise, and I know she's not exaggerating the use of "never" like so many people do.

She really hasn't gone to a big family dinner before.

I look away from the stove, not prepared for the sadness I see in her eyes. She forces a smile and pushes her shoulders back, a move I've seen her do before. It's a move I know, one that might fool the world but starts to break down over time. You can't lie to your own heart, after all.

"You're not close to your brother?"

"Oh, I am. I pretty much raised him. He's nineteen, so the

nine-year age difference made me feel more like his mother than anything else, though I guess you get that. You're the oldest."

I nod because I don't know what else to do. Quinn is eight years younger than me, but I never felt like a parent to her. I probably annoyed her growing up—and still to this day—by being an overprotective older brother, but that's all I was. Her *brother*. I never felt like I had to raise her or step in and fill a role.

"I have a sister too," she goes on, turning her head down to look at the dishes she's washing. "She's twenty. We didn't get along growing up much either. For the same reasons."

"What about now?"

She laughs. "Sometimes." She rinses the pan and sets it on the counter to dry. "My mom wasn't the best, and my dad wasn't in the picture until I was fifteen."

"Oh, I'm, uh, sorry."

She waves a hand in the air. "It's water under the bridge. What doesn't kill us makes us stronger and all shit, right?" She goes back to washing dishes, closing the conversation about her family. I know there is more to be told, and I know emotional scars when I see them.

"We can bring wine," I suggest. "My mom likes wine."

Scarlet looks up with a smile. "That's something we have in common."

I laugh. "You're off to a good start."

13

WESTON

I've never once been nervous bringing a girl home to meet my parents. And Scarlet is far from *my girl*. Still, my heart is beating faster than normal when we get into my Jeep. Scarlet is dressed in a simple black dress. It's long-sleeved and ends above her knees, with a scoop neckline that shows off her large tits just enough to cause me to want to stare. She curled her hair and put on makeup, looking perfect as usual.

But the way she's clutching the bottle of wine makes me think she's nervous too.

"Is there anything I should know about your family?" she asks as I back out of the garage and into the alley that runs behind our house. "Any dark secrets or things?"

There really isn't. Daisy's betrayal is the only dark secret in the Dawson family...that I know about, at least. We might not be the most exciting bunch, but I wouldn't trade my family for anything.

"Don't bring up cats," I tell her. "Quinn is almost married and successful, but still very much a crazy cat lady at heart. If she starts talking about cats, she won't stop."

"Cats? Well, I wasn't going to bring them up, but now I'm terrified I'm going to. You're putting too much pressure on me. Don't get mad if I start meowing at the dinner table."

"Funny." I steal a glance at her, heart hammering even faster when I see her smiling.

"I'm serious. I don't know if I can handle this kind of pressure right meow." She looks at me with a straight face. I roll to a stop at a stop sign and stare right back at her. We hold each other's gaze for a few seconds before we both start to laugh.

"So that's your family's deepest, darkest secret? Your rich and successful sister is a crazy cat lady?"

"I never said she was rich."

Scarlet's cheeks flush. "I kinda assumed so from meeting her. Not that she was stuck-up or anything. She had a lot of designer items."

"Oh, I guess." I turn down the main street that runs through Eastwood. "I don't pay attention to that stuff. And she is, so you weren't wrong. And yeah…I guess that's the worst of it. Quinn's fiancé is my brother Dean's best friend. There was some drama there for a while, but everyone is over it."

"Ohhh, falling for her older brother's best friend. That is good drama."

"And Dean's wife is kind of a…a…" I trail off, not wanting to badmouth family.

"A bitch?" Scarlet finishes for me, mouthing the word so Jackson doesn't hear.

"You said it, not me. But yes."

She smiles again. "Your secret's safe with me." She turns her head, looking out the window. She hasn't seen any of Eastwood yet, and now I feel like an ass about it. I'm off tomorrow as well, and I'm going to make it a point to show her around town.

"Do you like dogs?" I ask, turning off the main road and heading toward the outskirts of town.

"I'm more of a cat person. I think I'll get along well with your sister." Her cherry-red lips pull into a smile. "Why?"

"My mom has four dogs. Now that we're all grown, she's a *dog mom*."

Scarlet laughs. "She's one of those."

"You know the type?"

"I do."

Jackson looks up from the backseat. "I like dogs."

"I know you do, buddy," I tell him. He's been asking for one for a while now. I briefly considered letting him take home one of the kittens Quinn's been caring for once it's old enough, but I wasn't home enough to feel like it'd be fair to any animal. Though now that Scarlet's here...

"I like dogs too," Scarlet tells him. "But I like cats more. They're elegant and so mysterious."

I laugh. "You are going to get along with my sister."

∽

"How's everything going?" Quinn whispers, giving me a hug.

"Pretty good," I say, unable to keep the smile off my face.

Quinn leans back, eyebrows going up. Damn her and her ability to read me like an open book.

"Not like that. Jackson is happy, and I think I can trust her around him."

"She's hot, you know."

I unzip my coat and shake my head at my sister. "Having you tell me she's hot doesn't make me want to date her. She's Jackson's nanny. You and Mom need to get off this, okay?" My words come out harsher than I mean to. I'm yelling at myself, not at my well-meaning baby sister. "Sorry. I just—"

"It's fine," Quinn says, green eyes flashing. "I want you to be happy, so shoot me."

Like Dean, Quinn has a flare for dramatics when she's angry or hurt. "I know," I say gently. "And thanks. Just...let me find happiness on my own?"

"But playing matchmaker is so fun."

"Play it for Logan and Owen."

"I said 'matchmaker,' not 'miracle worker.' Which is what they need."

We both laugh, and I turn around to introduce Scarlet to everyone. We're the last to arrive, and I'm pretty sure the only reason Logan and Owen got here before us is because they knew Scarlet was joining tonight.

"Hi, Quinn," Scarlet says, bending over to unzip her boots. Oh God, I shouldn't have looked. The feel of her breasts pressed against my chest is seared into me like muscle memory, and I can't go down that road right now.

"Hey." Quinn drops to her knees to hug Jackson. "How are you liking it here so far?"

"So far so good," Scarlet tells her and flicks her eyes to me. "Everyone has been very welcoming. Though I haven't seen much of the town yet."

Quinn eyes me, and I smile guiltily. "It's supposed to be nice tomorrow. We can walk around downtown in the morning."

Jackson grabs Scarlet's hand and pulls her through the foyer. My parents' house is also historical and fully restored, but on a much bigger level than mine. This place was a dump when we first moved in, and my brothers and I might have had fun teasing Quinn about how haunted it was since it looked like something out a horror movie.

Slowly over the years and in between projects for clients, my dad did most of the renovations himself. He taught us all how to be handy, and there aren't many home improvement projects I can't handle myself because of it.

"Your parents' house is gorgeous," Scarlet says, looking around with wide eyes. "I feel like I'm going to a dinner party with Chip and Joanna."

"Who?" I ask, following after her and Jackson.

"I'll tell you later," Scarlet says over her shoulder. The whole family is gathered in the kitchen, like always. This place is really the heart of the house, and the custom-built island is always a topic of conversation. It's huge, long enough for us all to have a seat at, and is the perfect place for everyone to converge, eating, talking, and drinking.

I watch Scarlet's face as we enter, and she does her little trick again, inhaling and pushing her shoulders back, acting like she's ready to take on the world. Emma, who's being held by my mom, coos when she sees Quinn and extends her chubby little arms for her mother.

"Hey, sweet pea," Quinn says and takes her baby. Jackson runs through the kitchen, excited to see everyone. And then all eyes fall on us. Scarlet stays close to me, holding the bottle of wine so tight in her hands I fear the bottle might break. I'm comfortable around everyone in this room. My siblings, obviously. Archer feels just like another younger brother since he and Dean have had a serious bromance going on since they met their freshman year of college, and Kara's been part of the family for the last four years.

We don't bring home dates unless it's serious, and I need to keep reminding myself that Scarlet isn't my date. There's nothing going on between us, and there never will be, even though I very much want it.

"This is Scarlet," I say, putting my hand on her shoulder. She's nervous, and her words come back, echoing through my head. She's never been to a family dinner, and while this doesn't seem like anything special to the rest of us, it's probably overwhelming to her.

"Hey, I'm Owen." My little shit of a brother gets up, flashing her a charming smile, and shakes her hand, taking the wine from her. "It's nice to meet you."

"You too." Scarlet returns his smile.

I spread my fingers over her shoulder, and the warmth of her skin through the material of her dress feels like fire. It's burning me, but I can't remove my hand.

"And that's Logan," I say, pointing to him. "Don't feel bad if you can't tell them apart."

"I'm the better-looking one," Owen says with a grin as he opens the wine.

Scarlet laughs and looks from Logan to Owen. "Logan's in the black, and Owen's in the blue. I'm good for now at least."

"That's Dean, his wife Kara, and Archer, Quinn's fiancé." We take a few steps forward into the kitchen. "This is my mom, and my dad is somewhere."

"He's getting Nana," Mom tells me, striding over. "It's nice to meet you, Scarlet."

"You too," Scarlet says with a sweet smile.

"Nana?" I question, trying not to grimace. Our Nana has a few screws loose and suffers from what we've dubbed Old Lady Syndrome, meaning she's lost her filter and it's gotten worse since last year.

"It's been a while since we had her over," Mom reminds me. "How are you liking it in Eastwood?" she asks Scarlet. "You're from Chicago, right?"

"I am," Scarlet answers. "And it's nice here. Very quiet."

"Quinn lived in Chicago for a few years, and I used to enjoy going for a visit. Though a visit is all I could stand. I was born and raised here. I like my yard and my privacy."

Scarlet laughs, nodding in agreement. "I could see that. I'm used to hearing the L and the constant chatter of people on my street."

"The L?"

"It's a train, Mom," Quinn answers, sitting down next to Archer.

"Oh, right." Mom nods. "Anyway, welcome to Eastwood." She looks down at Jackson and smiles. "And I hope this little guy is being a perfect gentleman."

Jackson giggles. "I always am, Grammy!"

"He has been perfect," Scarlet agrees.

"Just wait," I warn her with a wink. "He's still in the honeymoon phase, trust me."

Scarlet smiles down at Jackson. "I think I can handle it."

Owen comes back over with two wine glasses, offering one to Scarlet and keeping the other for himself.

"We got that for Mom," I deadpan. Owen gives me a look and then gives Mom the glass.

"I prefer beer anyway," he says.

"What happened to that moonshine you were raving about?"

Logan snorts a laugh. "Yeah...what did happen to it?"

Owen glares at Logan, and I motion for Scarlet to sit with me at the island. "I'd rather not talk about it," he mutters.

"You don't have to." Logan takes his phone from his pocket. "I have evidence."

Mom shakes her head. "I don't think I want to see this, do I?"

"No one wants to see it," Owen interjects, going over and trying to steal Logan's phone. Mom shakes her head and goes into the living room to play with Jackson. Giving up trying to get the phone, Owen takes Emma from Quinn and pulls a silly face, making her laugh.

"Your baby is adorable," Scarlet tells Quinn, taking a drink of her wine.

"Thanks," Quinn and Archer say at the same time. All the bar stools are taken now, so Quinn sits on Archer's lap. He wraps his arms around her and leans in for a kiss.

"Get a room," Logan teases.

"Don't encourage them," Dean replies dryly.

"Upstairs is free," Owen goes on, blowing a raspberry on Emma's cheek. She lets out a shriek of laughter. "They need to have another baby for me to play with."

"You could have your own," Archer counters.

Owen's eyes widen, and he shakes his head. "Nope. It's not for me."

"Not yet," I tell him with a laugh.

"You and Quinn can have the babies. I like being an uncle."

Kara flicks her eyes up from her phone. "Are you going to have another?" she asks.

"Not soon," Quinn answers, looking into Archer's eyes. "I want to be able to drink at our wedding and go on all the rides at Disney. Ideally, I'll be pregnant by the time we come back from our honeymoon."

"Gross," Dean mumbles.

"Stop envisioning it," Archer teases.

Dean gives him a dead stare. "I'm still scarred by that time I walked in on you two."

"Dean!" Quinn squeals, eyes wide. If looks could kill, he'd be dead on the floor.

Logan laughs. "When did this happen?"

"A long time ago. Before Emma was born," Quinn laughs, burying her head against Archer.

"At least he never saw the picture," Archer whisper-yells to Quinn.

"Picture?" Owen asks, cuddling Emma against his chest.

"No," Quinn says, putting her hand up to Archer's mouth to silence him. Everyone laughs, and I lean back in my chair to look at Scarlet. A small smile is on her face, and she's watching us almost as if she's in a lab observing our behavior. Rufus, the biggest and oldest of Mom's dogs, jumps up at the back door, startling Scarlet a bit.

Dean gets up to let him in. I'd already moved out and was overseas when she got him, but he's the family dog to the rest of the family. Without thinking, Dean opens the glass doors, and all four dogs come barreling in. Most are friendly, but Rufus can be finicky with new people. He's a German Shepherd mixed with a Malamute and is big and intimidating.

Scarlet tenses, bringing her wine glass to her lips and taking a big sip. I slip off the stool and take a hold of his collar as he sniffs her.

"This is Rufus," I say. "He's a cranky old dog but will leave you alone."

"Hey, Rufus," Scarlet says and holds out her hand for him to sniff. His fur raises for a few seconds, and then he decides she's not a threat.

"I found my wedding dress," Quinn tells me, looking over Archer's shoulder. She beams, and I'm so damn happy for her. She's my baby sister, one of the nicest people in the whole fucking world, and I want nothing but the best for her.

"When are you getting married?" Scarlet asks.

"June. At Disney World!"

"Ohhh, that sounds awesome. Have you picked out the rest of the wedding, uh, stuff?"

Scarlet's trying, and I give her props for that. She doesn't have to. It doesn't really matter if she gets along with my family. She's Jackson's nanny...*not my girlfriend.* I've never really cared if my boss's family liked me before. It actually never even crossed my mind.

"Most of it," Quinn tells her. "Disney takes care of a lot of stuff, which makes it easy. All I'm really concerned about is having good food."

Scarlet smiles. "I think that's how I'd be too. Do you have a picture of your dress?"

"Of course. Want to see?"

"Heck yes!"

Quinn moves off Archer's lap. "I don't want to risk him seeing."

"Oh, definitely." Scarlet gets up and follows Quinn into the living room. The moment she steps out, my brothers round on me.

"Dude," Owen starts, still holding Emma against his chest. "What the fuck?"

I shake my head, playing dumb. "What?"

"Your nanny is fucking hot."

"Shut up," I snap.

Owen raises an eyebrow. "You disagree?"

"I don't agree or disagree."

Logan chuckles. "Spoken like a true politician. Has this election gone to your head already?"

"Funny," I tell him. "Yeah, she's good-looking. But she's here for Jackson so I can work."

"Of course she is." Dean raises his eyebrows. "Why else would she be here?"

"Sorry," Archer starts. "I know Quinn had a secret agenda hiring her. She means well."

"I know," I tell him. "She does. And so far, Scarlet is great with Jackson. But it's only been a few days so…"

"Who knows?" Logan finishes for me. I meet his eyes and nod.

"Right." I get up and go to the fridge to get a beer. And who the fuck knows? I return to my seat and suck down a few gulps of the beer. I'm on edge, fighting my own attraction to Scarlet, and I feel like everyone can see right through me. That's the only downfall of having a close-knit family like this.

The garage door opens, and Dad and Nana come in. Things get rolling after that, and Jackson throws a little fit when I tell him to wash his hands before dinner. I look at Scarlet.

"Told you so," I mouth, and she laughs. She picks him up off the floor and takes him to the bathroom to wash his hands. Finally, we're all seated around the table. Scarlet's at my side, and Jackson ended up across the table by Mom. I've introduced Scarlet to Nana twice now, and she's staring at her, questioning who she is for the third time.

"I'm Scarlet, Jackson's nanny," Scarlet says sweetly.

"What the fuck happened to Daisy?" Nana asks, trying to steal Logan's beer. He takes it from her and slides her water glass into her reach. She bats his hand away and goes for the beer again.

"Mom," my own mother scolds. "We don't swear at the dinner table."

"Daisy is my mom," Jackson says slowly, as if he's not sure of himself. Silence falls over the table, and it's taking everything inside me not to pound my fist before getting up and storming out. I'm not mad at my nana. Her mind has been going at a scary rate the last few months, and she doesn't remember much of what's happened recently.

I'm mad at Daisy and what she did to Jackson.

No one speaks, and each second that ticks by gives Jackson more and more time to think, to let his own mind question *what the fuck happened to my mom?* Dean opens his mouth only to snap it shut again, and Dad looks just as stunned as the rest of us.

"So, Quinn," Scarlet says, reaching for her wine. Well, what's left of it. "I hear you like cats."

"Yes," Quinn says, eyes meeting mine. I can see the relief on her face and, more importantly, the relief on Weston's face. Poor little Jackson is still sitting there with a spoonful of mashed potatoes hovering on his spoon in front of his face, not knowing what to think. "I do."

"How many cats do you have?" I flick my eyes to Wes's not knowing if I should be apologetic for going into forbidden territory or not. He meets my gaze and offers a small smile.

"Eight."

"Eight?" I echo.

"One or two might be temporary."

Quinn's fiancé, Archer, raises an eyebrow. "Only one or two?"

Quinn smiles guiltily. "They're all so cute."

"I want a cat!" Jackson says, face lighting up. He eats his mashed potatoes and bounces in his seat. "Daddy, can we take Dobby home?"

"We'll see," Wes tells him, and I know it's a firm *no* from him.

"Please! I want a pet." Jackson drops his spoon and glares at Wes, crossing his arms. I don't mean to laugh, but the over-the-top dramatics are a little cute.

"Dobby is really nice," Quinn goes on. "And will be able to leave in a few weeks."

Dean shakes his head, looking at Archer. "I can't believe you let her keep the others. Eight cats? That's crazy."

Archer's eyes fall on Quinn, and the way he looks at her makes me want to turn around and throw up. But mostly because I'd give anything to have someone look at me like that. On its own accord, my head jerks toward Wes.

Nope. Can't happen. He's my boss. And he'd never go for someone like me...the real me.

"I have a hard time saying no to Quinn," Archer says, and I want to gag.

"That's why they have a baby out of wedlock," Wes's grandma says. Everyone at the table rolls their eyes and ignores her. I'm guessing this isn't the first time she's brought it up, and neither Quinn nor Archer seem bothered by it. "Though I can't blame her. I do like a man who's good with his hands. You know, doc, I'm overdue for my annual exam." She winks at Archer. Archer shakes his head and turns his face down to his food, concentrating really hard on cutting his steak.

I turn to Wes, trying not to laugh. He leans over, shaking his head.

"She hits on Archer every time they're together. Don't judge us."

"I'm not," I say honestly, and for the life of me, I can't come up with a single judgment against the Dawsons. And trust me, I'm trying. But they're all nice. Caring. No one tries to impress each other or puts up a front. Logan cuts up his grandma's steak for her, and Owen takes Emma again when she gets fussy so Quinn and Archer can eat a meal in peace. Mr. and Mrs. Dawson love each and every one of their children and grandchildren equally, and I can tell just from this brief interaction how proud they are of them.

They're the perfect American family, and I'm convinced they are the real deal. That families can be functional.

And I'm not sure if I hate them or love them for it.

Thinking big family meals like this don't exist made it easier for me to handle knowing we were nowhere near perfect. Get-togethers with homemade food only happen in the movies.

Thinking it wasn't real helped me deal with the fact that there was a huge part of me missing.

Because I want a family. I want this. But I can't have it. People like the Dawsons would never want the likes of me sitting around their dinner table if they knew the truth.

I'm Scarlet Cooper, a thief from the South Side with no college education, a former drunk for a father, a sister in jail, and heir to a fortress of lies.

I sɪᴛ on the living room couch next to Wes, a hot mug of coffee in my hand. His dad and his brother Dean are in his dad's study going over something for work, and the rest of his family is still in the kitchen.

"Have we scared you off yet?" Wes asks, leaning against the arm of the couch. "We can be a little loud and overwhelming."

"Not overwhelming. Your family is super nice. Well, except for Kara. You were right about her being a bitch."

"I never actually said that."

"You didn't have to. It's written all over your face."

Wes laughs and shifts his weight, moving a little closer to me. Things should be awkward with him, but they're not anymore. Being around him is as easy as breathing, and while he still holds up walls around him, they're starting to turn more into windows, letting me see inside.

"Hey," Logan says, stepping into the living room. Or maybe it's Owen. Shit. Who was wearing blue again? "You guys want dessert?" He eyes Wes, smirking. Owen. It's Owen. He's the smartass of the two, and it's oddly endearing.

"Yeah," Wes says quickly before Owen can slip in a line about Wes getting dessert elsewhere. We both know it's coming.

"Scarlet!" Jackson stops running around the kitchen and gives me a hug. "Will you do the Baby Shark Challenge with me?"

"Sure," I tell him. "But what is it?"

"What?" Wes's hand flies to his chest as he fakes his shock. "You don't know what Baby Shark is?"

"You're lucky," his mom says, raising her eyebrows. "It'll get stuck in your head for days."

"So it's a song?" I ask.

"And a movie," Jackson tells me.

"It's more like a music video. For kids," Wes says and shakes his head. "And you gave me crap for not seeing *Titanic* and here you are never having seen Baby Shark."

I laugh, heart skipping a beat when I look into his eyes and see that smirk on his face. "You've had years to see it, mister. Baby Shark can't be that old."

He laughs before shrugging. "You got me there." Motioning to the dining room, he puts his hand on Jackson's head and tousles his hair. "And we'll do one song after dessert. Then it'll be time to go home and get ready for bed."

"If you make me leave, I'm going to throw a fit," he threatens. His face crumples, and he tries to make himself cry but stops when Emma lets out a shriek.

"She's all yours," Dean says, handing the crying baby to Archer. "I think she pooped."

"You're welcome to change her diaper, Uncle Dean," Archer tells him, laughing. I look around the kitchen as this cute-as-hell family and might start throwing a fit like Jackson when it comes time to leave too.

Though getting back to late-night TV with Wes sounds nice…

"I think it's time to eat cake," I say, dropping down to Jackson's level. He beams and grabs my hand, hopping as he leads me into the dining room. I have another glass of wine and the best chocolate cake I've ever had in my entire life. Turns out Kara is a really good cook, which is probably one of the reasons Dean's with her. Or at least that's one theory I have.

"Scarlet," Quinn starts, looking at me from across the table. "Would you guys want to go to the farmers' market with us on Tuesday? It's supposed to be nice out and we can walk from Wes's place."

"Sure," I say, looking at Jackson, who nods excitedly. "I've never been to a farmers' market. Are they like the ones in movies?"

"This one isn't as big. Especially now that it's fall. I need some mums for our porch."

I don't know what a mum is, but I smile and nod anyway.

"And there's a local winery that sells the best sweet red wine and blueberry cider. Now that Emma is eating solid food I can half like an ounce of wine at night once she goes down."

"You had me at sweet red wine." I scrape the last bit of icing off my plate and wonder if it would look bad if I picked it up and licked it. This stuff is like crack. We stay for a bit longer after that, and I hang out with Jackson in the living room while Wes talks about the campaign with his dad and brothers.

It's dark when we go to leave, and I stop short in the driveway.

"You okay?" Wes asks, unlocking his Jeep.

My head is turned up to the sky. "I've never seen this many stars before." I exhale, and my breath clouds around me. "It's beautiful."

"Yeah," Wes agrees, and I can feel his eyes on me. "Beautiful."

"I could see them from my house, but not like this. It's...it's incredible. It makes me feel so...so..."

"Small?"

"No." I shake my head, unable to tear my eyes away from the heavens above. "Connected. It makes me feel so connected and grounded at the same time. It doesn't make sense, I know." I shake my head and shiver. I didn't put my coat on, not thinking I'd need it for the quick walk from the house to the Jeep. "Forget it," I say with a laugh. "It's stupid."

"I don't think it's stupid." Wes steps close next to me. Jackson's opening the back of the Jeep and climbing in. "When I was deployed, I'd look up at the sky and take comfort knowing I was under the same blanket of stars as the people I loved. The people I missed. So I get what you mean about having it make you feel connected."

I tip my head down, eyes meeting his. My lips part, and another chill goes right through me. Ignoring the fact that I'm dumbly holding my coat in my hands, Weston takes off his jacket and drapes it around my shoulders.

Dammit, Wes, stop being such a nice guy.

A nice guy who loves his son more than anything, has a family I wish could adopt me, and who may or may not be making me feel things I didn't think I was capable of feeling.

I'm in over my head here, and it won't be long before the waves crash against the shore and pull me out with the undertow. But being washed out into dark waters isn't scary.

It's that I want it to happen.

15

$\mathcal{I}$ push Jackson's hair back, feeling bad that I forgot to take him for a haircut—again. It's hard juggling everything, but now it should be easier. Scarlet is here to help with housework, make dinner, and most of all, to care for the single most important person in my life.

"Love you," I whisper and kiss his forehead before quietly slipping out of his room. Light pours into the dark hall, coming from Scarlet's room. She's sitting on her bed, with one hand pressed to her forehead and the other holding her phone. I can tell right away she's upset.

"Yes, I'm fully aware he needs that medication, but insurance denied it. I've been working on it and will pay out of pocket if I have to." She pauses, listening to whoever is on the phone. "Sure. If the doctor thinks he needs it, then yeah." Another pause. I should go and not listen to her conversation, but I'm fighting hard against myself and the urge to go comfort her. "How many falls does that make this month? Fuck—sorry. It's just…I didn't realize he'd fallen so many times."

She exhales, and I turn away, giving her privacy. I head into the bathroom to shower and then put on sweatpants and a T-shirt. Mom packed a plate of leftovers, and it's calling my name. The light is off in Scarlet's room when I step back into the hall, but her door is open, leading me to believe she's downstairs.

But she's not.

She's nowhere to be found, and I actually go back up and peek in her room—she's not there—and she's not in Jackson's room, either.

"Scarlet?" I call quietly when I get to the bottom of the stairs. I'm starting to get concerned when I see her sitting on the back porch, arms wrapped tightly around herself and her head tipped up to the sky. She's not wearing a coat and has to be cold.

Grabbing a blanket from the living room, I put on my jacket and step onto the porch.

"Hey," she says, flicking her eyes to me for a nanosecond before looking away.

"It's freezing out here."

"I know." Her breath leaves in silver wisps, hanging in the air. "I didn't mean to stay out here for so long."

I go to the steps and sit next to her. "Here."

"Thanks," she says and takes the blanket from me. She wraps it around herself and looks back up at the sky.

"Do you believe in aliens?"

"Kind of," I admit. "I think there has to be other life forces out there, and I do enjoy the *Ancient Aliens* show on the History Channel."

"Nerd." She bumps me with her elbow and smiles.

"What about you?"

"Not in the traditional sense. I don't think little green Martians are going to come abduct us and probe our butts, but I agree that we can't be the only life in the universe."

I laugh. "Not probing butts is a good thing."

She turns her head down and meets my eyes. "Well, sometimes it can be a good thing."

Dammit, Scarlet. Leave it to her to turn a tender moment borderline erotic. Though she could read the phone book and I'd get turned on.

"It's so quiet here," she says and rests her head on my shoulder. I clench my fists, trying to keep my hands to myself.

I know how good her lips feel against mine.

If I touch her, I'm going to kiss her again, and there's a good chance we'll make love right here on the stairs.

"It is."

"I thought downtown would be a little louder than this."

I chuckle. "Main Street is, and we're three blocks away. Though everything shuts down around ten or eleven. There are a fair amount of festivals in the summer, though, and we have one twenty-four-hour diner. And, of course, Getaway, my brothers' bar is open until two or three. Friday and Saturday nights are a different story, though once the weather starts to turn, it does quiet down a lot."

"Do you like it here?"

"I do. I was born and raised here, so maybe I'm biased. But it's a good town with good people and it's a safe place to raise a kid."

She nods and gently touches a scar on the back of my hand. "What is this from?"

I swallow my pounding heart. "Dean threw a glass bottle at me when we were kids. I needed a ton of stitches, and he got grounded for a week. I was the one who told him to throw the bottle in the first place, but I never told my parents that."

She laughs. "I'm surprised he forgave you."

"I was able to convince him it was all his fault, and he felt bad about it for like a year. I milked it for all it was worth, of course."

"I would too."

"Do you have any scars?" I hear the words leave my lips but don't know where they came from. Clearly, my upstairs brain has checked out.

"I do. Nothing too interesting, though. I have a cigarette burn on the back of my left shoulder."

"How'd that happen?"

"My mom fell asleep with a cigarette in her hand, and it dropped on me."

"Damn."

"Yeah." She takes her head off my shoulder and raises her eyebrows. "I think I had an entirely different childhood than you."

I'm not quite sure what to say. I know Scarlet isn't one to want pity. She said what she did factually and only because I asked. She's not trying to make me feel bad for her.

"Oh!" She jerks up and points to the sky. "I think I saw a shooting star!"

"Make a wish." I look up, breath catching just a bit when I see how sparkly the night sky is above us. Then I look at Scarlet, and my breath does more than catch. It stops.

Her eyes are closed, lips curved into a slight smile, and her head is tipped up to the sky.

"You should make one too," she whispers.

I look back at the stars and wish for self-control. Because Lord knows I need it tonight. Scarlet gathers up the blanket and lays back, eyes fluttering shut.

"What do you do if you're hungry in the middle of the night?"

"What do you mean?" I lick my lips, watching her breasts rise and fall beneath her shirt as she fixes the blanket around herself.

"Does the diner deliver?"

"No. I'd just go get something from the kitchen." I raise an eyebrow. "You can't possibly be hungry."

"Oh, I'm not. I'm preparing for future nights. Sometimes I have a hard time falling asleep, so I get up and eat my feelings."

I'm usually good at reading people, but I'm struggling with Scarlet. Because she spits out her truths like they're lies, saying serious things so casually it's like a joke.

"Make sure to keep the fridge stocked," I tease and lay back with her, scooting closer, but only so I can see the stars. Not so I can feel her against me. "What'd you wish for?"

"Wes Dawson," she scolds. "I can't tell you."

"Right. It won't come true if you do."

"Oh, I didn't think of it like that. I was going to be cliché and say if I tell you I have to kill you, but you're so big and tall. It'll be such a pain to chop you up and bury your body."

I laugh, and her hand brushes against mine. "You're different than I expected."

"Is that bad?"

"No, it's perfect."

She turns to me, face inches from mine. Suddenly, the humor in her eyes goes away, and I see darkness reflected back at me. I get a glimpse of her, and if I hadn't felt the same thing when I came back after my first tour overseas, I wouldn't have noticed.

She's struggling, fighting tooth and nail to stay afloat in choppy waters.

And then she blinks, and the moment is gone. Slowly, she reaches out and runs her finger over the scar on my hand again.

"Remember you said that," she whispers. Her eyes fall shut, and she turns her head away, sitting up and pulling the blanket tight around her shoulders. "Want to finish that ghost show?"

I do, but now that I've seen inside, and it was like looking into a mirror, I can't. "Maybe tomorrow." I get up and extend a hand. "I'm pretty beat, and I have work tomorrow night."

"Right." She gives me a tight smile and takes my hand, letting me pull her to her feet. "Then you should get to bed."

I sit on the couch, twisting Ray's yarn mane through my fingers. It's worn and frayed by now, but the sensation still gives me comfort. I cheat and lie for a living but still take solace in a stuffed animal I've had since I was a child.

Psychologists would have a field day with me.

After going out for breakfast at the cutest little mom-and-pop diner this morning, Wes showed me around town, and we ended the tour at the library. Jackson likes to play there, and we left with an armload of picture books, as well as a few paranormal romances for me.

One of the books is on the coffee table next to me, and I intended on reading it. Jackson fell asleep pretty quickly tonight, and once he was down, I took a quick shower, changed into my PJs, and came downstairs to have a cup of tea and read.

It's so domestic it's weird.

It's not me at all, and yet I'm finding myself liking this more and more. It's putting me in the middle of an existential crisis that I certainly don't have time for. My whole life, I've identified as Scarlet from the hood, the girl who had to grow up too fast, who had to raise her siblings as well as take care of her inebriated mother, cleaning up vomit and dragging her inside when she passed out in the yard. Some days she'd be covered in frost by the time I found her, and I'd spend my morning carefully soaking her fingers in bowls of warm water to try and prevent frostbite.

I wasn't always successful.

The simple fact that I like this—putting Jackson to bed, straightening up the house, and sitting down with a cup of fucking tea and a book—is rocking my whole sense of identity right now. I never understood why some people criticized women who chose to stay at home and look after their household. If that's what they want and aren't being repressed into anything against their will, then it's no different than a woman going out and getting a job. She's doing what she wants. What makes her happy.

I didn't realize this could make me happy.

"It's only been a few days," I tell myself and stand, needing to reheat my tea by now. Before I make it into the kitchen, the alarm beeps, and Wes steps into the house. I get to the keypad first and punch in the code to disarm the system.

"Hey," he says, closing the door behind him. I open my mouth to say hi back, but the words die in my throat. I was not prepared to see what I'm seeing.

Weston is wearing a fitted suit, and dear God, it's worse than if he were standing naked before me. I want to throw myself at him, wrapping my fingers around his sleek black tie and using it to pull him up to the bedroom with me. His hair is neatly pulled back away from his face, and a slight five o'clock shadow covers his strong jawline.

And I thought he looked good in his uniform.

"Look at you," I say, raising my eyebrows. "Looking all GQ."

He smiles and looks down at himself, almost as if he forgot what he's wearing. Fuck, it's adorable.

"I had a debate tonight."

"For the race?"

He nods and takes his suit jacket off. "Yeah, and then I had a meet-and-greet." His face tightens, and he shakes his head. "I don't like this part of it. I just want to do my job as the Sheriff and not convince Mr. and Mrs. Johnson why they should donate to my campaign over anyone else's."

I smile at him, body still tingling. He hangs his jacket on the back of a kitchen chair. Then he starts to roll up the sleeves on his button-up dress shirt.

And now I'm dead, lying motionless on the kitchen floor.

"That's why you'll be good at the job," I say, words coming out thinner than I'd like. I tear my eyes away, trying to convince myself that Weston looks like the homeless man who used to sleep in our crawlspace instead of Chris Hemsworth at the Met Gala.

It doesn't work.

"You want to do the job for the job. Not many people in politics are that way."

He chuckles. "It doesn't feel that political, to be honest. I'll be the Sheriff of our county, not governor of Indiana."

"You'd be good at that too." I put my mug in the microwave.

"How'd Jackson do at bedtime?"

"He was good. I ended up reading like four extra stories. Maybe I'll get used to saying no when he asks for another with time, right?"

Wes smiles. "I have a hard time saying no to books, too. Someday he's not going to want me to sit in bed with him and read."

"Right. They don't stay little for long."

He holds my gaze for a moment too long, and blood rushes to my cheeks. He goes upstairs to change, and I take my tea back to the living room. I read a few pages, and already I'm imagining the alpha werewolf in my book to look like Weston.

Dammit.

"I have something for you," he says, coming back down the stairs. He's wearing black athletic pants and a Chicago Bears hoodie. I'm not a big sports fan, but I do support my city.

"You do?"

"Well, kind of." He crosses the room. "Grab your coat."

Setting my book down, I get up and hurry after him. "If it's a cat, you should have waited until Jackson wakes up."

He gives me a playful glare. "It's not a cat."

"Darn."

We put our shoes on, and I grab my coat, following him to the back porch. There's a telescope standing on the sidewalk, pointed up at the night sky. I pause, suddenly forgetting how to move my feet.

"So you can see the stars." Wes is standing by the telescope, a smile on his face. He takes a cover off the lens and wipes away dust. "It was mine when I was a kid. It's been at my parents', and I grabbed it on my way home. I have no idea if it still works, but it's not like these things go bad, right?"

I fumble with the zipper on my coat, and for some reason, I'm still unable to move. I stare down the telescope feeling the weirdest sensation prick at the corners of my eyes. And an even weirder one inside my chest.

Wes holds my gaze, waiting for me to come down the stairs. To say something. Anything. But I'm still standing there like a statue.

"Anyway," Wes goes on, bringing his hand up to his hair. He pulls the band out and lets his long locks fall around his face. I can feel his eyes on me, and I know he's waiting. The longer I go without reacting, the more he's going to think I don't appreciate the gesture or that I think it's stupid.

Which couldn't be farther from the truth.

He went to his parents' house, which I know isn't on the way home from anything. They live on the edge of Eastwood, away from the police station and the town hall where the council meetings are held.

No one has ever done anything like this for me before.

"Jackson might think it's cool at least," he says, and I shake myself.

"It is cool." I inhale, finally get my zipper to go up, and dash down the stairs. I stand close to him, feeling the heat radiating from his large body. I look into eyes, seeing the stars reflected before me, and want to tell him just what this means to me. Attraction aside, this was the most thoughtful thing he could have done.

"How does it work?"

"I have to put a different lens on," he starts and opens a bag. "We might have to watch YouTube tutorials on this."

I laugh and use the sleeve of my coat to carefully wipe the dust off the metal. It takes us a while, but we finally get the thing ready. Wes goes inside to quickly check on Jackson and to turn off the back porch light.

"You know," I say when he comes back. "We could totally spy on your neighbors."

He raises his eyebrows. "Why do you think I wanted to get one of these in the first place?"

"Seriously?" I laugh.

"No. I went through a phase where I wanted to be an astronaut. Like all kids, I suppose."

"Not me." I bend over and put my eye to the focuser. "I wanted to be a professional mermaid."

"That's a thing?"

"Yeah. You swim around at aquariums or shows."

"Shows?"

"Yeah." I carefully move the telescope until I see the fuzzy bright light of what I think is a star. "Like carnivals."

"You'd be a mermaid carnie," he snickers.

"It sounds not as fun when you say it like that. But yeah...and come on. It sounds like a sweet deal. I'd get to swim all day, wear pretty seashell bras, and have lots of glittery makeup on my face."

He laughs and helps me adjust the telescope. "When you put it that way, maybe I'll be a professional merman."

"We could make a career out of it, traveling the country together."

"Clearly I chose the wrong profession." His hand drops from the telescope, and he inches closer. I swallow hard.

"Oh, I see the moon!" I spend a minute adjusting everything, and it comes into focus. "Holy shit, this is amazing." My heart hammers away in my chest, and a chill goes through me, but it's not from the cold. I stare at the moon, and that weird feeling comes back. It's so overwhelming I break away, telling Wes he should take a look as well. His large frame leans over, and he looks at the moon.

"Now I want to be an astronaut again," he says after looking up at the moon for a moment. "It's incredible."

I'm looking at him when I agree. "It is."

He straightens up and reaches back into the bag. "There's a map of the stars. I never was able to make much sense of it."

Another chill goes through me, and I'm unable to hide the shiver.

"Cold?" Wes asks.

I shake my head, not wanting to go in just yet. "I'll survive. Let's try to read this map."

He unfolds the paper and gets out his phone to use as a flashlight. His lock screen is a recent picture of Jackson, and I just about die all over again.

"I can see the Big Dipper," I say, pointing to the sky. "And that's it."

Wes smiles, still looking at the sky. "Same here." We stand there in silence for another moment, looking up at the stars. Something streaks across the sky.

"Did you see that?" I gasp.

"I did." He tips his head down to mine, and there will never be a more perfect moment for him to kiss me. It's like we're floating amongst the stars and nothing matters. Not the past. Not the mistakes I've made.

Just this moment.

But he doesn't kiss me.

Instead, he folds the map and puts it back in the bag. "It's cold out here, and I have an early morning tomorrow. And Jackson has school."

"Right." Back to earth I go, free falling from outer space. "He picked out his outfit for tomorrow," I go on. "With approval, of course. He has really cute clothes."

"I enjoy shopping for him," Wes admits. "So does my mom."

"I can tell."

Wes picks up the heavy telescope with ease, putting it on the back porch for the night. I don't think theft is a worry around here. We step back into the house, and the warm air feels hot against my cheeks.

"You're all set for the morning?" he asks, taking off his shoes. He's nervous about me driving Jackson, and usually something like this would annoy me. I'm capable. Trustworthy, well, that's questionable, but this time there's nothing to worry about.

"Yes. His bag is ready to go, and you showed me the drop-off and pick-up procedure twice today."

He laughs. "Sorry. He's only been in school a few weeks, and I don't know if he's used to his new routine or not yet."

"Don't be sorry. I'd rather see you be a little overprotective than too carefree with him. I know you love him, and you're a good dad."

"Thanks," he says, almost as if my statement caught him off guard. "It's not always easy, ya know, doing things alone." He goes to the fridge and grabs the plate of leftovers. Jackson helped me make chicken enchiladas tonight, and while I don't mean to toot my own horn, we both went back for seconds.

"This looks good," Wes says as he sticks his plate in the microwave.

"I enjoyed it. Jackson did too." There's still nearly a minute left on his food, and suddenly the silence feels awkward. I go into the living room, fold the blanket I was using, and grab my tea to reheat again.

I add another spoonful of sugar to it, stirring it, and stick it in the microwave once Wes's food is done heating. We both sit at the table.

"Do you have campaign stuff tomorrow too?"

He shakes his head. "No, just the gym and then work. I'll go grocery shopping on the way home. If there's anything you want, I can grab it for you."

"I do like chocolate an awful lot."

He smiles. "Noted. Any kind or something special?"

"I guess any kind. But not dark chocolate. That shit is nasty."

Wes laughs, cutting into another piece of his food. "Agreed. And you know you don't have to make dinner every night. I'll do it the nights I'm home."

"I don't mind," I say honestly. And really, I want to stay busy. Being busy keeps me from thinking.

"Oh, and I'm off all day Wednesday, so if there was something you want to do, feel free."

"I might go visit my dad and my sis
should, especially since Dad fell again yes
paid, I'm going to burn through half my
medication for him. Since my food and lodging
my pay, I'm more or less living here for free. I *coul*
money over to Dad and Heather. Yeah, I want stuff for m
I don't need stuff.

Wes nods. "I'm sure they'd like that."

"Yeah. I think so." Heather will, at least. Dad might not remember who I am. I finish my tea, put the mug in the dishwasher and wipe down the already-clean counter just so I have something to do. Wes is done now, and we both look at each other in an awkward stand-off.

He has to be thinking the same thing I am. We kissed, and it was a damn good kiss. I felt his hard cock against me. My breasts pressed against his firm chest, and we both wanted more. If Jackson hadn't come down the steps, we *would* have had more.

And then what?

Would we be in an even more awkward situation than we are right now? I've never had someone resist me like this, and it sucks. Only because I want him something terrible...and not just physically, as much as I don't want to admit that to myself.

I should hate him, but I can't. Because, without a doubt, Weston is making me feel.

ter," I tell him. And I really
erday. As soon as I get
money just buying
are figured into
send all my
yself. But

LET   111

"I thought maybe you forgot about me now that you're a working girl and all," Heather says, sitting back in the plastic chair. Her hair is even worse than before, and she has a bruise on her cheek.

"What happened?" I ask, ignoring her subtle jab.

She shrugs. "Kickball got a little rough in the yard."

"You're allowed to play kickball?" I shake my head. "That's not the point. Please don't get in fights."

"Seriously, Scar? Like I want to get in fights?"

I let out a breath. "Sorry. I didn't mean it like that. Just...don't get into fights."

Heather rolls her eyes. "How's the new job? Are you ready to slit your wrists yet?"

"No. It's not bad at all. I kinda like it."

Heather cocks an eyebrow. "You hate kids. This guy must be loaded for you to say you like being a nanny for a rich, spoiled brat."

Her words piss me off, and I try hard not to let myself recognize it. Because you only get upset when someone insults someone you care about. "He doesn't have the money I thought he did. And the kid isn't spoiled or bratty at all. He's sweet."

"Are you fucking him? He must have one magic cock for you to hang around now."

I want to be fucking Wes. I have no doubt his cock *is* magic. "Nope. Not sleeping with him."

"You mean not yet, right? That's how you pull your tricks, isn't it? Sex and blackmail are like your claim to fame."

"They're not," I say, fully aware of another visitor eavesdropping. I get it, our conversation is unorthodox at best, but geez, be a little discreet.

"So what are you going to do? We need money."

"My job."

Heather's eyebrows push together, and she stares at me for a good few seconds. "Wait. You took a job as a nanny for a rich couple so you could con them out of their money, but you're just going to be a fucking nanny and earn minimum wage?"

Hearing her say it out loud makes me realize how terrible a person I am. "I'm doing the job I was hired to do. And it's not a rich couple. Wes is a single dad."

"Ohh, his name is Wes. You must be hot for him or something. Because my badass big sister doesn't work petty jobs."

I roll my eyes. "Stop bragging about me to your prison friends, okay? You're going to get me caught or something."

"Please." She runs a hand through her butchered hair. Fixing it is the first thing I'm going to do once she's out of here.

"And I don't get hot for people. I think all that love shit is that just that: shit."

Heather drums her fingers on the table. "Have you seen Dad lately?"

"Yeah. I saw him before I came here."

"How'd he look today?" she asks apprehensively.

"Okay. He has a big bump on his head from falling face first out of his wheelchair. I guess he was reaching for something and hit the floor." I rub my forehead, feeling a headache coming on. "I was able to talk to the doctor today about switching medications. I don't want him to be drugged up, but something needs to change so he doesn't bust his head open."

"Yeah, we need to get him into a better place with more staff."

"Oh, that would help for sure. But places like that are expensive."

Heather looks down at the table, dropping her *I don't give a shit* attitude. She knows the stunt she pulled that got her arrested took away a lot from Dad. I spent money on her lawyer, and she obviously can't work and contribute to the medical bills anymore.

"Why do you have so many scratches on your hands?" she asks.

"Kittens."

"Awww, I want a kitten. Are they at the house?"

"No, Wes—my boss—has a sister who really likes cats. We hung out yesterday." I say it almost like a confession, because Heather knows how far from normal this is for me. After picking up Jackson from school, I met Quinn and Emma at the farmers' market downtown. I really like her, which surprised me more than anyone. Never in a million years would I think I'd be talking and laughing with someone like Quinn.

"You're really making yourself at home. I thought one of your cardinal rules was not to get involved and make personal attachments or whatever."

I shake my head, stomach tightening. "This isn't my usual situation. I told you, Wes doesn't have a trust fund. I don't know…" I pick at the lint that's stuck to the sleeves of my sweater, angling myself away from the chick who's still looking at me. Judge away, bitch. You can't be much better considering we're both visiting someone in prison. "I'll figure it out."

Heather lets out a huff. "Do it fast. I'm almost out of money, and I really like being able to buy snacks."

I can't help but laugh. "I'm glad you have your priorities in check."

∼

"Is everything okay?" Wes asks softly. We just finished dinner, and I've hardly said a word throughout the meal. Going back to the south side, seeing my sister and my dad, and walking down the streets I've haunted since I was old enough to venture out on my own…it reminded me who I am.

Of the shit I've done.

And all the thoughts I've wrestled down are fighting to come up. To remind me how shitty of a person I am.

That there is no such thing as redemption.

"Yeah, just…just thinking." I force a smile.

"Okay." He doesn't believe me, but he's not going to press it. His phone buzzes again, and I eye it.

"You're mister popular tonight."

He flips it over and glances at the text. "It's my brothers trying to get me to go out to the bar tonight."

"On a Wednesday?"

"Yeah. There's a twenty-first birthday celebration going on, and it's always entertaining to watch."

"You should go," I tell him. "I'm here to look after Jackson after he's asleep."

Wes considers it for a whole two seconds. "Honestly, I feel bad going out."

"Don't. I'm here, and if you put Jackson to bed, then it's not like you're missing out on time with him, which is what I think you feel bad about, right?"

He smiles. "Right. They have been bugging me for ages. And I'll only stay for an hour."

"Stay as long as you'd like. I have a wild night planned, and having the law here is going to cramp my style."

Wes laughs. "Then maybe I should stay."

I gather the plates from the table and take them to the sink. "It's going to get crazy up in here. It'll start with me singing off-key to Def Leppard and will end with tea and a few more chapters of a rather steamy werewolf-vampire romance."

"You like Def Leppard?"

"I do. Motley Crue, KISS, and Skid Row will be on repeat as well." I turn on the sink to rinse the dishes. "You sound surprised. Are you judging me, Mr. Dawson?"

"I am. I am judging you hard, and I will admit you do not look like someone who'd be a fan of 80s hair bands."

"Looks can be deceiving."

"Apparently so."

I laugh and start loading the dishwasher. "Don't be mad if I teach Jackson the words to 'Pour Some Sugar on Me.'"

"Oh, he already knows them."

"Seriously?"

"Seriously." Weston comes up behind me and grabs a plate from the sink to put into the dishwasher. "Add in Bon Jovi, Poison, Van Halen, and Ratt and you've pretty much named my whole playlist."

"Did we just become best friends?"

"You like 80s rock and you made a *Stepbrothers* reference? It's like you're not real."

I laugh, finding twisted humor in his words. I've never been this real with someone before.

"I'm not. You're imagining everything right now. It's all a dream."

"At least it's a good one."

Dammit, Weston...if only you knew.

His phone rings, and he wipes his hands on a towel with a sigh.

"Your brothers really want you to go out."

"They won't stop until I do."

"It's cute, you know. And nice to see you all still be close as adults."

"So close I'm going to send this call to voice—oh, it's my mom. Never mind." I finish loading the dishwasher as he talks to his mom, and it sounds like she's stopping by to drop something off.

"Remember how I said my mom likes buying Jackson clothes?"

I start the dishwasher and grab a rag to wipe down the counter. "Yeah."

"She's bought 'a few things' and is bringing them over."

"Awww, that's so sweet."

"Hey, Jackson!" Wes calls, and Jackson comes in from the living room. "Grammy is bringing you something."

"A kitten?"

I can't help but laugh.

"No, not a kitten."

"Oh, man!" Jackson throws his head back dramatically. "But I really, really want one."

"You should let him get a kitten," I say, flashing Wes a sweet smile. "We played with them yesterday, and they're so sweet."

"I'll think about it," Wes says flatly, and Jackson starts jumping up and down. He runs back into the living room to look out the window for his grandma.

"The kittens are cute," Wes agrees.

"They are so stinking cute, and oh my God, your sister's house is huge," I blurt, and it feels good to finally say it out loud.

Wes laughs. "Yeah, it's…it's something."

"She has enough room for more cats."

"Don't encourage her," he chuckles and goes to get the vacuum. We work together to get the kitchen cleaned up, falling into a rhythm without even meaning to. The front door opens, and Mrs. Dawson steps in, carrying two large shopping bags.

"Hi, Scarlet," she says, setting the bags down. Jackson drags one into the living room and dumps it out, sorting through his clothes. There are new figures for his farm set at the bottom of the second bag, and Jackson races up the stairs to put them in his barn.

Wes's phone starts buzzing again, and this time it is his brothers.

"Who's texting you so much?" Mrs. Dawson asks, trying to look over Wes's shoulder at his phone. He's too tall to get a look.

"Dean, Logan, and Owen. They've been annoying me all night about going out with them."

"You should!" Mrs. Dawson says right away. "Both of you should. I'll stay and put Jackson to bed." She looks at me and smiles. "He told me you're more fun, but I do miss that little rascal."

"It's a school night," Wes counters.

"I know. I can get him to bed. You should go out. You don't," his mom says gently. "And you should."

"You're encouraging me to go to a bar on a weekday. Such good parenting, Mom."

Mrs. Dawson laughs. "Take that as a sign of how much you need to get out of the house. And I'm sure Scarlet would appreciate it too, right?"

"Uh, right," I agree, even though a quiet night alone not being able to sleep due to excessive amounts of guilt was what I had on my agenda. "I'm curious to see this bar too."

"Fine," Weston huffs. "But only for an hour. I do have to work tomorrow."

"Let me go get changed," I say and dash up the stairs. Usually, if I go to a bar, I'm pulling out all the stops. But tonight, I'm brushing through my messy hair, putting on just enough makeup to look presentable, and am wearing leggings.

Scratch that. I'm wearing a v-neck black sweater dress that hugs my curves and shows the perfect amount of cleavage. I do enjoy dressing up for myself every now and then. Not wanting to keep Wes or his mom waiting, I hurry out of my room.

Wes and Jackson are coming up the stairs right as I step into the hall.

"He wants me to give him a bath," Wes says before he sees me. He does a double-take, and I'd be lying if I said it didn't feel good to see his reaction.

"Oh, okay."

"I'll try to be fast. Give us twenty minutes."

Jackson races ahead, already stripping out of his clothes. Twenty minutes is all I need to put on more makeup and curl my hair. I finish getting ready a few minutes after Wes and Jackson are downstairs.

"Wow!" Jackson says when he sees me. "Your hair is so bouncy."

I run my hand over a curl. "Yeah, I guess it is. Do you like it or is it too bouncy?"

"I like it! You look like a princess!"

"Thank you. And you look super cute in those Mickey Mouse jammies."

Jackson narrows his eyes. "I'm not cute. I'm handsome."

"Ohhh, I'm sorry," I say with a laugh. "You are very handsome."

Jackson beams and looks at Wes. "Like Daddy."

I can't disagree. Wes *is* very handsome. He changed too, and the dark jeans and gray Henley shirt look so good on him.

"We won't be out too long," Wes tells his mom, dropping down to his knees to give Jackson a hug and a kiss. "Be good for Grammy. And don't stay up too late. You have school in the morning."

"Yay, school!" Jackson throws his arms around Wes, hugging him goodbye. I grab my coat and put on my favorite over-the-knee boots and follow Wes outside.

"You look nice," I tell him, looking over my shoulder at him.

He looks a little surprised by the compliment. "Thanks. And you...you look beautiful." The headlights of the Jeep flash as he unlocks it. I turn around, twisting the strap of my purse in my hands, and look at Wes. There's an undeniable hunger in his eyes, and I know it'll only take one move to be devoured.

I part my lips, eyeing Wes up and down. He steps in, loose stones on the pavement rolling under his feet. The chill in the air starts to disappear the closer he gets, and I want so badly to reach out and pull him to me. He hesitates, holding my gaze for a moment.

And then he steps around, going to the driver's side of the Jeep. I exhale heavily, just now realizing that my heart is racing. What the hell is wrong with me? It's not like it's been that long since I've had sex that I'm desperate to hook up with the first attractive man I can find. He's my boss. We can't just hook up and go on like everything is fine and dandy the next day.

And really...I don't want to hook up with him. I want more, but I know Wes wouldn't date someone like me. Not the real me.

∽

"SOMETHING TELLS me he's not going to make it through the first three shots, let alone the twenty-one he wants to do," Logan laughs, wiping up a spilled drink from the wooden surface of the bar.

"People still try that?" I ask.

Logan nods. "They do. We'd cut them off before they get close, but I've never seen anyone get past four shots in a row like that." He shakes his head. "It wasn't pretty."

I wrinkle my nose. "I actually never thought about that before. You probably have your fair share of vomit to clean up."

"We really try to cut people off before they get to that point, but it's not always possible. Luckily most people somehow get outside and puke in the parking lot. It's easy to hose away."

"Glamorous."

Logan laughs and steps away to take drink orders from two girls who just walked up. Wes is throwing darts with Dean, and I turn around to watch for a minute. The bar is pretty crowded for a Wednesday, even without the birthday party. The bar itself is amazing and much bigger than I imagined.

"Do you want a drink?" Logan asks, coming back over.

"Sure. Do you have wine?"

"We do.

"Give me a glass of whatever's cheapest," I say

"You don't want what's cheapest. It's shit."

I laugh, looking Logan over. Physically, he looks exactly like his twin. They wear their hair the same and probably share clothes. But there's a distinct difference between the two, with the biggest being how obviously Logan is crushing on fellow bartender, Danielle. I've been watching him flirt and get flustered when she's around, and she's giving it right back.

"You work for Wes. I'll put it on his tab." Logan steps away and returns a minute later with a glass of sweet red wine.

"This is good," I say after I take a sip.

"It is, isn't it?" Logan looks across the bar at Danielle, spacing out for a second before turning back to me. "What's it like living with my brother? He can be very, uh, uptight at times. Though he's dealt with an unfair amount of shit in his life."

"He's great. Jackson too."

"You can be honest," Logan jokes.

"Really," I laugh. "We get along well, which is nic[e]
for Jackson, but it helps, ya know? We eat dinner and [w]
together and it's not weird."

"That's good. Going and living with someone would be w[
on its own."

I nod and take another drink of wine. "It takes a while to get
used to. I know he wishes he didn't have to have a nanny for
Jackson." I look over at Wes again. "He'll never admit it, but I
think he feels guilty for being away."

"He does. My big brother might be a tad prickly at times, but
nothing is more important to him than family."

"I can tell," I say as my gaze drifts back to Wes. "It's a very
admirable quality, and if I'm being honest, it's not one I see too
often."

"Right," Logan agrees.

I can't help the smile that pulls up my lips or the flush that
colors my cheeks. I'm still looking at Wes, and Logan catches me
watching.

"So your place is really nice," I blurt, feeling almost as if I'm
having an out-of-body experience. The last time I was at a bar,
things went very different. I actually can't remember the last time
I went to a bar just for fun like this. This isn't me. It's so far from
the version of myself I usually am it's jarring.

But I like it.

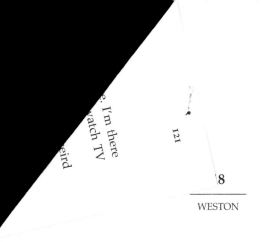

8

WESTON

I put my squad car in park and get out, stepping into the quiet night that surrounds my house. It's been a long week, and I'm looking forward to having the weekend off. The living room light is on, and I can see the fuzzy outline of Scarlet sitting on the couch through the sheer curtains.

Several pumpkins and a few pots of mums are on the porch steps, and it looks like she and Jackson finished putting up the little graveyard scene in the lawn today, finally decorating for Halloween. She's been here for two weeks now, and we've fallen into a good routine.

A good routine that involves awkwardly avoiding the very obvious fact that we're both extremely attracted to each other.

We eat meals together whenever I'm home, and on the nights the sky is clear, Scarlet goes outside to look at the stars. I've joined her a few times, but it's harder and harder to keep my hands to myself and my heart in my chest whenever I'm around her.

Jackson loves her, and having the stability has already made a difference in his behavior and mood. He's always a happy kid, but not having to get up at the crack of dawn makes a huge difference on the kid. He's not a morning person.

My life has been simplified in some aspects as well, and not having to try to fit in cleaning and making dinner has been a huge relief. I shouldn't be as tired as I am, but I've had a hard time falling asleep knowing Scarlet is just down the hall. I wake up almost every night after dreaming of her, cock hard and heart racing.

She's beautiful, but it's more than that. She's good with my son. Takes care of him and makes him happy. The rare times I'd let my mind wander and would think of dating again, I always came back to the same issue: Jackson.

Dating isn't easy. Dating with kids is even harder. Not only do I need to find someone who is fine with me having a kid, they'd have to bond with Jackson before I considered moving into anything serious. It's almost like things have been done in reverse with Scarlet. She came here for Jackson, and I know he'd approve if we—

"Stop," I say out loud to myself. It's not going to happen.

A gust of wind blows through, rattling the trees. Misty rain begins to fall, and I hurry into the house. I take off my shoes and coat, and head upstairs to lock up my gun for the night.

"Hey," Scarlet says, looking up from her phone. "How was work?"

"Work was fine. The meetings…" I shake my head. "They went all right too. But you know how I don't like them."

"I do." She sets her phone down on the coffee table. "Jackson polished off the leftovers, but I can make something for you if you want."

"Thanks, but I'm good. I picked up fast food on the way home." I pat my stomach. "I undid my workout from this morning, I know. But those fries were worth it."

Scarlet laughs. "I admire your dedication." She stretches her legs out in front of her. "I was just about to start the new season of *American Horror Story*. Want to watch it with me?"

We haven't sat on the couch like this since *the incident*. I think we're both afraid of what might happen if we stay up late and sit in the dark together again. And good Lord, I want it to happen again. I've been able to use work as an excuse before. I can't stay up late because I have to get up early, and obviously working the night shifts prevented any such offerings.

But tonight…tonight I have no reason to say no, and I do want to watch the show. I'm off all weekend, and so is Scarlet. She's going to Chicago to see her dad again tomorrow. I haven't asked, and she hasn't said anything, but I get the feeling her dad is sick or something. I've heard her a few times on the phone, talking about treatments, and once she seemed close to tears while arguing with insurance about getting a medication covered.

"Yeah," I tell her. "I'll watch it."

"Great. So you said no to food, but what about popcorn?"

"I never say no to popcorn."

Scarlet smiles and gets up to make some while I change. She's still in the kitchen when I come back down. Her phone is set to silent and is still on the coffee table. It vibrates, getting my attention. A text comes through from someone named Corbin. Two black hearts follow his name, and I divert my eyes, not wanting to so much as read a word he's saying.

I never really thought about Scarlet dating, and I assumed she was single from 1) taking a job where she moved two hours away from home and in with another family and 2) that kiss was pretty intense the other night.

Scarlet comes back, smile on her face, and sits on the couch next to me. There are three cushions on the couch, and there's an unwritten rule of leaving the middle one free when two people who aren't romantically involved sit together. But Scarlet ignores the rule and puts the popcorn in her lap.

Her phone vibrates again, and as soon as she reads the texts, her smile disappears and a line of worry forms between her eyes. She hands me the popcorn and texts back, making sure her phone is angled away so I can't see it.

With a sigh, she sets her phone down next to her and picks up the remote. Her face is tight as she turns on the TV.

"Everything okay?"

"Yeah," she says back without missing a beat. She puts on her front again, pushing her shoulders back and lifting her eyebrows just enough to cover the worry. She holds that stance for a while, and I wonder if it's subconscious or if she's really good at understanding body language and is doing it on purpose.

Either way, something is upsetting her, and it upsets me. I don't want to pry, because I know Scarlet isn't throwing out the "it's fine" line just to see if I'll keep digging. She wants me to believe things are fine so I don't pressure her.

"Okay. If you need anything…just let me know," I say quietly.

Her smile trembles for a quick second. "Thanks. And I will. Actually, I'll probably leave early tomorrow to beat the traffic."

"You can take my Jeep," I offer, knowing she's been Ubering to Chicago and back. It's not cheap.

"Don't you need it?"

"I don't plan on going anywhere tomorrow, to be honest, and I have my squad car if I absolutely need to leave the house."

"You're sure?" she asks again.

"Yeah. This might be a stupid question, but do you drive a lot in the city?"

"Where I lived, yeah, I did. Well, when I had a car. I sold it for drug money."

I raise an eyebrow, waiting for her to laugh so I know she's joking. She doesn't.

"Drugs for my dad," she goes on, seeing the blank expression on my face. "And not illegal drugs. Prescription. My dad is…" She lets out a breath and, at the same time, lets go of the air she's putting on. Her shoulders sag forward, and her smile is nowhere to be seen. "My dad is sick."

"Shit, I'm so sorry."

She pulls her arms in around herself. "He's been sick for a while, and the medical bills won't pay themselves."

"It's bullshit how much healthcare costs."

"Yeah, you're telling me." She pushes her hair back and lets out a deep sigh. "We missed the beginning." Turning her attention back to the TV, she rewinds the minute or so we missed. Halfway through the episode, Scarlet's rests her head on my shoulder. Only a minute or two later, she's asleep.

Guess I'm not the only one having a hard time sleeping at night.

"I don't get it," I say, cutting apart a piece of chicken. Well, if you can consider this over-processed mess chicken. "If the issue is he wants to get up and walk, then why can't someone walk with him?" I stab a small piece of chicken on the fork and feed it to my father. "He wouldn't fall then because someone would be helping him, right?"

"Girl," Corbin says, feeding two patients at once. "We are so understaffed I'm thrilled if we get through our shower list. You're right, and it's not fucking fair, but it's all I can do just to get two aides to cover the south wing with me."

"It's not your fault," I say, making sure he knows I don't hold any blame on him. Corbin works his ass off, as do many of the others here. The problem is there aren't enough of them. This place is a dump, and nobody wants to work here. Unfortunately, most of the residents here have similar financial situations to mine and can't go anywhere else.

"You need to get out of here," Corbin says quietly, as if he's reading my mind. "I'm trying to, and I have an interview at the hospital next week." He looks around the table and shakes his head. "I don't want to leave these guys, though."

"You deserve better," I tell him.

"So do they."

I give Dad another bite of chicken. "This fucking sucks."

"I know it." Corbin shakes his head. "It's lose-lose no matter what we do."

I let out a sigh. "Yeah, it is." I pick up the water and put the straw to Dad's lips. He swats my hand away.

"I can feed myself, Wendy."

It's not the first time he's called me by my mother's name. Once upon a time, before the meth and the heroin, my mother and I shared a resemblance. I remember looking through her high school yearbook once and thinking she was the most beautiful woman in the world.

Ignoring my father, I move the water away and wait a few seconds before trying again. This time he takes a drink.

"So," Corbin starts. "You pulled up here in a Jeep Wrangler, not a Caddy. Did the new job not work out?"

My stomach tightens. I'd moved past conning Wes, and dare I say I almost forgot about it? I didn't, not by a long shot, but a girl can dream, right?

"I'm still working as a nanny, but in the traditional sense this time."

Corbin gives me a quizzical look. We never hang out, but he's the closest thing I have to a friend. He's one of the least judgmental people I know, and there's just something humbling about the guy who wipes my dad's ass and gives him a shower. There are two people in this world who know the nitty-gritty details of my life. One is my sister, and the other is Corbin.

"But you don't like kids."

I shrug. "This kid isn't so bad." I smile. "He's great, actually. And his dad—my boss—is a great guy too. His whole family is great, and now I've said great like a million times."

"They must really be great."

I roll my eyes at Corbin. "They are, though, and it's been nice hanging out with them," I say, lowering my voice. I'm not sure what state of mind Dad is in, but there's always a chance he'll hear me, and I don't want to make him feel bad.

Not that his behavior is excused. He and Mom had a tumultuous relationship that imploded when Mom cheated on him. Dad always drank too much but spiraled after that. He left us, and Mom went into a depression. She wasn't without her vices before, of course, and things got worse from there on out. We never realized how much Dad tried to keep Mom clean until he left.

He wanted to leave her, but he also left us. When he showed back up in our lives, I refused to talk to him for half a year. I caved only because I wanted to go back and graduate high school.

"And his wife?" Corbin asks, raising his eyebrows.

"He doesn't have one."

"Ohhhh."

"It's not like that." I shake my head and trade the fork for a spoon and test the soup before giving some to Dad. It's not terrible, but it is lacking a bit in flavor. I add some salt, stirring it up. "They're just good people. Maybe they'll rub off on me. They all get together on Sundays for dinner, and by all, I mean my boss and his four siblings. At their parents' house. Like a TV family."

Corbin shakes his head. "Perfect families like that freak me out. Lord knows what's hiding in their closets."

I smile and laugh, but I know the Dawsons aren't like that. They're perfect in my eyes. But they're not without their faults.

Maybe we're not so different after all.

"I THOUGHT they misspoke when they called my name." Heather's arms are crossed tightly over her chest, and she's sporting a new bruise on her temple. I'm not even going to ask.

"Funny, Heather."

"It's been, what, two weeks since I've seen you?" She cocks her eyebrows and stares me down as if she just caught me with my hand in the cookie jar.

"That's not my fault."

"What's that supposed to mean?"

"It means the reason I haven't seen you is because you're in jail." My words come out harsher than I meant. Trumpets will sound the day she grows the fuck up and takes responsibility for her actions. "I've been busy."

"Too busy to see Dad?"

"I saw him today."

"And that was the first time since you came out this way last?"

The woman who obviously eavesdropped on our conversation the last time I was here comes into the room. Her eyes fall on me for a few seconds before she moves in and takes a seat at a nearby table.

"No, I saw him last week."

"And you didn't come see me?" The pitch of Heather's voice goes up. Dammit. She takes things too personally, and I know she has to be miserable in here. Knowing I was in the area but didn't stop by stings, but it's not like that.

"It's a two-and-a-half-hour drive from here to Eastwood, and I was tired. Plus, I needed to get back for…for dinner."

"You couldn't come see me so you could fucking eat dinner? It better have been a damn good meal."

"The food was good," I admit. Though the company is even better. "What happened to your face?" I change the subject, knowing asking about her injuries will piss her off too, but at least she'll be pissed off for a different reason.

"This is what happens when you try and stay out of trouble." She motions to her face. "But it's been handled."

"Handled?"

Heather lets out an exasperated sigh. "It's hard to explain unless you've been in here, okay?"

I nod. "Okay. I just want you to come home."

"Do we even have a home anymore? Aren't you living with some rich family in East-something-or-other."

"Eastwood, and I told you, he's a single dad and not rich."

"So that's *your* home. Where am I going to go?"

I shake my head. "I'll figure it out."

"What if I get out tomorrow?"

She won't, so that's not even a concern. "I'll come get you."

"And then what?"

"I'll take you back with me."

She lets out a snort of laughter. She's angry at something else and is taking it out on me. "And I could stay in the house you're living at?"

"No, I don't think Wes would be okay with that," I say honestly. "But we'd get you a hotel room until we could set up something more permanent."

"We?"

"Yes, I know Wes would help me. He's a good guy."

Instead of coming back with a sassy comment, Heather smiles. "You really like this guy, don't you?"

"I do like him, but not in the way you're insinuating. He's a good guy."

"Yeah, you said that."

Heat rushes through me. "Okay, yeah...he's attractive, and if I wasn't his son's nanny, I'd make a move. Another move, since Jackson kind of cock-blocked us the first time." I shake my head. "But he's a *good guy*, Heather. One of the rare, really good ones. And I'm, well, not. I took the job as a nanny with the intentions of conning money out of him. I'm a horrible person."

Heather laughs and reaches across the table, taking my hands. "Scar, don't even say that. You're not a horrible person. We've all done things we're not proud of. And this orange jumpsuit proves it on my end." She gives my hands a squeeze. "So what are you going to do about it?"

"Nothing."

"Nothing? That's not my older sister talking."

"He's my boss. What if we hook up and then it's weird? I live with him and his son."

"But what if it's not weird?"

I shrug. "I don't know. He doesn't strike me as the kind who would be okay with a fuck-buddy type of relationship. If we hooked up, things between us would go to the next level."

"Isn't that what you want?"

God yes. I'd love to be Weston's girlfriend. To go out together and actually cuddle on the couch as we're watching horror movies, staying up way too late and then crawling up to bed together. We'd be so tired but unable to keep our hands off each other, and we'd have sleepy, lazy sex that only couples who have reached a deep level of comfort have.

"I wouldn't mind," I tell my sister. "But then I'd have to disclose personal info, and I don't know how he'd feel about me if he knew, well, everything."

"That you've been conning people for years, Dad was a drunk, Mom died with a needle in her arm, and your baby sister is in jail?"

"Yeah. That."

"Just brag about Jason a bit first."

I give her a lopsided smile. "I already have. It doesn't matter. He won't understand where we came from, and more importantly, I'm not going to sleep with my boss."

"You're in love with him."

"No. I don't believe in love." The words escape my lips and feel like a lie. I *didn't* believe in love, but now I'm not so sure. Being in love meant having a heart, and I convinced myself mine stopped working long ago.

But now when I close my eyes and the world becomes still, I feel it fluttering back to life.

"*W*hat about this one?" Jackson races forward to the biggest pumpkin he can find.

"I think that might be a little too heavy," I laugh. It's late Monday morning, and Jackson and I are at the pumpkin patch with Quinn, Archer, and Emma. "How about this one?" I point to a round, white pumpkin.

"It lost all its color!" Jackson's eye widen in shock, making both Quinn and I laugh.

"It's supposed to be like that," Quinn explains, adjusting Emma in the baby carrier she's wearing. "Ohh, a cat!"

"Don't even think about it," Archer says, slipping his arm around Quinn's waist. "Pretty sure it belongs to the orchard."

"I didn't say I was going to take it."

Archer gives her side a squeeze. They're gag-worthy cute together, but Quinn is quickly becoming a friend, so it doesn't bother me like it normally would. "I know the way your mind works."

"Look at this one! It's all bumpy!" Jackson laughs, looking at the pumpkin with a look of disgust on his face.

"You don't like it?" I ask.

"It has warts!"

"It does?" I make a move to touch it, and Jackson grabs my hand, laughing.

"You'll get warts too!"

I take Jackson's hand and lead him to another row of pumpkins. He goes to a large, oval-shaped one that has to be heavy.

"I like this one!"

"I think it's perfect," I tell him.

Archer picks up the heavy pumpkin for us and puts it on the wagon he's pulling. We make it through the rest of pumpkins, grabbing a few more little ones along the way. Jackson and I grabbed pumpkins from the store not long ago, but this is way more fun. I've never been to a pumpkin patch like this before. We go into a big barn to pay for our pumpkins and to get apple cider. The sun is out in full force today, making the fifty-degree air comfortable.

I'm having fun, and while I'm working, it doesn't feel like it. I really care about Jackson, and seeing him light up and have fun makes me happy. We get our cider and take it outside, enjoying what could very likely be one of the last warm days this fall. Archer's loading the pumpkins into the back of the SUV when Quinn's phone rings.

"It's Wes," she says, brows coming together. Weston is at work today, and his call isn't expected. "Hey, Wes. What's up?" She waits a moment, listening to her brother. "Oh no. Yeah, yeah, we'll be right there." Another pause. "Archer's with me. I'll let him know."

Archer, having heard his name, looks up. Once he sees the worry on Quinn's face, he comes over. "What's wrong?"

Quinn shakes her head. "Thanks, Wes. Just, uh, keep him calm if you can. We'll be right there." She ends the call and readjusts Emma on her chest. "It's Bobby."

Archer's face falls. "Is he…is he…"

"He's alive," Quinn answers and starts to take Emma out of the carrier. "Wes has him."

"Where is he?" Archer asks, fumbling with the last pumpkin.

Obviously, something is going on and Bobby has significance to both Quinn and Archer.

"Wes has him."

"Jackson," I call, taking his hand and leading him over to Quinn and Archer. "Is everything okay?" I ask Quinn.

"No, it's Archer's brother, Bobby. He's an addict, and Wes found him passed out in the park. He's been clean for the last few months." She lets out a sigh and shakes her head. "I guess he relapsed."

"Oh my God, I'm so sorry."

Quinn frowns, looking at Archer as he hurries to put the wagon away. "He'd been doing so well."

I swallow hard. That's something I know all about, and the disappointment crashes down on you hard.

"How long had he been clean?"

"A couple months, which is the longest ever." Quinn starts to take Emma out of her carrier. "Archer really thought it was for real this time."

"It's hard," I say with too much emotion. Quinn catches on and tips her head slightly, flicking her eyes to mine. "You said Wes has him...did you mean in jail?"

"No, and thank God it was my brother who responded to the call about a drunk in the park. He took him to a cafe that's like five minutes away and got him coffee instead of taking him to the station."

"Is he supposed to do that?"

"Probably not, but he knows how hard Bobby's been working...and how much this means to Archer."

I feel a tug on my heart, pulling it up from the dark pit I shoved it in, bringing it closer to the spot it's supposed to be in.

"Do you need to go get him?"

"Yeah. We can take you home first."

"No, you don't have to. You said he's only five minutes away, so we should go."

"Are you sure?"

I nod, words of truth bubbling inside of me. I know what it's like to have a family member be an addict, and I want to tell her that she and Archer are good fucking people. And Wes too, but dammit, his goodness is so bad for me.

"Yeah, and I can hold Emma for you if you need help."

"Thank you."

It's a tense ride to the diner, and when we get there, Jackson says he has to go potty. Emma is asleep in her car seat, and Quinn carries her in. Wes is sitting in the back, looking all gorgeous and heroic in his uniform.

"Daddy!" Jackson calls and runs to him. Wes gets up, face tight but smiling as soon as he sees his son. Jackson throws his arms around Wes's neck, and my ovaries explode.

Then I notice the guy who's sitting at the table with Wes. He looks like Archer but is dirty, tired, and worn. It's a look I know, one I used to see on my own mother's face.

Archer rushes forward, and Bobby stands, face falling. Tears well in his eyes.

"I'm sorry, Arch."

"It's okay," Archer tells him, pulling him into a hug. Quinn sets Emma's car seat on the table and puts her hand on Archer's back. Bobby breaks away and looks at Quinn and then Emma. His face falls, and he hefts back into the booth, covering his hands with his face.

"Hey, buddy," I say, dropping down to Jackson's level. "Do you still need to go potty?"

He does, and I take him into the bathroom. When we get back, Bobby is drinking coffee with Archer, and Quinn is talking to Wes near the door. Jackson goes to his dad, and Wes scoops him up. I slowly make my way over, giving them some space.

"Thank you, Wes," Quinn tells him.

"It's no problem." Wes pats Quinn's shoulder. "I'm glad I was the one who responded."

Quinn nods. "Me too. The last thing we need is for him to get arrested again."

I watch them and then look back at Archer. He's ordering food for Bobby, who is still very much drunk and overly emotional.

"Do you guys have this?" Wes asks his sister.

"Yeah. We'll order him some food and take him home. The

Joneses are out of town this week, and we thought Bobby would be okay on his own. We'll bring him home with us and look into rehab again."

"Can I get food too?" Jackson asks.

"Of course you can," Quinn tells him with a smile. "But you have to share your fries with me."

"No!" he laughs. "Order your own!"

"I will. But I'll still steal one of yours." She smiles, and Wes looks up at me. His navy eyes meet mine and, Lord have mercy, that man is fine. Out of the corner of my eye, I see Quinn look from Wes to me and back again. "Can you join us for lunch?" she asks him.

"Yeah, I'm not doing much else, and I eat lunch around now anyway."

"Can I show you my pumpkin?" Jackson asks Wes. "It's so big!"

"Sure, on our way out," Wes tells him, setting him down. Jackson takes my hand and pulls me over.

"Hungry?" Quinn asks, giving a guilty smile. "Sorry if this isn't how you imagined your day would go."

"It's fine," I assure her, though she's right. This isn't how I thought my day would go. I didn't think I'd see Wes and Quinn deal with a sensitive issue with nothing but concern and care.

Maybe there's hope for me after all.

I zip up my coat, feeling chilled despite the warm sun beating down on me. Maybe I shouldn't have ignored the fact that I woke up with a sore throat. But the day is over, and I'm looking forward to going home and having dinner with Jackson and Scarlet.

I call Quinn on the way and check on Bobby. He's at their house and has been sleeping it off for hours. I remember the first time Archer stayed with us while he and Dean roomed together in college because his brother got himself into trouble with drinking. They've been trying to help Bobby get clean for so long. It's starting to get hard to think he ever will.

Scarlet and Jackson are outside when I get home, and she's chasing him around like a zombie again. He fakes a fall, dramatically rolling through fallen leaves. Scarlet sees me first and stops dragging one foot with her arms out in front of her. She smiles, and I have to work hard at ignoring the rush that goes through me, making my cock jump.

Her hair is a mess and leaves are stuck to the back of her sweater. Knowing she was rolling around in the leaves with my son makes her all the more attractive, and after the dream I had about her last night, I'm going to have a hard time looking her in the eye.

"Hey," she calls, giving me a wave. Jackson gets up, smiling, and starts running again for Scarlet to chase him. "Your dad's home," she tells him, but he doesn't stop. "Jackson," she calls again, and this time he stops.

"Hi, Dad!" He gives me a quick wave and turns to Scarlet again. "Can we keep playing now?"

"Dinner's ready and waiting," she reminds him. "I know it's not Tuesday, but we're having tacos."

"Sounds good." I stop a few feet from Scarlet, and suddenly everything feels so fucking weird. We function like a couple but don't touch each other. She takes care of my son, and he's enamored with her. She's a little odd, but it's one of the many things I find so damn attractive about her.

And that kiss we shared her first weekend here...there's no denying we have chemistry.

"Have you heard from your sister?" Scarlet asks, brushing leaves out of Jackson's hair. "I was going to text her and see how things are going but didn't know if that would be overstepping."

"I don't think it would be, and yeah, I did. Things are going as well as they can, considering."

Scarlet nods. Her concern is genuine, and her friendship with my sister makes this even weirder. No one in my family liked Daisy much. They tolerated her for my sake, but she never even made an effort to hang out with Quinn.

"That's good, I guess. It's hard when you think someone is doing well and then things go right back to the beginning." She gets a distant look in her eyes, and I get a feeling she's speaking from experience. "And Wes..."

"Yeah?"

"What you did for him was really nice."

"Bobby's not a terrible person, and arresting him is hard on Quinn and Archer."

"You really care about your family. It's not something I see too often." A slight flush colors her cheeks. She pushes her hair back, finding leaves at the end of her long locks, and shakes her head. "We should get in and eat."

"Yeah," I agree. We all go into the house, and by the time I get changed and back down, the table is set, and Mexican music is playing from Scarlet's phone.

"We're having a fee-yes-ta," Jackson tells me, proud of himself for learning a new word. He takes my hand and leads me to the table. There are chips and salsa already out on the table, and Scarlet brings over two margaritas.

"They're virgin, obviously, since there's no tequila in the house."

"I have one too!" Jackson picks up his plastic up and wants to "do cheers" with everyone. Dinner is good, and Jackson tells me about his trip to the orchard. My sore throat gets worse, and by the time I get Jackson bathed and in bed, I have a bad headache.

"Not feeling well?" Scarlet asks when she sees me get a bottle of painkillers from a cabinet in the kitchen.

"I think I'm getting sick," I admit.

She sets her book down on the table and gets up, coming right over to me. She doesn't stop until her small frame is lined up with mine, and she presses the back of her hand to my forehead. "You have a fever."

"You don't know that."

Pursing her lips, she turns around and gets the thermometer and swipes it across my forehead. "See?" She flips it over to show me my temperature. "One hundred and one point seven. You are sick."

"I'll be fine in the morning."

"Hopefully. You should go to bed and try to rest."

I make a face. "I'll go to bed later. I want to watch TV for a while."

She raises her eyebrows. "You sound like a child."

"And do you go to bed at eight-thirty when you're sick?"

"Oh, of course. And I drink extra water and always make sure to take my vitamins."

"Don't give up your day job to pursue stand-up comedy."

She laughs. "But my witty sarcasm is everyone's cup of tea." She sets the thermometer down and goes back to her book. "Do you want to continue *American Horror Story*?"

"Sure," I say, and we go into the living room together. I make it through one episode before I start to feel worse, and as much as I want to stay on the couch and imagine taking things farther with Scarlet, I go up to bed.

I feel even worse when I wake up in the morning. Scarlet is already downstairs making Jackson breakfast.

"How are you feeling?" she asks, cutting up an apple.

"I've been better."

She trades the knife for the thermometer and takes my temp again. "Your temp went up. You should stay home."

"I'll take some Tylenol and my fever will go down. I'll be fine."

~

"Wes?"

The kitchen light turns on and I look up, blinking. Scarlet stands in the threshold, hand still on the light switch, eyes narrowed as they adjust to the dark.

"You okay?"

I pick up the pill bottle I dropped, head throbbing so bad it's hard to function. "A little shitty," I admit. I felt like shit when I came home from work, and the fever never went away. I don't get sick often, but when I do, it's usually bad.

And right now, I feel like I'm dying.

She crosses the kitchen, stopping in front of me and putting her hand on my cheek. "Jesus, you're burning up." She grabs the thermometer. "One-oh-three point four. That's really high, and you've had a fever for over twenty-four hours. Maybe you should go into the ER or something. You could be dehydrated."

"I don't need to go to the ER."

She takes the pill bottle from me, looking worried. "Trust me, I'm not one to suggest going to the hospital, like ever, since they rip you off on bills." She rolls her eyes. "It's bullshit, but having a high fever for this long isn't good for you."

"Are you worried about me?"

"Maybe."

She takes out two pills and hands them to me. I grab a glass and fill it with water.

"No need to worry." I try to smile, but the lights above me are making my headache worse. I'm not entirely sure I won't throw up. "I'm gonna go back to bed."

"I'm going to come check on you in twenty minutes," she says seriously, "and make sure your brain hasn't fried."

Bringing my hand to my forehead, I nod, wincing from the movement, before dragging my ass back up the stairs. I crash into bed, closing my eyes and praying for the Tylenol to bring down this damn fever and make the headache go away.

It doesn't.

I toss and turn, trying to get comfortable, which is hard to do since every bone in my body is aching now. Scarlet softly knocks on the door.

"Wes?" she whispers. "Are you awake?"

"Yeah." I sit up, squinting in the dark. I can see the glow of the thermometer in her hand as she draws near. She sits on the edge of the bed and brushes my hair back. Her touch is soft and gentle, instantly comforting me.

"You still feel warm."

"It's been twenty minutes already?" I mumble.

"Eighteen. I've been timing it."

My eyes fall shut, and I smile. "You really are worried, aren't you?"

"I am." She takes my temperature. "And I have good reason to be. Your fever went up."

"That's probably because I'm covered up."

She presses her lips into a thin line, not convinced. "You can get brain damage from high fevers."

"They have to be higher."

"Wes," she stresses, hand falling to my thigh. I've imagined her here, in my room...in my bed...touching me so many times before. But not like this. Still, having her here is nice. "It'd be one thing if you woke up with a really high fever and we waited it out. But this has been going on for over a day. You probably have the flu. People die from the flu. And you could give it to Jackson."

Dammit, she knows exactly what to say to make me bend.

"Fine. If I still have a fever in the morning, I'll go in to the doctor."

"Thanks." She brushes my hair back again. "Lay down. I'm bringing you a wet rag and some cold water."

"You don't have to," I tell her, though that sounds heavenly right now. "And I don't want you to get sick."

"I'm already exposed. Jackson too."

"He's probably the one who gave this to me," I say with a smile. Then my headache intensifies, and I squeeze my eyes shut, laying back down. Scarlet leaves, coming back a minute later. Ice clinks against the sides of the water glass, and she makes me get up and take a drink before gently pressing the wet rag to my forehead.

I don't remember the last time someone took care of me like this. Daisy was never very maternal—obviously—and while she cared and really did love me for a while there, so much of our time was spent fighting or ignoring each other that it's hard to remember the good times.

"Do you have another thermometer?" she asked, picking up the rag and flipping it to the cool side. "Because the forehead one won't work now."

"Yeah, there's one in Jackson's bathroom."

"It's not a rectal thermometer, is it?" she jokes.

"That's actually the kind I prefer."

She laughs and runs her fingers through my hair. I'm feeling a little out of it thanks to the fever. I'm not going to kiss her again because I'm sick, but I wouldn't be surprised if I confess what I'm feeling.

Because right now I know that I'm starting to fall for her.

*T*he bed frame creaks, and I startle awake. I sit up, goosebumps covering my arms, and blink in the dark.

"Wes?" I whisper, feeling the mattress shake beneath me. I didn't mean to fall asleep in Weston's bed. I'm on top of the covers and he's underneath, and we're on the opposite sides of this king bed.

The sheets rustle, and I see the outline of Weston's large body moving. Red hot fear pulses over me, and my heart immediately starts racing. I reach for Wes, hand landing on his shoulder.

"Scarlet?" he croaks, throat dry. "What's wrong?" He sits up too fast and winces. I squeeze my eyes shut, having a hard time blocking out the memory.

"I thought you were having a seizure." A chill rips through me, causing me to tremble.

"Why would you think that?"

The words want to come out, and the fear I had before of him judging me, of being looked at differently—as unworthy—is gone. "When my sister was little, she got really sick with a bad fever." I wrap my arms around myself, shivering harder. "Our mom was too drunk to care or take her to the doctor. Her fever got so high she started convulsing. It still scares me to this day."

It's hard to read Weston's expression in the dark. He feebly sits up and puts his hand on my arm.

"You're freezing."

"And you're still hot."

"Come here," he whispers, pulling back the blankets. My fingers shake as I move in, sticking my feet under the warm sheets. Wes wraps his arms around me, and his warmth goes right down to my very core. "That's why you're so worried."

"Yeah," I say in a small voice.

"I'm sorry."

"Why are you sorry?" My eyes flutter shut, and I put my hand on top of Weston's, apprehensively bringing it around me. He wiggles in a little closer while keeping a careful distance at the same time. If I scoot back a mere inch or two, my ass will press against his cock. My body craves it, but now's not the time. He's sick and needs to rest.

"If I would have known you were scared like that, I would have gone to the ER."

"Just to appease me?"

"Just to put your mind at ease."

I close my eyes before I run the risk of having them get glossy. "Thank you," I whisper so quietly I'm not sure he can hear me. "And be warned, if Jackson spikes a fever, I'll be even more paranoid."

"I will too," Wes agrees, tightening his grip on me. "That's one ER trip you won't have to pressure me to take."

"I should check your temperature again," I say but don't make a move to get up. "I don't even know what time it is. I didn't mean to fall asleep."

"It's three-thirty, and you need to sleep. There's a good chance you're already sick and it's just a matter of time before the symptoms hit you."

"I have a pretty strong immune system," I tell him. "That's one good thing that came out of having a drunk for a mother. She wasn't a good housekeeper, and I think it helped me build up a strong immunity."

"I don't know if you're joking or not," Wes admits.

"You know what? I don't either." I open my eyes, looking around the dark room. I can't see Wes, and even if I roll over and look him in the eyes, his expression will be hard to read. It doesn't make sense, but there's something safe about the dark. It hides the truth, and sometimes the truth hurts. "I say things like that with sarcasm and dark humor, but it's not really funny, is it?"

"Sometimes you laugh so you don't cry."

"I think that's what I've been doing my whole life."

"You don't have to anymore," he mumbles, lips brushing against the back of my neck as he talks. "At least not for tonight."

I roll over in his arms and brush his wavy hair back out of his face. His cheeks are warm, and his forehead is even hotter. If it really is three-thirty, then he should sit up and drink some more cold water and take another dosage of Tylenol.

But his arms are locked around me and he's drifted back to sleep. I bend my leg up, hooking my ankle over his calf, and run my fingers through his hair, lulling myself back to sleep.

"Daddy?"

My eyes wake up before my mind, and I can't make sense of the small figure standing before me for a good three seconds. I'm still in Weston's bed. His arm is still draped over me.

And Jackson is standing at the side, looking curiously at the both of us.

"Hey, buddy," I whisper. The sun hasn't fully risen yet, and I'm so tired. I want to go back to sleep. "What are you doing up so early?"

"I had a bad dream."

"Want me to tuck you back into bed?"

He shakes his head. "I want Daddy."

"Daddy's not feeling too well," I softly explain.

"Is that why you're in bed with him?"

It is one-hundred percent why I'm in bed with him, but I still cringe. "Yeah. I've been taking care of him."

"Is Daddy okay?"

"He will be."

Wes stirs behind me, and his hand slides along my side.

"Daddy?" Jackson asks, climbing onto the bed.

"Jackson," Wes murmurs, eyes fluttering open. "Shit," he says under his breath. Shit is right. We're in bed together, though I don't think Jackson is jumping to conclusions. He has no idea what being in bed together can imply.

"Can I watch videos on your phone?" Jackson asks.

"Yeah, this morning you can."

"Thanks, Daddy."

Wes feels around his nightstand for his phone, unlocks it, and gives it to Jackson, who takes it back into his room.

"Don't judge me."

"That's the last thing I'll do," I tell Wes. "You're sick. A little screen time isn't going to hurt anything." I sit up. "Do you want me to leave?"

"No." Wes blinks a few times, face tight. I can tell he doesn't feel well. I reach over and grab the thermometer to take his temp again.

"Still high."

"How high?"

"Hundred and two point eight."

"Dammit," he mumbles.

"I should probably take you to the doctor now." I grab the glass of water and hand it to him. He takes a drink and shakes his head.

"It's not open yet. Doctor, not ER, remember."

"Oh, right. Lay back down then."

"You too." He sets the water down and snakes his arm around me, pulling me back to him. We lay back down, and I rub his back until I fall asleep, not waking for another hour. I slip out of bed and into my room to change out of my PJs and into black leggings and an oversized gray sweater. Jackson fell back asleep, and I carefully take Wes's phone from his hands, turning it off as I walk back into Weston's room.

I gather up the damp rag and the water glass, take them downstairs, and then go back into my room to run a brush through my hair and brush my teeth. Going back into Wes's room, I slip under the covers with him, heart going a million miles an hour.

I'm worried about Wes. Whatever virus he has is hanging on strong with no signs of leaving. But I'm also feeling more for him than I have before. Realizing how scared I am of something bad happening to him, of him being really sick, makes it pretty much impossible to deny that I more than like him.

He's making me believe in love, and I think I'm falling for him.

∾

"THANKS FOR COMING OVER," I tell Owen, shutting the door behind him.

"No problem," Owen says, looking concerned. "Wes must be really sick to willingly go into the doctor."

"He's had a high fever for three days now."

"Oh, shit." Owen unzips his coat and steps out of his shoes. Jackson is finishing his breakfast and gets so excited when he sees his uncle he almost spills his milk.

"Hey, Jackson!" Owen calls. "Ready to have some fun?"

"Yeah!"

"I'm going to teach you all about cars and picking up women." Owen's face tightens when he sees Wes sitting at the table, hunched forward with his head in his hands.

"Thanks for getting up and coming over," Wes mumbles.

Owen pulls out the chair next to him and sits, looking at his oldest brother with worry. "Of course. And you look terrible."

"I still look better than you."

Owen laughs. "You wish. Take care of yourself, bro. And I get to have some fun with my favorite nephew. We don't spend enough one-on-one time together, do we, buddy? What do you want to do first?"

"Brush teeth after breakfast," I suggest, and Owen nods. I grab the keys to the Jeep and put on my coat and shoes. Wes moves slowly on his way to the car, and I keep looking over to check on him as we go to the clinic.

Wes rests his head on my shoulder as we wait, and when the nurse calls his name, I look at Weston.

"Do you want me to stay out here?"

"It doesn't matter to me," he says. I don't think much of anything matters to him right now. He's pretty damn sick. I loop my arm through his and walk with him into the examination room.

Not surprisingly, he's dehydrated, and the doctor wants to send him to the hospital for a bag of IV fluids and monitoring until his fever goes down. Wes doesn't even argue, which lets me know just how shitty he's feeling at this point.

"How far is the hospital?" I ask, unlocking the Jeep as we walk through the parking lot.

"About twenty minutes," he tells me, moving slow.

"Can you tell me how to get there or should I program it into the GPS?"

Wes gives me a look. "I'm sick, but I still know how to get to the hospital."

"Just making sure," I say with a smile and try to rush forward and open the car door for him, but he beats me to it. "Are you going to call Owen?"

"I'll text him. Hopefully this shit doesn't take long," he grumbles. "I'd be fine if I went home, you know."

I start the Jeep and shake my head. "Why must you perpetuate the stereotype and be so difficult? Though you're not complaining nearly as much as the average man."

"Being sick is too time-consuming."

"I totally agree. It's a huge inconvenience. But taking care of yourself—like going to the hospital—will speed up your recovery. Who knows? Maybe by tomorrow, you'll feel a lot better because you got treatment. And if you didn't…"

"I would have suffered miserably for weeks."

"There's that overdramatic attitude I was looking for." I take my eyes off the road to look over and see the small smile on his face. He's quiet the rest of the way to the hospital, and we end up waiting over half an hour before we're taken back into a room in the ER. Things drag again after that, and it's been over an hour before he's finally given an IV and meds.

"Thanks for coming," Wes says, looking into my eyes for a quick second before diverting his gaze to the floor. "You didn't have to."

"I know," I say softly, shifting my weight. I'm sitting in an uncomfortable chair next to the bed. "But I'm glad I did."

"Me too." He starts to reach for my hand but is stopped by his IV line. My heart skips a beat, and I get to my feet, words burning in my throat. Words that want to come out. Words I'm not entirely sure I know the meaning of.

"Scarlet," he starts and pushes himself up. My lips part and my heart pounds away in my chest, so loud I'm sure Wes can hear it.

"Weston," I say back with a smile, shuffling closer. I take his hand, and he links his fingers through mine. He circles his thumb along the soft flesh on the inside of my wrist. I bring my free hand forward, brushing his hair back behind his ear.

There's nothing romantic about this moment. We're standing in a crammed ER room while Wes gets IV fluids due to dehydration. And yet I've never felt something more intimate. Then again, I know nothing about love.

I bring my hand down and cup his face. Wes closes his eyes and leans his face into my palm. He tightens his grip on my hand, and I can feel his heart racing along with mine.

And then someone knocks on the door. I drop my hand that's on Weston's face but keep a hold of his hand.

"Hey." Archer pulls back the curtain, and Wes takes his hand out of mine. "I saw your name in the system. How are you feeling?"

"I've been better," Wes tells his almost brother-in-law.

"I'm surprised you didn't say 'fine,'" I tease.

"I didn't read your chart," Archer says. "What's going on?"

"He's had a high fever for three days and finally let me take him to the doctor this morning." I give Wes a telling look and then smile.

"There's a nasty virus going around," Archer tells us. "The ER has been busy." He pulls out the little rolling stool I've always been too afraid to sit on. What if the doctor came in and yelled at me? "Are you being admitted overnight?"

"No," Wes says. "And I won't stay even if they say I should. I'll be fine at home."

Archer and I give Wes the same dubious look.

"This virus is serious. It's put a few people in the ICU already. Take care of yourself so you can take care of Jackson," Archer tells Wes, using his *you better listen to me because I'm a doctor* tone. Wes just grumbles in response, and Archer tells him he'll check back later if we're still here. He's off to perform another surgery.

"Oh shit," Wes says after Archer leaves.

"What?"

"I didn't tell him not to tell Quinn."

"You think he will?"

Wes raises an eyebrow. "I know he will."

"That's not a bad thing. They're concerned about you because they care." *Like I do.*

"Once Quinn knows, she'll tell our mother."

"That's not a bad thing, either," I press. "It's nice the way you guys all look out for each other."

His eyes meet mine, and something passes between us, something unsaid, something I can't describe, but it's in that moment it's like he knows.

He knows I'd give anything to have a family like his.

"I know," he says softly. "It's really nice, and I shouldn't complain about it. I don't like people doting over me."

"Well, you're still a big, strong man even when you're lying here in the hospital, you know."

His eyes narrow into a playful glare, and then he sighs. "I know. It's more that I don't want to burden others."

"Taking care of people you care about isn't a burden. People like doing it, and it makes you feel good."

"Does it make you feel good?"

My mouth goes dry, and I forget how to breathe for a second. If his hand was still surrounding mine, there'd be no way to deny just how good this is making me feel.

"Yes," I whisper. "It does. Because I care about you." I swallow hard and inch closer to the bed. The moment is becoming too intense, and suddenly I'm hot and sweat breaks out along my hairline.

Someone else knocks on the door, and this time I'm thankful for the interruption. Because I'm feeling things I've never felt before, and I'm not sure what to do with all these fucking feelings. Moving back to the chair, I pull out my phone and text Corbin, asking for an update on Dad.

The nurse leaves, telling Wes to try and rest and she'll be back in half an hour to check on him.

"You don't have to stay," Wes says, looking tired.

"I'll probably wander around and see if I can find something to eat." He'll be more likely to fall asleep if I'm not in here. "Are you allowed to eat?"

"No one told me no."

"I'll bring you something." Standing, I fight back the urge to go to him, brush his hair back, and kiss his forehead.

"Hey," Wes says, catching my hand as I walk by. His fingers walk up my wrist, and a shiver runs down my spine. I inhale sharply, knees weakening. How can he affect me so much with just his fingers on my wrist?

"Yeah?"

"Thank you, Scarlet, for everything."

I put my free hand on top of his hand and close my eyes in a long blink. "Of course, Wes." I look into his eyes. "Get some rest so you get better. We still have Netflix to binge."

His lips curve into a small smile. "That's good motivation."

∿

I TAKE a drink of ice water, debating pouring it over my head while I sit in the middle of the hospital cafeteria. After practically running out of the room, I hid in an elevator with my back against the wall until my heart stopped pounding.

I don't know what is happening to me...even though I really do.

But I won't say it. I don't believe in love. My heart isn't capable of it.

My phone buzzes in my purse, pulling me out of the reverie I was in. It's Quinn, and I'm sure she's calling to check on Wes.

"Hello?"

"Hey, Scarlet. Are you with Wes?"

"Not currently. I went to the cafeteria to get some food."

"Oh, okay. How's he doing?"

"He's looking better."

"Thanks for taking him. Wes doesn't go to the doctor willingly."

I lean back and smile. "I noticed. Did you happen to call your mom and tell her Wes is sick?"

Quinn laughs. "I know better."

"Wes said she freaks out a little."

"That's an understatement." Emma starts crying in the background. "I gotta go, but thanks for looking out for my brother. Can you text me an update later?"

"Yeah, I will. Give Emma a hug for me."

"I will. Bye!"

I hang up and finish my food, then grab a drink and a snack to take up to Wes. He's asleep, so I quietly slip in and try to get comfortable in the chair next to the bed. The nurse comes in a few minutes later, looks him over but doesn't wake him, and then all is quiet again. I read a book on my phone and end up drifting off, not waking until the doctor comes back in to look Wes over.

His fever went down to a manageable level, and Wes can go home.

"You're still sick," the doctor tells him. "Rest the remainder of today and take it easy tomorrow."

"I will," Wes agrees, eager to get out of here. The doctor leaves, and a few minutes later a nurse comes in with discharge paperwork.

"Is your girlfriend driving you home?" the nurse asks, going over the standard questions.

I look at Wes, who hesitates but doesn't take the time to correct her. Maybe it's because he's too tired to bother, or maybe because he's pretending we're together too, like I am.

I grab Wes's coat, taking it to him once the nurse leaves.

"Thanks again," he tells me.

"You're welcome. You look better already."

I text Quinn as we're walking out, letting her know Wes is on the mend and is heading home. Logan is at the house along with Owen. They're both wearing jeans and gray T-shirts, making it hard to tell them apart.

Jackson has his play doctor kit out on the coffee table and immediately leads Weston to the couch for a check-up.

"Did you mean to dress alike?" I ask the twins, going right to the bathroom to wash the hospital germs off my hands.

Logan and Owen look at each other and then down at their own clothes.

"I didn't even realize it," Logan admits with a laugh. "It's a twin thing, I guess."

"That's funny and very interesting at the same time." I join everyone in the living room, sitting on the edge of the couch. Wes bends his legs up, giving me more space.

"Well," Owen says, giving his twin a look. Logan widens his eyes and ever so slightly shakes his head. "You're in good hands here. We gotta head out and get the bar ready for tonight."

"Thanks, guys," Wes says, sounding like he's about ready to fall asleep again.

"No problem." Logan gives Jackson a hug goodbye. "Take care of your dad, okay?"

"I will," Jackson promises.

"Thanks for looking out for Wes," Owen tells me quietly before they leave. Jackson cuddles up with Weston on the couch, and I slip upstairs for a quick shower. When I get out, I hear voices coming from downstairs. I pause by my bedroom door, recognizing Mrs. Dawson's voice. Towel drying my hair, I quickly get dressed and go downstairs.

Wes is still on the couch, looking tired and a little annoyed by his mother's presence. She's fussing over him, taking his temperature and removing the blanket Jackson had covered him with.

"Hi, Mrs. Dawson," I say.

"Scarlet, hi." She stands, setting a Tupperware bowl on the coffee table. She comes over and gives me a hug. "Thank you so much for making my stubborn son go to the doctor."

"You're welcome. I wanted him to go yesterday, but he swore he'd be better."

"I would have been," Wes counters, and I laugh. Mrs. Dawson looks from Wes to me and back again.

"I brought chicken noodle soup. Is anyone hungry? I can heat it up."

"I am, Grammy!" Jackson exclaims but makes no move to get up and away from the cartoons he's watching. Mrs. Dawson goes into the kitchen, and I move closer to Wes.

"Make her leave," he whispers.

"She's just worried."

Wes rolls his eyes. "I have the flu, not a rare jungle disease. I'll be fine, really." He sighs. "I'm tired."

My heart lurches in my chest, and I want nothing more than to crawl under the blanket with him, run my hands up and down his muscular arms until he falls asleep.

"I'll try to speed things up," I promise.

"Thanks."

Going into the kitchen, I plug in the coffee pot.

"Tired, honey?" Mrs. Dawson asks.

"Yes. I was worried about Wes and didn't sleep much through the night," I admit before I realize how that sounds. He's my boss.

Instead of looking shocked, Mrs. Dawson's face lights up. "I'm glad you're here for him."

"For Jackson?"

"For them both." She takes the lid off the Tupperware. "Weston's always been the strong, responsible one. The last few years haven't been easy on him, though he'll never admit it. It's nice seeing him happy again."

Is she saying what I think she's saying? "Well, I'm sure it's because he doesn't have to worry about Jackson's schedule as much anymore."

Mrs. Dawson gives me a wink. "Sure. That's all it is."

Yes, she is saying what I think she's saying. And dammit, I want it to be true. In fact, I've never wanted anything more in my whole life.

SCARLET

"You could take another day off," I tell Wes, looking up from Jackson's bed. I'm stripping the sheets and replacing them with new ones. Wes slept pretty much all day after we got home from the hospital and took it easy the next day. Now he's ready for a long day of work.

"I don't need to," he tells me, leaning against the door frame. "I don't have a fever anymore. And you and Jackson are fine, so the virus is gone."

"Don't you dare jinx us. Those things can lay dormant for days."

"If you get sick, I'll take care of you."

The elastic slips out of my fingers, and the fitted sheet pops off the mattress. Heat rushes through me, and my pussy quivers at the thought of him *taking care of me*. Yesterday, the three of us lounged around and watched movies for most of the day. It was more than just nice.

It was perfect.

Well, except how fucking horny Weston makes me. We get along. He makes me laugh. And I want him so bad I'm going to have to change my underwear the moment he leaves. My body craves him, making it physically hard to *not* touch him when we're near.

Just to see what will happen.

He kissed me once. I'm sure he'll do it again.

I kneel on the mattress, bending forward to stick the corner of the fitted sheet back on. My ass is in Weston's direct line of sight, and part of me hopes I'm driving him as wild as he drives me.

Because this is really un-fucking-fair.

"I'm sure you will," I say in a tight voice. "Though if I do get sick, it'll be your fault, for one, bringing home the virus, and two, having just jinxed me like a minute ago."

Wes laughs and steps in, grabbing the other end of the sheet. He helps me make the bed and gathers up the laundry Jackson left on the floor. He adds it to the laundry basket in the closet.

I could sit back and watch him clean all day.

"When will you be home?" I ask, crossing my arms tightly across my chest.

"Around nine."

"Okay. I'll keep a plate of dinner in the fridge for you."

"Thanks."

He's in uniform, looking hot with his hair pulled back. The color is back to his face, and he looks better. Though a proper inspection is probably a good idea. "Hot in Here" plays in my head again as I imagine him stripping naked in front of me. I'm getting so wound up and sexually frustrated. I need to stop.

"I'll see you tonight."

"Right," I say. "Tonight."

∼

"TIME FOR BED, BUDDY," I tell Jackson, eyeing the time.

"Aww man," he says, throwing his head back. "But we just got the farm all set up."

"I'll tell you what. Let's leave it out until morning and we can play again after breakfast."

"Okay!"

I get up and offer him a hand. He lets me pull him off the ground—and I mean literally pull him up—and we go into the bathroom to brush his teeth and go potty before bedtime. We read a dozen books, and I'm starting to drift off during the last one.

"Lights out," I yawn. Jackson starts to freak out the moment the light goes off. "What's going on?" I ask.

"The Tall Man might get me in the dark. Can you leave the light on?"

"The Tall Man isn't here. Are you scared of the dark tonight?"

He nods, and I flick the bedside lamp back on. "Hang on a second. I have something for you. Stay here."

I get to his door before he scrambles after me, following me into my room at the end of the hall.

"This is Ray," I say, taking my scruffy unicorn from my bed. "He was mine when I was a kid, and he kept me safe. He'll keep you safe too."

Jackson looks at the stuffed animal, not sure whether to believe me or not. A few seconds pass and he hugs Ray.

"Can you feel his protection powers?"

"I do!"

"Good." Taking his hand, I lead him back into his room and into bed. I shut off the lights and pull the blankets back up, gently tucking Jackson in. He cuddles the dingy yellow unicorn against his chest and closes his eyes for half a second before opening them again.

"Are you still here?" he asks, voice thin.

"Yes," I assure him. "I am."

"Can you sleep without Ray?" He eyes the unicorn, face tight. "You can have him if you need him."

"He's yours now," I say with a smile. "I think he'll have more fun hanging out in your room with your other toys than he did sitting alone on my bed."

Jackson nods. "And you're kind of old to have toys."

I laugh and lean forward, kissing his forehead. "I suppose I am. Try to get some sleep, buddy." Smoothing out his blankets, I get up to leave.

"Scarlet?" Jackson sits up right before I close the door.

"Yeah?"

He twists the frayed yarn that makes up Ray's mane through his fingers. "Will I always be scared of the dark?"

"No," I say with a shake of my head. I go back into his room and sit on the edge of his bed. "You won't be. I used to be scared of the dark, you know."

"You were?"

"Yeah. But I'm not anymore."

"How do you stop being scared of the dark?" His eyes meet mine, and something pulls on my heart. I look at him and see everything a child should be. Innocent. Playful. Pure. Kind-hearted and carefree. It's then I realize that I'll do anything to keep him that way, to make sure he lives the best life he can, the life he deserves to live.

It's then that I realize I love him.

"I don't really know," I start. My eyes flutter shut, and I think of my own life, of the darkness that grew around me, suffocating and deafening at the same time. The darkness that spread so deep within, it turned everything inside of me black, and the numbness took over, like poison ivy twisting on vines, wrapping around my head and eventually my heart.

I think of the numbness that was so vast and hollow it reverberated through my soul with an emptiness that hurt more than anything I've ever experienced. That isolated me and made me feel alone even when I was standing in a room full of people. That made me do bad things just so I'd feel anything other than nothing.

I open my eyes, and Jackson clicks on his flashlight. The tightness in my chest releases, and it's here, in this moment, I realize how I stopped being afraid of the dark.

"You stop being afraid of the dark when you learn how to make your own light."

Jackson tips his head. "Like my flashlight."

"Yes," I say, tears pricking the corners of my eyes. "Like your flashlight."

"Can I keep it on all night?"

"Of course. And I'll be just downstairs in the kitchen. I have dishes to wash. But if you need me, call for me and I'll be back here."

"Okay. I love you, Scarlet."

I smile, heart pounding inside my chest. "Love you, too, buddy."

*F*uck. Me. I'm in trouble.

It's Friday night, and while I'm still not at one hundred percent, I agreed to go out with everyone to Getaway tonight. And I mean everyone. Logan and Owen are there already, of course. Dean and Kara are going, as well as Quinn and Archer. Quinn invited Scarlet to hang out with her and her friend Jamie, and I can tell Scarlet's looking forward to it.

"Ready?" Scarlet asks, coming down the stairs as if she has no idea she looks like a temptress. Swallowing hard, I shift my weight to hide my hardening cock. It's going to be one hell of a night. She curled her hair and is wearing a simple, curve-hugging black dress and heels. My mind jumps ahead, and I imagine myself pushing her up against the wall. I can almost feel her legs around me as I inch the hem of her black dress up and over her ass.

Dammit. Now I have an erection.

"Just a second," I mumble and go into the kitchen, clenching the muscles in my thighs to try and get rid of this thing. I open the fridge, pretending to dig around for something to eat until my cock goes down.

"Are you seriously eating again?" Scarlet asks, voice coming from behind me.

"I'm always hungry."

She laughs. "We literally just ate."

And we did. I put the food away while Scarlet brushed her teeth upstairs. I waste some more time before grabbing an apple and closing the fridge. Feeling like a teenage boy at the risk of popping a boner just from looking at a hot girl, I grab my coat and hold it in front of me as we walk to my Jeep.

"It was nice of your parents to watch Jackson tonight," she comments.

"Yeah. I think my mom misses having him around even though it made it hard for her to do her job."

"I can see that. He's a great kid."

We get in, and we both reach for the radio at the same time. The slight feeling of Scarlet's skin against mine sends a jolt right to the tip of my cock. She took such good care of me when I was sick, balancing helping me out but not being overbearing. Every minute I'm around her puts me more and more at risk for spilling my guts. Or maybe I'll cut through all the verbal nonsense and kiss her.

Again.

But this time I won't stop.

~

"STRIKE OUT ALREADY?" I ask Logan, taking a drink of my beer.

"Not as bad as you," he fires back, pulling out a chair and joining me at the table. "Though we think you're holding out for your new nanny."

I shake my head, flicking my eyes to Scarlet. She's sitting at the bar with Quinn, Kara, and Jamie, sipping a vodka tonic and laughing at something Quinn just said. "She's Jackson's nanny. I'm not getting involved with her."

"I'll get involved with her," Owen says, coming up behind us. He's on his third—maybe fourth—beer already.

"No," I say a little too sternly. Dammit. "Besides…you seemed to be getting involved with the chick in the leopard skirt."

Owen grins. "Yeah, I am." He motions for Logan to follow him. "Her friend thinks I'm hot, which translates into thinking you're hot. Kind of. We might look alike, but I have the winning personality."

Logan brings his beer to his lips and doesn't say anything. Owen stands there, looking at Logan as if there's something seriously wrong with him. I lean back, always amused by these two.

"Nah, I'm staying here." Logan rests his arms on the table, taking another swig of beer.

"What the fuck?" Owen's eyes widen.

Logan shrugs. "I'm not feeling a one-night stand tonight." He flicks his eyes to mine, knowing I understand where he's coming from. With Dean married and Quinn engaged and planning her wedding, thoughts of settling down are hanging heavy above him too.

"Are you sick?" Owen sinks into the chair next to Logan. "Should I get Archer?"

Logan rolls his eyes. "Fuck you. Don't you want something more?"

"As long as I'm getting laid, I'm happy," Owen says, and I believe him. Sometimes I wish I could be as carefree as him, but having a kid changed all that. Jackson is my world, and I won't even think about bringing anyone new into our lives unless it's the real deal.

Logan shifts his gaze to the girls Owen was talking to. "Don't you want someone a little more...uh...cultured?"

"She's cultured, all right," Owen says and holds up his hand. "Pop-cultured. I bet she knows everything there is to know about the Kardashians."

"Go get em', tiger," Logan says, making a shooing gesture with his hands. Owen mumbles something incoherent and wanders off. Dean and Archer, who've been playing pool since we got here, come over and join us at the table.

"You're not out there on the prowl?" Dean asks Logan, grabbing his beer from the table and taking a swig.

"Nope. It's more fun sitting here giving Wes shit about his hot nanny. He says there's nothing going on between them."

"Her name is Scarlet, and there's nothing going on between us."

"Don't lie to us, man." Dean raises his eyebrows. "We've seen you two flirting and giving each other fuck-me eyes. You're sleeping with her, aren't you?"

"Nope."

"Why not? You two obviously want each other."

I shake my head. "Just because I want her doesn't mean I should go for it." Everyone looks at me like I'm crazy. With a sigh, I pick at the label on my beer. "What if things don't work out? I wouldn't just be losing a friend, I'd be losing a nanny, one Jackson really likes and one I actually trust."

"But what if they don't?" Archer says, and all eyes fall on him. "Trust me, I understand where you're coming from. I waited years to tell Quinn how I felt because I was afraid of what would happen when I finally did." He looks across the bar at her and smiles without meaning to. "I'll spare you the details since she's your sister, and you guys know how happy we are. But I do regret the time I lost every now and then." He looks back at me. "If you like her, tell her. At least you'll know one way or another."

"She's into you," Dean goes on. "I can tell. And she already lives with you and knows what a tyrant you can be."

"I'm not a tyrant," I say, and both my brothers give me dubious looks. "It's not the right time."

"Weston," Logan starts, and I know whatever he has to say is going to be seriously simply by the fact that he called me by my whole name. "You can date again. You can hook up again. You can have no-strings sex with anyone who wants to participate. And you should. Daisy is gone, and if she comes back, she's going to know she's not welcome."

I peel the label down the bottle and nod. "You're right."

"What?" Logan asks, blinking. "Did I hear you correctly?"

"Yeah," I say with a laugh. I look across the bar at Scarlet again, and my heart lurches in my chest. "You're right. Daisy is gone, and it's time to move on." I look my brother in the eye. "And this time, I want to."

"THAT WAS FUN," Scarlet says, looping her arm through mine. We're leaving the bar, and I think she's a little drunk. I swallow hard, soaking in the warmth of her skin. I'm carrying a take-out bag full of burgers and fries for us to eat once we get back to the house.

"It was," I agree, aware of the way my heart speeds up as soon as she's near. "I haven't gone out like that in a while."

"I know. Quinn told me. She's really talkative when she drinks."

I laugh. "She drank tonight?"

"She had one glass of wine and it was more than enough to make her loopy." Scarlet tightens her hold on my arm, having a bit of difficulty walking through the uneven gravel in her tall heels. "This was her first time going out and having a drink since before she got pregnant, but something tells me she's always a lightweight."

"She is, but Dean's worse. Don't tell him I told you."

Scarlet laughs, clinging to me after her ankle almost twists. We get to the Jeep and she lets go of my arm, walking around to the edge of the parking lot. It butts up to a cornfield, and a big half-moon hangs high above it. Stars dot the black sky, and the night is quiet.

"What are you looking at?" I ask her, setting the food down on the hood of my Jeep and unzipping my jacket. She has a black sweater over her dress but no coat. I take mine off and drape it around her shoulders.

"Thanks," she says quietly and pulls the coat tightly around herself. "And nothing."

"Nothing?"

"I'm looking at nothing. And I like it." She tips her head back and reaches for me. My heart pounds, and I think back to what was said in the bar. I like her—more than like her. I step forward and wrap her in my arms.

"I never thought I'd end up in a place like this," she says quietly. I'm behind her, with my arms wrapped tightly around her waist. She leans back against me.

"Like this?"

"Quiet. Safe. A place I'd like to call home."

"You can call it home," I say without thinking. "I mean, you're here for a job, I know, but once Jackson is too old for a nan—or if you want to leave or…or—"

"You're cute when you get flustered." She smiles as she turns around to look at me. "And maybe I will." She takes a few steps out in the dirt that leads to the cornfield and holds out her hands. "Look at this. I'm behind a bar and don't feel threatened for my life. Partly because you're with me."

"Was it really that bad where you lived in Chicago?"

She turns around and nods. "Yeah, but you learn how to deal. Don't go out at night alone…carry something that either is a weapon or looks like a weapon…avoid certain streets and places after dark." She shakes her head and puts on her mask again, pretending everything is okay. Looking up at the sky again, she becomes completely still for a moment. "I think I saw a shooting —wait, it's an airplane."

I laugh. "We do get a lot of flyover traffic to the Chicago airports."

She takes a few steps back, and I find myself moving toward her. My arms fold around her slender waist and my cock jumps. I turn my head to the side, fighting with myself. I want to kiss her and tell her how I feel…but she's more than a little tipsy.

I'll wait.

"The food is probably getting cold," she says, eyeing the bag. "And those fries smell amazing."

I unlock the Jeep and open the passenger door for her, then quickly go around and get in. Scarlet turns up the heat and plays with the radio as I drive us home, stopping on a classic rock station. "Living on a Prayer" is playing, and she looks at me with a smile before cranking the volume. We belt it out together, laughing and dancing in our seats. I don't realize it until a car comes up behind me, but I've slowed down, going less than half the speed limit on this country road.

Speeding up, I glance over at Scarlet, watching her move her seatbelt to the side so she can take off my coat. Her dress gets caught when she pulls it off, and the low-cut neckline of the dress moves to the side, exposing part of her lacy black bra. Fuck, she's gorgeous.

I clench my jaw and grip the steering wheel, keeping my eyes on the road the rest of the way home. Parking in front of the house, Scarlet and I walk up the sidewalk together. She stops a foot before the porch and looks up at the sky again.

"It's so beautiful, isn't it?"

"Is it making you believe in aliens?"

She laughs, and the way her face lights up is even more beautiful than the sky above us. "It's starting to convince me."

I pull my keys from my pocket to unlock the front door.

"Can we eat on the porch?" Scarlet asks. "So I can look for shooting stars?"

"I can do you one better."

~

"CAREFUL." I hold out my hand, planting my foot down on the shingles of the roof. Scarlet steps through the open window, gripping my hand tight.

"I'm not really scared of heights," she starts, holding onto the window frame. "But I'm afraid of falling from heights."

"I won't let you fall."

She looks me right in the eye. "You sure about that?"

"I'll catch you."

Her lips curve into a smile. "You better."

"You can trust me."

"I know."

She steps onto the roof, and I help her down a few feet. We're on top of the covered back porch, and while the roof still angles down a bit, it's level enough to sit. Once she's settled, I reach back inside and grab a blanket and the food. I take a seat close to Scarlet, draping the blanket around both of us.

Scarlet opens the take-out bag, and we eat together in a silence that's anything but awkward. Once we're done with our food, I gather up the wrappers and toss them along with our empty water bottles into the house through the open window.

"You know Jackson is going to come out here once he's older, right?" Scarlet says, resting her head on my shoulder.

"I'll nail the windows shut before then." I slip my arm around her.

She laughs. "I'd be out here every night if I were a kid."

"Just wait until winter."

"I can tough it out."

She could, and she would just to see the stars. "Have you been to the Alder Planetarium?" I ask.

She shakes her head. "I've always wanted to go, but I haven't been. I used to take my brother and sister to the Field Museum, though. It was within walking distance of our house. Well, a long walk. We'd make a day out of it. Then when my dad came back into the picture, he'd meet us there." She closes her eyes and rests her head on my shoulder. "I haven't been in a while. A long while. I haven't even thought about it but now I really miss it."

"Do you want to go? We can take Jackson and drive up next week."

She lifts her head up and looks at me. "Really?"

Her smile is making me smile. "Yeah. I haven't been since probably high school, and Jackson's never been. You could invite your dad and sister, if you want."

She stiffens, and the smile is gone from her face. "They...they won't be able to come."

"Shit, right. Your dad is sick. How's he doing?"

With furrowed brows, she turns to me. "I need to tell you something."

"*Y*ou can tell me anything," I say. Unable to help myself, I put my arms around her again. Scarlet tenses, and for a moment I think she's going to pull away from me. Then she relaxes in my arms, leaning back against me. Holding her is one of the best feelings in the world.

"My dad is sick, but it's not the kind of sick he'll get better from."

"I'm sorry."

"Don't be. He more or less did it to himself. Years of heavy drinking and getting into fights takes its toll on the body." She inhales, breath catching. I hold her closer, pressing my lips to the back of her neck. I can tell this is painful for her, and the confession is like pulling the bullet out of the wound. It hurt going in, and it'll hurt coming out, but once it's gone, the wound can begin to heal.

"He's in a nursing home, a really shitty one at that, but it's the best I can do. And my sister can't join us because she's in jail."

I blink but don't say anything. I was not expecting any of that. Waiting for her to go on, I run my fingers up and down her arm.

"Why is she in jail?"

"She got caught up with the wrong crowd." She shakes her head. "She's so desperate to fit in she went along with this stupid idea to rob a store and got caught. Her friend had a gun, and even though my sister didn't, she still got charged with armed robbery."

"Damn."

"My sister and my dad...they're not bad people, though. They've just...they've made bad choices. Hell, I've made bad choices."

"Haven't we all?"

She turns, eyes glossy. "You have no idea." Slowly, she twists in my arms and cups my face with her hands. "You're a good person, Weston. A good dad, a good brother, a good cop. I used to think people like you only existed in fairytales."

I rest my hands on the curve of her hips. "No one has ever compared me to a fairytale before."

"Well, they should have. You're everything I could have—"

I can't stop myself any longer. I pull Scarlet to me and kiss her. She melts against me, arms flying around my neck. Everything disappears in that moment, and it's like it's just us and the stars.

Scarlet's lips, soft and warm, press against mine with a passion that matches my own. I slide one hand down to the small of her back, feeling the heat of her skin. The blanket falls from her shoulders and she shivers, pressing herself closer to me. The desire I've been trying to ignore, trying to convince myself isn't there, comes rushing back, and my need to be inside her is the most intense thing I've ever felt.

"Scarlet," I say, breaking away and not having my lips on hers feels like I've dived underwater and have no air. "You were a little drunk when we left the bar. Are you sure you want to do this?"

"I was a little drunk then," she says, holding tightly to my shoulders. "But I'm not now. And yes, Wes, I want to do this. I've wanted to do this pretty much since the moment I saw you."

Her brazen confession turns me on even more. I kiss her again and forget we're on an angled roof. Scarlet pushes up with the intention of moving into my lap but slips and starts to fall. I grab her around the waist, pulling her against me.

"You did catch me," she whispers.

"I told you I would." I press my foot down on the roof and steady her. "Let's go in."

She nods and turns, reaching for the window frame. She gets in first, and I follow behind, tossing the blanket in behind us and closing the window. We're in my bedroom, and light from the hall spills in.

"Scarlet," I say again, heart still racing. Blood rushes through me, and every nerve in my body is alive. "Are you sure you—"

She doesn't give me a chance to get the rest of the question out. Her lips meet mine again, and it's all I can do not to throw her down onto the mattress. I kiss her hard, tongue pushing into her mouth, and run a hand through her hair, over her back, and down to her supple ass. Heat rushes through me, and the tip of my cock tingles with anticipation. She puts one of her hands on my chest, slowly raking her fingers down until they rest above the button of my jeans.

I pull back, needing to look at her, needing to make sure this is real. I've dreamed about this more times than I can count since the first time I saw her. Taking her chin in my hand, I tip her head up and kiss her, eyes falling shut. My tongue pushes into her mouth, and I slide my hands down her back.

Scarlet fastens her arms around me, standing on her toes to better kiss me. She presses herself against me, and her desperation is almost enough to undo me. *Almost.* It's been a long time since I've been with a woman.

I'm going to take my time with Scarlet. Make her feel, pleasuring her until she's screaming my name, writhing on the bed beneath me. I take a tangle of her hair in my hand, kissing her harder.

"Are you ready, Scarlet?" I pant, barely taking my lips off hers. My cock pulses, begging to be inside of her. "Are you ready for me to fuck you?"

I f my arms weren't wrapped around Weston's neck, my weakened knees might have given out. He's standing before me, with one hand wrapped in my hair and the other planted on the base of my back, fingers inching down my ass. His legs are slightly spread, hips close to mine.

I open my mouth to tell him I've been ready for him to fuck me, but no words come out. I'm breathless before him, excited and intimidated all at the same time. Tingles are running rampant through my body, and I'm as hot as I am cold from the chilly night air.

He steps forward, closing the distance between us. His hard cock presses against me, and holy shit, that thing is big. I shouldn't be surprised since he towers over me. Every aspect of Weston is big, and his cock is no exception. I bring my hand down, fingers trembling, and feel its length through his pants. Wes grunts, pushing himself forward. It will be a tight fit inside of me, and the thought of having him push that big dick all the way in makes a shiver run down my spine.

"Do you want this?" he says, voice low.

"Yes." The word escapes my lips in a single breath. Wes brings his head back down to kiss me again. The desperation is here again, and I can't get enough of him fast enough. But this time is different. This time we're not going to stop. We're going to go all the way, and Lord help me, I want it.

I want him.

I've never wanted anything more in my life.

Desire for him swells inside of me, growing hotter and hotter. It'll only take a spark to start this fire, and I know we're going to burn hot and bright together. You can tell a lot about a person from the way they kiss, and I knew the first time Weston kissed me that he's the kind of man who takes his damn time.

I push up against him, lips crashing against his. His fingers press into my ass and a guttural growl comes from deep inside his throat, vibrating against my lips. I moan, growing wetter by the second.

There's no going back after tonight. We can't ignore this kiss like we did last time. We're in too deep, feeling too much. Wes picks me up as if I weigh nothing and strides forward, pressing my back against the wall. His cock is so hard beneath me, fighting against his jeans. I slide my hand up the back of his head, running my fingers through his hair, and buck my hips against his.

I'm so wound up and turned on, but it's more than that. The connection is emotional as well as physical, and my heart is yearning for his to beat along with mine just as much as my clit begs to be touched. I don't want to think about it and risk ruining the moment, though something tells me nothing could ruin this moment. Zombies could be scratching at the door and I wouldn't be fazed. Not when this monster cock is rubbing over my clit, nearly bringing me to come right here and now.

He grinds himself against me, and my dress bunches up around my ass. I'm so wet that if he reaches down, he'll be able to feel it through my panties. Taking his lips off mine, he kisses my neck, sucking at my skin in a way that drives me crazy. Pleasure shoots through me, going right to my pussy. It pulses, needing to be touched. I rub myself against him again, needing to come before I explode.

"Wes," I pant, letting my head fall to the side. I don't know how he's standing so steady, supporting all my weight nonetheless. His hands are under my ass, fingers digging into my skin.

As suddenly as he picked me up, Wes puts me back on my feet. For a split second my heart stops, thinking he's having second thoughts and is going to pull away, taking his body away from mine. It would be as painful as sucking all the oxygen out of the air, which is basically what he does to me anyway.

He takes it all away and the only way to breathe is to put my mouth on his and inhale him all in. I swallow hard, pulse bounding, and stare at him. My lips are parted, and I've never felt so empowered and so helpless at the same time. This beast of a man is standing in front of me. I'm so small compared to him, yet I know he's as much of a slave to the desire to lose ourselves in each other as I am.

Suddenly, he drops to his knees, pushing my dress up to my stomach. I lean back against the wall, gasping. My breasts rise and fall rapidly, and I look down, watching him slowly slide a hand up my leg.

He starts at the inside of my knee, touching my soft flesh with only his fingertips. I shiver from his touch, and every single nerve in my body is humming with pleasure. My eyes flutter shut, and I surrender to him.

I'm usually the one who stays in power, who always has to be on top. But not tonight. Weston won't allow it even if I tried, and being with a man who's as gentle and caring as he is domineering and demanding is throwing me for a loop, and it feels so fucking good.

Slowly, he slides his hand up the back of my thigh, pushing his fingers up inch by inch until they're right below my entrance. I'm burning hot for him and don't know how much of this teasing I can handle before I bring my foot up, push it against his chest, and force him back so I can climb on top.

No one has ever made me this wound up before, and I'm entirely sure it's because no one has ever made me feel this much outside of the bedroom before. Wes has done something to me, damn him. He didn't mean to, didn't set out to get under my skin and into my heart.

But he did, and now I want him in every way possible.

He pushes his hand up to my ass and brings me to his face. I'm trembling with anticipation, almost nervous to take things to the next step with him. I've been with my fair share of lovers, but no one compares to Weston. He's uncharted territory, and the thrill of setting sail in unfamiliar waters is shadowed only a bit by the fear of not being enough for him.

I want to offer him everything. I want to give him all of me.

"Ohhh," I moan when his lips gently brush over my stomach. He kisses me softly, and my entire body hums in rhythm to him. He moves closer, parting my legs, and I reach out, grabbing the edge of his dresser to steady myself.

And then he moves in, slipping his hand up under my panties and pushing them to my side. There's no easing into it. No warning. His tongue lashes out against my clit and my mouth falls open, but I'm unable to make a sound.

He licks and sucks, speeding up and slowing down, going at me hard and soft and he's paying attention to my reaction the entire time, taking note of what I like better, and then he does it again. And again. And again.

I feel the orgasm coiling tight inside of me, and he brings his free hand up, nails dragging over the flesh of my ass and pushes a finger inside of me. He rubs against my inner walls, finding my g-spot. He pushes against it, holding the pressure there for a moment before releasing. *Holy shit.* I press my head against the wall behind me. This feels so fucking good.

He does it again, moving his fingers in more of a circular motion. It's a different stimulation, one that sends another wave of pleasure through me. Part of me thinks it's going to all come crashing down soon, and I'll be left with female blue-balls. Because this build-up is too good. And things that are too good to be true usually are.

"Ohhh my god," I moan, and everything inside of me becomes alive. Weston sucks my clit, while at the same time he flicks his tongue against it. He continues to finger-fuck me, rubbing my g-spot with two fingers. If my eyes were open, they'd roll back in my head.

My mouth is hanging open, and I grip tighter onto the dresser, feeling my knees threaten to buckle. If I fall, he'll stop, and having him take his mouth off my pussy would be a sin right now.

I need to come.

He knows it, and as soon as I'm close, he pulls back.

"Wes," I growl, trying to find my voice. I reach down with my free hand and take a tangle of his hair, keeping his head against me. "Weston Dawson," I say, forcing my eyes open. "If you stop—"

"What?" He looks up with so much lust in his eyes I could drown. "What will you do if I stop?"

Holy fuck, this man. I arch my back, pushing my pussy forward and in his face.

"If you stop, I'll be forced to finish myself while you watch, and then I won't let you lay a finger on me."

Wes inhales and dives back in with an open mouth. He licks and sucks with fury, and only a minute later I'm hardly able to hold myself up. The orgasm rolls through me, slow at first and then crashing in with fury. It floods every part of me, making my toes curl and my ears ring. I come so hard wetness spills from me.

"Holy shit," he pants, wiping his face.

"Should I be sorry?" I pant as stars dot my vision.

"Hell no. You are so fucking sexy, Scarlet."

I rapidly blink, still floating on ecstasy. I pitch forward, hands landing on Weston's broad shoulders. He stands, scooping me up. I'm like a rag doll in his hands. He brings me to the bed, gently laying me down. He moves on top of me, parting my legs and moving between.

I'm still fully dressed, with damp thighs and wet panties. He brushes my messy hair back, kissing me so that I taste myself on his lips. I feebly reach for the hem of his shirt, trying to pull it up over his head. It's a moot point; I'm not fully functional yet. My pussy is still spasming from the intense orgasm he just gave me, and we're not even close to being done.

"Weston," I breathe, so quiet I'm not sure if he can hear me.

"Scarlet," he whispers back, holding himself over me. I swallow hard and bite my lip.

Reaching down, I undo the button on his jeans, freeing his massive cock. The sheer size of that thing is hardly contained by his boxers, and it feels so fucking good in my hand. I push his pants and boxers down enough to free his cock. I let my eyes fall shut, waiting until my heart stops racing to sit up. I plant my hands on Weston's muscular chest and give him a shove. He's so big and so solid he doesn't move.

Instead, he takes my hands, moves them aside, and flips me over onto my stomach. With a slap to my ass, he gathers the hem of my dress in one hand and slips the other under the band of my panties. I arch my back, making it easy for him to pull them off me.

"Sit up," he grunts, and I obey without question. Licking his lips, he eyes me up and down. I push onto my knees, looking at his cock in all its massive glory. Precum wets the tip, spilling down the thick shaft.

Weston grabs the hem of my dress and pulls it over my head. He groans with want when he sees me. He inches closer, running a hand up and over my breasts. The dress I was wearing required a pushup bra, and I'm looking all cleavagey right now, with my tits pushed up and together. He brings his head in to my breasts, kissing his way up along my collarbone. With deft fingers, he unhooks my bra.

I hold the cups against me, slowly letting the straps fall down one at a time. Weston waits, licking his lips with anticipation. I smile coyly, watching his face as I let my bra fall to the mattress. He sweeps his hands over me, thumbs circling my nipples.

"You're beautiful," he says and moves back to me, kissing me with fervor. I'm on my knees, naked before this man, but I'm anything but shy. I push him back, wanting to level the playing field. He needs to be naked too.

Biting my lip, I inch forward, hands going to his pants. I pull them the rest of the way down, after struggling to get them over his ass, Wes gets impatient and yanks them off.

"Your shirt," I say, leaning back a bit. "Take it off."

Wes looks me right in the eye and gives me a devilish smile before pulling his shirt over his head.

I want him to go down on me again, make me come so hard the entire world falls off its axis again. But there's another thing I want more than coming so hard nothing else matters.

Him.

I want to feel him push inside me. I want to join together, even briefly, and exist as one. It's fucking lame, I know, but dammit, I'm craving him like a starving man craves food.

"I need you," I whisper, body coming alive at the thought of that big, muscular man lying down on top of me. "Now."

"You're sure?" he asks, and having him make sure I'm good with this is such a turn on.

"I've never been more sure of anything in my whole life."

He lets out a growl and moves on top of me, spreading my legs as wide as they'll go and lining his cock up to my entrance. He pauses, kissing me first, and then pushes that big cock inside of me.

He fills every single inch, and I cry out with pleasure as he pulls out only to push back in. I bend my knees, hooking a leg around him. He rocks his hips, thrusting in and out slowly at first and then speeding up his movements. He's doing everything he can not to come right now, and I'm getting closer and closer to coming again myself. My eyes are shut, and my head is to the side. I have one hand on Westin's ass, feeling him drive that big dick in and out of me.

The other hand is gripping the sheets beneath us. Because I've never felt anything this intense in my whole life. I'm not just having amazing sex with Weston. We have a connection, and being together like this only furthers that.

I squeeze the leg that's wrapped around him, bringing myself up against him. Wes moans, head falling forward. He buries it in my neck, teeth nipping at my skin. Then he pushes in balls deep, biting at my neck as he comes. Feeling his cock pulse inside of me pushes me over the edge, and I dig my nails into his skin as I climax again.

Weston holds himself in me for a moment and then moves back, holding himself above me just enough to look into my eyes.

Brushing my hair back, he kisses me softly and pulls out, lying down on the mattress next to me.

We're more than aware of the mess we've made, but neither of us cares. Weston pulls me into his arms, spooning his body against mine. We stay like that for a moment, neither of us wanting to move. But I have to pee, so I force myself up and hurry to the bathroom. I clean myself up and dash back to bed. Wes pulled the covers down, and I climb in next to him.

Moonlight spills in through the window, illuminating Weston's face. I sit up, sheet falling off my shoulder, and gently brush his hair back. My heart is still hammering away in my chest, breasts rising and falling. I've never felt so much with anyone before.

I've never let myself.

I've been afraid, though laying here next to Wes, I don't know what I was afraid of.

"Tired?" I ask him, snuggling back down against his muscular chest.

"Not really." He folds me up in his arms, and it's like I'm where I'm supposed to be. Where I'm meant to be. Soon enough, the effects of the intense orgasms he just gave me will wear off and the gravity of the situation will hit me.

Whether or not I'll survive impact is still up in the air.

But I do know I *want* to survive it. Even though I've stayed in the same place for so long, I've spent my whole life running. Trying to escape what was right in front of me, and it's not until this very moment that I realize I was running in circles.

"Are you?" His lips brush against the back of my neck as he talks.

"No, but I don't plan on getting up any time soon." I roll over and hook my leg over his. He sweeps his hand across my waist, splaying his fingers over the small of my back. I push one arm under his pillow, pulling myself closer to him. He kisses my forehead, and I close my eyes, relishing his warmth.

"We should have done this the first time I kissed you," Wes says softly.

"We're quite good at it," I say, nuzzling my head against him. "We could have been doing it the whole time. But that's okay because we get to keep doing it now." I don't realize what I'm saying until it's said. I'm implying we're taking thing to the next level, that we're in a relationship more than boss and employee now.

He's my boyfriend.

Previously, the thought would have made me go running for the hills without a look back. But now…now things are different. Wes is different.

He made me different.

Or maybe…maybe he brought out exactly who I always was. Who I was always meant to me. He showed me that there's nothing to fear, that surrendering to someone isn't scary. It's exhilarating. It's freeing.

That admitting I'm happier with him doesn't make me weak. It makes me stronger, and having my heart beat right along his is the thing I was missing my whole life. He makes me want to be a better person and leave the past behind me. He even makes me think it's possible to move on and start over.

Simply put, he makes me happy. Nothing will bring me down from the high I'm on right now.

"Scarlet, we need to talk."

27

SCARLET

he way he says my name makes my heart skip a beat, but not in a good way. I tense and sit up, suddenly cold now that I'm away from his body heat. He swallows hard, doesn't look me in the eye, and pushes himself up on the mattress. Moving his pillow behind him, he leans against the headboard.

"You regret sleeping with me?" I blurt.

"Fuck no." He shakes his head and reaches for me. I tense, heart hammering away and feeling like I might throw up. I open my heart to a man for all of half a night and he's already dropping the *we need to talk* line.

What is wrong with me? Why did I think things would be different with Wes? I've been burned by love so many times in the past, starting with my own mother. Love isn't real, and I need to pull away now before I die in a sea of flames.

"Scarlet," he says again and takes a hold of my waist. He's stronger than me and he knows it, but I'll be damned before I let him get the best of me.

"I can just go if you want me to." I pull away and start to get out of bed.

"What?" he rushes up, moving toward me. "No. I don't want you to leave. Please."

I stop, turning around and looking at the man before me. He's so big, so muscular and strong. And yet he looks so vulnerable right now. Letting out a shaky breath, I inch closer. "I'm no good at this, Wes," I admit. "I usually avoid my feelings and try not to let myself get attached to anyone or anything. It's hard for me to trust people, and you're freaking me out."

"I know," he says, snaking his arms around me again. I should protest, but dammit, it feels so good to have his body against mine. I cave and let him pull me close, and I snuggle up with my head on his chest. "That's why I need to tell you something."

"Okay." I run my hand up his side, bracing myself.

"Maybe I should have told you before I slept with you."

I sit up, eyes wide. "You're not helping your case."

He nods and closes his eyes in a long blink. "I'm still married," he says and waits, expecting the bomb to go off.

"Oh. That's it?"

His eyebrows go up. "You're not mad?"

I shake my head. "I already knew that."

"You did?"

"Quinn told me at the bar tonight."

His brow furrows. "Oh, well that's good I guess."

I smile. "So does that solve our issue?"

He doesn't look at me. "It feels unfair to you to start something when I haven't ended things with Daisy."

"Do you want to end things?" I ask carefully, afraid of his answer. My heart is on the line here, and one word can change everything. I inhale and brace myself for the worst. That he doesn't want to end things. Daisy is Jackson's mother, after all.

"I wanted to end things before she left," Weston admits, and his words throw me.

"Really?"

He nods and looks away. "We were together for a long time. Being with her was easy because it was familiar. But that didn't mean we were meant for each other, and we kept waiting for things to get better. Obviously, you know how that turned out. So, yeah...I want to end things."

"Why haven't you?"

"I didn't see the point. If I dated again at all, it wouldn't be for a long time. I can't do that to Jackson...bring someone into our lives and risk them leaving."

"But didn't you want to date?"

"Of course I did. And I do. But Jackson comes first." He flicks his eyes to me, and my heart skips a beat. I look at this beautiful man before me, realizing now more than ever that he's everything I never knew I wanted. I used to think my dream man had to be a rich alpha asshole, but now I know how wrong I was.

My dream man is kind and caring, fiercely protecting those he loves. He's willing to put his own happiness on hold for the sake of another. He's brave and stands up for the right thing. My dream man values his family, doesn't get caught up in petty drama and...and is sitting right next to me.

"How long has she been gone?"

"She left when Jackson was almost two months old."

"Oh, wow. I mean, I'm sorry. Can I call her an idiot? Because she is to leave both Jackson and you."

Wes smiles, and the tension leaves his face. "Yeah, you can call her an idiot."

"I'm not sure how the laws work in Indiana, but I know some places have abandonment of marriage rules or whatever they're called so you can get a divorce without her signature."

"I know. I've thought about it but never saw the point. But now..."

My heart flutters, and he takes me in his arms again. "Now?"

"Now I want to." He holds me tight against his chest and brings one hand up, combing his fingers through my hair. "I didn't think I'd find someone who'd fit."

"Fit?"

"Into our family," he says quietly. "Someone who I want to be with and someone who's good with Jackson."

I blink rapidly, keeping tears at bay. I'm not a crier. Damn you, Weston.

"You think I fit?" I ask, each word coming out a little stronger than the last.

"Yes," he says.

I close my eyes and lose my battle with the tears. One slips out, cascading down my cheek and landing on Weston's chest.

"Scarlet?" He tips my head up to him. "Did I say something wrong?"

"The opposite of wrong."

He hugs me tight and presses his lips to mine. Another tear falls, and he wipes it away with his thumb as he cups my face. I inhale deep, trying to calm myself down. This is everything I wanted and now that it's happening, I'm already panicking about it coming crashing down around me.

"If it's too much pressure to date someone with a kid, I understand," Wes starts.

I stop fighting my tears and kiss him. To anyone else, maybe this isn't a big deal. It's not like a marriage proposal or anything, but to me, this means so much.

He looks at me and sees something more than the girl from the ghetto.

"So," he goes on, kissing me once more. "I'm going to talk to a lawyer. Tomorrow."

I can't stop smiling. "I think that's a good thing."

He rolls over, pinning me between his large body and the mattress. Heat rushes through me and my pussy contracts. I can still feel him in between my legs, as I'm sure I will in the morning. I curl my legs up around him. His cock jumps and knowing I'm turning him on just from my slight touch makes me horny all over again.

I buck my hips, rubbing myself against him. The tip of his semi-hard cock rubs my clit, and I let out a moan. I do it again, feeling his cock get hard as I use him like a sex toy. Wes takes hold of his cock and rubs it against me, not stopping until I'm squirming against him, mouth falling open as I come.

I'm still riding high, unable to form a coherent thought or even lift my head off the mattress. Wes doesn't wait, doesn't give me time to come down from the high. He moves to the edge of the bed, grabs my ankles, and pulls me toward him in one swift movement.

He stands before me, eyes full of hunger as he looks me over.

I'm still panting, breasts rising and falling rapidly. Wes leans forward, precum pooling on the tip of his cock, and slips his arms around me. I think he's going to pull me to him and kiss me, but instead, he flips me over and grabs my ass, bringing his cock to it.

Breathing hard, I push myself up, looking behind me at this beast of a man. He has one hand on his cock, face set, and slips his free hand down between my thighs, spreading my wetness along my opening. His finger sweeps over my clit, sending another jolt through me.

Guiding his cock to me, he slowly pushes into my pussy. Taking a hold of my hips, he thrusts in hard, pulling back until only the tip remains. He pauses, leaving me waiting with bated breath to feel him fill me, every single inch of me, again. Pushing in slow, he teases me, and it hurts so good.

And then he lets loose, fucking me hard and fast. My eyes flutter shut, moaning loudly as I'm overcome with pleasure. Wes's breathing quickens, and I know he's close to coming. His fingers press into the flesh on my hips and he pitches forward, hitting me at a new angle. He slides one hand down my hip, going between my legs. He moves his fingers in circles over my sensitive clit, and my god that man is good with his hands. He's balls deep inside of me, moments away from coming, and he's reacting to me as if he can read my mind and knows exactly how to touch me.

My muscles tense, and I feel the orgasm building inside me. My mouth falls open, but no sound comes out. My breath hitches, and the orgasm rolls over me, coming in waves. The first feels amazing. The second knocks me senseless. I collapse down onto the mattress, pussy spasming tightly around Wes's cock, wetness spilling onto the sheets beneath us.

Wes pulls out, hand going to his cock, pumping his dick as I fall back onto the mattress. He dives on top of me, falling between my legs, and kisses me as he enters me again. I can hardly kiss him back, and I'm not even going to attempt lifting my arms to wrap around his neck. I know I can't.

Stars dot my vision, and my ears ring. Wes buries his head against my neck, pumping in and out of me faster and faster until he lets out a guttural growl as he comes. He lowers himself to the mattress, panting.

"That was incredible," I breathe, blinking open my eyes.

"I am incredible." He smirks and rolls over, getting out of bed to grab a towel from the bathroom. I clean myself up and snuggle up with him. "Not to ruin the mood," he starts. "But we didn't use protection."

"I don't have anything," I tell him. "And I'm assuming you don't, either."

"Right. But I don't want you to get pregnant."

"It's a fat chance. But we should probably use protection or pull out just to be safe."

"I can do that."

I could easily fall asleep right now, but I don't want to miss a minute with Wes.

∾

I WAKE up to the smell of coffee and bacon wafting up the stairs. I'm still naked in Weston's bed. My heart is still soaring as I get up, use the bathroom, and put on a robe. I brush my teeth, twist my hair into a messy bun, and go downstairs.

Wes is standing at the oven, flipping pancakes. He's wearing just a pair of boxers, and seeing that muscular man making breakfast does me in and I'm ready for round three.

"Good morning," I say, smiling as I step into the kitchen.

Wes looks away from the stove. "Morning. Are you hungry?"

"Starving. You wore me out last night."

He smirks. "I plan to wear you out again if you're up for it."

I drop my eye to his crotch. "I'm sure you'll be."

"Don't tease me. The bacon might burn."

Laughing, I cross the kitchen and go to him, wrapping my arms around his waist. Wes turns down the burner and twists in my arms, taking a hold of me. He picks me up and sets me on the counter.

I rake my fingers through his messy hair, pressing my forehead to his. He steps in, fingers inching down my spine.

"Bacon," I whisper, knowing if we start kissing, we won't be able to stop. "Is breakfast almost ready?"

"Yeah." He doesn't step away, and the bacon on the cast iron skillet starts to sizzle and pop. It takes a joint effort to separate from each other. Wes goes back to the stove, and I get out plates and fill two glasses with orange juice, sitting at the table and admiring him cooking.

He serves the food on the plates and brings them over to the table. We eat a few bites in silence, just enjoying each other's company.

"So," I start, picking up my glass of orange juice. "Now what?"

"We keep eating?" Wes says, cocking an eyebrow.

"I plan to, but I meant with us." I look down at my plate, suddenly feeling a little shy.

"Last night wasn't a one-time thing for me," he says with no hesitation. "I meant what I said. You fit with us, and I really like you, Scarlet. I want more."

"Me too." I look up and smile, resisting the urge to reach across the table and take his hand. I refuse to be one of those couples. "This means we get to change our Facebook statuses, right?"

He laughs. "I don't have a Facebook account. Shocking, right?"

"I got rid of mine." I wrinkle my nose. "My life isn't that interesting." That part is true, but another reason I took myself off social media was because I didn't want to be easily found. Being unrecognized comes in handy when you're conning people.

"But I do like the idea of being able to show off my hot new girlfriend." Wes wiggles his eyebrows. "We'll have to get T-shirts instead."

"Ohhh, I do like obnoxious couples' T-shirts. I'm going to get you at least a dozen T-shirts that say *Property of Scarlet Cooper*."

He chuckles. "If being your property means we get to do what we did last night again, then I'm okay with it."

"I can be a very selfish lover," I warn. "I expect you to pleasure me at least once a day and always be enthusiastic about it."

"I don't think I'll have a problem with that. In fact," he says and stands, chair scooting out fast behind him. "I'll pleasure you right now."

"Here?" I ask, trying to keep the school-girl-in-love smile off my face. "At the table?"

He grabs my chair and turns me around. Tingles make their way through my body. Wes leans forward, eyes full of lust and hunger. "Yes, Scarlet," he growls. "I'm going to fuck you right here on the table."

And, Lord have mercy, he does.

~

"Hey, Mom." Wes sits up, pulling the blankets down with him. After breakfast, sex, and a shower, we got back into bed and passed out. "Yeah, I just woke up." He pauses. "No, I'm not sick again. Just tired from working night shifts all week."

I'm half asleep and don't want to move, but I'm cold. I wiggle closer to Wes, and he lays back down, wrapping his arm around me.

"I'll get dressed and come get him. Is that Quinn in the background I hear? Tell her we'll be over." He looks at me with a smile. "And that I'm considering letting Jackson take one of the kittens."

I sit up, eyes flying open, and nod encouragingly. The only pet I had growing up was the raccoon who lived under our stoop for a few weeks. I named him Ringo—original, I know—and fed him scraps. He started waiting for me at dusk, and it still makes me sad to think back to the evening I went outside to feed him and he never came.

"Yeah, you too," Wes says and ends the call. He puts his phone on the nightstand and pulls me on top of him. We're both naked, and his cock starts getting hard against my stomach.

"Again?" I ask, raising my eyebrows. "I'm gonna go back on my multiple-times thing and add in spacing it out."

Wes laughs and kisses my neck.

"Well, maybe I can make an exception."

"Should I be sorry?" His hands wander over my body. "You're beautiful…and it's been a long time since I've been with anyone."

I push up so I can look him in the eyes. "You haven't slept with anyone since your wife left?"

He shakes his head. "I'm still married…technically, I mean. But it felt wrong. Like I was cheating."

I push his hair back. "You're a good man, Weston Dawson. And she's been gone for four years. It's not cheating at this point."

"It doesn't feel like it. I don't feel like I'm married," he tells me. "But legally we still are."

"Is she still on your insurance and everything?"

"No. I took her off the first time she left me. She did take a car that was in both our names."

"What about the house?" I ask, not sure if I'm overstepping. He's my boyfriend now, I suppose I should know some of this stuff.

"It's in my name. I bought it before we were married."

"That's good." I brush his hair back. "Do we have to go get Jackson?"

"Yeah, we should. It's ten-thirty. I didn't realize how late it was."

"Ten-thirty is late?"

He laughs. "For me it is. We should—dammit."

"What?"

He rolls off and grabs his phone. "I want to talk to Mr. Williams. He's in his office sometimes on Saturday."

"Is he the lawyer?"

"Yeah."

"You go. I'll get Jackson. You said Quinn was there? I wouldn't mind hanging out with her a bit."

Wes smiles, blue eyes sparkling. "I like that you two are friends."

"Me too."

It takes us a few minutes to untangle, and the moment we do, I miss him. "So...I'm guessing I shouldn't give Quinn the gritty details of my night."

Wes laughs. "I don't think she'd appreciate it. And now I kinda get why Dean acts like such a baby about Quinn and Archer." He shakes his head and gets out of bed. I admire his muscular ass for a moment before reaching over the bed for Wes's T-shirt I'd been wearing. "But if you're asking if I want to keep our relationship secret or anything...no."

"What about Jackson?" I ask quietly, getting back into bed. I'm cold already. "Do we tell him?"

Wes shakes his head. "Honestly, I'm not sure how to go about that. There are guidelines and rules, but most of them have already been met since you already live here, and I know you get along." He shakes his head.

"Do kids his age understand dating? He knows what it means to be married, well, kind of."

"If I told him you were my girlfriend, he'd know it was important. He doesn't really seem to get that Quinn and Archer aren't married yet since they live together." Wes shakes his head. "Sorry I don't have a better answer."

"Don't be sorry. It makes me feel a little better for being clueless. In the movies, they always do things slow. Date for a while, make sure things are getting serious before the kid even meets whoever is dating their mom or dad. But like you said, Jackson already knows me."

Wes pulls on boxers, and I'm disappointed to see that gorgeous ass covered up. "As much as I like to have a plan and know what I'm doing, I think we should wing it." He turns, smile on his face. "We kind of already function like a couple."

"Yeah, we do." I smile right back.

Wes dives back onto the bed, snaking his arms around me, tickling me and making me laugh. He presses his lips to mine. "But now I get to do this whenever I want."

28

$\mathcal{S}$carlet and Jackson are back at the house by the time I'm done talking with Mr. Williams. I'm not officially divorced yet, but the process has started. And it feels so fucking good.

My heart lurches in my chest, and I can't stop smiling when I step onto the porch carrying a pizza. Jackson's sitting on Scarlet's lap on the couch, and she's reading him a book. His eyes are heavy, and he looks like he'll fall asleep at any minute. They haven't noticed me yet, and I stop to watch them through the window for another few seconds.

Jackson rests his head against Scarlet's shoulder, and she brings her hand up, running her fingers through his hair. His eyes start to flutter closed, making me almost feel bad for coming into the house and waking him up. It's impossible to sneak in and out with our current alarm system, which is why I have it set up the way I do.

I unlock the front door and step in. Scarlet smiles the moment she sees me, and Jackson is more excited about the pizza. I set it on the coffee table and tell Jackson to go wash his hands before we dig in. The second he runs into the bathroom, I pull Scarlet into my arms.

Feeling her body against mine sends a rush through me, and I can't kiss her fast enough. She hooks her arms around my neck and leans in, lips parting. I bring my head down, lips crashing against hers. Once I start, I can't stop. My cock jumps, and I want to carry her upstairs, stripping her out of her clothes and burying my cock inside of her.

"I take it things went well with the lawyer?" Scarlet asks. Her arms are still around me and my hands are still firmly planted on her waist. Jackson will be out of the bathroom at any second, but even one more second with my lips on Scarlet's is worth it.

"Yes," I growl and go in for another kiss, which isn't the smartest idea because I'm starting to get a hard-on, and now I'm thinking of how good it feels to make love to her. As if she can read my mind, she brings one hand down, sweeping it over my chest, and cups my balls.

"Jackson is pretty tired. He was up late at your parents' last night. I think an early bedtime would actually do him some good."

"It'll do me good too." I push my pelvis against her hand and she closes her eyes, moaning. "You're killing me, Scarlet."

"That's all part of my master plan."

"Oh, is it now?"

"Mh-hm."

I raise an eyebrow. "What happened to me being too big to chop up and bury?"

"Now that it's getting colder out, I'll wrap you in a tarp and keep you in the shed."

"I'd rot and would start to smell in a few days. It's not cold enough yet."

"Dammit." She shakes her head. "I forgot you were a cop and know how these things work. So tell me, Officer, what's the perfect murder?"

I laugh, but before I can get any words out, Jackson calls for help.

"What's wrong, buddy?" I ask.

"I had to go potty, and I missed."

Scarlet slides her other hand down my chest. "Good thing you're home."

"Fine. I'll clean up the pee."

"You're a good dad." She gives me a smile and steps away, going into the kitchen to get plates and drinks while I clean up the floor as well as Jackson, who requires new underwear, pants, and socks.

Finally, we gather in the living room, eating pizza while watching a movie. When we're done eating, Scarlet scoots closer to me on the couch, and I drape my arm around her. Jackson gets a blanket and sits close to Scarlet, leaning against her. Scarlet helps him fix the blanket, draping it over both their legs.

"Are you comfortable?" I ask Scarlet, aware of how uncomfortable it can be when Jackson decides to use you as his personal pillow. Though at the same time, having him close like that is the best thing in the world. There really is nothing like snuggling up with your child.

"Yeah," she says, turning her head to look at me. I sneak in a quick kiss, pressing my lips to hers. She puts her hand on top of mine and leans back against me. Sitting here with Scarlet and Jackson is such a simple thing, yet it means so much. We just admitted our feelings last night, finally hooking up after weeks of ignoring the spark. It's not like we're going out and getting married tomorrow, but I know I want her to be part of this family.

~

"Every time the weather turns, I question why I live in the Midwest." Scarlet zips up her coat. We just got to my parents' for Sunday dinner, and freezing rain is falling down on us. "And it's not even winter yet."

"I used to want to move out west. Though spending years in the desert kind of changed my mind. I like snow."

Scarlet makes a face. "Not me. It's too cold."

"Come sledding with us this winter and maybe I can change your mind."

She opens the back door to the Jeep, getting Jackson out of his car seat. She puts his coat on before he's even out of the car, zipping him up and making him wear his hood.

"We're walking fifty feet from the driveway to the house," I tease. "We're not going to die of hypothermia in that time."

"You never know." She snaps the top button on Jackson's coat and takes his hand. She's so good with him, and he's so responsive with her. Seeing them together makes me so fucking happy, and I can't stop smiling right now.

I let out a snort of laughter when I see the magnet on the back of Owen's truck that reads *Big Truck, Small Penis*.

"What's so funny?" Scarlet asks.

"Owen and Logan must be at it again," I tell Scarlet, pointing to the magnet. "They put ridiculous and usually vulgar magnets on each other's cars and see how long it takes before the other notices."

She laughs. "That's actually hilarious. I wonder how long that's been on."

"No clue. A few months ago, Logan drove around with a big smiley-face magnet that said, 'I have herpes' for four days before he noticed."

"Can we get a magnet like that for your car, Daddy?" Jackson asks, and his innocence pulls on my heart.

"Sure," I tell him. "Something similar but not the exact same."

"Yay!"

We hurry into the garage, shaking off the slushy rain from our coats before stepping in and being bombarded by my mom's dogs. Logan and Owen are in the kitchen at the big island counter, eating chips and salsa. Meat for tacos is simmering on the stove, and tequila and margarita mix sit out on the counter next to the fridge.

"Hey," Logan says, and Jackson rushes over, getting excited to see his uncles. He flicks his eyes to Scarlet and then me in question, and I know he's thinking about what we discussed back at the bar Friday night.

"Hi, Logan," Scarlet says, pointing to him. "And Owen. I got it right this time, didn't I?"

Logan nods. "Right, but it's not hard. I'm much better looking than he is."

Scarlet laughs and takes off her shoes and coat. "You dress alike, and even your mannerisms are the same."

Jackson slides out of Owen's lap, wanting to show him the farm set-up he worked on while he was here yesterday. Logan starts to get up to follow them, but I stop him.

"Does he know Charlie is engaged?" I ask in a hushed voice.

"Charlie's engaged?" Logan's eyebrows go up. Fuck. Owen doesn't know.

Scarlet takes a seat next to Logan and pulls the bag of chips over. "Who's Charlie?"

"Owen's ex who he's not over," Logan tells her. "He won't admit it, but we all know he still has feelings for her."

"Poor guy." Scarlet shakes her head.

"How'd you find out she's engaged? Last I heard she was living in New York," Logan says.

"I met with her dad today," I tell him, and he puts two-and-two together right away.

"Are you free?" His lips curve into a smile. "Can I pour a round to celebrate?"

"What are we celebrating?" Mom asks, coming into the kitchen carrying an armload of Mason jars. "Oh, hello, Scarlet. It's so good to see you again."

"It's nice to see you too. Need any help?"

"No, but thank you. I'm canning tomorrow and just brought these up from the basement." Mom puts everything in the sink. "Is there really a celebration? I'll drink to it if there is."

"You'll drink to anything," Logan quips.

Mom nods. "That is true. I do enjoy wine, though tonight I'm having a marg to go with my taco."

"Don't call it a marg, Mom." Logan shakes his head.

"Why not?"

Logan laughs. "Just don't. And Wes said he talked to a lawyer today. So I'm assuming that means…"

"I petitioned for a divorce," I finish, feeling a huge sense of relief as soon as the words come out of my mouth. "Given the circumstances, how long Daisy has been gone, and the fact that she hasn't provided any sort of support for our son, Mr. Williams thinks he can have things handled fairly quickly and I'll be granted full custody of Jackson."

Mom gasps and claps her hands together. "I have been praying for this!" She pulls me into a hug.

"You know how weird it sounds to admit you've been praying for me to get divorced?"

Mom laughs, giving me one more squeeze. "Oh, stop it. I want you to be happy."

"I am, Mom. I am."

The garage door opens, sending the dogs running in a frenzy. Quinn and Archer make their way in, trying to make it to the kitchen table without being tripped by the dogs. Archer sets Emma's car seat on the table, folding back the blanket she's covered with. Somehow she stayed asleep through all the noise.

"Hey, guys," Quinn says and notices Mom's watery eyes. "What's wrong?"

"Nothing," I assure her. "Mom's being overly emotional."

"Shocker, right?" Logan laughs.

"About what?" Quinn goes right for the tequila and unscrews the lid.

"I finally filed for a divorce," I say.

Quinn reacts just like our mother, running over to hug me. "Yes! Can you make her take her maiden name back too? I don't even want her to be a Dawson anymore."

"Having your name be Daisy Dawson forever is almost a punishment," Logan says.

"It's pretty awful," Archer agrees. "Sounds like a cheap porn star." He yawns, and I notice he looks dead on his feet.

"Long day at work?" I ask.

"I had a nine-hour surgery and then spent forty-five minutes arguing with a patient's insurance company." He shakes his head. "I don't know if want to punch someone or take a nap."

"Have a drink first," Quinn says, going back to the margarita. "Then take a nap."

"Why are you here?" Logan asks, grabbing another chip. "I'd be passed the fuck out if I did anything for nine straight hours."

"I'm hungry," Archer says, and we laugh. "And it's nice coming here and being together. It means a lot to Quinn."

"You're so whipped," Logan teases.

"I don't mind it. Not one bit." Archer watches Quinn mix him a drink. Gaining my approval to date my baby sister isn't easy. But Archer's a good guy, and I know he really cares about her.

"I think it's sweet," Scarlet says with a smile. "And it is nice that you all get together like this."

"I love it." Quinn pours way too much tequila into the drink, making Logan wince. "I missed it when I lived in Chicago." She mixes up the drink and pours it into a glass. "Anyone else want one?"

"Let me take over, sis." Logan gets up, patting Quinn on the shoulder and takes the margarita from her hand. He smells it and shakes his head. "Are you trying to get Archer drunk?"

"Kind of. Then I'll ask for another cat." She flashes Archer a smile. "Kidding. Eight is enough."

"More than enough."

"Actually," I start, sure I'm going to regret this. "If you still want to get rid of one...Jackson keeps asking."

"You guys need a pet," Mom says, taking Emma out of her car seat. "But dogs are much friendlier."

"Cats are easier," I counter. "I'm not home enough for a dog."

"But Scarlet is," Mom goes on.

Scarlet wrinkles her nose. "I'm more of a cat person."

"I knew there was a reason I liked you." Quinn beams, going over to the chips and salsa. Dad, who was grilling corn on the covered patio, comes in. He's a die-hard griller and will stand out there in the middle of winter.

Owen and Jackson come back to the kitchen, ready to eat. Dean and Kara aren't here yet, and we all try to convince Mom to let us go ahead and eat without them. Right when we've just about got her to cave, we see Dean's car pull into the driveway.

"I need to update Jackson's forms at school," I start, turning to Logan. "I'm putting you as an emergency contact after Scarlet. I had Quinn on there, but now it's easier for you to get over to the school than it would be for her with Emma."

Logan nods. "Okay."

"I can be an emergency contact," Owen offers, and I make a face. He'd do a good job looking after Jackson, I know, but it's fun hassling him.

"You're the last person I'd put on the list," I tell him. "Quinn is first, and then Logan, then Dean, then Quinn's cats, and then you."

"You're so fucking hilarious," Owen says dryly.

"Finally! We're starving," Quinn says dramatically when Dean and Kara step into the house.

"Sorry." Dean unzips his coat. "We couldn't leave with the dishwasher going." He rolls his eyes. Kara shakes her head, clenching her jaw. I can tell they were fighting, and I don't think the dishwasher was the only issue.

"It might leak," Kara says through gritted teeth. "Like it did before."

"I fixed it," Dean spits.

"Hey!" Quinn blurts, trying to be the peacekeeper. "Wes has good news!"

"Yeah, I do." I put my arm around Scarlet. I look into her beautiful blue eyes and smile. "I filed for divorce, and Scarlet and I are dating."

I've never felt more welcome, more at home, than I do with the Dawsons. Everyone was thrilled when Wes told them we were dating. I think I smiled the entire time we ate, the whole way home, and while I straightened up the house when Wes put Jackson to bed.

"I have to work in the morning," Wes reminds me when I get into bed next to him.

"I know. You're leaving at seven, right?"

"Yeah. And then I have some campaign shit to do." He turns off the bedside light and takes me in his arms. "I want to stay home with you."

"I'd like that too." I curl a leg up around him.

"Is it presumptuous to open that box of condoms now?" he asks with a cheeky grin.

"No. Not at all."

He kisses my neck and moves on top of me. "So, we had sex," he starts.

"We did? When?"

"Just now. You didn't feel it?"

"Ohhh, that's what that was." I laugh, and he nibbles at my neck.

"What I mean is, we had sex without protection. I know you

said you don't think you can get pregnant, but…well…are you sure?"

"Yes. If you knock me up, it would be a miracle."

"What do you mean?"

I let out a breath. "I don't think I can have kids." As soon as I say it out loud, I wish I could take it back. What if Wes wants another kid? Is that a deal-breaker? Thinking of him not wanting to be with me is like a stake through the heart.

"Why do you think that?"

"The last time I saw my OB, she said I only have one functioning ovary and my cycles are extremely random. Like I only have a few periods a year."

"Oh." Wes's face is unreadable. He's thinking, but I can't tell what he's thinking about. "I'm glad an unplanned pregnancy isn't likely, but, uh, sorry? I don't know what to say."

"I don't either. But I really like how honest you are." A twinge of guilt hits me. I'm honest with him now, and I plan to be from here on out. But I wasn't, and thinking back to the woman I was when I stepped out of the car, remembering the disappointment I felt when I realized he wasn't some rich asshole I could charm money out of…it makes me hate myself.

"Does that change how you feel about me?"

"No, of course not."

"Good." I let my eyes fall shut and realize how fast my heart is beating. "Do you want more kids?"

"I don't know. I used to. Coming from a big family, I thought I'd want that too. But things didn't work out as I expected, and I'm happy. Now more so than before. What about you?"

"I think I've always wanted kids," I admit, not letting myself stop and think. "But I didn't want to raise them in the same situation I was in when I grew up."

"You've never mentioned your mom," he says carefully. "Is she out of the picture?"

"Yes. She's dead."

"Oh, fuck. I'm sorry."

"I'm not." I'm speaking my truths. Why stop now? "It sounds terrible, I know. But she was a terrible mother who had me young and should have given me up for adoption and gotten her tubes tied. She died of an overdose, and I'm the one who found her. The worst part wasn't her dying. It was having to tell my sister and brother." My eyes fill with tears, and all the emotions I've denied myself of feeling over the years come rushing back. "I dropped out of school to take care of them." Hot tears roll down my cheeks. "I wasn't able to go back to school until our dad came back." I break off, choking up.

"It's okay," Wes soothes, gently wiping away my tears.

"But it's not. You're such a good person, Wes. I'm not. I've done so many things I wish I could take back. My life sucked but that's no excuse. I could have done better. I should have. You need to know this if you want to be with me. That's who I am. Scarlet Cooper: South Side trash with a dead mother, a sister in jail, and a father who poisoned his own brain with drugs and alcohol."

"That doesn't define you."

"But that's the thing." More tears spill from my eyes. "Nothing defines me. I...I don't know who I am."

"You're Scarlet Cooper," he says slowly, looking right into my eyes. "A little quirky and a lot amazing. You like shifter romance and classic rock. A certain four year old who I happen to think is the coolest kid in the world really likes you."

I smile.

"And I do too."

"I've done bad things, Wes." My jaw quivers and I want to tell him the truth as much as I don't. I want to start fresh, confess everything.

Because I'm in love with Wes Dawson.

"It's okay," he says like he believes it. "It's in the past."

"But I still did them."

His brows pinch together. "We live by going forward, not backward." He wipes away a tear.

I sniffle, turning my head to the side to mop up my messy face. This is only part of the reason why I hate crying. "I wish I could see myself the way you see me."

"You'd see how incredible you are."

"Weston," I start, ready to tell him everything. But he cuts me off with a kiss, and I give in, surrendering myself to him.

∼

"WHAT'S YOUR EXCUSE THIS TIME?" Heather asks before she even sits down at the table. I haven't seen her in a while, and I feel bad about it. But I'm here now, right? The last few weeks have passed in a whirlwind. A wonderful whirlwind, but they've been crazy nonetheless.

The closer we got to the election, the busier Wes was, and he's barely been home this week. Logan and Owen came over to pass out candy yesterday so I could take Jackson trick-or-treating. Wes made it home in time to do the last two blocks with him, and we pigged out on candy as soon as we got back to the house.

"Things have been busy at home."

"You call it home now?" Heather's sporting a fresh cut on her lip and has more bruises on her cheek and arms.

"What the hell is this?" I reach forward and push up the sleeve of her shirt.

"Nothing." She smirks. "You should see the other guy."

"This isn't funny, Heather. I want you out of here." I close my eyes and let out a breath. There's no point in arguing with her. I don't know what it's like to be in her shoes. My knowledge of how prison is run is limited to what I've seen on *Orange is the New Black*.

"Home?" she questions again.

"It feels like home," I admit. And it does. Everything I own is there. It's filled with people I care a lot about. I'm sleeping in Wes's room every night, even when he's working nights.

"You look different." Heather eyes me up and down.

"How?" I ask, looking around the visitation room. That one annoying woman isn't here, thankfully. She listened in on my conversations with my sister and just gave off a bad vibe.

"You're not wearing black, for one."

I look down at my wine-colored sweater. "I don't always wear black."

"Nine times out of ten, you do." Heather shrugs. "But it works for you."

"It's the color of my soul. What can I say?"

"Sure. Keep telling yourself that, sis." She shakes her head. "It's almost like you're glowing. You had sex, didn't you?"

"Maybe."

"With your boss?"

"He's my boyfriend now." A smile takes over my face.

"Seriously?"

"Yeah." I lean back, heart swelling in my chest. "He's...he's amazing."

"You're so in love with him."

"He's a good guy."

"Who you *love*," Heather presses.

"I care a lot about him."

"Oh my God, Scar, just say it."

"I don't want to jinx anything," I admit. "Because I'm happy. Things are finally going right in my life, and I'm terrified they're going to crash and burn. That tends to happen to me, you know."

"Because you're usually the one causing the crash. And then pouring gasoline on the fire. I love the shit out of you, big sis, but you're a bit self-destructive at times."

"I know," I admit with a sigh. "I'd rather end things on my terms...do whatever I can to stay in control." Shaking my head, I lean back. "Is it crazy to think things can work out for me?"

"No, not at all." She puts her hand on mine. "You deserve to be happy, Scar. I've had a lot of time to think in here—shocking, I know—and I realized how much you gave up for us. You dropped out of school, and you fucking loved school. You were such a nerd."

"Yeah," I say with a smile. "I was. I still am."

"And everything you did to take care of Mom and me and Jason...it was a lot to put on you. No one asked you to do any of that. You just did it. And then you did it again when Dad got sick."

"It had to be done."

"Yeah, and you never once complained. You've always taken care of us. Now someone is taking care of you. And I don't mean just financially."

I wiggle my eyebrows. "You mean sexually?"

Heather laughs. "That's not what I meant, but it's good to know he's adequate in all aspects."

"Very adequate." My heart skips a beat, and warmth floods through my veins at the thought of Wes.

"I want you to be happy. You deserve it, Scar, so much."

"Thanks. I...I don't feel like I do," I admit. "I've been thinking a lot too, and I want to do better. Wes makes me want to be a better person."

"And you say you don't love him."

"I didn't say that I didn't love him."

An inmate a few tables over stands up, yelling at her baby daddy. Heather and I turn, distracted by the drama.

"That's Jasmine," Heather whispers. "She's not sure if he's really her baby's father or not. It might be his cousin."

"Damn. And you say jail time is boring. It's like a real-life soap opera."

"Oh, I could write a sitcom with all the shit I've seen and heard. Half of which no one would even believe. Like the chick a few cells down from me." Heather shakes her head. "She had a cell phone up her snatch for over a week."

"Ew. And ouch. But mostly...how?"

Heather slowly shakes her head. "No clue. But can you imagine the smell? And rumor has it, it was an iPhone."

I shudder. "I have all sorts of questions, but I don't think I even want to know."

"I've learned not asking is the way to go."

I lean back in the uncomfortable chair. "I talked to Jason yesterday."

Heather's eye light up. "How is he? Is he coming home anytime soon?"

"He said he's doing good, and he sounded like it. I think he's a little homesick and he's hoping to be able to come home in January."

"If he does, please bring him to see me! I miss that little twerp."

"I don't think he's a twerp anymore."

Heather laughs, wiping her eyes. Unlike me, she's emotional. Cries during commercials and during certain songs no matter how many times she's heard them.

"And I will."

"What else did he say?"

A few more visitors shuffle in and the room gets louder. I fill Heather in on everything Jason told me, which isn't much.

"I should get going," I tell Heather, feeling bad. "It's a long drive back to Eastwood." I go to stand, and Heather reaches forward, taking my necklace between her fingers.

"You're wearing a cat charm?"

"Oh, yeah. I almost forgot. It's a joke."

"A joke?"

"Wes's sister, Quinn, is kind of a crazy cat lady, and their mom is very much a dog person. Their house is more divided than Bears and Packers fans living under the same roof."

"So you've sided with Team Cat."

"I do like cats."

Heather laughs and stands with me, giving me a hug before I leave. I spot that one annoying eavesdropper on my way out. I wouldn't think much of it, but she won't stop looking at me. I put on my coat and glance her way.

She's not just staring at me. She's glaring, seething with hatred.

"You're officially a heartbreaker, Weston." Scarlet turns away from the stove, setting down a wooden spoon. I just got home from work and the house smells amazing.

"How so?" I ask, amused. I take off my shoes. "And what is that?"

"Spiced cider. We can add rum to ours if you want."

"That sounds good." It's a cold and windy day, and I spent the last hour and a half of my shift outside in it, dealing with a car accident. No one was seriously hurt, but both people involved had flaring tempers, which made everything take twice as long. I unzip my coat, longing to feel Scarlet's warm body pressed against me. "How am I a heartbreaker?"

Scarlet strides over and wraps her arms around my neck. I slip a cold hand under her shirt, making her shriek and squirm away. I hold her tighter, laughing.

"Your hands are like ice!"

"It's cold out."

"Don't you have gloves to wear?"

"Yeah, but I didn't wear them."

"Obviously," she laughs. "And Mrs. Hills stopped me when I

picked up Jackson from school today. She was very upset to learn you were off the market."

"How did that even come up?" I slide my hands to Scarlet's ass. She's wearing leggings, and I don't think she has panties on underneath. I bring my head down, lips going to her neck.

"My dress blew up in the wind and she saw my *Wes Dawson's tight end* panties."

I laugh. "That's what I figured happened." I kiss her neck, and Scarlet arches her back, pressing herself against me.

"Really, she said she saw us at the diner last week and we seemed close."

I step in, widening my legs. "Well, we are." We kiss, and just seconds later Jackson comes down the stairs. He runs over for a hug, and I scoop him up, pulling Scarlet to me with my other arm.

Things are so fucking perfect.

"Is dinner ready?" Jackson asks.

"Let me check it." Scarlet gets a pot pie from the oven. "It's done. It needs to sit for like five minutes to cool first." She taps her chin, looking at Jackson. "I wonder what we could do in that time? Oh no. I think the zombies are back!"

Jackson wiggles out of my arms and takes off, laughing and screaming as he starts to run around the house. Scarlet and I both chase after him, and we run around the house for more than five minutes.

I go upstairs to change while Scarlet cuts into the pot pie and has Jackson help set the table. We function so well together. I don't want to get ahead of myself, but I'm already thinking about the future.

Never in a million years did I think I'd want to get married again, but my mind has drifted to proposing to Scarlet. I want us to be a family.

"What are you guys looking at?" I ask, coming down the stairs. Scarlet and Jackson are peering out of the blinds in the living room with the lights off.

"That white car has been by twice," Scarlet says. "And Jackson told me it was stopped in front of the house earlier."

"Really?" I go right to the front door, not bothering with socks.

"Wes, wait!" Scarlet springs up and comes after me, telling Jackson to stay in the house. "Shouldn't you go back and get your gun before you go up to a creepy car?" She grabs my arm.

The car goes from *park* to *drive* and moves down the street. People do stop along the side of the road sometimes, whether to text or mess with something in their car. But if Scarlet has seen this car before, and they left as soon as we stepped onto the porch, something is up.

"That's weird, isn't it?" Scarlet says, and I wrap my arm around her, keeping her warm. I watch the car go down the street, stopping and making a turn onto a one-way road.

"Yeah. That is a little weird. Let's go in." I lock the door behind us and pull my phone from my pocket, arming the house.

"Hopefully the crust is cooked through this time," Scarlet says as we sit down. "I undercooked it last time." She wrinkles her nose and looks so damn adorable.

"I liked the mushy-crust," Jackson tells her.

"You were the only one," I loudly whisper.

"Hey now." Scarlet gives me a pointed look and we dig in. After dinner, I give Jackson a bath and put him to bed. Scarlet is sitting on the couch when I come back down, wrapped in a blanket. She's holding a cup of tea in one hand and her book in the other.

"Want me to make a fire?" I ask, eyeing the brick fireplace that we rarely use. Call me paranoid or overprotective, but it makes me nervous to have the fire going with Jackson around. The fireplace is original to the house, and the entire hearth gets pretty warm when a fire is going.

"That would be amazing." She puts her book down. "And a little romantic."

I wiggle my eyebrows and go to the couch first, needing to feel my lips against hers before I go outside and get firewood off the back porch.

"Do you want any tea?" she asks as I work on getting the fire going. It's not as easy as it looks.

"No, but I will take some of that spiked cider."

"Ohh, right. I almost forgot! I'll heat us both a glass."

I have a small, rather pathetic fire going by the time Scarlet comes back into the living room, carrying two mugs of steaming cider. We sit together in silence, drinking our cider and watching the flames.

"I could do this every night until summer," she says, putting her mug down and snuggling up against me.

"Me too." And then do it again next fall. And the one after that…and the one after that…

"Quinn asked if we wanted to double-date with her and Archer to dinner and a movie tomorrow. She already talked to your parents about watching both of the grandkids."

"Yeah, that'd be fun. Are Dean and Kara going too?"

"She didn't say they were. Is that weird to go and hang out with Archer when he's Dean's friend?"

"It's not weird for me. Archer's like another brother. But Dean can be possessive," I say with a laugh. "I haven't gone to see a movie that wasn't G-rated in years."

"I haven't seen one in a while, either. And just to warn you, I'm probably going to hog the popcorn, which has to have extra salt and tons of butter."

"That's the only way to eat movie-theater popcorn."

"I'll text Quinn back now before I forget." She grabs her phone and fires off a text.

"You and Quinn seem to really get along."

Scarlet smiles. "She's great."

"She is." I put my empty mug on the coffee table. I don't drink very often, and I think Scarlet put too much rum in the cider. Or maybe I'm feeling buzzed because I'm with Scarlet. "Having Jackson and Emma will be interesting."

Scarlet laughs. "I think your parents can handle it. And Jackson loves Emma."

"He does because they're not together all that often. And he's been difficult lately."

"Yeah," Scarlet agrees. "He was difficult today a few times."

"What'd he do?"

"Nothing serious. Just defiant and I had to tell him multiple times to pick up. And I pretty much ruined his afternoon by giving him a green cup instead of a blue one."

I chuckle and shake my head. "Don't be afraid to discipline him," I remind her. We went over ways to handle his bad behavior from the start, but I know Scarlet still feels a little awkward. I don't want her to, especially with the way things are going.

"I know. And after his meltdown at the grocery store the other day…" She shakes her head. "I got this."

Fuck, I love this woman. "You do."

She climbs into my lap and rakes her fingers across my back. It drives me crazy and she knows it. "I know it's borderline arctic outside, but it's a full moon. Want to look at it with your telescope with me?"

"Why does that sound dirty?"

"Everything sounds dirty to you."

"That's your fault," I tell her. "I think about your pussy all damn day."

"Weston," she exclaims, faking shock and bringing her hand to her chest. "I'm a lady. How dare you speak like that in front of me."

"You were not a lady last night when you had me pull your hair and fuck you from behind."

A little moan escapes her lips. "Fuck that was good."

"We can do it again."

"Oh, we will. But…the moon."

"Yeah, let's go look at it."

I check on Jackson before we go outside. He kicked off his blankets and is covered in goosebumps. After fixing the covers and adding one more blanket to make sure he's not cold, I grab socks and a sweatshirt from my room and meet Scarlet in the kitchen.

"It's not *that* cold," I tease, seeing her bundle up like it's the middle of winter.

"Promise you'll warm me up later?"

"You know I will."

We go outside onto the back porch and bring the telescope into the middle of the backyard, trying to get a good view of the moon. Trees and the roof of the house obstruct our vision. I pick the heavy thing up and lug it around to the front, even though Scarlet protests and says I shouldn't go through any trouble.

But doing anything to see her smile will never be trouble for me.

"I'm starting to really love this quiet," she whispers, looking up and down the street. It's dimly lit from a few street lamps and porch lights. I set the telescope down on the sidewalk and adjust it until the moon comes into view.

"It's really bright tonight. It looks awesome," I tell her and step aside so she can have a look. A car drives by on the street perpendicular to ours, rolling through the stop sign. Things are pretty quiet downtown once night falls, but it doesn't become a ghost town.

"It's amazing," Scarlet whispers, and I find myself smiling as I watch her. "I can see so much detail."

I zip up my coat and stick my hands in my pockets, turning around. It feels like someone is watching us, and unease creeps over me. After years as a soldier and then a cop, I know to trust my gut. I take a few steps away from Scarlet and look down the narrow stretch of grass that separates my house from the neighbors'. I don't see anything…and then I remember that we went out the back door and walked around to the front.

The back door is unlocked.

Jackson is inside.

"I'll be right back," I say and start forward, only to stop. "Come with me."

Scarlet looks up from the telescope. "Where?"

"Inside. The back door is unlocked."

"Oh, shit. Go lock it." She waves me away and bends her head back down.

"Come in with me. Please?"

"I thought you said this was a safe town."

"It is." I inch toward the house. "But I'd feel better if you came in with me."

She looks up and sees the worry in my eyes. "Yeah, I'll come in. I need more warm cider anyway."

I run around the house and leap up the porch steps. The door is still closed, but that doesn't mean anything. I don't stop until I'm in Jackson's room, seeing him safely sleeping in bed.

I sit on the edge of his bed, resting one hand on his back. I used to sit up with him like this when he was an infant, making sure he was still breathing. I still do this when he's sick. I'll probably always do this.

"Everything okay?" Scarlet whispers, appearing in the doorway.

"Yeah." I pull my phone from my pocket and log into the alarm system app, checking the activity. Other than me opening the door less than a minute ago, the last time the back door was opened was when Scarlet and I left the house. "I worry about him."

"I know." Scarlet comes into the room and perches on the bed next to me. "I do too." She takes my hand and brings it to her lips. "He's lucky to have such a caring father."

I give her hand a squeeze. The words are burning in my mouth, wanting to come out.

Wanting to tell her I love her.

31

"*A*re you getting nervous?" Scarlet asks, pouring herself a cup of coffee.

"No."

She looks at me incredulously. "Not at all?"

"Honestly, I'm looking forward to election day so this campaigning bullshit will be over."

She laughs. "I don't blame you there. You'll know if you won that night, right?"

"In theory."

"I have a good feeling about this. Come Tuesday night, I'll be calling you Sheriff."

"Even if I do win, I won't be the Sheriff until the term ends."

She sits at the table next to me. It's early Friday morning, and she woke up when my alarm when off. Instead of going back to sleep, she came downstairs with me for breakfast. "I'm still calling you it. And I'll make sure to be a bad girl who needs to be arrested and appropriately punished."

"It is my duty to uphold the law."

She takes a sip of her coffee, smiling. "I'll make sure you catch me jay-walking or something."

I laugh. "Living on the edge."

"I'm a regular criminal."

"Please. Like you've ever broken a law."

She chokes on her coffee, eyes going wide.

"Forget how to drink?" I raise my eyebrows.

"Went down the wrong pipe," she says between coughs. "And it's hot."

"You okay?"

"Yeah. And I have broken laws before."

"Really?"

She casts her eyes down. "Yeah. What if I told you I did some bad things but never got caught?"

With one question, she's back to being hard to read. I think she's joking, but she says it seriously. Her body language changes as well, and she's still looking down at the table. Before I can question her, my phone rings.

"It's the station." I answer, talk to my boss for a minute, and then stand. "Gotta go."

"Already?"

"Yeah. We got a lead on a meth lab in a garage."

"Be careful."

"I will." I grab my plate and carry it to the sink. "We bust meth labs more often than you'd think around here."

"Is it like *Breaking Bad*?"

"Most aren't that cool-looking."

"Sounds dangerous, though."

I nod, not one to sugarcoat anything. "I know what I'm doing."

"Good. Because I need you home tonight."

I'm tempted to tell her I love her again, because I never really do know what the day will bring. I suppose the danger is there for anyone who leaves the house: car accidents claim the lives of many every day, but it's a little different when you're leaving the house to go running into danger.

"I'm gonna go give Jackson a kiss goodbye," I tell her and hurry up the stairs, sneaking into his room so I don't wake him. I pause in the doorway, looking at his handsome little face. We finally took him to get a haircut, and the shorter locks make him look older. He's four and a half already. Time is fucking flying by.

"See you later, buddy," I whisper. "I love you."

If Scarlet weren't here, I would have had to wake Jackson up already, fight with him to eat breakfast and get dressed, and probably deal with a tantrum or two as I get him to put his shoes on and get buckled into his car seat. I'd drop him off with my mom before heading into the station, tired and most likely irritated from dealing with his attitude. It's inevitable that all parents feel frustrated with their own children. I still get frustrated with him. But having him on a solid schedule where he's developed a routine and gets plenty of sleep has been so good for us.

"Can you call me when you're done?" Scarlet asks before I head out the door. "So I know you're okay?"

"Yeah. I will."

"Thanks." She brushes her blonde hair over her shoulder. "I'm going to sit here worrying, you know."

"I do. And not that I want you to worry, but it's nice knowing you are. If that makes any sense at all."

"It does. You know that I lo—that I care a lot about you."

Was she going to say she loves me? I look into her blue eyes and my heart hammers away. Fuck this. Life is too short to live cautiously when it comes to matters of the heart.

I stride over, take her in my arms, and plant a big kiss on her lips.

"Scarlet?"

"Yeah?" She fastens her arms around my neck.

"I love you."

Her lips curve into a smile and her eyes get misty. "Are you sure about that?"

"Yes," I chuckle. "I'm very sure. I am in love with you, Scarlet Cooper."

"I didn't think I'd ever love anyone, because I was convinced love didn't exist." Her eyes flutter shut, and my heart starts to beat faster and faster. "Then I met you, and I realized that love is real, and I don't just mean romantic love. You have so much love for your son...and your family...every one of you." She swallows hard, having a hard time with the words. Tipping her head up, she locks her eyes with mine. "I love you, too, Weston."

We kiss, and my heart explodes with happiness. For the first time in years, everything is perfect.

～

"Look at him," Scarlet whispers, leaning in. "He totally wants her!"

"Do you think she knows?" Quinn whispers back. We're sitting at the bar at Getaway, and are currently watching Logan painfully try to get out of the friend-zone with fellow bartender, Danielle.

"She messes with her hair when they talk." Scarlet slides her drink in front of her and looks at Danielle. "And they're so flirty, you'd think so. How long has she worked here?"

"I think like a year," Quinn answers. "Or at least that's about how long ago he started mentioning her. As his friend, of course." She slides her drink in front of her and takes a sip. "I have to pee. Want to come with me?"

"Sure." Scarlet slides off her bar stool and follows Quinn to the ladies' room. Dean ended up joining us after the movie, and he and Archer are playing pool. I grab Quinn's drink, not wanting to leave it sitting on the bar unattended and join them.

"Ditching the girls already?" Dean asks, glancing up from the pool table.

"They went to the bathroom together."

"Oh. Scarlet and Quinn have become good friends."

"Yeah," I say, not meaning to smile as much as I do. "It's nice."

"I guess," Dean says flatly, and I look at Archer and roll my eyes. We both know what he's getting at. Kara is—for some stupid fucking reason—annoyed at the new friendship. If she weren't so uptight, we could all hang out together and it'd be fun. Though I suppose when I stop and think about it, it's kind of a weird situation.

Archer and Dean have been best friends for years. Quinn is

marrying her brother's best friend. My girlfriend is now good friends with my sister, so when those two hang out and we double-date, Archer comes with.

Whatever. We're all family now.

"How's Bobby?" I ask Archer.

"He's doing all right. Supposedly he made a breakthrough during group therapy yesterday. Like he did the last time he was there. And the time before that."

"I'm sorry, man. That's rough."

"You can't help someone who doesn't want to help themselves." He moves around the pool table. "Speaking of help…you are taking a cat, right? Quinn mentioned that you wanted one for Jackson."

"I did, and I'm considering it. Scarlet would like it too."

"Getting her a pet already?" Dean trades his pool stick for his beer. "Are you ready for that type of commitment?"

He's joking, but my answer is serious. "Yeah. I am." I look in the direction of the bathrooms, hoping to see Scarlet walking out. "She's perfect."

"It's nice seeing you happy," Dean tells me. "We all like Scarlet, which is a welcome change from—what the fuck?" He cuts off and almost drops his beer, eyes going wide. "Daisy."

He doesn't have to say the words for me to know. The look of horror on his face says it all. Daisy is here, and I turn just in time to see her stop in her tracks. We make eye contact, and she doesn't so much as smile. Then she turns and makes a beeline to Scarlet.

"*I* swear to you, it burned my mouth," Quinn says, and we both laugh. "I told Archer I would never go down on him again if he eats spicy food. I know he likes it, but for the sake of a blow job he'll give it—what the fuck?"

She grabs my arm and comes to a dead stop.

"What's wrong?" I face Quinn. Her green eyes are wide, and it's like she just saw a ghost. Following her line of sight, I turn and do a double-take. The annoying eavesdropping woman from the visitation room at the prison is standing a few feet from us.

Is this a strange coincidence or is she—

"What the fuck are you doing here?" Quinn demands, and a darkness that I've never seen before comes out in here. "Get the hell out of here before I beat your ass."

The annoying lady puts her hand on her hip and shakes her head. "Nice to see you too, Quinn."

Wait a minute. She knows Quinn?

"Get out of here," Quinn says through gritted teeth. "Now."

"Or what?"

"I'll force you outside myself."

Annoying Lady leans in. "We both know you don't have it in you."

"But I do." Logan rushes forward, putting himself between

Annoying Lady and Quinn. "This is my bar and I can kick whoever I want out. So get out."

"That's no way to treat a lady."

"You're not a lady," Logan spits. "Get the fuck out of my bar, Daisy."

Daisy? I blink. Once. Twice. She's still there. Owen and Archer are coming over, and Dean is standing in the back of the bar, hands raised a bit as he tries to talk down Wes.

And now it makes perfect sense.

The Dawson siblings are ready to tear this woman apart because she's Weston's wife. She's Weston's wife who sat next to me while I poured my fucking heart out to my sister. While I admitted every bad thing I've done and planned to do.

I can't breathe.

"Babe, you okay?" Archer puts his arm around Quinn's shoulder, trying to turn her away. She's still seething with anger, ready to throw the first punch.

"Archer Jones?" Daisy tips her head. "Wait a minute—you two are together?" She laughs. "I did not see that coming. How'd Dean take it?"

"Stop acting like you know us," Logan warns. "And get out before I call the cops."

"But one is already here." Daisy smiles. "I'd like to talk to my husband now." She looks right at me. "You do know you've been sleeping with a married man, right? Though I suppose breaking up a marriage is a cake-walk for you."

She knows. She fucking knows.

The world spins around me, threatening to swallow me whole at any second. And I think this time I'll let it.

"You okay?" Owen puts his hand on my shoulder.

"Yeah." I blink and shake my head. "Shocked, that's all."

"You knew about her, right?"

I move my head up and down, unable to force out more words. Owen gives me a gentle nudge, leading me away. My feet don't want to cooperate, and part of me knows that if I walk away, anything is fair game.

She'll tell Weston what she overheard.

He'll know the truth. Know what a horrible person I am.

And he'll hate me for it.

I squeeze my eyes shut, trying to block out the noise. My mind races, going into self-preservation mode. There's no reason for Weston to believe a word this bitch says, right? I'll tell him she made it all up. I'll admit to some of the less terrible things I did, like steal a few bucks from assholes who got a little too handsy at the bar.

And then we can go on like nothing happened, because it *has* to go on like nothing happened. I love this man so much. And I love Jackson.

I can't lose them. I won't lose them.

But maybe I should.

I'm obviously not the woman Weston thinks I am. I love him. I really, truly love him. I don't want to live the rest of my life lying to him.

"I'm not your husband anymore," Wes says, and hearing his voice makes me feel sick, because I'm already thinking of losing him, of never hearing his deep voice again. Daisy whips around, and I see the remorse in her eyes the second she looks at Weston.

She messed up big time, and she knows it.

We already have one thing in common.

"What do you mean?" she asks.

Wes sidesteps Daisy and puts his arm around me. "I mean I filed for divorce."

"But I didn't sign anything." She smiles again, trying to look victorious. Really, she's terrified that she just lost the one angle she thought she could play.

Which is bad news for me.

"Doesn't matter. The papers are already being processed. It'll be official soon enough."

"Why, Wes?"

"I haven't seen you in three years, Daisy. What did you expect?"

She lets out a breath and shakes her head so fast it looks like a nervous tic. "I want to see my son."

"No."

"You can't keep my son from me."

Wes's grip on me tightens, and I know he's working hard to keep calm. I can't imagine how pissed he is. "You can take it up with the court. You haven't seen him for over three years. You haven't provided any sort of support for him since he was two months old."

"He's *my* son."

"He is. And he's a fucking awesome kid. It's a damn shame you missed out on him."

"I want to see him."

Wes slowly shakes his head. "He doesn't even know who you are."

Daisy's eyes fill with tears that she angrily wipes away. She looks at me. "There's a lot of that going around."

Feeling like I might puke, I turn in toward Wes. "She's not worth it," I whisper, unable to make my voice any louder. We need to get away. Maybe she'll disappear again, and we can go back to how things were before.

Because things were perfect.

"Let's go," I tell him.

"Yeah." Wes brings his arm down and takes my hand. "Let's."

"Wes, wait. Please," Daisy pleads.

"You heard him," Dean says through gritted teeth. "He doesn't want to talk to you. None of us do, so do yourself a favor and get the hell out of here. And don't stop until you're out of Eastwood."

"I have a right to be here." Daisy pushes her shoulders back, trying to hang onto what's left of her dignity. There isn't much to hold onto. "And I have a right to see my son."

"You forfeited that right when you abandoned him," Logan interjects. "As my brother said, take it up with the court if you want to see him again. Though if you really care about Jackson at all, you'll stay away. He doesn't know you. Best to keep it that way."

"He can get to know me," Daisy pleads. I watch her body language, breaking her down as if she were a potential client to scam. She's desperate all right, and I think some of it is genuine.

"For how long?" Wes spits. "How long before you take off again? It won't be any different than the last time."

"It might be," Daisy goes on. "I deserve a chance."

"Not with me." Wes shakes his head and squeezes my hand. "And not with Jackson. We're leaving, and if you even think of coming to the house and seeing Jackson, I'll arrest you for trespassing myself."

"Wes, stop! Let's just talk."

Wes turns, pulling me with him. Logan and Owen move in, blocking the way so Daisy can't chase after us. Wes storms out of the bar, letting go of my hand the moment we get outside. He's upset, and I should comfort him.

Better yet, I should tell him the truth. It will sound better coming from me than from that crazy bitch. All I need to do is open my mouth and confess. Just get this over with.

But I can't.

We get into the Jeep and Wes pulls out of the parking lot. Now's another good time to come clean.

But I don't.

"I'm so sorry, Scarlet."

"Don't be," I tell Wes, reaching over and putting my hand on his thigh. I close my eyes, clenching my jaw to keep my teeth from chattering. If anything, I'll blame it on the cold. "It's not your fault."

"I feel like it is. I have no idea why she showed up."

I do. She showed up because she heard me running my mouth about this nanny job I took, thinking I could con money out of my new boss. She showed up because I talked about her soon to be ex-husband and son.

I was careless, thinking it was damn near impossible that someone would overhear me and know exactly who I was talking about. It has to be fucking fate. The universe is finally giving me the middle finger, getting back at me for all the shit I did.

Just a few days ago, she heard me say I was in love with Weston, and now she's here. Which only means one thing.

She's here to break us up. She's here to tell him everything she knows about me.

33

"Wes?" I ask quietly. We're at a four-way stop and need to turn left to get to his house. There are no other cars around us, and we're still sitting there. I take my hand off his thigh to turn on the heater. The cold has crept through me, going straight to my heart.

I want to shove it back down into the hole it crawled out of. But it's beating strong inside my chest, making me feel so much. Too much.

I can't do this.

Not to Weston. Not to Jackson.

My jaw trembles, and I think about how far I've come, how much I've changed. *How happy I've been.* Weston has given me everything without even offering. He showed me love, real, unconditional love.

"Wes," I start again, voice breaking. I bring my hands into my lap and swallow the lump in my throat. I need to say it. Now. Get it out. One way or the other, Wes deserves to know, doesn't he? I'm not stupid. These things have a way of coming out when you least expect it, and even if Daisy goes away and never returns, I can't live with this hiding in the closet.

His phone rings and Logan's name pops up on the display screen on the dash.

"Daisy just left," Logan rushes out as soon as Wes connects the call. "And she said something about finding Jackson one way or another. We think she's headed to Mom and Dad's. Owen's on the phone with Mom now. Dean, Quinn, and Archer went after her."

"You let Quinn—never mind." Wes grips the steering wheel. "I'm headed there now. Thanks, Logan."

Wes hangs up, and I know I can't drop a bomb on him now. Though maybe it would be a good time. He's more distracted with Jackson that what I did might not seem so—God, listen to me? I'm going into self-preservation mode again.

And then it hits me. Hard. Harder than the thought of Daisy telling Wes that I took the nanny job thinking I'd sleep with him and would blackmail him into paying me for my silence or something.

She might try to kidnap Jackson.

"Drive faster," I say through clenched teeth. Wes doesn't say anything but steps on the gas, jerking the Jeep forward. We make it a few miles before I speak again. "Should you call this in or something? Get a squad car to go to their house?"

"I can get there faster."

I'm so tense the rest of the way that my back hurts by the time we peel into the gravel driveway of the Dawsons' farmhouse. The kitchen light is on, as is one upstairs. Quinn and Archer's Escalade is parked in front of the garage, and they're just now getting out. Wes really did drive fast.

Wes kills the ignition and rushes out of the Jeep, running to the garage.

"I already disarmed it," Quinn says, face illuminated by light from her phone. She has to be freaked out almost as much as Weston. I know she loves her nephew fiercely, but Emma is inside too.

Wes pushes the door open, and the five of us rush in. Mr. Dawson is in the kitchen, wearing plaid pajama pants and a white T-shirt. He was obviously settled in for the night and is already putting on a pot of coffee.

"He's upstairs sleeping," Mr. Dawson assures Wes, knowing

he's going to go up there anyway. "Mom's in the room with him. Emma just finished a bottle and went back to sleep too."

"Thanks, Dad," Quinn says, shrugging off her coat. She sets it down and wraps her arms around herself. "I'm still shivering."

"It's from adrenaline and nerves." Archer steps in, wrapping her in a tight embrace. Wes disappears up the stairs, needing to see Jackson for himself.

"Well, now you've met Daisy," Dean says, pulling out a bar stool. He sits, letting out a heavy sigh. "She's lovely, isn't she?"

"She seems great." I force a smile, feeling myself slipping back into the shadow of Old Scarlet. It feels weird, though familiar, and I don't like it. I wasn't a happy person before I met Weston. I barely got by, and I don't just mean with money.

Every day was a struggle to keep my head above water. Some days, just waking up and facing the day was hard to deal with. I had no purpose, no drive…no meaning. Life sucked and that was just the way it was. I didn't think things could ever get better.

That I'd actually be happy.

And yet here I am, feeling it all slipping out from underneath me like sand being washed out with the tide.

"Do you really think she'll show up?" Quinn asks, sitting down on the floor to pet the dogs. The biggest one—Rufus, I think?—pushes into her lap, and she nervously twists his long fur around her fingers.

"Who knows?" Archer takes a seat next to Dean and shakes his head.

Mr. Dawson gets out coffee cups and sets them on the island counter. I'm still standing awkwardly in the hallway leading into the kitchen, feeling unworthy of sharing the company of these people.

"I always knew she'd show back up again," Mr. Dawson says. "Thank God Wes filed for divorce and primary custody of Jackson a few weeks ago." He looks at me and smiles. "We have you to thank for that."

It's like the real Scarlet checked out and took a first-class ticket to hell, being forced to watch things unfold before me with no control.

"Yeah, I did push him a little," I say with a smile. *But it's my fault she's here in the first place, and it'll be my fault when Wes learns the truth.* Hurting him is the last thing I ever wanted. Even when I hoped he was a rich asshole, I didn't necessarily want to hurt him. Teach him a lesson in fidelity maybe, but not crush his heart with my bare hands.

And Jackson—oh my God, Jackson. Tears fill my eyes, and I pull my boots off, knowing Mrs. Dawson has a strict no-shoes rule, and start to cross the kitchen, mumbling that I needed to check on Jackson too. I've never been upstairs in this house, and each wooden plank creaks slightly under my feet.

Daisy is in town, adamant about seeing Jackson. Most kidnappings happen when a non-custodial parent takes the child. We have a recipe for disaster and I have no idea how long the danger will be there. Everyone is freaked out enough right now, making me think there's a good chance Daisy will actually try to do it.

Suddenly, the thought of dropping Jackson off at school on Tuesday terrifies me so much dizziness crashes down on me. My heart hurts and I can't bear the thought of anything bad happening to that sweet little boy.

"Scarlet?" Mrs. Dawson calls softly. I blink away tears and look up the stairs. "Is that you?

"Yeah." I dash up the rest of the stairs and step into the dim light spilling out of the open bedroom door. Weston's large frame is bent over a bed. He kisses Jackson's forehead and pulls up the blankets.

"Come here, honey." Mrs. Dawson picks up on how upset I am right away and pulls me into a hug. If only she knew...

"Do you really think she'll do it?" I whisper, not needing to explain what I'm referring to.

"I don't know." Mrs. Dawson pats my back, stepping away and motioning for me to follow her. She steps into the room across the hall, going right to the window which looks out at the street in front of the house. "I'll be honest and say I never really liked Daisy, not even when she was just a teenager. I questioned her faithfulness to Wes while he was deployed, but that's not the issue at hand." She lets the curtains fall shut and turns back around to face me.

"Motherhood isn't easy, and I'll be the first to admit that. There were times when the idea of running away seemed like a dream come true. But never forever. A childless vacation can be a welcome—and needed—escape, but the thought of being away from my children…" She shakes her head. "I don't understand how she did it. We thought maybe it was post-partum depression, and Wes did everything he could to find her the first time she left. They weren't on good terms, but he was worried sick. And then she showed up at Jackson's first birthday party, acting like nothing happened."

She lets out a heavy sigh. "I've accepted that there are certain things you'll never understand. People do unspeakable things for reasons that make sense to them and them alone. I've stopped seeking answers for questions that shouldn't be answered."

"That's…that's very wise." My throat feels thick. Like I might burst into tears or puke or something.

"And don't worry, honey. Weston cares deeply for you. He's been smitten from the start. It was pretty obvious."

I smile, wishing I could close my eyes and erase my past. "Yeah, it was obvious." The stairs creak, and Quinn stops in the threshold of the room. She's holding a phone, and the screen is glowing.

"Do you know the passcode to Wes's phone?" she asks me.

I shake my head. "Why?"

"His motion sensors are going off." She holds it up, and I see the alerts.

"Try Jackson's birthday," Mrs. Dawson suggests.

Quinn looks down at the phone. "Wes wouldn't be that predictable—well, I guess he is."

She opens up the security system app, impatiently tapping her fingers on the back of the phone case as she waits for it to load.

"Oh shit. It's Daisy."

"What?" Mrs. Dawson rushes over.

"She's just sitting on the front porch. Looks like she's waiting for someone to answer the door." Quinn shakes her head. "She did say she wants to talk to Wes." With a sigh, Quinn turns and goes down the hall.

And I'm back to not being able to breathe.

My heart beats loudly, echoing in my ears. I clench my fists, digging my nails into my palm. Wes's deep voice comes from the hallway, and the second he comes into view, I spring forward, wrapping my arms around him.

"Maybe if you ignore her, she'll go away?" I say, attempting to make a joke. I'm shaking, and Wes holds me against his firm chest. Even now he's calm and collected.

"I wish."

"Then we should." I don't want to let him go. If I let him go, he'll talk to Daisy. He'll find out everything.

"Come get some coffee and something to eat," Mrs. Dawson says softly. "Jackson and I made chocolate cake that I could use some help eating."

"That sounds good," Quinn says. She peeks in at Jackson before turning down the stairs. Mrs. Dawson goes down with her.

"You okay?" Wes asks, running his hands down my arms. "You seem freaked out."

"Well, it's not every day your boyfriend's ex-wife storms back into town and under-the-table insinuates she's going to kidnap her son."

"I'm sorry."

"Don't be," I interrupt before he can go on. "This'll blow over, right? It has before."

"Yeah." He lets out a deep sigh. "Fuck, it's weird seeing her."

"Yeah, that would be. Was she like this the last time she showed up?"

"No, not at all. The last time was even more fucked up. I came home from work and she was just there in the kitchen making dinner like it was something we did every night."

"That is fucked up."

"Yeah." His eyes fall shut for a few seconds. "I don't have feelings for her anymore. I need you to know that."

"I know you don't."

He cups my face. "You're the only one I want."

Tears burn my eyes. Thankfully it's too dark in the hall for Wes to see them. He puts his mouth to mine, kissing me hard and desperate.

"Do you want cake?" I ask, stepping in closer.

"Yeah." He rests his head on mine for a moment. Then he steps back, takes my hand and goes downstairs.

The kitchen isn't nearly as tense as it was a few minutes ago. Mrs. Dawson is talking to one of the twins on the phone, and Dean and Archer are very animatedly telling a story to Quinn about something that happened back in their college days. I can tell by the look on her face this isn't the first time she's heard the story.

Mr. Dawson brings Wes a cup of coffee and pats his back. God, this family is perfect, and their faults and flaws are exactly what make it so.

"What's the plan?" Mr. Dawson asks Wes.

"I don't know." Wes takes a drink of coffee. "She's not going to leave until I talk to her, so I should bite the bullet and just do it. I'll give her copies of the papers I filed so she knows what's going on. Part of me doubts she'll even fight for Jackson."

Mr. Dawson nods. "I agree. Lay everything out so she knows exactly what's going on and then tell her if she wants to see or talk to you again, she'll have to go through the legal system."

Wes pinches the bridge of his nose. "This is the last thing I need right now."

Shit, I almost forgot amidst all this chaos that the election is only days away. He told me he wasn't nervous or stressed over it, but I know better.

"It'll be okay in the end," Mr. Dawson assures his son. "She's been gone his whole life. There's no way she can take him away from you."

"Right." Wes doesn't look convinced. He takes another drink of coffee. "All right. Time to get this over with."

I step forward, thinking I'm going with Wes. His face says otherwise.

"I think it'd be best if I go alone," he tells me.

No. He can't go alone. Because if he's alone with her, there's no telling what she'll say. I won't know. I'm slipping into panic mode, and part of me wants to run for the hills, seek cover, and never come back up to see the light of day again.

"Are you sure that's a good idea?" I put one hand on the counter to steady myself. "I can stay in the car or go inside."

"It's late. Stay here. And I'll grab some things and come back." Wes frowns. "I don't want to wake up Jackson and worry him. I'm staying with him tonight."

"Good idea." I swallow hard, doing everything I can, not to freak out. My life as I know it might be over in a few short hours. "So you're going to wait until morning to talk with her?"

"No, I'll go now. Or else she'll be on the porch all night and I don't want attention drawn to this matter. The quieter I can handle this, the better it'll be for Jackson's sake."

"Are you two staying?" Wes asks his sister.

"If Emma wakes up, we can stick her in her car seat and head home," Archer says. "But I don't want to wake her up either." He rests a hand on Quinn's shoulder.

"You guys can come stay with us," Quinn says, looking at Wes and then me. "Daisy might not know where we live yet, and I think she'd have a tough time sneaking around or breaking into our house."

"Right," Archer says dryly. "We'll throw a cat at her. We have enough of them."

"No one is throwing my cats. I was referring to the upgrades I did for our home security system."

Quinn and Archer's house is more secure than Fort Knox, and I wouldn't be surprised to find out they have a panic room.

"Thanks," Wes says. "But we'll be fine at home. I'll talk to her and try to diffuse the situation. If we're lucky, she'll be gone by morning."

Poor Wes. He looks so tired, and I want nothing more than to go home together, taking advantage of an empty house. We'd have sex—and I wouldn't have to muffle my moans—and then I'd rub his back until he falls asleep.

But after Wes talks to Daisy, there's a chance that'll never happen again. And it will be totally my fault.

34

*T*his is the last fucking thing I want to be doing right now. I used to hope Daisy would show up like this just so I could serve her with divorce papers, but things are already in the works and can get taken care of. I'll have to call Mr. Williams tomorrow and see how her showing up like this affects my case.

Exhaustion hits me, making the short drive from my parents' house to my house challenging. All I want to do is take Scarlet up to bed, fuck her senseless, and pass out naked next to her.

We have a good thing going, and I can't help the sick feeling that's forming in the pit of my stomach that all this soon-to-be ex-wife drama is too much for her. I'm terrified of losing her, of having her decide this isn't what she signed up for and take off running for someone with less baggage.

I know events unfolded in such a way tonight that anyone would be shocked, but there's something different about Scarlet. I don't know what it is, but it has something to do with Daisy showing up announced. I suppose I can't blame Scarlet if she doesn't want to be involved with all this.

Just the thought of her leaving makes me feel sick to my stomach. I don't like very many people, and I love even fewer. Scarlet is one of those people who I like a whole lot and also love with my whole heart.

She's the perfect fit for our family. We just click, as lame as that sounds. I get her, and she gets me. She and Jackson get along perfectly, and she's been more of a loving mother to him than Daisy ever was. Actually, Scarlet has been here for nearly two months. That's longer than Daisy stuck around after Jackson was born.

I slow at a stop sign and see a shooting star streak across the dark night sky. My mind immediately goes to Scarlet, and I can hear her honey-smooth voice whispering *make a wish*.

I don't believe in wishes. You make your own dreams come true, and it has nothing to do with a wish. But right now, I'm desperate. I close my eyes. "I wish Daisy would go the fuck away and Scarlet, Jackson, and I can get back to being a family."

Feeling stupid, I open my eyes and shake my head at myself. I let off the brake, and the Jeep inches forward, getting closer and closer to home.

Daisy is still on the porch when I pull up in front of the house. A white car is parked in front of me. It's the white car we saw the other night. Fuck, that makes me even more pissed. She was driving around spying on us.

"Wes, you came." Daisy stands, stiff from the cold, and comes over.

"Stop." I close the Jeep door behind me and hold up a hand. "I'm not here to be won over or any of your other bullshit. I'm here so you'll go home."

"Can I at least come in? I'm freezing."

"Fine. But when I say we're done, we're done."

"Fair enough." Daisy goes up the porch steps and picks up the doormat. "You got rid of the key?"

"That was an obvious place to hide the key. I took it out the day you put it there, but you weren't around enough after that to figure it out, were you?"

"Wes, I'm…"

"Save it." I use my body to block her line of sight when I punch in the alarm code and turn off the system.

"I'm sorry."

I wasn't expecting an apology this early on in our conversation. She wants something, I'm sure of it.

"Wow." She looks around the living room. "It's different yet the same."

"What do you want?" I ask her. "It's late, and I'm tired and want to get this over with."

"How's Jackson? He's at your parents, isn't he?"

"Maybe."

"Oh, please, Wes. I know you and know you'd only trust your mom with our son."

I don't like hearing her say *our son*. It's what he is, and I'm well aware she's his mother, but it sounds so wrong. She hasn't raised him. Hasn't been here to sit up with him when he's sick. To calm his fears in the middle of the night.

"What do you want?" I ask again, taking a seat on the stairs.

"I want to give us another shot."

"No." I shake my head. "Daisy, I don't love you anymore. I stopped being in love with you before you left and we both know that. You didn't love me either. We had issues from the start and should never have gotten married to begin with."

She folds her arms over her chest, and I look at her, really look at her for the first time. We were freshmen in high school when we met. She was a cheerleader and I was a football player. She went to Greendale, another small town in this county and Eastwood's rival when it comes to high school sports. We dated on and off throughout high school, and I proposed before I left for my first tour overseas. We got married shortly after that, and she moved around from base to base with me until my time in the army ended.

We should have broken things off then, but we wanted to give it one last shot. Daisy's mother was the one who put the idea in her mind that we'd magically fix things if we had a baby, and neither of us expected it to happen the first time we tried.

The moment we knew we were having a baby, things changed. For me. Daisy didn't want a kid, and I'm sure the resentment started there. I hoped things would change when she gave birth and held our sweet, tiny son in her arms, but it didn't.

Not everyone is cut out for motherhood, she told me just a few days after Jackson was born. I chalked it up to pain and exhaustion. It was a red flag of a warning. Several weeks later, I came home from work to find Jackson screaming and crying in his crib and Daisy nowhere to be seen. Judging by how dirty his diaper was, we guessed she'd been gone at least half my shift, having left poor little Jackson alone in his crib.

The raw, painful emotions come back with a vengeance, and I remember it all too well: sitting in this living room, holding my crying baby to my chest and having no idea what the fuck I was going to do. I didn't know anything about babies. How was I going to raise one alone?

"You left us," I say slowly. "And now we've started a life. A *good* life. Why do you want to take that away?"

"I don't, Weston. We were happy once. We can be again."

"It's not that easy."

"It can be." She walks through the living room, going to the photos hanging on the wall. She stops before one of Jackson, and her face pulls down with emotion. "He looks just like you."

"Luckily."

She turns, eyes brimming with tears. "Wes," she pleads.

"Don't."

Sniffling, she wipes her eyes and looks back at the photos. "Whose baby is this? One of your brothers'?" She's looking at a family photo we took over the summer, and Jackson is sitting front and center with Emma on his lap.

"No."

"Quinn?"

"Yes."

Daisy turns, eyebrows raised. "Wait...she and Archer?"

"Stop, Daisy. It doesn't matter. You left us," I repeat. "All of us."

"I miss your family."

I let out a sigh. "They don't miss you." She's been gone for so long but still knows about us. I wish I could take the memories back. I just want her gone.

"I'm really sorry."

"You already said that." I rub my forehead. It's been years, but the same round-and-round arguments are certain to take place. "Look, Daisy...I'm sorry too." I get up and step around the stairs. "I'm sorry for the way things worked out. But you made your choice and now you have to deal with it. You can't come back into our lives and expect everyone to just accept you."

"But a girl can dream, right?" She unzips her coat and lets it slide to the floor. "You're even more handsome than I remember." Running her eyes over my body, she advances, wrapping her arms around me and trying to go in for a kiss.

"What the hell?" I push her away.

"Wes," she cries. "You were the first man I slept with. I want you to be my last."

"No." I shake my head, wanting her out of my house. "What don't you get, Daisy? I. Don't. Love. You." I reach into my jacket pocket and pull out my wallet, getting out enough cash to cover one night at the local motel. "Here, get a room for the night. This isn't happening."

"We were good at it."

"It was the only thing we were good at." And it wasn't all that great, if I'm being honest. "I don't want this. I don't want you." The words sound harsh coming out of my mouth, but she needs to hear them. "I love someone else."

"That blonde whore?"

"Don't talk about her like that."

Daisy laughs. "Like she's so innocent."

"She's perfect just the way she is, and we're happy. All three of us are happy."

"Sure you are. How well do you know this woman? Maybe I don't want her around my son."

"Then you should have stuck around so you'd be able to make such decisions. It's late and I want to sleep. It's time for you to leave."

"One more thing, Wes, and then I promise I'll leave."

"Fine. One more thing."

35

SCARLET

I pull the blankets tighter around my shoulders, unable to stop shivering. Wes has been gone for nearly an hour now, and I haven't heard from him. Every minute that passes makes me more anxious.

I've shut down, told everyone I was tired and wanted to sit in silence on the couch. Dean went upstairs to sleep, and Quinn and Archer left about half an hour ago. Emma woke up crying, and after nursing her back to sleep, Quinn was able to slip her into her car seat and leave.

Mrs. Dawson walks out from the kitchen to check on me, and I close my eyes and pretend that I'm asleep. I have no idea what will happen. I'm in the middle of nowhere at their farm. While this place feels safe and I trust the Dawsons as if they were my own family—actually I trust them more than my own—I want out of here. Because shit is going to hit the fan at any minute and I don't think I can stand to see the disappointment in Mrs. Dawson's eyes.

My phone vibrates in my hand and I shoot up. It's Weston, and for a split second, I'm scared to answer.

"Hello?" My voice is shaky and thin.

"Hey." He's not yelling. Not telling me to fuck off or run away and never return. "She's finally gone…for now. I'm changing into pajamas and will head back. What do you want me to bring for you?"

Wait, what? He's not mad. Does he not know? Did I get a Christmas miracle in No-fucking-vember?

"Scarlet?"

"Sorry," I rush out. "I'm tired. Um, just my toothbrush and some leggings and a sweatshirt or something for the morning. I don't really care."

"Any preference?"

"Something black."

I can hear Weston walking down the hall and into my room. My clothes are still mostly in that closet. "That's easy. About ninety percent of what you own is black."

"It's a flattering color."

"Anything is flattering on you."

I close my eyes and lean back, eyes filling with tears. He doesn't know. I will live to see another day.

"Just pick the first thing you grab and get back here. I miss you."

"I miss you too." He zips a bag and moves through the house. "I'll be there soon. I love you."

"I love you too." I hang up, too relieved to realize Mrs. Dawson has come back into the room.

"Is everything okay, dear?" she asks.

"Uh, yeah. I think so." I pull the blankets up and cast my eyes down, trying to cover up how emotional I am right now. "Wes is coming back. He wants to stay here just in case."

"I figured he would. I can show you to the guest room upstairs if you'd like."

"Yeah, sure. Thanks." We go upstairs.

"This used to be Quinn's room, and when she lived in Chicago, she'd come and stay for the weekend. There should be face wash and soap in the bathroom if you need any."

"Thank you."

Mrs. Dawson looks at me and smiles. "And thank you, Scarlet, for making my Weston happy again."

Don't thank me yet, lady.

~

WES ROLLS over and pulls me to him. The rough skin on the palm of his hand slides under my shirt and over my stomach, and I inhale deeply, not opening my eyes. It's early in the morning, and we're still at his parents' house.

He didn't talk about what happened when he came in last night. He looked tired and worn and not even his mom questioned him on it. I've been dying to ask, but I'm going on the whole *no news is good news* thing.

Once we were in bed together, Wes kissed me hard and made love to me. I know he's worried this whole mess with Daisy will send me running, but he has nothing to worry about. The expectation of finding someone with no baggage, with nothing from their past that could come back to haunt them, is ridiculous. We've all done things we're not proud of. We've all had the best-laid plans come crashing down.

It's not the past that makes up who you are. It's how you continue forward with your life. Which is why I know we can work out. I'm not the same girl I was when I first laid eyes on him, when my only thought was *oh shit*, both because I knew he was the right amount of brooding and gorgeous to get under my skin and because he wasn't the rich asshole I thought I'd be working for.

And even if I had started working for Quinn and Archer...I don't think I would have gone through with things. They're both good fucking people. Quinn is my friend now.

I swallow hard and let out a shaky breath. I fell in love with Weston, but it's deeper than that. There's Jackson, of course, and the rest of the Dawsons. I love that whole family.

The toilet flushes in the jack-and-jill bathroom, and I sit up, peering in. Jackson steps onto a stool at the sink to wash his hands. He doesn't know we're here. I wait until he's drying his hands to whisper his name. He does a double-take and then runs in, jumping on the bed.

"Shhh," I whisper. "Your dad is still sleeping."

Jackson hugs me and then squirms out of bed, running back into his room and returning with Ray, who's looking more tattered and worn as each day goes by.

"He told me he gets lonely," Jackson says, situating the unicorn under the covers with us. He's sandwiched between Weston and me, and Wes wakes up with a smile.

"Hey, buddy."

"What are you doing here, Daddy?"

"I missed you too much." Wes wraps his muscular arms around his son, making Jackson look so small nestled against Wes's large frame. "Did you have fun with Grammy and Papa?"

"Yes! We made cake, and I helped change a poopy diaper," he says proudly. "And I was the only one who got Emma to stop crying."

"You're a good cousin," I tell him, pulling the blankets up over all of us. We lay in bed for a few more minutes. Then Jackson says he's hungry and gets crabby when Wes tells him to let us go back to sleep.

"Go find Grammy," Wes mumbles, turning over. "You're at her house."

"I want you," Jackson whines.

"I'll take him down," I offer.

"You don't have to," Wes grumbles. "Jackson, it's early. Lay back down."

That starts a crying fit, and Wes gets up with a huff. It's not even seven AM yet, and the house is quiet. Well, until we go into the kitchen. Then all four dogs come running, thinking we're going to feed them breakfast. Wes lets them out and plugs in the coffee pot.

"Want any?" he asks, getting out a mug.

I shake my head. "I'll have tea instead if there is any."

Wes puts on a kettle and turns on cartoons for Jackson, who cuddles up with a blanket on the living room couch and isn't interested in breakfast anymore. But we're already up, so we might as well eat.

"Morning," Mrs. Dawson says, coming into the kitchen a few

minutes later. She looks at the cereal we're eating and shakes her head. "I'm going to make you a real breakfast."

"You don't have to," I tell her, rather enjoying my Crackling Oats.

"There's no point in arguing," Wes whisper-talks. "Food is love in Mom's eyes."

"Food is comforting, and I figured after last night you could use a little extra comfort." She pulls eggs and bacon from the fridge and looks at Wes, waiting for him to explain things.

"Yeah. In that case, make me lunch and dinner too."

"Is she coming back?" I ask quietly.

"I'm sure, but I think I made it clear I'll only handle this through a lawyer. I'm not making deals or promises with her." Wes takes a long drink of coffee. "I don't know what to do." He sets his mug down and puts his head in his hands. "He's her son too."

"It's a hard situation," I agree, putting my hand on Wes's shoulder.

"You said your dad wasn't around when you were a kid, right?"

"Right. I was glad when he came back into our lives, but mostly because my mom was a dead-beat drug addict who left me to raise my brother and sister."

Mrs. Dawson turns away from the stove to look at me, but her eyes aren't full of judgment. She feels bad for me, which is almost worse than being judged. I don't want anyone's pity.

"Jackson has you," I go on. "So it's a totally different situation."

"She's never been a mother to him," Mrs. Dawson says, and I know she's fighting hard not to scream profanities and curse Daisy's name. "Thank God you're in the process of being granted full custody of Jackson."

Wes nods. "She is his mother, but she's left him. Twice. I'm not risking him getting to know his mom only to have her leave again."

"That's smart," I agree. "She'll have to earn the right to see him. He's a great kid." I look into the living room, only able to see the top of Jackson's head from where I'm sitting. "I can't imagine leaving him like that."

Mrs. Dawson beams at me. "I've always been a believer in things happening for a reason. Sometimes the reason takes years to manifest, but it's there."

The tea kettle starts to whistle, and I get up to get it. Mrs. Dawson's words echo in my head, making me think I've been looking at this all wrong. Maybe everything in my shitty past happened to push me here right now.

I never would have met Wes in the South Side. And I never would have come to this small Indiana town. The only reason we met was because I took a job thinking I could con my new boss. If I didn't have such shitty moral character before, I wouldn't be where we are right now.

I'm happy.

Weston is happy.

Jackson is happy.

Maybe this did happen for a reason.

36

"*W*hat's all this?" I ask, looking at the papers and boxes cluttering the living room. We just got back to Weston's house. In the daylight, things never seen as scary as they do in the dark. And the more I think about the universe wanting me to meet Weston, the better I feel about this whole situation.

"Family heirlooms. Jackson, don't touch them," he adds quickly.

"Why are they out?" I take off my coat and move to the couch, curiously picking up an old book.

"You-know-who wore her mother's wedding dress at our wedding." He looks uncomfortable talking about it. "She wanted it back and I wasn't sure what box it was in."

"Oh. This stuff is cool."

"You like Civil War history?" he asks, looking a little amused.

"If I'm being honest, I don't know much about it. But I love antiques. Wait, all this stuff is from the Civil War?"

"Some of it is. Not all is that old. It's been in the Dawson family for years and gets passed down to the oldest son. Jackson will get it someday."

"Can I see it?" Jackson asks, peering into a box.

"Sure," Wes says, and we all sit on the floor together. There are books, handwritten letters, a World War II Army uniform, a saber, and a silver tea set that looks like it has to be worth a pretty penny.

"Can we use it?" Jackson asks as I carefully look at the teapot, feeling like I should be wearing those white gloves you see museum workers wearing when they handle artifacts.

"I don't know if it's safe to drink out of," Wes says, looking at the sugar bowl. "It might have traces of lead in it."

I gently set the teapot down and grab my phone, doing a Google search for more info on the tea set.

"Holy shit—I mean, shoot. But holy." I turn my phone around, showing Wes the value of the tea set.

He takes my phone from me, eyes going wide. "These aren't in as good of condition."

"They're tarnished, which can be cleaned. That's crazy, though."

Wes nods. "It is. I had no idea."

"That sword and the uniform are probably worth a lot too."

"I know the saber is," he tells me. "And we know the personal history of it." He sorts through a box for a minute, pulling out a photo of great-great-great Grandpa Dawson holding the exact sword.

"Wow. That's incredible."

"It is pretty cool," he agrees. We spend another half an hour looking through the stuff before putting it away. Wes tries to get Jackson to sit and watch a movie with us since we're tired. Any other time this kid would jump at the chance to watch TV, but since both Wes and I are dead tired, of course he wants to paint instead. Everything is fine at first, and then Jackson paints his face in the one minute Wes and I turned our backs, talking in hushed voices about being extra careful at preschool pick-up with Daisy back in town.

Wes takes Jackson upstairs for a bath, and I start cleaning up the paint mess on the table. Wes's phone is on the counter, and it vibrates with an alert from the motion sensor on the doorbell. Wiping my hands on a dishtowel, I rush through the house and see Daisy standing at the front door.

Anger surges through me, and I storm out of the house before thinking it through.

"You are not welcome here," I say, clenching my fists. "Leave before I call the cops. Or better yet. Watch Wes cart your ass off to jail."

"Please." She rolls her eyes. "And it was you I wanted to talk to."

Oh shit. I cross my arms, trying to stay calm and keep warm. It's cold out here, and I'm not wearing shoes or a coat.

"You have two minutes."

"This won't take long. Good thing I already know all about you, Scarlet Cooper."

I try to swallow my fear and keep my cool. "What do you want?"

"I want my family back, and I want you out of the picture."

"That's not happening."

She laughs. "That's what you think. Come on, we both know Wes will kick you out when he learns the truth. And not just about you coming here to rob him blind, but about all the other cons you pulled. I think my favorite was the time you convinced a Fortune 500 CEO to donate thousands to a bullshit charity you made up."

The blood drains from my face. How does she—dammit, Heather. She was bragging about me to her prison friends, who relayed the message to Daisy.

"I'll tell him you're lying."

"I knew you'd say that." She bats her lashes and gives me a smile. "So I did some digging, and your sister has been so helpful. I should really send her a thank-you note or something." Daisy reaches into her pocket and pulls out a piece of paper with a name and number written on it.

Deven McAllister.

My old boss. The one I blackmailed into paying me for my silence. Shit. Shit Shit *Shhhiiitttt.*

"Why would you do that to Wes?"

"Because I want him back." Daisy shakes her head like it's obvious. "And you're going to help me get him back."

"Fuck that."

Daisy holds up her finger. "The election is coming up soon, isn't it? It'd be a shame if something were to happen."

"You wouldn't fucking dare."

"Oh, I will if you push me." She takes a step forward, and I feel like I'm standing at the edge of a slippery cliff, desperately trying to keep my footing. "Star County is small and full of closed-minded, simple people. If you haven't noticed, not everyone here is as open and understanding as the Dawsons. One little rumor about candidate Wes Dawson dating a known con-artist with a sister in jail, a mother who died of an overdose, and a father who drank himself into a stupor and, well…it's not something I'd risk."

The girl from the ghetto comes out, and I don't even think as I take a tangle of Daisy's hair and yank her to the ground.

"Stop!" she screams. "Or the article will go out now!"

I freeze, breath leaving in ragged huffs. "Article?"

"My sister works for the *Star County Post*. Ask Wes if you don't believe me." She scrambles up from the ground. "It's already written and ready to go out in the morning."

"They why would I do anything for you?"

"If you tell Wes he should give his wife, *Jackson's mother*, another chance and then get the hell out of here, I'll have her yank the article. And if not…you know what will be on the front page of the Sunday paper…two days before the election."

"You're a horrible fucking person."

"Like you're much better," she snorts. "How many people have you fucked over? Actually, I'm curious. How many other married men have you slept with? Wes can't be the first."

"He's not married to you anymore."

"It doesn't matter. He was mine first. And I want him back." She taps her watch. "Tick-tock. You don't have much time before the front page is drafted up. And even if you took your sorry ass out of here after that, there's nothing I can do to stop it."

With a triumphant smile, she turns and leaves, walking across the street and getting into a white sedan. I never stopped and thought about what the people I was conning felt. They were asshole men trying to pick me up at a bar, not even attempting to hide the fact they were married. They deserved it, or at least that's what I told myself. Maybe I deserve to have my happily ever after ripped away, but Weston doesn't.

I came here with the intentions of taking everything from him, and instead he took the one thing I thought I lost years ago: my heart. He taught me how to love, not just other people but myself. Leaving him will hurt, but having everything he's worked for fall apart will hurt worse.

And if he lost his job…nope. I can't even think about it. He has worked so hard to build a life for himself and Jackson. I won't let anyone take that away.

"What about this one?" I ask Jackson, picking up a pink teapot with little purple flowers painted along the base.

Jackson shakes his head. "Scarlet isn't really a girly girl, Dad."

"Good point. It's too pink for her. Too bad I didn't think of this around Halloween." I push the cart forward, browsing the shelves of a home decor store. We needed to go grocery shopping, and Scarlet said she wasn't feeling well. Telling her to stay home and rest, Jackson and I set out.

Something is off with her, and I'm sure it has to do with Daisy showing back up. I don't want Scarlet to think that old feelings came back the moment I saw my wife. It did the opposite, and if there was any good that came out of this, it's knowing that I can look at Daisy and feel absolutely nothing.

Scarlet is the only one I want.

"That one!" Jackson leans out of the cart and narrowly avoids knocking a glass candle holder off the shelf. "It has a skull on it."

Smiling, I carefully move things out of the way and find what has to be leftover Halloween-themed dishes. This teapot is pink too, but instead of flowers, it's decorated with skulls.

"It's perfect. Good eye, buddy."

Since Scarlet heats up her water for tea either in a saucepan or in the microwave, I get a kettle as well. We check out, go to the grocery store, and pick up Chinese takeout on the way home.

Jackson says he's tired, which is music to my ears. Maybe after lunch, we can all take a nap. And by that, I mean Jackson nap in his room and I take Scarlet into the bedroom. I think about it the whole way home, missing her already even though Jackson and I have only been gone for a few hours.

"Can I give Scarlet her tea set now?" Jackson asks when I get him out of the car. I look up and down the street, making sure Daisy isn't lurking about before I let go of his hand to reach inside and grab the bag.

"Soon. Let's get the groceries unloaded and eat lunch before we do." Keeping a tight hold of Jackson's hand, I take him inside. The house is still and quiet, making me think Scarlet is upstairs sleeping. "Stay right here on the couch," I tell Jackson, giving him my phone to watch YouTube. He doesn't get to watch it that often, so his butt will be glued to the couch as long as the phone is in his hands.

Hurrying back to the car, I bring the bags of groceries up to the porch, setting them all in front of the front door. I lock the Jeep once the last bag is out and rush to the house. Jackson hasn't moved, and I grab the three bags with the cold stuff to put away first.

I get the first bag completely put away before I notice the note on the counter. Setting the milk down, I grab it.

Wes-

I'm so sorry. I love you and Jackson more than you'll ever know. I didn't want to do this, but I have no choice. This is for the best.

Love always,

Scarlet

I blink, not understanding what I'm reading. Shaking my head, I refuse to understand it. The note floats to the floor, and I rush upstairs. Scarlet's room is empty. There are no clothes in the closet. The bathroom counter is free from her neatly cluttered makeup.

I exhale, feeling dizzy, and sink down onto her bed. What the fuck is happening? Why did she leave? And I still don't understand her note. She didn't want to do this? Then why did she?

Pain hits me hard in the center of my chest, spreading throughout my whole body. Is this what it feels like to have your heart break all at once? I dig my fingers into the mattress, fighting against everything inside of me not to feel.

"Dad?" Jackson calls from downstairs. I'm not sure how long I've been sitting there, zoning out, flashing between grief and anger. My foot has fallen asleep, and I can hardly move it.

"Yeah?" I call back, voice coming out weak.

"Someone is on the porch."

Inhaling, I push up, shaking my foot to get some feeling back to it. "Don't move. I'm coming down."

Blinking a few times, I realize my eyes are watery, and only get worse when I see Jackson. He put the phone down and carefully got out the tea set, arranging it on the coffee table. What the hell am I supposed to tell him? I don't even know what's going on.

My heart leaps in my chest, thinking maybe it's Scarlet at the door.

"Jackson, go up to your room," I say as soon as I see Daisy.

"Why?"

"Now," I say, and my tone scares him enough to grab the phone and run.

"Shut the door."

"Is it a bad guy?" he asks, looking down the stairs.

"Kind of," I say, knowing I shouldn't tell him that his mother is bad, but I need him to stay out of sight. Once his door closes, I throw back the front door.

"What the fuck do you want?" I bark.

"Nice to see you too, Wes. Can I come in?"

"No." I grab my coat that I left hanging on the banister and step outside. "What the fuck do you want?" I repeat.

"I came here to talk." Her brows push together, and she looks confused. "Didn't Scarlet tell you that we should—"

I rush forward. "Scarlet?" It's making sense now. "What the fuck did you do?"

"Nothing."

"Bullshit." I'm raging, wanting to turn around and put my fist through the windows on the front door. "Goddammit, Daisy," I say too loudly. There are people walking their dog down the street in front of our house, but I don't fucking care right now.

Daisy showed up and Scarlet left. It has to be why. Scarlet wouldn't just leave.

Trying to recover, Daisy puts a hand on her hip, ready to come at me with some ridiculous blow, just like she did back when we lived together. "Well, if she didn't tell you *that*, then I'm guessing she didn't tell you how she took this job thinking she could con you."

"What the hell are you talking about?"

"Yep. That little snake. I knew she wouldn't confess."

"Confess what? You're not making any sense."

"Your girlfriend, the woman you left alone with *our son,* is a con artist."

"No, she's not." I shake my head and point to the street. "Get off my porch, Daisy. You're sounding crazier and crazier by the minute."

"It's true."

"And how the hell would you know?"

"A friend got arrested and spent time at Cook County with someone named Heather Cooper. Ring a bell?"

I blink. Scarlet does have a sister in prison.

Daisy's lips curve into a smile. "I take your silence as a yes. Anyway, when I've been going to visit my friend—she shouldn't have been arrested, but that's not the point—and of course I noticed the bombshell blonde coming in. Everyone noticed her. I mean, how can you not?"

Daisy inches forward. "I didn't pay her much attention after that, until I heard her mention Eastwood. You know how it is when you hear something familiar. Turns out, she has quite the reputation with the inmates. You see, her sister thought bragging about her would earn her cred or something. Boy, the stories I could tell you. But back to you, Wes. Your darling Scarlet thought some rich couple was hiring her. And then she showed up at your place. There was one thing I couldn't figure out, but now that I know Quinn and Archer have a baby, it's them."

There's no way Daisy would know Quinn and Archer are actually the ones who hired Scarlet instead of me unless she really did overhear Scarlet talking. But everything else she's saying isn't true. It can't be.

"I know you won't believe me, so I got the name of the last couple she was a nanny for. Turns out, she seduced a married man and forced him to buy her expensive clothes and handbags in order for her not to tell his wife."

"You're making that up."

She digs a folded piece of paper from her purse. "Call him. Ask about Scarlet."

Could it be true? Did Scarlet take the job thinking she'd con money out of me? But then why'd she stay? I love her...and I know she loves me.

"What did you say to her?" I ask, rounding on Daisy, whose smile disappears. I don't know what she thought would happen. I'd take her in my arms and up to bed and we'd wake up like everything was fine?

"I didn't say anything."

"Then why did she leave?"

"She left?" Daisy acts shocked. "Wow, can't say I'm surprised. Better make sure nothing valuable is missing." Her face softens. "I miss us. And now that Scarlet is gone, we should try again."

"You did something to make her leave, didn't you?" I shake my head. "Did you think you'd come here with bad news and I'd welcome you home?"

"No, but I...I..." She squeezes her eyes shut.

"Let's just say everything you said was true. It wouldn't change things between us. You left me alone with an infant. And then you showed up again only to do the same thing. I'm not stupid, Daisy."

"I know, Wes, I know you're not."

"And now you're here again, telling me these things only to hurt me."

"Wes, no. You need to know the truth about her. I'd never hurt you."

"Really?" I question, and her face crumbles. "It's always been about you, Daisy. You need to leave."

"Wes, please."

"No. Get. Off. My. Porch." I open my clenched fists and go inside, slamming the door shut behind me harder than I meant to. It rattles the whole house and probably scared Jackson. I lock the deadbolt behind me and stride forward to go upstairs and check on Jackson.

And then I realize the boxes of valuable family heirlooms aren't in the living room anymore.

I can't move. Not yet, not while my mind is going a million miles an hour. Scarlet wouldn't steal them. She's not a bad person. She's not a con artist or a thief. She's Scarlet, a quirky girl from Chicago who likes paranormal romance, drinking tea, and looking at the stars.

She's the woman I love.

But the boxes...I shake my head and move through the small foyer, going to the other side of the house. The boxes came from the basement, and maybe she put them back. I run down the stairs, getting hit with cool, musty air, and pull the string light at the bottom of the stairs. The basement is cold and damp most of the time, typical of older houses in this area. We use it for storage, and the washer and dryer are down here too. I go around the stairs to the storage section and see the boxes neatly put away. I pull one out and open it. Everything is inside.

And now I'm feeling bad for even doubting her. I put my head in my hands and let out a breath. What the hell am I doing?

"Daddy?" Jackson's voice echoes through the house. Shaking myself, I go upstairs and find Jackson in the kitchen.

"Can we eat now? I'm hungry."

"Of course." Having forgotten about our food, I heat it up.

Jackson only wants an egg roll anyway and asks for a piece of toast with peanut butter on it instead.

"Is Scarlet still sleeping?" he asks. "Can I bring food up to her?"

I never lied to him about his mother, and I don't want to lie to him about Scarlet either. But—fuck—what do I say?

"She had to go visit her sister," I blurt the first thing that comes to mind.

"When will she be back?"

I swallow the lump in my throat. "I'm not sure."

I put the groceries away while Jackson eats. I should be hungry, but my appetite is gone. I can't get Daisy's words out of my head. I don't know what to believe, and the best thing is to ask Scarlet. I call her and get her voicemail.

"Scarlet, it's Wes…call me. Please."

I put my phone down and pace around the kitchen, feeling more and more anxious as the minutes tick by. It's like history is repeating itself and I'm damned to live through this again and again.

To be left over and over.

But this time, it's different. This time, I'm in love with the woman who left me. This time, there was no small relief in knowing she was gone, that our constant arguing was finally over. Daisy and I should have separated long before she left. I wouldn't change a thing that would take Jackson away, but if things came about differently…if we at least talked about the issue we ignored and hoped would go away things might have been a lot better for all of us.

Which is why I'm not going to sit back and hope things fix themselves. Not this time around.

∽

I PUSH open the door to Getaway, and bright sunlight spills into the dimly lit bar. Logan's car is parked out front.

"Oh, hey, Wes," Danielle, one of the other bartenders, says, looking up from behind the bar. It's Saturday, and the bar doesn't open for another few hours, but one of my twin brothers is always here getting things ready for the night.

"Is Logan here?" I set Jackson down and look around for him.

Danielle shakes her head. "No, we had an issue with our hard liquor delivery, so he ran to Newport to pick it up himself."

"Oh, bad timing on a Saturday."

"You're telling me. Owen is here, though. He's in the office. Want me to get him?"

"Yeah, thanks, Danielle."

She gives me a smile, looking a little concerned. I've never come in here during the day like this, so it's obvious something is up. Danielle disappears into the office behind the bar to get Owen. I was hoping to talk to Logan because he's a good voice of reason, but maybe Owen's the better one to give advice on this situation. We're the least alike, and hearing what he'd do could do me some good.

"Hey," he says, hurrying over. "What's going on?"

"You got a minute?"

"Of course." He looks at Jackson. "Is everything okay?"

"I'm not sure."

Danielle comes around the bar. "Hey, Jackson, want to play pool with me?"

"Thanks," I tell her, and she takes Jackson's hand, leading him across the bar to the pool table.

"You're freaking me out," Owen says, going to the bar. He grabs a bottle of top-shelf whiskey and pours us each a shot. I take mine and sip it.

"Scarlet left."

"What do you mean, she left?"

I finish the shot, feeling like I need another. "Daisy showed up at the house today."

"Oh, shit."

"Yeah. And she wouldn't admit it, but I think she said something to Scarlet and that's why she left." I pinch the bridge of my nose, and Owen fills the shot glass again. "But that's not all... Daisy told me Scarlet is a con artist and only took the job because she thought she was working for a rich couple—Quinn and Archer—and wanted to con money out of them."

Owen blinks. Once. Twice. "The fuck? Daisy's crazy. How would she even know that?"

"Supposedly, she has a friend who's at the same prison that Scarlet's sister is at and overheard them talking."

"Scarlet has a sister in prison?"

"Yeah, she does. I knew that already, though."

"Does she look like Scarlet? Is she single? You know I love bad girls."

For once, I'm thankful for Owen's smartass attitude. It makes me shake my head but smile. "I've never seen her."

Owen takes his shot and then slides the second one he poured for me over. "Tell me everything."

I take another look at Jackson, making sure he can't hear. He's distracted with Danielle, thankfully. Taking a deep breath, I tell Owen everything.

"I need a minute to process," he says, reaching around for more whiskey. "Do you think she's a con artist?"

"I don't want to, but I...I don't know."

"Okay." Owen nods, thinking. "Say everything is true. She took the job thinking she'd con some rich couple out of money. But she didn't. She stayed with you and Jackson and did her job. Really well." He wiggles his eyebrows. "Right?"

"She was great."

"You dog."

"Shut up," I say flatly. "She was a great nanny and did the job she was hired to do."

"Isn't that all that matters?"

I shake my head, unsure.

"Hey, Danielle?" Owen calls. "I have a moral question for you."

"Uh, sure?" Danielle looks up from the pool table.

"Two guys walk into the bar—"

"Are you forgetting little ears are present?" Danielle puts a hand on her hip and stares at Owen.

"It's not a dirty joke," he deadpans. "Two guys walk into the bar, both with the intent to rob the place at gunpoint. The first guy doesn't go through with it, even though he walked in the doors with the intention of doing it. The second guy does rob the place."

"Okay…what's the moral question?"

"Who's worse? Or are they both as bad since they both intended on doing the same thing?"

"The guy who actually robbed the place is worse. Though I suppose you'd need to know *why* the other guy didn't go through with the robbery. If it was for self-preservation, like he knew he couldn't get away so he decided to wait until another night when the bar was less crowded or something, then I suppose he's still as bad as the second guy. But if he didn't rob the place because he had a change of heart, then he's not as bad."

"Does that help?" Owen asks.

"I think so." I rub my forehead, feeling a migraine coming on. "What would you do if you were me?"

The smirk fades, and Owen unscrews the lid to the whiskey. "I wouldn't let her be the one that got away."

"You'd go after her."

"I'd run after her." He refills our shot glasses. "If she was going to con you, she would have. And once she realized you weren't who she thought she was going to work for, she would have left and moved onto another couple to con. But she stayed because she had a change of heart."

"But you don't know that."

"No." He shakes his head. "I don't. Just like you don't know she didn't. Where is she?"

"I don't know."

"Did she have a house back in Chicago?"

"No. She lived in an apartment and gave up her lease to take this job."

"Maybe Quinn can hack into her phone. Track her location or something."

"No, I don't want her involved." I don't want anyone else in the family involved, but that goes without saying to Owen. He'll tell Logan, I'm sure. They claim to have a hard time lying to each other, saying it's a "twin thing" and non-twins don't understand.

"I know where her sister is." I sit up. "And she'll know where Scarlet is."

"What are you waiting for?" Owen asks. "Go!"

"I can't just drive up to a prison and ask to see a random inmate."

"But you're a cop." He gives me a blank stare.

"I know, but it doesn't work that way. Though I might be able to get her on the phone." I pull out my cell to look up the number for the prison. "I'll have to make a few calls." I open the internet and type in the name of the prison. "I get no service here."

"I know. It's become a dead-zone after the old cell tower was replaced by a different carrier."

"What's your wifi password?"

"Shit. I don't remember. Quinn set it up...try *I love cats* or something."

"Even Quinn wouldn't be that obvious." Still, I try a handful of guesses, text Quinn for help, and wait a whole two seconds before getting frustrated with her lack of reply.

Owen gets up. "What do you need info on? We can look it up on the office computer."

"I'll be in here," I tell Jackson and Danielle, motioning to the office. He's using his hands to push in the balls on the pool table and is excited to be "winning." It'll be okay. I'll get Scarlet back. For me and for him.

Owen puts in the password and steps aside, letting me sit in the desk chair. "Are you in love with her?"

"Yes." I don't hesitate, don't try to hide my feelings. There's no point. I do love Scarlet, and I love her fiercely.

"Then you've got to do this, man. You have to go get her. Take it from me," he starts but doesn't finish. I write down the prison's phone number and address, closing the internet browser and letting out a breath. I'm so tense my shoulders are killing me. Standing, I turn to Owen.

"Thanks."

"No problem. But I do think we should mark this date down in history as the day you came to me for advice."

"I was actually hoping Logan was here."

"Fuck you."

I laugh. "He probably would have said the opposite."

"No shit. He plays it too safe." Owen shakes his head. "He's going to miss his chance with her," he says, meaning Danielle. "But what am I—"

He cuts off when he hears Danielle loudly tell someone the bar isn't open yet.

"Ah, shit. I bet that's Bart again."

"Your resident drunk?"

"Yeah. Poor bastard's drunk more than he is sober. We started giving him protein shakes and saying they're full of vodka. He drinks them at least. Hopefully it'll help him put on a few pounds before winter."

"Owen!" Danielle calls, and both my brother and I run. Danielle is standing behind the pool table, holding Jackson's hand. Her eyes are wide and full of fear, and Jackson looks confused.

"Daddy!" he yells and tries to make a run for me. But she's faster.

Daisy grabs Jackson, and he immediately starts to struggle, just like I taught him in the event someone tries to kidnap him.

"It's okay, I'm your mom," Daisy tells him, and he freezes.

"Daisy." I rush over, blood boiling. "Put him down."

"Dad?" Jackson asks, looking back and forth between Daisy and myself. "Is this Mommy?"

"Yes, baby!" Daisy hugs him and drops to her knees, tears falling from her eyes. "I'm your mommy."

"Let him go," I tell her. "You have no right to be here."

"He's my son! I have every right that you—"

"Legally," I interrupt. "You have no rights. Let him go and leave."

"No." She stands up, holding Jackson's hand. She looks down at him, smiling. "Want to go get ice cream? We can catch up."

"Okay," Jackson says, not too sure of himself.

I clench my fists. I could easily stride over and shove her away, but I don't want Jackson to see me lay a finger on Daisy. And I don't want to hurt her. Deep down, I feel bad for her.

She's missing out on the greatest kid in the whole fucking world.

"No. Let him go," I say again in a calm, level voice. Out of the corner of my eye, I see Owen pull out his phone and start recording a video. I know exactly what he's doing: getting proof of Daisy trying to take my son. Thank you, Owen, for thinking two steps ahead for once.

"You have no legal standing to take him," I repeat. "You gave up custody when you left us four years ago. Let him go."

"No," she says again and shuffles back. "I'm taking him and you can't stop me."

"Should I call the cops?" Danielle asks, voice trembling a bit.

"Yes," I tell her. "Tell them exactly what's going on. Jackson's non-custodial mother is trying to take him."

"Daddy, I'm scared." Jackson tries to pull away, and Daisy tightens her grip. I rush forward, and she picks him up, holding him so tight she's hurting him. He kicks and hits a table, knocking a few glasses onto the ground. They shatter, and glass crunches under her feet. If I try to wrestle him out of her arms, she could drop him or fall, and he'll get cut.

As she shuffles away from me and toward the door, I advance, going around a table and blocking the exit.

"Get the fuck out of my way!" Daisy struggles to keep a hold of Jackson. The kid is only four, but he takes after me and is solid.

"Put him down," I say again. If she gets out the door, she's going to take him. She came here to kidnap him, though she won't see it that way. But it's exactly what it is. There's no way I'm letting her out that door.

Or walk out of here free.

"Ow!" Jackson cries, twisting as he tries to get out of her arms. She adjusts him against her, gripping his arms so tight his skin is turning red.

"For God's sake, you're hurting him!" I yell. That's it. I'm getting Jackson back. But before I can make a move, Daisy puts Jackson down, takes a death grip on his wrist, and pulls a can of pepper spray from her purse, pointing it at me.

"Jackson, it's okay," I say, swallowing hard. She's really come unhinged. Or desperate. I don't know which is worse right now.

"You can't keep him away from me."

"Daisy." I hold up my hands, heart racing. Pepper spray is far from lethal, but I don't want Jackson to go through the pain of getting it in his eyes or inhaling it. "We can work something out. Just let Jackson go."

Jackson starts struggling again, crying and calling for me. "It's okay," I tell him again. "Daisy, think about this. Is this how you want to start a relationship with your son?"

Daisy's face goes slack, and she looks down, realizing what she's doing. She lets go of Jackson, and he runs to me, crying. Having him in my arms again is the best feeling. I scoop him up, never wanting to let go.

Daisy starts crying, and Owen rushes over. I hand him Jackson, heart aching a bit not to have him in my arms. I rush forward and take the pepper spray from Daisy.

"Don't do this to me," Daisy says, looking up.

"I'm not. You did this to yourself." I inhale and hear sirens in the distance. Thank fucking goodness. I didn't want to be the one to make Daisy's official arrest.

 $\mathscr{I}$ sit up, eyes waking up before my mind. I'm uncomfortable with stiff legs and an aching back, and for a split second, I think I fell asleep sitting up on the couch. Then I blink and realize my eyes are still sore and swollen from crying.

Yes, crying.

The room is dark, and I sit up, stretching my arms over my head. I didn't mean to fall asleep in the stiff armchair next to my father's bed at the nursing home. After leaving Weston's house, I walked into town, took Eastwood's only taxi to Newport, and was able to get an Uber to drive me up to Chicago.

I didn't know where else to go other than the nursing home. Dad was having a bad day and just sat in his chair not really paying attention to anything. So, for the first time in my entire life, I spilled my guts. Said everything I ever wanted to say. Confessed the bad things I've done as well as admit just how deep my love for Weston goes.

And Dad just sat there, staring blankly in my general direction. A little empathy would have been nice, and advice on how not to farther fuck up my life would have been welcome.

But I got nothing.

Rubbing my eyes, I get up, moving slowly in the dark. My phone is in my purse, and it's dead.

"Dammit," I mutter. I have no idea what time it is, and I think I left my phone charger in the kitchen at Weston's house. I left in such a rush I wouldn't be surprised if I left more behind. Moving slow so I don't wake up my dad or his roommate, I go into the hall, blinking from the bright lights.

"Oh!" a nurse exclaims, surprised to see me. "I thought you left."

"I fell asleep." I rub the back of my neck, trying to work out a knot. "What time is it?"

"A little after two AM."

"Shit. Sorry. I'll, uh, I'll go."

The nurse shakes her head. "Stay. It's late, and I know you walk back to your place. Just this one time, though, you hear?"

"Thank you." I go to the bathroom and then back to Dad's room. The nurse put an extra blanket on the chair for me, and I'm grateful. These rooms are fucking freezing.

"Scarlet?" Dad is sitting up in his bed.

"Dad." I rush over, clicking on the light over his bed so he can see me. "It's late. You should go back to sleep."

"You listen to me," he starts. I don't have the emotional bandwidth to deal with one of his flashback rants right now. "You're a Cooper, and Coopers don't give up."

"What?"

"You love that boy?"

I blink, unsure if I'm hearing him correctly. "Weston. Yes. I love him a lot."

"Then what the fuck are you doing here?"

"I...I..." I don't know what to say. "I had to leave or else his ex-wife was going to publish an article about him that made him seem unfit to be the county sheriff. It would have ruined his chances of winning, and he was so close. And besides...once he hears what I did—what I used to do—I don't think he'll see me the same."

"So you're running away with your tail tucked between your legs? I might not have raised you, but I know that's not the type of girl you are. You have more Cooper blood in you than that."

"I just...I..." I shake my head. Dad's having a rare moment of clarity, and I've been honest all night. Why stop here? "I'm scared. Scared to hear him tell me he doesn't want me. Scared to see the look of anger or disgust on his face when he sees me. I left to save his career but also to escape rejection."

"I've been waiting to hear you admit that." Wrinkles form around Dad's mouth as he smiles. "I was scared to come back to you for the same reason."

"Really?" I perch on the edge of the heater vent next to his bed. The air coming out is room temperature, which is why this place is so fucking cold.

"Yeah. I was sure you'd hate me."

"I did hate you."

"Only for a while." Dad yawns and looks around the room. "What time is it?"

"Two in the morning."

He yawns, and I know his mind is going to start slipping back into whatever fog it's usually in. He'll forget about our conversation in the morning. Memory is such a wondrous and confusing thing.

"You should get home. You have school in the morning. We'll talk about the boy tomorrow."

"Okay. Thanks, Dad."

"It will work out." He nods and reaches forward to pat my shoulder. His balance is off, and I don't want him to fall out of bed. I stand, moving closer. "If he's a decent boy at all, he'll see you for what you are."

"I hope so," I whisper and gently push Dad back down. I don't know what I am…but I know what I want to be.

I want to be with Weston and Jackson. I want to go back to Eastwood. I want us to be a family.

~

I tuck my legs up under myself, trying to get comfortable. About an hour after I got Dad back to sleep, his roommate woke up and has been in bed hollering for pain meds nonstop ever since. The nurse came in, told him he's not due to have any more for another few hours, and told me that he does this pretty much nightly.

Great. Just fucking great.

I put on my winter coat and folded up the blanket, trying to use it as a pillow. My suitcases full of all my possessions are cluttering up the room, and every time I see them my heart sinks even lower into my chest. It's going back to that dark crevice it clawed its way out of, and it hurts more and more the lower it gets.

I thought about Dad's words and see truth to them. But I'm still scared, both for myself and for Weston. I'll take his anger and disappointment in me any day over the possibility of ruining everything he's worked for. I'll get over it. Somehow, someway.

I know Jackson will someday face adversity in his life, but if I can keep him innocent and carefree, I will. Weston does a good fucking job hiding his trouble and stresses from the kid. But there's only so much he can handle. Having Daisy come back, finding out my dark past, and losing his job…nope. I won't have it.

I doze off for about an hour and wake up with terrible cramps in my legs. I roll my big suitcase over and stretch out my legs, trying to get comfortable again. I'm so tired, physically and emotionally. I close my eyes and drift to sleep, dreaming that I'm back at Weston's and everything is perfect.

Dad's roommate wakes me up. He gets out of bed, and some sort of alarm goes off. And off. And off. Finally, I get up, pull back the curtain that divides the room in half and see the guy sitting on the edge of his bed, about to face plant on the floor.

"Hey," I say to him, but it's no use. He's even farther gone than my own dad, and I don't think I'll get lucky with another moment of clarity. I duck into the hall, looking for someone to help me get him back into bed. There's no one in sight. Grumbling, I spend the next fifteen minutes trying to get him to lay back down.

Once he's down, I get my toothbrush and go to the bathroom, brush my teeth, and come back to the room. I pull my messy hair into a bun and grab a new sweater to change into. Dad is still asleep and should be getting up for breakfast soon. My stomach grumbles at the thought of food. There's a crappy diner that serves crappy food not far from here, and they open at six AM. I know this because I used to work there until I got laid off.

I grab my purse, shove my luggage into the corner of Dad's room and hope no one steals it while I'm out, and step into the cold November air, keeping my head down as I walk the streets.

I make it to the diner with only a few catcalls and one offer to take a ride on some guy's pogo stick. Not bad considering how hellish I look right now. I'm in no mood to talk to anyone I used to work with, and of course luck has it out for me again.

"Scarlet, hey!" Trisha, another waitress, says. "Haven't seen you in a long time. How've you been, girl?"

"Good." I put on my fake smile.

"You left for some fancy nanny job, right?"

"Right."

She raises her eyebrows. "But you're back. We're not hiring, hun."

"I'm visiting my dad. I just want breakfast."

"Oh, gotcha. Sit in section one and I'll get you."

I force a smile. "Okay." I slide into a booth, wishing for my phone to distract myself with. Instead, I pull out a paperback of a book that I've already read three times. It was at the top of my suitcase, and I didn't want to rustle through my stuff for another. The floor in the nursing home is gross and sticky. Risking my clothes falling out onto it isn't something I want to do.

I order tea, bacon, and French toast, and hunker down in the booth, not wanting to be disturbed by anyone or anything as I contemplate the next step in my life. After getting out of the slums the first time and living in the ritzy part of Chicago, it was hard coming back. It's even harder after Eastwood.

I love that little town.

I have no job now, and with it getting closer and closer to the holidays, I probably won't be able to find one. With Dad's medical bills, I'm going to need money. So I guess it'll be back to the old ways. Just the thought of it makes me feel sick.

Though I'm not as hungry as I should be, I force myself to eat every last bite of food on my plate. Who knows when I'll get out for lunch, and if I'm going back to Old Scarlet, it's going to take some time to get on my feet. I won't have money to burn. Mentally groaning at wasting money on a hotel room for the night, I finish my tea and zip up my coat, leaving Trisha a decent tip.

I trudge my way back to the nursing home, using everything I have inside of me not to think or feel. How did I do this so easily before? Every step hurts, as every footfall reverberates through my heart, jostling the broken pieces. The sharp edges hurt all over again as they slice into me.

Cold rain mists down on me, and I flip the hood up on my coat. Tears well in my eyes, and this time I make no attempt to keep them from falling. I'm sad, really fucking sad, and it's mostly my fault.

If I could take everything back, I would. I'd accept the nanny job in good faith and show up to actually do the job I was hired for. Crazy thought, right?

Wiping at my eyes, I enter the nursing home. My feet are sore from walking, and my fingers are cold and numb. I forgot my gloves at Weston's house as well. They're in his Jeep, I think.

The entrance of the nursing home opens up to the cafeteria, and right now the smell of coffee and breakfast masks the usual sickening odor of this place. I look around for Dad. He's not as his regular table, and for a minute, I think he'd been forgotten in his room. It wouldn't be the first time.

Corbin comes down the hall, pushing Dad in his new chair.

"Ohhh girl," he says, coming to a screeching halt.

"I know, I know," I say with a shake of my head. He's obviously seen my luggage in Dad's room. "I'll explain later. I just...I don't even know." I push my hood back and sigh. "I can't right now."

Corbin cocks an eyebrow. "Well you better, because there's a gorgeous hunk of man-meat looking for you."

"What?"

"Some guy named Weston is here."

"What?" I say again. This is a dream, right? Wes wouldn't...he couldn't...

"I told him to wait in the nurses' station. It's the least stinky place here."

"Yeah...good idea," I say, still in disbelief.

"Aren't you going to go to him? Because if you don't want him, I'll take him."

Weston is here. He came here for me.

"Scarlet?"

I shake myself and inhale, suddenly nervous. Did he come here to yell at me? No, that doesn't make sense.

"How do I look?"

"You've seen better days," Corbin says honestly. "But you're still hot."

"Thanks." I wipe my eyes and pull the tie out of my hair. Running my fingers through my messy locks, I hurry down the hall, fingers trembling.

Wes is standing in the nurses' station with his back to me. The moment I see him, tears spring to my eyes again. He turns as if he can sense me coming.

"Scarlet."

My name on his lips is the best thing he can say. His brow pinches together with emotion, and he strides forward, long legs bringing him to me. He doesn't speak, doesn't question me or raise a finger and start lecturing.

He envelops me in a hug, and I've never felt more at home than I do wrapped in his arms. It's safe. Familiar. Where I'm meant to be.

"What are you doing here?" I ask, fighting back tears.

"I came to find you."

"Why?"

He runs his hand over my hair and steps back, tipping my chin up. Leaning down, he kisses me, and a tear rolls down my cheek.

"Partly to do that."

"And the other part?" I slide my hands to his forearms, scared to let go. If I do, he might vanish into a puff of smoke.

"What the hell is going on?" His navy-blue eyes hold back a storm. "You left us."

As soon as he says it, I realize I did exactly what Daisy did.

"I'm so sorry," I say, voice breaking. Tears fall like rain, and Wes brings me to his chest, cradling me against him. "I didn't want to leave, but I had to."

"Why? Why did you have to leave?"

I sniffle, trying to compose myself. "Daisy came to the house when you were giving Jackson a bath. After he got paint on himself," I remind Wes. "She threatened to have her sister publish an article in the paper about me that would hurt your chances of winning the election."

"I knew she did something. She came by thinking you'd convinced me to give her another chance."

"That was part of her ultimatum, but not even I could go through with that. So I left, and I'm sorry. I just…I couldn't…"

"It's okay."

"No, no, Wes, it's not. What I did…who I am…" I squeeze my eyes shut.

"So it's true." He lets go of me, and my heart falls to the floor. "You really are a con artist."

I can't look at him. My heart is already shattered into a million pieces on the floor. If I see the disgust or disappointment in his eyes, my soul might break too.

"Yes."

"And you took the job thinking you'd be able to con me?"

"Yes."

"But you didn't."

I shake my head, hands shaking and breath coming out in huffs.

"Why?"

Lips quivering, I look up at Wes. "I fell in love with you. And Jackson. I think he stole my heart first if I'm being honest. I tried to resist you as long as I could." He doesn't say anything back. His jaw tenses, and he looks away. "Do you hate me now?"

"No. Maybe I should, but I don't." He takes a step away, bringing his hand to his forehead. "I need some time to think about this."

"I understand." I turn to walk away, going back toward Dad's room to hide from the world.

"Will you come home with me while I think about it?" Wes asks before I get too far.

I whirl around, blinking as if that would make me hear him more clearly. Because I must have misheard.

"Are you sure you want me to come home with you?"

"Yes. I missed you a lot last night. Jackson did too. And I have to work the night shift and could really use a nanny."

"You still trust me?"

"I don't know. I think so."

"That's fair." I swallow hard. "I'm not going to scam you."

"I know. I don't have much for you to take, anyway." He gives me a half-smile. "You stayed that first night when you realized I wasn't a rich doctor. Why?"

I shake my head. "For one, I had nowhere else to go. And from the start, as much as I didn't want to admit it, there was something about you and Jackson. You two are the perfect family...and then when I met the rest of your family..." I trail off, eyes filling with tears again. "I've wanted a family like that. I didn't think families like yours actually existed outside of Hallmark movies or fairy tales. You...you made me a better person, Wes. And even if you don't want anything to do with me ever again, I'll always be thankful for that."

Wes takes another step forward, and I can tell he's fighting against himself not to come any closer.

"Wait," he says, shaking his head, and I think he's going to take back the invitation to go home with him. "You left so Daisy wouldn't publish an article in the paper?"

"Right."

"What was the plan for after?"

"I don't know. Hide here and cry until I figured out something better to do."

Wes frowns, exhaling heavily. He looks so tired and worn.

"Do you want to go get some coffee?" I offer. "You look exhausted."

"I am. I didn't sleep well at all last night."

"I'm sorry."

"It is your fault." He steps in and takes both my hands in his. "I got used to sleeping next to you already. Please come home."

"You don't have to ask me twice."

I reach over and take Scarlet's hand. We're headed back to Eastwood, and though I should probably be a dozen other things, I'm happy. Scarlet is coming home with me.

"Why did you start conning people?" I ask, giving her hand a squeeze.

"I realized I could," she confesses. "It wasn't like a dream I had when I was a little girl to grow up and be a con artist."

"What did you want to be when you grew up?"

She shakes her head. "I don't know. For a while there, I wanted to work at a zoo, but then things changed and I realized I didn't have options. Especially after I dropped out of high school to take care of Heather and Jason."

"You did go back, right?"

"Right. My dad showed up again and was able to look after them. Luckily, because our mom died shortly after." She looks out the window, and it hits me how different our childhoods were. "I've always worked. I had to. Hell, someone had to, and it sure wasn't Mom. I busted my ass for my family, and when I realized I could get more money doing something as harmless as flirt with a guy...I still shouldn't have done it, but, well..."

I rub my thumb against her hand. I don't want to judge her. I don't want to look at her any differently than I did before. "How'd you pick people to scam?"

"Well, my go-to scam was to hang out in bars at expensive hotels. Men—usually married men away on business trips—were easy. I mean easy to con. Not easy to sleep with. I didn't sleep with them. I just took their money and left. Which was supposed to sound better but, fuck, I'm terrible."

I laugh, giving her hand a squeeze. "Honestly, I find this all really interesting."

"Well, that's good, I guess. And to answer your question, I'd read the room. Find a guy who had something to prove. The more desperate, the easier they were to take money from. And you'd be surprised at how distracting a low-cut top and a good pushup bra can be. I picked a lot of pockets after 'accidentally' spilling a few drops of whiskey down my cleavage."

"Yeah, that would be distracting. Even for me."

She smiles, but I can sense her discomfort. I don't approve of what she did, of course. It's illegal and I'm a cop.

"I used to think of myself as a version of Robin Hood who kept the money I hustled instead of giving it to the poor. My family was poor so it kind of makes sense." She shakes her head. "The people I conned were rich assholes who were more than willing to cheat on their wives. Losing a couple hundred bucks here or there wouldn't have hurt them and maybe it taught them a lesson in cheating. Instead of getting a sexy one-night stand, they got stood up and got their cash stolen."

"That's a way to look at it."

"It doesn't make it right. I know. If I could take it back, I would. There's a lot of stuff I'd take back, and I'm not just talking about cons."

"I've done things I'm not proud of too." She looks cold, so I take my hand from hers and turn up the heat. "I've never conned anyone, but there's plenty of things I'd do over. Specifically, my marriage."

"Has she been back?" Scarlet asks hesitantly, and I debate on telling her what happened at the bar yesterday. She's already upset.

"Yeah. She showed up at the house, and I told her to leave. Then Jackson and I went to Getaway—"

"You took Jackson to a bar?"

"During the day. They weren't open yet."

"Oh, that's better. I was going to say you really fell apart on me and I was only gone a day."

"I did fall apart. But anyway...we went to talk to my brothers, and Daisy followed. She tried to get Jackson to leave with her."

"Oh my God. What happened?"

"I had her arrested for an attempted kidnapping. Her parents got a fancy lawyer right away and she was released. We're supposed to have family court in the near future, so nothing will happen until it's reviewed then."

"Are you fucking serious?"

"Unfortunately."

"So she'll be back."

"Yes, but hopefully the next time she does, I'll be officially divorced and will have all the paperwork I need to legally have full custody of Jackson."

Scarlet nods and falls silent for a few minutes.

"Do you still want to be with me?"

"Yes." I slow, getting stuck in construction-zone traffic. The clouds are starting to give way to blue skies.

"Are you sure? I'm not a good person, Wes."

"What you've done and who are you are different from each other. You're not a bad person, Scarlet, and I believe that with my whole heart. I've seen you, the real you, and over the last few weeks, I fell in love with you. I never thought I'd love anyone again."

"And I never thought I'd love anyone at all." She pulls her arms in toward her body. "Not even myself."

I turn away from the crawling traffic to look at her beautiful face. Tears well in her eyes and she's working hard to keep them from falling.

"Loving you and Jackson came easy," she whispers. "But loving myself...hell, it was hard to remotely like myself most days."

"You're worthy of love, Scarlet. Admitting your faults isn't easy to do, and you have."

Scarlet nods, wiping away her tears. "Thank you, Weston."

"For what?"

"For believing in me. My past is dark, but the rest of my life doesn't have to be."

I take her hand again. "It won't be."

∽

I LUG the biggest suitcase to the top of the stairs. Scarlet is behind me, carrying her other bags. I pause at the top of the stairs, looking down the hall at the guest room. My bedroom is on the opposite end, and even before this whole mess, Scarlet kept her stuff in the guest room closet.

She dozed off on the way home, giving me time to think. I've always been cautious. Too cautious. I married Daisy because it made sense. We'd dated long enough to warrant a proposal. I loved her because she was safe and familiar, and look how that turned out.

I trust Scarlet when she says she wants to change. She did nothing to make me question her judgment before, and I know the worst thing you can do to someone who's trying to better themselves is to constantly remind them of the mistakes they made.

I'm done being cautious when it comes to love. I'm letting my heart guide me this time.

"Where are you going?" Scarlet asks when I take her stuff into my room.

"I love you." I set her suitcase on the floor by the bed. "I want us to be together and I want to make sure you know I'm not going to hold the past against you. We can't move on and enjoy the present if we're constantly looking backward. And I want to move forward with you."

Scarlet drops her bags to the ground. "I love you, too." She steps forward, closing the distance between us, and it's like I can't get enough of her. I grab her and throw her on the bed. I move over top, settling between her legs. She rakes her fingers up over my back, and I'm turned on already. I press my hardened cock against her, and she bucks her hips against me.

I bring my head down, kissing her hard before moving my lips to her neck. She reaches down, fumbling with the button on my jeans for a moment before popping it off and shimmying them down my legs. She pushes me to the side, hooking one leg over me and taking hold of my cock. I look down, groaning when I see her long and slender fingers wrapped around my dick. She pumps her hand up and down, swirling her thumb over the tip and spreading precum down my shaft.

Then she lets go and moves down. With a swift movement, she yanks my pants the rest of the way off and takes a hold of my cock again. But instead of moving back up to where she was before, she takes me in her mouth, tongue flicking the tip of my cock.

I let out a moan, falling back onto the mattress. I spread my legs, watching her suck my cock. She moves slow, teasing me, and then speeds up only to slow again. Fuck, she's good at this. My eyes flutter shut, and I enjoy her mouth on me for another minute before pushing her away.

"I wasn't done yet," she says coyly.

"You're going to make me come already."

"That's the plan. I want to take care of you."

I sit up, grabbing her by the waist. "Letting me fuck you is taking care of me."

She moans and falls back against the bed, one arm landing above her head. "I'm okay with that."

I kiss my way down her torso and pull her leggings down, dropping them on the floor. Then I trail kisses up her thigh, stopping right next to her tender core. She tenses, anticipating what's coming—which will be her in just a few minutes.

I put my mouth over her, letting out a breath of hot air and teasing her through her panties. Slowly, I stroke her, though so gently she's pressing herself against me.

"I need you, Wes," she groans, reaching down and taking my

hand. "I need you to make me come."

She doesn't have to tell me twice. With a growl I move back up, kissing her lips as I slip my hand inside her panties.

"You're so wet," I moan.

"You made me wet," she replies, and I might come right here without her even touching me. "Now make me come."

I circle her pussy with a finger, inching closer and closer to her clit. Her entire body is tensing as she waits, and as much as I want to keep teasing her, I know I can't hold out much longer. I stroke her clit, soft and gently at first. She's easy for me to read, but that's only because we're so in tune with each other while we're making love.

Going off her cues, I speed up my movements, rubbing her clit faster and faster until her body stiffens and she loudly cries out. With her pussy still spasming, I move down, removing her wet panties and parting her legs.

I put my mouth over her and flick her clit with my tongue.

"Oh, God," she moans, squirming against me. Her hands go to my hair. I lash my tongue out again and again, not stopping until she's coming so hard the sheets grow damp beneath her.

My cock is dripping, pulsing so hard and begging to be inside of her. Her head is to the side, mouth still open. One of her hands is gripping a handful of my hair so tight it's painful, but the pain feels good. I move up, cock going right to her center.

"Weston," she pants, feebly wrapping her arms around me. I push in, rocking my hips slow and steady. It feels so fucking good to be inside of her. I push my big cock in deeper, feeling my eyes roll back and an orgasm build inside me.

She curls one leg up, and I hit her at a new angle. Her pussy tightens around my cock, and my pleasure hits a peak. I come so hard my vision darkens, and I collapse on top of her, sweating and breathing hard.

I roll to the side, reaching for my boxers for her to use to wipe herself up with until she can get into the bathroom. I didn't mean to come inside of her, but I was too caught up in the moment to grab a condom.

Scarlet uses the bathroom and comes back to bed. I pull the

blankets over us both, and she snuggles in.

"Where's Jackson?"

"Quinn and Archer's. It's safe there with all their alarms, and Archer is home today."

"Good." She rolls over and cups my chin with her hand. "I love you, Weston Dawson."

"And I love you, Scarlet Cooper." I kiss her again and lay down, pulling her onto my chest.

I didn't play it safe. I listened to my heart instead of my head this time around, and right here in bed with Scarlet is exactly where we're supposed to be.

"Wes?"

"Yeah?"

"What if Daisy does run that article?"

"I don't think she will. Blackmailing me like that will look bad in family court. I reminded her of that when she was in handcuffs."

"But if she does anyway? Your family will hate me."

"They won't hate you," I assure her, though I am a little anxious about them finding out the truth. Dean can be judgy and Mom can hold a grudge like it's nobody's business. Dad is more practical, which is where I got it from, and while he might not have an easy time trusting Scarlet for a while, I don't think he'll object to us being together.

"I really like your family."

"They like you too. But," I start, being honest. "Finding out the truth from an article will be a hard pill to swallow."

"Maybe we should tell them. Now."

"Now?"

"Just in case."

I trace the curve of her hip with my finger. "I really don't think we have to. And if the people in the county can be that easily swayed in who to vote for, then maybe I don't want to be in charge of keeping them safe."

Scarlet laughs. "I'll still feel terrible."

"Don't. If losing the race means I get to be with you, then I've won."

"*H*ey, buddy!" I step past the dogs, holding the bag of takeout a little higher to keep Rufus from sniffing at it.

"Daddy!" Jackson comes running. "We have to be quiet," he says loudly. "Emma just fell asleep."

"Okay," I whisper back, shuffling into the kitchen. Archer got called in for surgery, so Quinn and the kids came over to our parents, just to be safe.

"Hey, Jackson." Scarlet takes her coat off, smiling down at him.

"Are you still sick?" he asks her, taking her hand. Both Scarlet and I pause for a moment until I remember telling Jackson Scarlet wasn't feeling well and that's why she wasn't home.

"She's better now," I tell him. "Are you hungry?"

Mom is sitting at the island counter, which is covered in blueprints. "You didn't have to bring fast food." She raises her eyebrows. "I could have cooked."

"I thought Jackson would like a Happy Meal," I say, and Jackson gets excited. "I got one for Quinn too."

Mom laughs. "She'll like that I'm sure."

I hand the bag of food to Scarlet, who gives me a little nod before ushering Jackson to the table.

"Mom?" I ask. "Can we talk in private?"

"Of course, honey. Is everything okay?"

"Yeah." I inhale slowly. Scarlet was right: it's better if the truth comes from me, no matter how uncomfortable this conversation will be. Mom follows me into the sunroom. We walk past Quinn, who fell asleep on the couch in the living room with Emma on her chest. "It's about Scarlet."

"Is she all right?"

"She is." I pace toward the windows overlooking the backyard. God, this is awkward. But I know it has to be said. I want to build a life with Scarlet, and we can't have this lingering. Well, she can't. I'm fine with letting the past be in the past.

"She told me she used to con people."

I can feel Mom's eyes on me. "What?"

I turn around, swallowing hard. "She used to be a con artist and would hustle money out of men at bars."

Mom doesn't say anything for a few seconds. "But she seems so sweet."

"Yeah, she does." I run my hand through my hair. "She wanted you all to know in case it ever came up again later."

"Does she still con people?"

"No."

Mom sinks down onto a lounge chair. "Why did she tell you?"

"Now that's a funny story." I pace to the other side of the room. "She has a sister…who's in jail."

"You're kidding."

"No. She said her sister got caught up with the wrong crowd and tried to rob a store."

"Jesus Christ, Wes!" Mom's eyes widen. "Scarlet is a con-artist and her sister is a robber. And you trust her with Jackson?"

"Yes," I say seriously. "I do. And I love her."

Mom's lips pull into a thin line. "Are you sure you're not too infatuated with her to see clearly?"

"I'm sure. She's had a hard life, Mom. Her own mother was an addict, and Scarlet dropped out of school to raise her brother and sister. She was only able to go back when her alcoholic father showed up, and then her mother OD'd and died. Scarlet is the one who found her and had to tell her siblings she was dead. Her father is in a shithole of a nursing home and she's the only one taking care of him."

Mom falls silent, and I pace back and forth, waiting to hear from her.

"Mom?" I finally ask. "Say something."

Mom flicks her eyes to mine. "Poor thing. She turned out better than most in her situation, I suppose." She leans back, rubbing her forehead. I'll leave out the part about Scarlet planning to con me for now.

"Do you think differently of her now?"

"Yes," Mom answers honestly. "But it doesn't make me like her any less. I feel bad for her, but I don't think being a victim of circumstance excuses poor choices."

"I don't either, and Scarlet will agree. She doesn't want that life anymore."

Mom, who's patience and understanding has always amazed me, looks up and smiles. "I don't think that's a problem now, is it?"

I smile back. "No. Her life is here now." With a sigh, I sit next to Mom. "Do you believe people can change?"

"Yes, but only if the change comes from within. You can't change a person, but they can change themselves. Do you think Scarlet wants to change?"

"I know she wants to. And she has. Who she is now…that's who she's meant to be."

Mom puts her arm around my shoulders. "You've changed too."

"I have?"

"For the better."

I look through the sunroom doors in the general direction of the kitchen. "We have Scarlet to thank for that."

"*I* think Salsa is a good name." I give Jackson an encouraging nod.

"It is cute," Quinn agrees.

"Do you think Daddy will let Salsa come home with us?" Jackson picks up the kitten and kisses her head. Wes got a little nervous around the time he was supposed to go into work. Instead of having Jackson come back here, I went over to Quinn's. Jackson and I are staying the night here, and Wes is coming by in the morning.

Even though Daisy was arrested and released with potential charges, we have no idea if she knows I'm back. And once she finds out her plans to sabotage the race, drive me out of town, and get Wes back didn't work, she'll be pissed. She might do something crazy.

Though if she's smart, she'll be on her perfect behavior so she can try to convince a judge that she's worthy of any sort of visitation rights with Jackson, which seem unlikely considering she basically tried to kidnap him.

Still, I'm worried. Worried she'll hurt Jackson and worried she'll ruin Weston's career. His parents know—more or less—of my colorful past, and while I can tell his mom was trying hard not to hold it against me, I know she doesn't fully trust me yet.

And I don't blame her.

At least she didn't come after me with a pitchfork or get the stake ready for a burning. The twins already know, which just leaves Dean, Archer...and Quinn. I don't want my boyfriend's sister to hate me. And I don't want to lose the woman who's quickly becoming my best friend.

"We'll work on it." I smile and pet the kitten. "He is very friendly. Are they ready to leave their mom yet?"

"They are, but don't tell Archer," Quinn whispers. "I'll miss them."

"Maybe we can take two," I say. "Then you'll be able to visit, and you can keep the others, right?"

"I'd like it."

"You have enough space."

"That's what I said!" Quinn laughs. We're sitting in her living room, and five of the eight cats are in here with us. Emma laughs when a fat orange cat comes over and rubs his head on her. He lazily saunters off, and she crawls after him.

"She's fast!"

"I know." Quinn gets up to grab her baby. "Too fast. I'm already getting anxiety about the balcony looking over the living room. I wake up in the middle of the night thinking she fell over."

"That's so unlikely to happen," I tell her. "Lots of people have fancy catwalk thingies like that in their houses."

"I know." She wrinkles her nose. "I told Archer I want to line the floor with mattresses just in case."

"You'll encourage her to jump," Archer teases, coming into the living room. "I would have if I were a kid."

"Don't give him ideas," Quinn whisper-yells, but Jackson is too enthralled in the kitten he's renamed Salsa to hear anything. I yawn and look at the clock. Thank God it's almost bedtime. I'm wiped out.

It's been a long fucking day, which I feel like is a summary of my life. Well, until Weston, that is. Things changed the moment I stepped foot on his front porch, and I think I knew, deep down, that I wanted that change.

I needed that change.

Emma slips as she's crawling and hits the floor. Her two little bottom teeth puncture her lip, and blood starts spilling out of her mouth. Quinn has a moment of panic, picking up Emma and going back and forth between checking her mouth and wanting to comfort her baby. I run into the kitchen to get a towel, and Archer calmly sits on the floor and tells Quinn it's okay.

"The blood is mixing with her saliva and it looks like she's bleeding more than she really is," he says.

Jackson gets freaked out, and I take him into the kitchen to avoid seeing the blood. Emma is screaming and crying, and he's upset that his cousin is hurt and upset. It's pure chaos for a good five minutes, but then we get everyone settled down and up to bed.

Half an hour later, I shut the door to the guest room, sneaking out. Jackson fell asleep fast tonight, and while I could lay there and snuggle with him, I know if I didn't get up, I'd end up falling asleep too.

"Should we have cake with our tea?" Quinn asks. I wash out the pink skull tea set Weston and Jackson got for me as a surprise.

"Of course."

"Good. Because I made one earlier today. I was craving Funfetti cake bad."

"Craving?" I raise my eyebrows.

"I'm not pregnant. Or else I better not be. I really want to go on Tower of Terror on our honeymoon," she laughs. "But I am dying to have another."

"You're a good mom. You should have at least one more."

"We want three or four." She opens the pantry and all the cats come running, circling her feet and meowing.

"I take that back. Maybe you shouldn't have this many cats."

"Their meowing is like singing." She looks at Archer, who's sitting at the large island counter eating. "Isn't it, babe?"

He rolls his eyes. "It's music to my ears."

I laugh and reach down, picking up one of the kittens. "Are you Salsa?"

"That's Binx," Archer says. "I mean, not like I can tell them apart or care or anything."

"He really likes Binx," Quinn loudly whispers.

"I guess you're staying then, huh, little guy?"

"He is."

Quinn sets the cake down, shoos the cats off the counter at least a dozen times, and heats up water for our tea. Archer goes upstairs to bed, saying he has early surgery in the morning, leaving Quinn and me downstairs to eat and talk until we go to bed as well.

I cut into my cake and sip my tea. I look at Quinn, excited to have someone I can actually call a friend. And she's my boyfriend's sister, which makes things ten times better.

Well, almost.

"Quinn?"

"Yeah?"

"I need to tell you something."

"Sure." She adds more sugar to her tea. "What is it?"

"It's more like a confession. Promise you won't judge me?"

"I promise."

And she doesn't.

THE MATTRESS SINKS DOWN next to me, and my eyes flutter open. I'm too tired to realize the body next to me is too large to be Jackson, and I lazily push myself up to tell him I'll be right up.

But then I see Wes, and my heart flutters.

"Morning, sunshine." He smiles down at me. He's in his uniform, and holy hell that man is fine. I sit up only to pull him down on me.

"What time is it?"

"Seven AM. I came here instead of going home. I don't think Quinn was too happy about having to let me in." He kisses me, brushes my hair from my face, and sits up. He's wearing a utility belt around his waist, which isn't comfortable to lay down on.

"We were up pretty late talking." I sit up again, resting my head on Wes's shoulder. "I told her everything."

"Everything-everything, or the version of everything I told my parents?"

"I was going to tell that version, then I drank half a bottle of wine."

Wes smiles. "And?"

"She didn't kick me out."

"That's a start."

I nod, not wanting to get up, but I have to pee and I'm pretty close to keeling over and dying of thirst. "Right. She might need some time to process, but I feel better. I want to start fresh."

"You are." He goes in to kiss me again, but Jackson comes in, excited to see his dad. I use the bathroom and we all go downstairs. Quinn is in the kitchen, and all the cats are following her around meowing.

"You really are a crazy cat lady, sis," Wes chuckles.

"Thank you." Quinn looks up with a smile. Her eyes meet mine, and the smile wavers. Shit.

"Once you're done feeding the beasts, can I talk with you?" Weston asks.

"Yeah, of course."

She gives Emma a few more Puffs and then feeds the cats. I pour Jackson a cup of milk, and we both get excited when we realize Wes brought us all donuts.

"What's Daddy talking to Aunt Winny about?" Jackson asks.

"I'm not sure," I tell him, though I have an idea. I set his milk on the table and see the paper under the donut box. My fingers shake as I reach for it.

My picture isn't on the front page. Or the second. Or third. Jackson laughs watching me thumb through the paper as fast as I can.

"We're good," Wes says, coming back into the room. He knows what I'm looking for.

"We are?"

Quinn takes Emma out of her highchair and sits at the table. "Yes." She meets my eye. "We are good."

∾

"You've already looked through it," Wes says, coming up behind me.It's Monday morning, and I keep going through the paper just to be sure I didn't miss anything. "There's nothing incriminating in there."

"Thank God." I exhale. "One more day."

"Yes, and I'm telling you, most people have already made up their minds when they wake up Tuesday morning."

"You're going to win."

"I might. Or I might not."

I pour myself a cup of coffee and join Wes at the table. Jackson is still sleeping, and Wes's alarm went off on accident this morning. He doesn't have to work today, but he forgot to turn off the alarm. Once he was awake, he came downstairs for breakfast. I was going to go back to sleep but got too anxious to see the paper.

"I'm going to talk to her today," Weston says. "I'm assuming she's at her parents'. I'll call over there and see."

"What are you going to talk about?"

"How we'll proceed with things. Actually," he says and stands up, "I'll call them now. Who cares if it's early?"

"So Jackson's other set of grandparents aren't involved at all?"

"They send him presents for his birthday and Christmas, but that's it."

"That's so weird."

Wes nods. "They feel like they have to side with Daisy on it. I think it's easier if they pretend like he's not here."

"Their loss."

"Yes, and a big one." He gets his phone and calls Daisy's parents. "Well, that's shocking," he says sarcastically when he hangs up.

"What?"

"She skipped town already and is back in Chicago."

I shake my head in disbelief. "Wow, though it is refreshing to hear about someone who makes worse choices than I do."

Wes sighs. "I don't know if this is good or bad. But I think I should call Mr. Williams and let him know what happened."

"Good idea. Get everything on record."

"Yeah, it'll come up again, I'm sure." He comes back to the table. "In the meantime, I got us tickets to go to the planetarium today."

"No way."

"Yes. And I thought maybe when we're done, we could visit your dad."

"You want to take Jackson there? My dad can be a little unfiltered."

Wes cocks an eyebrow. "You've met my nana, right?"

I laugh and reach for Wes. He takes my hands and pulls me to my feet. "I love you, Weston."

"And I love you."

I put my arm around Scarlet, smiling as we watch Jackson tear into his Christmas presents. The three of us are wearing matching pajamas, which was Scarlet's idea. Not mine. She said she bought them as a joke, but was rather insistent on all of us wearing them and taking a picture together last night on Christmas Eve.

No sooner than Scarlet gets comfortable against me, she jumps up.

"Salsa, get out of the tree." She grabs the black kitten and brings him to the couch with her. He stays for half a second and jumps down, pouncing on the pile of discarded wrapping paper.

Midnight, the mother cat to all the kittens, curiously walks over, batting a plastic bow across the living room. We were only going to take the kitten, but the mama cat really likes me for some reason. She's a bit annoying, really, and rubs her head all over me purring almost every night when I go to sleep.

Scarlet laughs, watching the cats have almost as much fun as Jackson with the presents. I take her in my arms again, stealing a kiss before Jackson moves onto the next present.

"I love you," she whispers, running her hands through my hair.

"I love you too," I tell her, and we settle back against the couch as Jackson finishes opening his presents. It doesn't take long. That kid could win an award for fastest present opening.

Once he's done, I deal with the aftermath of the wrapping paper, torn boxes, and toys scattered throughout the living room. Jackson plays with a new remote control dump truck, "helping" me clean up the mess.

The smell of cinnamon rolls fill the air, and Scarlet turns on Christmas music. She comes back into the living room with a cup of tea in her hand, stopping in the threshold of the room with a smile on her face.

"Breakfast will be ready soon," she says, taking a drink of tea. She sets her cup down and pulls Salsa from the tree again. I stashed all our breakable ornaments when Jackson was a baby, replacing the pretty glass balls with shatterproof plastic ones that actually look just as good as the others. I almost dug them out of the basement this Christmas, and I'm glad we didn't.

"Then I need to shower so we can get ready to leave."

I scoop up another armload of wrapping paper and add it to the big gift bag a toy came in. We have a lot of stops to make on the way to my parents' for their big Christmas party.

The first stop is to Eastwood's Senior Care Center, where Mr. Cooper now lives. We were able to get him a room there around the first of the month, and it's been a big weight off Scarlet's shoulders. The old nursing home was a dump. I didn't want to say anything and make Scarlet feel worse, but I was shocked when I walked in, and not in a good way.

The second stop we have to make won't be fun. It'll be awkward and uncomfortable, but it's something I couldn't rightfully refuse to do.

Daisy's parents want to see Jackson on Christmas. They got him presents and asked if he could come over for lunch. Scarlet and I are going with, and I'm not sure if Daisy will be there or not. The judge let her off easy, and she's going to court-ordered therapy. I haven't seen her since she left the last time, and now all the paperwork is official and filed.

I'm not married to her anymore. I'm free to remarry anyone I want, and that person is standing in the living room with a squirming kitten in her hands. Quinn suggested I propose while we're all at Disney World together after her wedding. Scarlet's never been and is just as excited as Jackson to go.

It's a damn good idea and would be magical and fitting for Scarlet, but I don't know if I can wait that long. I love her, and I know there will never be another who fits with us as well as she does.

Things were awkward for a while after we told the rest of my family the truth. I was good with not ever bringing it up, but Scarlet insisted she come clean and start with no secrets. Dean and Archer had the hardest time with it, convinced she wasn't trustworthy. Owen already knew, of course, and told Logan later that day after I left the bar. And Mom and Dad didn't know what to say, though I think they were both so relieved to hear that I was finally free of Daisy they didn't care who I was dating now. Dad didn't understand how I could be so understanding and forgiving, and when I tell the whole story, it surprises me too.

But Scarlet isn't that person anymore. I don't think that's ever who she really was in the first place. She's a good person, and I know one day soon she'll make a good wife.

"MERRY CHRISTMAS!" Jackson shouts, running through the kitchen. He's on the lookout for more presents.

"Hey, Sheriff," Owen says, piling more cookies on his plate. Ever since I won the election, that's all he'll call me. He knows it annoys me.

"Hey," I say back, letting it go this time. "Save some for the rest of us."

"You should have gotten here sooner."

Mom comes in, shooing Owen away with her hand. "Those are for dessert. We haven't even had dinner yet." She gives me a hug and moves on to Scarlet.

"You look lovely, dear. And I love your necklace."

"Thanks," Scarlet says, hand going to her neck. "Wes got it for me for Christmas."

"He has good taste." Mom smiles and goes to the stove to check on dinner.

"Yeah," Scarlet says with a smile. "He does." The necklace is a little star, encrusted with diamonds. I know how much she loves to look at the stars. I fill a plate with appetizers and take Scarlet's hand, going into the living room to find my other siblings. We're early, but soon my extended family will shuffle into the house and things will get loud.

"Logan brought Danielle?" Scarlet whispers, slowing before we get into the living room. "I thought they were *just friends*?"

"That's what he tells us."

No one believes them, and if they really are just friends, then they're both missing out. I don't know Danielle well, but she seems nice enough and gets along with Logan better than anyone I've seen him with.

He brought her to Thanksgiving too, which threw us all for a loop. He's never brought anyone home for a holiday. He claims it was because Danielle's at odds with her family right now. They're rather conservative and had a whole plan laid out for the rest of her life that she had no say in. She basically ran away from it all last year, coming to live at her grandfather's farm here in Eastwood.

"Quinn and I had an idea and we think—"

"No," I say with a laugh. "We shouldn't get involved. And you know by now how much my sister likes to play matchmaker."

Scarlet smiles and gives my hand a squeeze. "Maybe just a little push?"

I shrug, not seeing how any harm can come from that. "Fine. But nothing more than a little push."

I don't see how the push can hurt, and if one of them confesses how they really feel they finally won't be able to deny it anymore. I want my brother to be happy, and I know he'll be happy with Danielle.

A push could be a good thing.

Unless they're pushed too far.

"Merry Christmas," Quinn says, coming into the room. She's holding Emma, who's dressed like a little elf.

"Oh my God," Scarlet coos, going over. "This is the cutest thing I've ever seen!"

"She's adorable!" Kara agrees.

"Does it make you want one?" Quinn teases.

"Nope. No way."

Scarlet takes Emma from Quinn's arms, cradling her against her chest. Her eyes meet mine and I know what she's thinking, because right now I'm thinking the same thing.

It's making us both want a baby.

"Did you get everything you wanted for Christmas?" Archer asks Jackson, scooping him up.

"I did!" Jackson says excitedly and goes on to list all the new toys he got. I step next to Scarlet, putting my arm around her shoulder. I got everything I want too.

Scarlet's phone rings, and she scrambles to get it from her purse. Her brother is supposed to be calling today and was trying to call around this time. He's stationed somewhere new and it's looking like he'll come home in January.

I go into the kitchen, finding Owen stealing more cookies, and take one too. Mom comes in and shoos us both away. Scarlet is in the dining room, and I want to give her some space while she talks to her brother. I go back into the living room with the rest of my family, hanging out and talking until it's time for dinner.

Scarlet, Jackson, and I are stuffed and tired by the time we get home several hours later. I changed Jackson into his PJs and brushed his teeth at my parents, knowing he'd fall asleep on the short ride home. I carry him upstairs and lay him in bed.

"Dad?" he grumbles, eyes fluttering open.

"Yeah?"

"I love you."

"I love you too, buddy."

He closes his eyes and reaches for the yellow unicorn. "And I love Scarlet."

"That's something we both have in common." I run my fingers through his hair and kiss his forehead. The kid is wiped out and falls asleep within minutes. I tuck him in and go downstairs to find Scarlet.

Only, she's not in the house. This time, there's no panic or worry. I know exactly where she is.

Grabbing a blanket from the couch, I find her on the back porch steps, looking up at the clear sky above us. I sit next to her, draping the blanket around our shoulders.

"This is perfect," she whispers, wrapping her arm around me. "I'm kind of sad Christmas is over."

"We'll get to do it again next year."

She looks at me with a smile. "Are you sure you want that?"

"More than anything. I want *you* next year. And the year after that. And the one after that. Actually," I start and get up, extending a hand. Scarlet takes it, eyes sparkling with amusement. "I love you, Scarlet Cooper. This isn't how I planned it, because I don't even have a ring yet, but you're right. This is perfect."

"Wes, what are you—"

I get down on one knee. "Will you marry me?"

The blanket slides off her shoulders and tears fill her eyes. She stares at me in disbelief, and for a moment I think I asked too soon.

Then the biggest smile takes over her face. "Yes! Yes, of course I will marry you!"

I get up and pull her into my arms. "I love you. Today, tomorrow, and every day after that. I will always love you."

EPILOGUE

SCARLET

Seven months later...

"Thank you so much," Quinn says, pushing her messy hair out of her face and taking Emma from my arms. "With Archer's parents up in Michigan visiting Bobby and my own consumed with construction on the hospital, I'm dying."

"It's no big deal." I look down at Jackson. "We had fun. Emma was perfect."

Quinn raises an eyebrow in disbelief. Now that she's over a year and is walking, Emma is a handful. And poor Quinn has been puking nonstop pretty much since the day she conceived her second child. She said she went through the same thing with Emma, making me question her sanity on getting pregnant again.

"Is Archer going to be home soon?"

"Yeah, thankfully." We move into Quinn's house, which is far from neat and tidy like it usually is. I hope when I'm finally pregnant I don't get hit with morning sickness like this.

Right after Wes proposed we started trying in a sense. I knew it would take a miracle to knock me up, but I was hopeful. We had a small but beautiful wedding on Valentine's Day, and then I had a sit down with my OB to talk about what was really wrong with me. After a slew of tests, I've been taking fertility drugs and we've still had no luck.

I know many couples try much longer than we have, but it's starting to really weigh on me. Jackson is dying for a sibling.

"How's your sister?" Quinn asks, sinking down on the couch in the family room. Three of her six cats are in here, lounging around.

"She's doing pretty well, actually. I think the group home is a good adjustment for her. She got a job last week at a bookstore."

"That's great!"

"Baby steps, but a step is a step." Heather got out of prison last month. Around the New Year, she started going to a church group with a few other inmates, and it actually turned her around. She still goes to church and is currently living in a group home for troubled young adults with mental health issues. She's still in Chicago, but we try to see each other at least once a week.

"When will your belly get big?" Jackson asks, looking at Quinn's stomach.

Quinn puts her hand on her belly. "You'll probably notice a baby bump in a month or so. I've heard you show sooner with the second."

"You're totally going to be one of those pregnant ladies who's all belly and boob, aren't you?" I ask.

Quinn smiles. "I was last time." She makes a sour face and then gets up, rushing to the bathroom to throw up. Jackson and I stay a little longer, waiting to leave until Archer gets home. He thanks me as well for helping out with Emma today so Quinn can rest.

"Are you tried?" I ask Jackson when we get home. "I'm tired. Emma wore me out."

"I'm not tired," he says with a yawn. "Can I go play now?"

"Yeah, that'd be great. Dinner will be ready in about an hour."

He goes upstairs and I have every intention of starting dinner, but I fall asleep on the couch, not waking until Wes comes home.

"You feeling okay, babe?" he asks when I get up.

"Yeah, I've been tired all day. Maybe I'm coming down with something."

Wes raises his eyebrows. "Or maybe…"

"I wish." I shake my head. I've been pretty good about waiting until after my period is supposed to begin before taking a test.

"You've been tired all week."

"That's just one symptom," I remind him, though after watching poor Quinn puke her brains out I just kind of assumed I'd be like that too and I'd know with absolute certainty that I was pregnant.

Still, Wes's question hangs over me throughout dinner. And dessert. And bedtime. So much so that I break a rule and bust out a test.

Jackson is fast asleep, and Wes is watching TV downstairs. I said I was going to change into PJs and be right back. Taking one test won't take long. And I have to pee anyway.

My hands shake, and I close my eyes, talking myself down. Flipping that test over and seeing a big fat negative is more disappointing than I ever expected.

But this time…

"Wes!" I blink. Once. Twice. "Wes!"

I hear him running up the stairs. "What's wrong?" he asks, pushing open the bathroom door. I'm standing in front of the sink, too stunned to talk. I hold up the test.

Wes looks at it, at me, and back at the test again. Then he pulls me into his arms. "You're pregnant!"

AFTERWORD

Thank you so much for reading Side Hustle! Out of all the books in the world, I'm humbled and grateful you picked up mine to read! I hope you loved Wes and Scarlet (and the other Dawsons of course!). If you could leave a review, that would be amazing and I'd appreciate it so much! I had such a fun time with Weston and Scarlet's story. Writing about their love was just one of the many things I enjoyed about this book, but I have to say Scarlet's discovery of self-worth was probably my favorite. It's often hard to love ourselves, so I want to remind you that you are enough. Never forget that.

∿

I LOVE connecting with readers and would be thrilled if you joined my Facebook group :) I post sneak peaks, early cover reveals, and lots of giveaways along with the occasional awkward live video or two. Search "Emily Goodwin Books" on Facebook to join!

∿

I'm also on Instagram and would be honored if you followed me! I'm "authoremilygoodwin" on Instagram in case you want to head over and check out my profile and see if it's something you'd like to see more of.

~

www.emilygoodwinbooks.com

ABOUT THE AUTHOR

Emily Goodwin is the New York Times and USA Today Bestselling author of over a dozen of romantic titles. Emily writes the kind of books she likes to read, and is a sucker for a swoon-worthy bad boy and happily ever afters.

She lives in the midwest with her husband and two daughters. When she's not writing, you can find her riding her horses, hiking, reading, or drinking wine with friends.

Emily is represented by Julie Gwinn of the Seymour Agency.

Stalk me:
www.emilygoodwinbooks.com
emily@emilygoodwinbooks.com

ALSO BY EMILY GOODWIN

Standalone Novels

One Call Away

Never Say Never

Outside the Lines

First Comes Love

Then Comes Marriage

Stay

All I Need

Love is Messy Duet Series

Hot Mess (Luke & Lexi, book 1)

Twice Burned (Luke & Lexi, book 2)

Bad Things (Cole & Ana, book 3)

Battle Scars (Cole & Ana, book 4)

Dawson Family Series

Cheat Codes

End Game

Side Hustle

Printed in Great Britain
by Amazon